In his *New York Times* bestselling trilogy of
post-apocalyptic America, Robert Ferrigno "has imagined
a world that's enough like our own, yet still shockingly
different, to send chills down anyone's spine" (*Chicago
Sun-Times*). . . . "Enjoy the vast breadth of what is truly a
remarkable achievement" (*Publishers Weekly*, starred
review) by delving into his acclaimed thrillers . . .

Prayers for the Assassin • *Sins of the Assassin* • *Heart of the Assassin*

Praise for
HEART OF THE ASSASSIN

"Ferrigno wraps up his provocative trilogy in grand style, alternating scenes of inventive mayhem with sweeping indictments of spineless politicians and political extremists."

—*Booklist*

SINS OF THE ASSASSIN
2009 Edgar Award finalist!

"One of the most gripping thrillers of the year . . . also one of the smartest. . . . Brilliant characters, well-choreographed action, and white-knuckle suspense."

—*Chicago Sun-Times*

"*Sins of the Assassin* is terrific—all killer, no filler. . . . Gripping. . . . Integrates the futuristic setting . . . with flashes of Ferrigno's mordant wit."

—*The Seattle Times*

Heart of the Assassin is also available as an eBook

ROBERT FERRIGNO

HEART OF THE ASSASSIN

POCKET STAR BOOKS

NEW YORK   LONDON   TORONTO   SYDNEY

Pocket Star Books
A Division of Simon & Schuster, Inc.
1230 Avenue of the Americas
New York, NY 10020

This book is a work of fiction. Names, characters, places, and incidents either are products of the author's imagination or are used fictitiously. Any resemblance to actual events or locales or persons, living or dead, is entirely coincidental.

First Pocket Star Books paperback edition September 2010

POCKET STAR BOOKS and colophon are registered trademarks of Simon & Schuster, Inc.

For information about special discounts for bulk purchases, please contact Simon & Schuster Special Sales at 1-866-506-1949 or business@simonandschuster.com.

The Simon & Schuster Speakers Bureau can bring authors to your live event. For more information or to book an event, contact the Simon & Schuster Speakers Bureau at 1-866-248-3049 or visit our website at www.simonspeakers.com.

Cover design and digital imaging by Jae Song
Capitol building by Randy McWilson

Manufactured in the United States of America

10 9 8 7 6 5 4 3 2 1

ISBN 978-1-4165-3772-4
ISBN 978-1-4391-6600-0 (ebook)

To my wonderful aunts,
Marge Macneil and Rose Iuzzolino,
who read to me when I was a child,
and opened up the world.

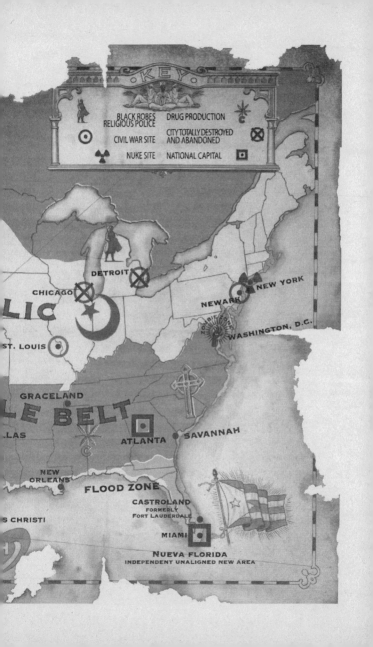

Civilizations do not fall because of the barbarians at the gates. Nor does a great city fall from the death wish of bored and morally bankrupt stewards presumably sworn to its defense. Civilizations fall only because each citizen of the city comes to accept that nothing can be done to rally and rebuild broken walls; that ground lost may never be recovered; and that greatness lived in our grandparents but not our grandchildren. Yes, our betters tell us these things daily. But that doesn't mean we have to believe it.

—BILL WHITTLE,
"THE UNDEFENDED CITY"

CHAPTER 1

Lester Gravenholtz stood beside an old-fashioned red phone booth, stood there in the Florida sun waiting to kill the Aztlán oil minister and get back into some air-conditioning. Sweat rolled down his bare scalp as a tour bus filled with tourists drove past, their voices going silent as they caught sight of him. He scratched his nose, fingers bumping up against the mottled blue prosthetic that covered half his face. He couldn't remember what kind of genetic disorder he was supposed to have, but the plasti-flesh molding was so realistic that when he checked himself out in the mirror he wanted to puke. Sweat burned his eyes. The Old One had insisted on his head being shaved, leaving only a few tufts of reddish hair sticking out at odd angles to complete the picture. He looked like a hyena with mange.

Over six feet tall, fish-belly white, with a heavily muscled torso and huge hands, Gravenholtz wore a filthy, oversize coat that concealed his powerful frame but left him steaming hot, itchy and miserable. Thirty-nine years old and this is what it had come down to. Two days he'd been standing out here—if he hadn't wanted to kill somebody before, he sure wanted to do it now. Actually . . . he was always ready to do some damage. That's what the Old One liked about him. A natural aptitude, that's what he called it. Gravenholtz had killed a dozen men in the last year, here, there and everywhere the Old One had sent him. He shifted in the sun, wished this Mexican oil minister would show up so his aptitude could kick in, and he could get back to his air-conditioned suite and those frosty rum drinks that Baby had introduced him to. He rubbed the fake pustules dappled across his forehead, wanting to tear his face off.

Don't fret, Lester, Baby had said after the makeup techs had finished with him. *You're going to be as handsome as ever when this is over.*

Maybe handsome enough to throw a fuck to, that's what Gravenholtz had thought. Ever since they had shown up at the Old One's Miami hideaway, Baby had stayed in her own bed. Turns out the old man was her daddy, which was some big dark secret, and since the Old One was Muslim, and Baby was still technically a married woman, that was that. Last night, while the two of them watched the beach from her veranda, she had given him a perfunctory jerkoff, not even taking his dick out of his pants, laughing as he popped his cork within moments. Ha-ha.

The *Old One.* What a crock. Baby tried to tell him that her father was at least 130 years old, but the geezer wasn't a day over seventy, tops. Gravenholtz played along—guy was a billionaire with his own private army, he could call himself fucking Methuselah for all Gravenholtz cared. He remembered hearing some big news about how it wasn't the Jews dirty-bombed New York and D.C. and Mecca thirty years ago—it was the Old One and his crazy-ass master plan. The Muslim messiah come to bring on the Caliphate, which was evidently dancing girls and flying carpets from sea to shining sea. Truth be told, Gravenholtz didn't give a shit if the Jews toasted New York, or if it was the Old One or the Sugarplum Fairy. That was ancient history and somebody else's bad luck, not his.

One thing for certain, the old man had enough enemies for more than one lifetime. Not that it seemed to concern him much. Baby said the only one he was really worried about was Rakkim Epps. That was all it took to convince him to sign on with the Old One. Gravenholtz would have paid money for the chance to kill Rakkim.

Gravenholtz squinted in the sun, amazed at all the sky tattoos. He had seen them in the Bible Belt a few times, a baby Jesus in the manger sketched over Atlanta at Christmas, and the stars and bars on Independence Day, but *here* . . . there were all kinds of ads plastered across the sky here, offering everything from time-share underwater condos to sex drink specials at the beachfront nightclubs. One of the largest tattoos looked just like the ocean, a full-on underwater scene up there in the clouds, manta rays and dolphins swimming in perfect unison.

He changed position, his pants sticking to him in the heat so he had to adjust his pecker, and he thought about the hump-girl in the pigtails last night. The old man might be territorial about his daughter, but he didn't mind importing pussy for Graven-holtz. Every night a new one appeared at his door. All colors and ages, from young to younger. Slim ones and big ripe ones with hungry eyes and soft mouths. Some of them spoke English and some didn't speak at all, which was just as well. Gravenholtz let them in, gave them the best workout they had probably ever had and sent them on their way. It didn't help. They weren't Baby. He requested ones that looked like her—long-legged Southern girls with honey hair, all pouty and pink as far as the eye could see. . . . He would close his eyes and pretend they were her, but he didn't really have that kind of imagination. He got mad some-times, busted a few of the girls up pretty bad. That helped, but it didn't last.

A party bus drove by, music blaring out this chunky Latin beat that he could feel running up his thighbones. People danced on the top deck of the bus, hoisted pastel umbrella drinks, women shaking their bare brown titties for all the world to see. Nueva Florida, where the world comes to cut loose. Bon-erama, nonstop.

Say what you want, the Cubans who ran Nueva Florida knew how to have fun. The couple hundred miles of white-sand beach fronting the Atlantic were covered with luxury resorts: Alligator Ballet, the Fountain of Youth, Everglades Under Glass . . . but it was Viva Libertad! that drew the most tourists, Viva Libertad!, a thousand acre thumb in the eye to that bearded commie prick who ruled Cuba once upon a time. No fun in that Cuba, just work work work and rationed toilet paper. Viva Libertad! was all glitz and glamour, a theme park development of manicured beaches and luxury hotels. At the center of the resort was Castro-land, a run-down slum modeled after old Havana, a crumbling facade of cheap buildings, falling-apart cars and beggars hustling handouts.

He watched the legless teenager across the street, saw him hop over and take a beer from a cooler hidden in an abandoned sofa. Stumpy popped the beer — his fourth of the afternoon — and finished it in two long swallows. He smiled at Gravenholtz as his belch echoed, tossed the empty bottle against a brick wall, sprayed broken glass. Happiest dead man Gravenholtz had ever seen, probably already thinking about the virgins waiting for him in Paradise, ready to do a dance on his dick. The Old One had the assassination of the oil minister all worked out, but he forgot to ask Gravenholtz how he felt about being Stumpy's decoy. Where's the fun in that? No, if there was anyone going to get his hands dirty, it was going to be Gravenholtz. If the Old One didn't like it . . . well, they could discuss that when he got back to the hotel.

Gravenholtz sweated as the buses and limos rolled past, thinking how much he missed the Belt. He had been happy working for the Colonel back in Tennessee. The Colonel was the most powerful warlord in the Belt, Gravenholtz his special enforcer, keeping the shitbirds in line and loving every minute of it. Yeah, it was one sweet situation, until Baby gave him the look that one afternoon, the Colonel's young wife back from horseback riding, sitting up on that white stallion like the queen of Sheba. *How you doing, Lester?* she said, staring down at him with those green eyes, the top button of her blouse undone so he could see the beauty mark between her breasts. The Colonel had been gone that day, and when Baby shook out her hair it was like a golden net he couldn't escape. *I'm bored, Lester Gravenholtz.*

If he had said no to Baby that day Gravenholtz would still be the Colonel's chief ass kicker. Instead . . . he waved at the gnats that buzzed his mouth . . . instead, he was standing under a phony banyan tree while tourists hurried past, crossed themselves and thanked God that they didn't have whatever the fuck he was supposed to have. Welcome to Castroland. Stumpy across the street did a flip, walked around on his hands to applause from the small crowd gathered around him. Gravenholtz squeezed out a dry fart.

A South American tour group walked past Gravenholtz, Brazilians with their emerald jewelry flashing, hurrying now as they got a good look at him. A little girl with short black hair started crying, buried her face into her mother's hips, was quickly lifted into the señora's arms. The elephant man prosthetic scared off normal folk, but according to the Old One it was just the thing to reel in the oil minister, make him go all gooey inside.

Gravenholtz watched the helicopters fluttering overhead, hotel guests heading out to what was left of the Bahamas. A year ago, he and Baby had stolen the Colonel's prize Chinese helicopter and flown to Florida, along with three of Gravenholtz's men. Supposed to sell the bird for enough that they could all live high and easy for a while. Good plan, but Baby changed it.

She had them set down the chopper in the Everglades. They barely got out before Baby shot his boys in the head, one-two-three, just like that. You'd think she'd been waiting forever to do it from the look on her face. *Come on, Lester honey,* she had said, tugging on his earlobe, *I want you to meet my daddy.* Good thing Baby hadn't tried shooting him—bullets just stung, but the betrayal might have pissed him off so bad he forgot himself.

He watched a barefoot mamacita waddle out of a shanty and start hanging clothes on a line. Bright colored tops with frayed sleeves, shorts with holes in them. He could hear her huffing and puffing from where he stood, raising herself up to pin the clothes.

The Islamic Republic had the Fedayeen, best fighters in the world maybe, so to counter that, twenty years ago some generals in the Bible Belt set up a secret project. They brought over this Jap scientist to build their own supersoldiers, augment the raw human material, so to speak, the psychos and sadists used for the experiments. Jap jobs, they called them, like that name might keep them in their place. Turned out the Belt generals were afraid of the Jap jobs almost as much as they were afraid of the Fedayeen.

Took at least thirty operations to make a Jap job, painful too . . . not that he remembered much about it, just dreams of bright lights and sharp knives peeling him open layer by layer like a pink onion. The Jap scientist had done something else to them . . . tweaked their frontal lobes a little bit, removing some moral governor that most human beings had. You ask Gravenholtz, there wasn't more than a smidge in him anyway.

Gravenholtz inhaled as he spotted a dark blue limo approaching. It looked just like the other hotel limos, but this one rode a little low from the added weight, one of the VIP German models, fully armored, top, bottom and sides. He kept his head down as the limo slowed . . . slowed . . . finally came to a stop in front of him and stayed there, idling softly.

Gravenholtz shuffled closer, edged his begging basket ahead of him with the toe of his shoe. The sun burned the back of his neck, heat rippling through him clear down to his fingertips. He could see the legless kid reflected in the security glass of the limo, the kid swinging along on his hands, begging basket clenched between his teeth.

The passenger door of the limo opened and a slender, light-skinned Mexican got out, a machine pistol swinging from a shoulder rig. Gravenholtz glimpsed the driver looking over at him, disgusted, before the door thudded shut.

He stared blankly ahead as the Mexican wanded him, taking his time. Explosives, metal, nuclear or biologic toxins, the wand screened for everything . . . but there wasn't any metal in Gravenholtz. None of those other things either.

The Jap scientist had used biologic body armor on Gravenholtz. Flexible body armor with hardly any seams. Made of some unique material where the more it was compressed, the stronger it got. The early jobs relied on their reinforced fists and feet, their heavy-density joints, but Gravenholtz was the prototype for the new model. New and improved, just like laundry detergent and mouth rinse. Might have made a real difference if they were ever put into full production . . . might have ended the stalemate between the Belt and the Republic, but something happened. Gravenholtz was on a solo training mission, doing what he did best, and when he came back to the lab complex everyone was dead. All the other Jap jobs, the head scientist and his team. Must have taken a full Fedayeen strike force. Gravenholtz had been shocked at first, then he thought, maybe it wasn't so bad to be the last of his kind. Made him even more special.

The light-skinned Mexican had him raise his shoes so he could test the soles, and when the man bent forward, Gravenholtz could see a tiny bald spot on the crown of his head, right there among that nest of fine brown hair. Would have been a problem for him in a few years . . . so there was that to thank him for. Not that anyone ever did. In the smoked glass, he could see the legless kid hovering nearby, keeping just out of range of the wand.

The Mexican nodded to somebody inside the limo, then pivoted, the machine pistol making a slow arc. He jerked his chin at the legless kid, ordered him back.

Stumpy did a one-armed push-up.

The Mexican laughed.

The rear door of the limo slid open, another bodyguard in the doorway, beckoning. *"Andale!"*

Gravenholtz moved closer, dragging one foot. He stepped into the limo, swayed in the doorway.

At that moment, the legless kid bounded toward the limo.

Gravenholtz was supposed to hold the door open just long enough for the kid to fling himself inside, then step out and slam it shut. The blast would pulverize everyone inside the limo, leaving Gravenholtz free to kill the remaining bodyguard and escape. He and Stumpy had practiced the move for the last two days until it was perfect. Kid never said a word the whole time, just had that same weird little smile like he had now as he launched himself at the open door, bullets ricocheting off the pavement.

The bodyguard tried to shove him aside, but Gravenholtz held his ground inside the limo, his eyes on the kid and the smile that got bigger and bigger as he shot through the air . . . until Gravenholtz slammed the door in his face.

The blast rocked the limo, the light blinding for an instant, even through the security glass. Gravenholtz fell back against the bodyguard, the man cursing as the limo raced erratically down the street, tires squealing.

"*Jefe . . . Jefe, está usted bien?*" gasped the bodyguard, pulling himself to his feet. He looked out the back window for pursuers. There were none. "*Jefe?*"

"*Estoy bien, Esteban. Muy bien.*" The oil minister nestled in the plush leather bench seat facing Gravenholtz, his hands gripped together to hide their trembling.

The bodyguard sat back down, one hand resting on his pistol.

"*Hablas español, señor?*" the oil minister said to Gravenholtz.

Gravenholtz watched a police helicopter circling the blast site.

"Do you speak English, sir?" said the oil minister without a trace of an accent.

Gravenholtz cocked his head at the tooth lodged in the pitted blastproof window. His mollusk mouth twisted, plasti-flesh flapping around his gums. He tapped the glass. "If you put that under your pillow tonight, the tooth fairy will leave you money."

"Yes . . . yes, I've heard that," said the oil minister. "Thank you for saving my life."

Gravenholtz scratched at his matted hair. "I didn't want to let the cold air out."

"Of course. It's very hot outside, isn't it?" said the oil minister.

"I like cold air," said Gravenholtz.

"*Jefe, por favor—*" started the bodyguard.

The oil minister silenced him with a glance, pressed a finger to his ear, listening. "I'm fine. No, that won't be necessary." His eyes stayed on Gravenholtz. "I don't *want* an escort, is that clear?" He settled back in his seat. "What is your name, señor?"

"Lester."

"Do you know who I am, Lester?"

"A man with air-conditioning," said Lester.

The oil minister smiled. "Yes, Lester, I *am* a man with air-conditioning." He had eyes like gray pearls, smooth brown skin and a trimmed mustache. Shiny black suit and a necktie of woven platinum. "I am also a man with a son who looks very much like you."

"There . . . there ain't nobody like me," said Gravenholtz.

"My son feels exactly the same way. He's twenty-four years old next month . . . and very lonely." The oil minister plucked at the crease in his slacks. "I'm afraid I don't get to spend much time with him. Hardly anyone even knows of his existence. A man in my position . . ." He winced. "Are *you* lonely, Lester?"

"Not really."

"I see," said the oil minister. "Do you have family?"

Gravenholtz shook his head.

"Well, then, perhaps you could do me a favor. Would you like to come live with my son? Keep him company? Be his friend?"

Gravenholtz pondered the questions. "Will there be air-conditioning?"

"Cold as you want, Lester. I'll fly in a mountain of snow for you two to sled down if you like. My son has never had anyone to play with . . . no one who really wanted to play with him." The oil minister leaned forward slightly. "You could have anything you ask for."

Gravenholtz nodded. He was tired of the game. "Anything?"

"Absolutely."

Gravenholtz pointed at the bodyguard. "Could I kill that pissant 'fore I kill you?"

The bodyguard was already raising his pistol when Gravenholtz chopped him across the bridge of the nose, the armored edge of his hand driving the facial bones deep into the man's brain.

The oil minister must have hit the emergency button, because the driver braked *hard*, the limo skidding across the road, knocking oncoming cars aside as if they were made of aluminum cans. They finally came to rest after crashing through a billboard advertising canned banana daiquiris that froze to a perfect slush when you opened the top.

Gravenholtz grabbed the oil minister by the necktie, jerked him close, close enough to smell the huevos rancheros the man had had for breakfast. "I ain't *nobody's* playmate, Pancho," he said, twisting the necktie, platinum links breaking off between his fingers as blood leaked from the oil minister's tear ducts. Gravenholtz jerked forward as the driver unloaded into his back. He broke the oil minister's neck and threw open the door.

A Hotel Viva! van on the way back from the beach had pulled over, tourists in bathing suits standing around ready to help. Until they saw Gravenholtz get out.

Gravenholtz tore open the door, dragged the driver out, the man still clutching the machine pistol, crying out for somebody, Mama, Papa, Jesus H. Christ or the presidente of Aztlán, it didn't make no difference. Gravenholtz drove his fist into the man's chest, ribs splintering like a bag of sticks, then tossed him aside and slid behind the wheel.

He backed out of the daiquiri billboard and peeled out into traffic. The front end wobbled a little bit, but it was a good ride. The old man and Baby would be pissed at him for changing the plan, but too bad. Hold the door open for Stumpy? *Yaz, boss.* Like Gravenholtz was some hotel doorman with gold brushes on his shoulders.

Gravenholtz maxed the air-conditioning, basking in the cold air. His back itched where the driver had shot him, the seat soaked with blood. No big deal. Only man who had ever really put a hurt on him was Rakkim. He had slipped a Fedayeen blade into Gravenholtz at the Colonel's base camp, found a seam in his armor and cut through to the soft parts like he had X-ray vision. Done it right in front of Baby too. Rakkim almost killed him, which was reason enough for Gravenholtz to go looking for him, prove to the man that he had just gotten lucky. It was more than that, though. He had seen the way that Baby looked at Rakkim, heating things up. Gravenholtz accelerated, one hand on the wheel. Revenge or jealousy, it didn't matter. Either way, that shit couldn't stand.

CHAPTER 2

Rakkim saw the fire as he left the mosque, a greasy red glow rising over the darkened buildings of New Fallujah like a sunrise in hell. Imam Jenkins stood outlined against the glow for a moment, then started up the cobblestone streets toward the blaze, his robe a billow of coarse, black fabric in the wind. Rakkim joined the faithful as they followed the cleric, and the faithful, seeing Rakkim's green jihadi headband, lowered their eyes and gave him room, fearful of incurring his wrath. He didn't blame them.

Jihadis were unstable cowards drunk with death, suicide bombers waiting for the call to heaven, eager to prove their devotion to the Grand Mullah. Last month a jihadi had blown himself up in a packed movie theater in Los Angeles, killed over a hundred Christians watching a new Brazilian romantic comedy. A second bomber detonated himself as the ambulances arrived. You'd think that Allah loved loud noises. If so, God was going to be disappointed, because the jihadi that Rakkim took the headband from got his ticket to Paradise punched without making a sound.

Jenkins increased his pace, his long garments flapping in the storm, dust swirling around his scrawny frame. Head shaved, his beard gone to gray, he was part of the Grand Mullah's inner circle, a Black Robe, one of those grim guardians of public virtue who dominated the fundamentalist stronghold once known as San Francisco.

No cars allowed on the streets after late-night prayers, no stores or cafés open, no satellite dishes on the roofs. Just the faithful. And Rakkim. A deep-cover agent for the moderates who governed the Islamic Republic, he was thirty-four years old, lean and tautly muscled, poised as a tightrope walker in loose-fitting pants and a thin jacket. Like the other men from the mosque his dark hair was cut short, his beard no longer than a fist. Unlike the rest of them, he wasn't out of breath as he climbed the hill. Rakkim moved effortlessly up the steep slope . . . just like Jenkins.

Rakkim stepped over the rusted cable car tracks and spotted a data chip peeking out from under the rails in the dim light. He bent down quickly, pulled it free. The crowd parted around him, flowed on either side, no one daring to make contact.

The chip gleamed in the moonlight. Must have dated from around the transition forty years ago, a thin black plastic rectangle with a platinum edge. Maximum limit. The hologram of the owner's face was faded, but she had been beautiful, with long, black hair, her head cocked playfully. No idea why he had used the past tense in speaking of the woman, but she had hidden the chip away for safekeeping and not come back for it in thirty years. Jewish, maybe, or accused of witchcraft . . . or just too proud to stay silent when silence was called for. Whatever her supposed crime, she was gone, the chip and the hope for escape it contained long since abandoned. Rakkim lightly touched her holographic face, whispered a prayer for her soul, then tucked the chip back under the rail. Maybe someone else would retrieve it someday and find out who she was, and what had happened to her. Someone in a more peaceful time. He hurried on through the crowd, moving through them with gentle touches on shoulders and hips, a shadow warrior technique, men giving him room without them even being aware of it.

Two lower-ranking Black Robes watched the crowd pass from a side street—they bowed to Jenkins but made no move to join the throng. Black Robes patrolled the city day and night, alert for signs of sin: a careless profanity or the sound of singing from inside a home, a woman with an improperly fitted burqa, or children playing too enthusiastically. So many sins to keep track of, so many punishments to mete out.

Rakkim heard sirens in the distance, fire trucks approaching from the opposite direction. Two trucks . . . one about ten blocks ahead of the other, driving faster, the engine misfiring. He could smell the fire now, burning wood and plaster and many coats of paint. An old building. They burned hot and fast. No one around him reacted, oblivious, their senses dull in comparison with his.

Put Rakkim in a small, dark room, not a speck of light, put him there alone in the dark except for four scorpions scattered about, four pale yellow scorpions from the North African desert. Androctonus australis, highly aggressive and deadly as a cobra. Put Rakkim in that room and tell him to find the scorpions before they found him. You had to know how to listen to survive in that room. You had to know exactly where you were in space without any reference points. Most of all, you had to be patient, to wait for the scorpions to move. Without patience you'd never get out alive. Rakkim was in that room eleven hours before he killed all four of them. He was already a Fedayeen when he walked into the room, first in his class . . . he was a shadow warrior when he walked out.

Fedayeen were the elite warriors of the Islamic Republic, genetically altered to be stronger and faster, go days without sleep and recover from injuries that would kill a normal man. Only one in a thousand qualified for Fedayeen, and only one in a thousand Fedayeen qualified to be a shadow warrior, men able to blend into any social environment, from the Bible Belt to the Mormon territories, to a Black Robe stronghold like New Fallujah. Hard work to stay invisible. The wrong accent, the wrong shoes or simply holding a fork in an improper manner could draw attention, and attention could bring death.

Wind whipped through the narrow streets, howling like a wounded ghost, the smell of smoke stronger now. The city always had lousy weather, but the storms were getting worse, part of a global climate change. The monsoons had shifted, China was in the tenth year of drought and Europe had the worst flash floods in history. If the wind was right, there were days when the West Coast from L.A. to Seattle was cloaked in smog from the firestorms burning up Australia. Sarah said New Orleans sinking was a warning of things to come, then got mad at him when he shrugged and said he'd buy her a boat.

The crowd trudged on, past boarded-up storefronts and apartment buildings where the residents peeked out from behind closed curtains. Most of the men around Rakkim were tech workers from nearby factories, sullen men in plain overalls and cheap, down-filled jackets. They worked twelve-hour shifts churning out cheap parts for Chinese nanocomputers, dangerous work, the fumes toxic but a steady source of hard currency. Rakkim made his way near the front of the moving throng, close enough to see the age spots on the back of Jenkins's bald head. The women from the mosque lumbered behind, slowed by their voluminous black burqas, barely able to see out of the eye slits.

Rakkim remembered Jenkins's sermon an hour ago, haranguing the believers to remain morally ruthless. *A woman who does not fear her husband is already a harlot in her dreams, her husband already a pimp by his weakness!* Jenkins had shouted, voice echoing off the dome of the mosque. Kneeling on their prayer rugs, the men nodded in agreement. From the other side of the mosque, half hidden behind a decorative grate, many of the women had nodded too.

He hated New Fallujah. Christians in the Belt were all over each other, skin to skin, sweating and cursing so easily it was part of the environment, like the humidity and gardenia blooms perfuming the air. He came back from a mission in the Belt, all he wanted to do was make love with Sarah, rest his cheek against the heat of her belly afterward, then make love some more. When he came back from New Fallujah . . . he was just going to play with Michael, listen to his three-year-old son giggle and try to forget all the ugly things fundamentalists did to each other in the name of God.

Rats skittered underfoot, darting among the crowd, but Rakkim seemed to be the only one who noticed.

Rakkim lived in Seattle, the capital of the Republic, a bastion of moderate Islam, where even Catholics could get an education. You heard music in Seattle, saw women in public with their heads bare and couples holding hands. New Fallujah was a city without bright colors or laughter, just the tightening vise of piety squeezing the life out of people.

Ibn-Azziz, Grand Mullah of the Black Robes, considered Seattle a non-Islamic cesspool. There were Black Robe senators in the congress, and what they lacked in numbers they made up for in intensity. President Brandt had been in office barely a year and already ibn-Azziz was demanding Shar'ia law be extended throughout the nation. His demand had been rejected . . . for now. The president thought the matter was settled, but he was naive. The Fedayeen commander, General Kidd, knew better. That's why he had sent Rakkim into New Fallujah.

Rakkim saw the fire now—the Ayman al-Zawahiri madrassa, a girls' boarding school housed in the former St. Regis Hotel, was ablaze. Flames shot fifty feet into the air, gray smoke boiling up into the night, driven higher and higher by the wind roaring off the bay. He heard the whoosh of burning lumber, paint bubbling off the outside of the building and the screams. Fire engines idled nearby, but the water pressure in the aging underground pipes was weak, the firefighters' trucks ineffectually shooting water onto the flames. The spray drifted across the yellow streetlights . . . gleaming in the moonlight.

Worshipers from the mosque joined the onlookers, neighbors and family of the children inside the school pressing against the police cordon that surrounded the burning madrassa. Women watched from behind their eye slits, flames reflected in their steady gaze. Firefighters dashed into the building, retreated as the wind kicked the blaze higher, then charged up the stairs again. Voices muffled, the girls' mothers wailed, the sound seeming to float in the air, while the police stood silently, blue uniforms covered in ash.

Cheers erupted, mothers ululating with joy as two firefighters ran out of the madrassa, each carrying a couple of small girls over their shoulders. Mothers rushed the firemen, grabbed their children, sobbing, the children coughing into their mothers' necks.

Jenkins pushed past the police, pulled a long, flexible flail from under his robes and began whipping the women, the girls screaming as their mothers turned, taking the lashing on their backs.

"Return them to where they came!" demanded Jenkins.

The women clutched their children.

"Would you consign your daughters to the darkest pit of hell?" Jenkins shouted, veins bulging in his scrawny neck. "Would you prefer a child steeped in wickedness or a child raised among the blessed in Paradise?"

"Save their honor," said one of the fathers, eyes downcast. "I . . . I have other daughters, imam."

"No, save *them*!" A woman broke from the crowd, confronted Jenkins, her voice booming through the burqa. "Let Allah decide who is virtuous and who is wicked—"

Jenkins cuffed the woman to the ground. "The world has enough whores."

"*Allahu Akbar!*" called other voices in the crowd, other women, other parents kicking at the woman, shouting their agreement. "*Allahu Akbar!*"

The upper windows of the madrassa blew out, glass shimmering as it fell through the air. Five girls clustered on the outer balcony, far above the street, raising their arms to the sky, howling, their white night clothes billowing up past their knees. Rakkim felt sick. Jenkins had decided it was better that the girls burn than be exposed in their underclothes. Better to burn than be seen by men not of their family, their reputation destroyed and along with it, the good name of their relatives.

Rats scurried from the burning building, their tails on fire.

Three teenagers leaped through a ground-floor window, sprawled on the ground for a moment, bleeding, then ran toward their parents. Jenkins intercepted them, whipped them back, the tips of his beard smoldering, pinpricks of red light surrounding his face as the flail rose and fell. Police joined in, pushing the girls back into the flames.

Rakkim worked his way around to the opposite side of the building, the east side where the smoke was thickest. No crowd here, no security cameras, just a few women huddled in the shadows, wailing and fingering prayer beads, and two burly policemen, their eyes watering from the smoke. An eight-foot chain-link fence surrounded this side of the madrassa, the links glowing in the heat.

A blond girl stumbled out of one of the lower windows, her nightgown smoldering. She sprang onto the fence, but fell back, hands scorched. She spit on her palms, started climbing again, ignoring the pain, her bare legs golden in the firelight. She had almost made it to the top when one of the cops ambled over, zapped her with his stun-stick. She fell back inside the fence, twitching.

Rakkim killed the cop with a single blow to the base of his skull, dropped him like a bag of wet cement. The other cop charged, but Rakkim dodged the stun-stick, crushed the man's windpipe with a thrust of his hand and kept moving. Rakkim walked into the oily black smoke, slashed the fence with his Fedayeen knife, the carbon-polymer blade slicing through the metal links as though they were cobwebs. Rakkim slipped through the gap, grabbed the blond girl and carried her through, the girl clutching at his chest, still dazed. She smelled of smoke and pine tar soap. Rakkim set the blond girl down, then rushed back for the others, who were staggering out of the madrassa.

He gathered up three of them like a bouquet of flowers, brought them through the fence. Women beckoned from the shadows, and the girls ran to them, disappeared into the night. He was going back for the others when the madrassa groaned as though it were alive, one whole side erupting in a ball of blue fire.

Face stinging, Rakkim ran forward, snatched the remaining two girls off the ground. He looked behind him, saw more girls stumbling down the stairs, fire everywhere, and then the whole madrassa collapsed—sparks erupted like fireflies rising up into the night, followed by a wall of heat that blistered the back of his neck. He turned as he fell, protected the girls from the worst of it, then passed them on to the women . . . who took care not to touch him, this man who was not part of their family. He watched them go. The women would hide the girls as best they could, but it wouldn't be enough. Rakkim hadn't really saved them, merely postponed their fate. The girls were still breathing, but they were already dead, condemned by the imam's decree.

He glimpsed the crescent moon low over the city, bloodred through the haze, which probably meant something, but he didn't know what, or care, either. Omens, signs and portents . . . that was for weaklings looking for some sort of edge. Like Allah was signaling his intentions in code, with only the initiated privy to his will. No . . . God didn't play games. He wasn't a co-conspirator. God either hit you hard and fast, and that was *that*, or he sat back and watched things spool out, laughing all the way.

Rakkim dragged the bodies of the two dead policemen to the gutter, pushed them into the sewer below. Then he circled the site, knife nestled in his hand, rage in his heart. He eased through the crowd, barely stirring their awareness, until he stood beside Imam Jenkins, stood right there on his left side, a half step behind. A blind spot.

Jenkins watched the burning madrassa as Rakkim stepped forward, his knife cutting through the coarse material of Jenkins's robe, sliding just under the imam's armpit. A gentle stroke would sever the man's brachial artery, bleed him out onto the cobblestones in a gush. Rakkim felt the imam shiver against the blade, but the man didn't shout for help or try to escape.

"The molten torments of hell await the one who harms a servant of Allah," Jenkins said quietly, looking straight ahead.

"I'll take my chances." Rakkim stepped closer, blocking anyone's view as the knife caressed the man's flesh. "How about you?"

"You smell of fire . . . and the soap used in the madrassa," whispered Jenkins.

"Your senses are sharp as ever. It's a burden sometimes, isn't it?"

"*Rakkim?*"

Rakkim's lips brushed the man's ear. "You're going to give new orders, old friend. You're going to declare the girls who escaped the flames innocent of immorality."

"Why . . . why are you doing this?"

Rakkim twisted the blade ever so slightly.

Jenkins kept his gaze on the burning embers. "So my choice is to be murdered by you . . . or executed by the Grand Mullah for encouraging lust?"

"Not at all," murmured Rakkim. "Wonder of wonders, *imam*, it was the grace of Allah that led them through the fire. Is this not a clear sign of God's intention?" He felt Jenkins tremble, a trickle of blood running warm across Rakkim's fingers. "The Grand Mullah will applaud your decision, imam. Think of the babies these girls will someday present to Allah, the future warriors and wives of warriors."

"You don't know the Grand Mullah."

"A man of your talents," said Rakkim, "you could convince the stones to sing."

Firefighters hosed down the wreckage, steam rising, red in the firelight.

"*Give* the proclamation," said Rakkim, the blade cutting deeper with every beat of Jenkins's heart. "Declare the girls innocent."

"Hear me!" Jenkins's voice echoed across the site, the command voice that cut through outside noise and reached directly to believers.

Rakkim listened as the imam spoke of the girls spared from the flames and the infinite mercy of Allah. Listened as the crowd blessed this news, women weeping with joy, men falling to their knees. The firefighters continued to spray down the embers.

Jenkins remained standing as the crowd dispersed, letting the night close in around them before he turned to Rakkim. "A shadow warrior who brings attention to himself," said Jenkins, as the wreckage popped and hissed. "Threatening me . . . playing the hero . . . and for what? *Schoolgirls.*" His mouth twisted. "You're a disgrace to the Fedayeen."

Rakkim slipped the knife free, wiped Jenkins's blood on his black robe, the stain shiny in the moonlight. "Alas, I had a poor teacher."

CHAPTER 3

Sarah glowered at the wallscreen in Spider's bedroom, watching a news conference from earlier today—Aztlán's Presidente Argusto at his hacienda outside Tucson; chair tilted back, silver-heeled boots on the desk as he lectured the press. Sarah was glad the sound was off; she couldn't stand hearing that strutting popinjay's voice. The narco-billionaires who had formerly ruled Mexico had been morally reprehensible, but at least their concerns were money and power, not territorial expansion. Not so the Aztec militarists like Argusto who had ousted the drug lords and resurrected the empire. El Presidente had already peeled a chunk of Texas off from the Belt; now he had turned his attention back to the Republic, and he wasn't going to be happy until he gobbled up the whole Southwest. *Reclaimed* it, while President Brandt dithered in the Oval Office, more concerned with the state of his hair than the state of the nation. She looked over at Leo, Spider's son, who slumped in a chair. "Are you *sure* of your information?"

"I don't *make* mistakes," Leo sniffed, a teenage brainiac with a pale pudding face and soft hands, awkward and arrogant and allergic to everything from dust mites to roses.

"Encryption was nine levels deep, Sarah, they don't waste that kind of effort on trial balloons," explained Spider, propped up in bed, head lolling on the pillows. The room smelled faintly of ozone from the static generators that prevented eavesdropping. The house was a run-down two-story box in a Catholic neighborhood of Seattle, a ramshackle Craftsman with buckled floors, peeling paint and state-of-the-art security. "The memo Leo decoded said the president will issue an executive order on water rights next week."

"What a coward." Sarah adjusted Spider's pillows, noted his shallow breathing. A short, paunchy gnome and brilliant mathematician, Spider had led the Jewish resistance during the early years of Muslim rule, hiding in the tunnels under the capital for twenty years. Jews were no longer hunted, but the decades spent without sunlight or fresh air had taken a toll. "Wait until the people find out Brandt's in negotiations to give Aztlán water rights to the Colorado River itself."

"The *people*?" Spider's voice cracked. "You're a historian, you should know better."

"Have you heard from Rikki?" asked Spider. "I wanted to ask him—"

Sarah shook her head.

"Do you know where he is?"

"Yes." The word left a bad taste in her mouth. "Honoring a request from General Kidd."

Spider patted her hand. "No wonder you look worried."

Sarah and Rakkim had argued before he left. They were doing a lot of that lately.

Let General Kidd send someone else, she had said.

There is no one else.

There's always someone else.

I'm the one he asked.

No, said Sarah, *you're the one who said yes.*

There had barely been time to make up before he left early that morning, and the making up was just a prelude to the next argument. Terrible thing to be in love with someone as hardheaded as herself. Better she had married a weakling from a good family, a foppish modern who did as he was told. Still . . . there was something to be said for making up with Rakkim as dawn streaked the sky.

"It's good to see you smile," said Spider. "You've been too serious lately."

"Can you blame me?"

"Surviving dangerous times requires a sense of humor,"

said Spider. "That's why I love Rikki. I wish he was here now."

"Me too," said Leo.

Sarah blinked back tears, annoyed at herself for her weakness. "I . . . I want you both to see something." She pulled a thumb projector out of her pocket, sent the wallscreen flickering, replacing Presidente Argusto with a cityscape breaking up, jumpy.

Leo rummaged in his ear with a fingertip. "Where are we?"

"Washington, D.C.," said Sarah.

Leo involuntarily curled into his chair.

The camera panned across a street filled with rubble and stalled cars, zoomed in on a ragged American flag lying against the curb. An insulated boot entered the frame, nudged the flag. *Found this in an office at the Pentagon,* drawled the voice-over, the sound muffled. *Probably some general's. Very rare. Open for bids.*

For an instant the cameraman's image was reflected in a sheet of cracked glass, a wiry man in a decontamination suit, his sunken cheeks visible through the plexi-hood, hair plastered against his scalp. The dirty bomb had done more than incinerate D.C.; it had started a chain reaction in the covert facilities that ringed the capital, the very sites whose wall of directed gamma radiation was intended to protect the city. Forty years later the capital was still a hot zone.

"This footage is from Eldon Harrison, one of the scavengers working the D.C. site," said Sarah. "You'd be surprised what they find, and there's an international clientele of collectors and historians eager to buy. I purchased a White House license plate from this particular man for the university a few years ago. Encased in leaded acrylic, of course—"

"D.C.'s a deathtrap," said Leo. "Don't they know that?"

"They know it better than anyone," Sarah said, "but the locals have to feed their families. They gear up in surplus decon suits and homemade adaptations when they go on salvage runs . . . and they die young. The lucky ones, anyway. They call themselves zombies, proud of the risks they take."

"They should call themselves dumbasses," said Leo. "Why don't they move?"

"Because their people have lived there for three hundred years and it's home," Sarah said. "And sometimes they find things that can make them rich overnight. Last year, a piece of the Declaration of Independence sold to a private collector in Capetown for seventeen million Mandelas." She shrugged. "It was fake, but even so . . ."

More interference onscreen, then the image stabilized on a brass plaque etched with the words *Watergate Hotel*, the plaque dented where it had been pried off a wall. *All kinds of sex scandals at the Watergate, politicians grinding away like millstones.* Cut to the front page of a newspaper . . . yellowed and brittle but real paper, *The Washington Post* . . . children pictured frolicking in a fountain . . . the date was July 18, 2015, the day the dirty bomb went off. *I got a few of these babies, one to a customer. Put your bid in fast.*

Sarah leaned forward. "Pay attention."

Static onscreen for at least ten seconds, then the image returned to a completely different location, the image flipping, more static. *Julia, put this up on the restricted section of the Web site. Eyes only, client BK-271. She has the access code.* The light bounced off the walls of a half-collapsed tunnel, claustrophobic, the zombie's breathing heavier now, his decon suit scraping against the sides as he scooted forward on his belly. *Are you seeing this, Sarah? If . . . if I'm right, this is going to change everything, just like you wanted,* he said, trying to catch his breath. The light bounced off a small hatch at the end of the tunnel. Fumbling sounds and the zombie's laser torch snapped on.

The wallscreen went dark, then came back on, a ragged cut around the hatch now. The zombie beat on the hatch with a small hammer until it fell into the space beyond with a crash. He scooted forward. Dust shimmered in the camera beam, reflected off the inside of a larger room, the image jumping wildly. The steel hatch had fallen beside an antique desk. Oil paintings on the walls . . . men in high ruffled collars and clerical garb, serious faces, most of them in profile, their eyes fixed on something unseen. The beam touched the slightly ajar door of the secure room . . . heavily reinforced, touchpad locks, DNA encryption, all useless now. *This is it. I knew . . . I knew I'd find it if I just kept . . . kept searching.* Sound of the zombie trying to squirm through the tight opening.

The light moved across the room. A pair of flintlock dueling pistols rested in an open case against the far wall. Another case showed parchment under armored glass. The light beam swept the room, the zombie looking for something. A large painted wooden globe, the continents wrong somehow. On the floor . . . something white, a skeleton hand emerging from the sleeve of a dark blue suit, the rest of the man hidden behind the desk. A gold wedding band gleamed among the finger bones. Near the hand . . . a small chunk of wood on the floor. A bud vase lay on the desk, directly in the zombie's line of vision; any water had long since evaporated, but the red rose was intact. *Yes, yes, yes, there it is.*

"What's with the flower?" said Leo. "I didn't think there was anything alive in D.C."

"There's not," said Sarah. "I've seen cherry trees from the tidal basin offered for sale, some even with blossoms intact. They look perfect, but the whole tree disintegrates as soon as someone tries to move them."

"Then why's he so excited?" said Leo.

"It's not the flower he's excited about," said Sarah.

Spider looked over at her, then back to the wallscreen.

The zombie tried again to get a shoulder through the narrow opening, camera jiggling on the raw metal. *Gonna need . . . Oh . . . shit.* The zombie turned the camera on himself, used his light to see something. *Damn.* The man blinked behind the scratched plexi-hood, clutched at the tear in the shoulder of his homemade decon suit. He fumbled out a quick-patch, slapped it over the metallic fabric, but the tear had spread down his arm, the material weakened from years of toxic exposure. The man looked into the camera, his breath momentarily fogging the hood. *Sorry . . . I'm sorry.* His yellowed teeth chattered, but he clamped his jaw shut, held himself together. Even through the transmission static they could see the effort it took, but he managed it.

The camera wobbled. *Been looking for this my whole life . . . finally found it and look where it gets me.* A jagged piece of metal could be seen at the lower edge of the frame where the man had cracked the room. The same sharp edge that had torn his decon suit. *Gonna try and get a better shot of it.* He scooted forward, extended the camera through the opening with one hand, the room sparkling in the bright light. *I'm beaming this to my Web site as a single data packet. This . . . this is what you wanted, Sarah.* He coughed and his hand bumped the edge of the entrance, knocked the camera loose from his thick glove. The camera bounced off the floor of the safe room, the image dizzying for a moment. Just as the light went out, the red rose collapsed, petals shattering onto the desk. The wallscreen went black.

Sarah switched off the thumb drive. "I used my access code to pull that sequence off Eldon's restricted site. He never made it home." She turned to Spider. "Can you and Leo walk back the signal and find out where it originated?"

"I doubt it," said Spider. "There's too much interference in D.C. Even when the surveillance satellites were working—"

"He would have used a dedicated signal to send the data packet," said Leo. "It's the only way to get through that soup, but without knowing the precise algorithm—"

"I need to find that safe room," said Sarah.

"What's so important about some old junk anyway?" said Leo. "Might as well collect bottle caps or baseball cards."

"Why not just admit you can't do it?" said Sarah.

"I didn't say that," said Leo.

"I understand," said Sarah. "It's too complicated. There's too much interference—"

"You still haven't told us what the zombie was looking for," said Leo. " 'This is what you wanted, Sarah.' What did you send him after?"

Sarah hesitated. "A piece of the cross Jesus was crucified—"

Leo burst out laughing.

Sarah ignored him, turned to Spider. "There's a school of revisionist history that says one reason the USA achieved greatness was because the founders possessed part of the true cross. As long as they were faithful, they were blessed."

"Supposedly why they had the eye in the pyramid on their money?" said Spider.

"They used to have Easter egg hunts on the White House lawn," said Leo. "Maybe the Easter bunny was the secret of their success."

"That's a full-security safe room that Eldon Harrison found." Sarah backed up the download. Froze on the chunk of wood lying on the floor. "Last room like that was discovered under the Capitol building sixteen years ago, and it contained the *real* Warren Report on the Kennedy assassination."

"Yes, I can understand your excitement," said Spider. "Still . . . the cross is a strange relic for a good Muslim to be interested in."

"I'm interested in its symbolic, not religious, value," said Sarah.

"If you were really interested in something valuable," said Leo, "why didn't you go looking for the missing gold from Fort Knox?"

She looked at Leo. "Isn't there something you can do to trace the signal?"

"It's late and I'm tired," said Spider. "If Leo says it can't be done, it can't be done."

"I didn't say it *couldn't* be done," Leo grumbled as he and Sarah slipped out of the bedroom. "Let's go for a walk. I wanted to talk to you anyway."

CHAPTER 4

"You've made things very difficult for me," said Jenkins. "I hope you appreciate that."

"Yeah, it's been gnawing at me," said Rakkim.

The Bridge of Skulls bucked so hard in the high wind that Rakkim had to put one hand out to steady himself, his clothes flapping like a distress flag. He looked back to shore. The guards assigned to patrol the bridge stayed on solid ground, huddled behind a concrete barricade. Jenkins clutched the railing beside Rakkim, hanging on with both hands as he faced the storm. Once vigorous and muscular, his face was now sallow and unhealthy, his cheeks hollowed out, dark circles under his eyes.

Rakkim shifted his grip, brushed against one of the thousands of skulls that lined the railings, this one long since plucked clean by the seagulls except for a patch of long brown hair. A small skull. A woman or a child. One of the multitudes of accused sodomites and idolaters, witches and blasphemers on display for the education of the faithful. He looked over at Jenkins, saw him watching.

"An adulteress, if I remember correctly." Jenkins's robe caught the wind, puffed up around him like a gigantic black toadstool. "A sinner, that much is certain."

Rakkim felt the bridge shift underfoot. "Like the girls at the madrassa?"

Jenkins looked down into the dark water below. "Duty . . . duty requires terrible things of us sometimes. You should know that as well as I."

"They were *children*."

Jenkins's face was pale in the moonlight. "They're already in Paradise."

"They should be with their families."

Jenkins cupped the skull in his hands, his knuckles red and raw. "I remember this one now. So adamant of her innocence. They all are at first, but they give that up soon enough. Not *her,* though. Kept going on about her husband's eagerness to trade her in for a more attractive wife and not wanting to pay alimony. She was homely, but such gentle eyes . . . you could see straight to her heart." He idly wrapped the strand of hair around his forefinger. "Impossible to free her, of course, his word against hers, but a few months after her execution, I had him buried alive for possession of pornography." He rubbed her hair between his spindly fingers. "Most shocking holo you could imagine . . . I hated to part with it." He plucked the skull free of the spike that held it on the railing. Caressed the cheekbones, then let it drop over the side, that single strand of brown hair spinning around and around until it disappeared into the darkness below.

The bridge shuddered in the gale, salt spray drenching them. Rakkim was grateful for the wind—it cut down on the stink.

Jenkins looked over at Rakkim. "I remember hearing that you had retired—what was it, five or six years ago?—and thinking, good for him, but here you are, another patriot sent where he doesn't belong. Hurray for God and country."

"I'm not doing it for my country. General Kidd asked me to do a favor for him—"

"Ah, yes, a *favor* . . . a secret mission known only to the two of you." Jenkins's eyes were sunk so deeply you couldn't see the bottom. "I wonder if anyone tells the general no."

Jenkins was the longest-serving shadow warrior in the history of the Fedayeen. Called back from teaching at the academy, he had disappeared into New Fallujah eleven years ago . . . right after Rakkim's second excursion into the Belt. Most missions lasted two years or less and shadow warriors were forcibly retired after ten. Shadow warriors might be needed, but they were never fully trusted. Sooner or later, they always went native, always turned traitor. Or went mad, lost among the masks, unable to find their true face.

"The jihadi you took the headband from . . . do you know his name?" asked Jenkins.

"Tamar."

"And where was his mission?"

"Santa Barbara. He said he wanted to detonate himself among a crowd of picnickers on the beach."

Jenkins nodded. "Are you still a good Muslim, Rakkim?"

"I was never a very good Muslim. I still truthfully declare the Shahada . . . I believe there is but one God, and that Muhammad is His prophet, but as for the rest . . ."

"Hard for a shadow warrior to keep his faith, but without faith . . ." Jenkins's eyes drifted off. "No God, no country, we might as well be devils." His black robe billowed around him. "Is that what you've become, Rakkim? Are you some devil sent to torment me?"

"I'm the man sent to *squeeze* you. It's been a while since you checked in."

"I send General Kidd regular transmissions—"

"Never received," said Rakkim.

"That's not my fault. Our satellite feeds are offline most of the time now." Jenkins glanced up at the stars. "Thought things were supposed to be getting better."

"It *was*, until a Nigerian weather satellite got rear-ended by an uncataloged chunk of debris, probably from one of the old lunar probes. Pieces of the Nigerian took out a couple Russian spy birds and so on and so on. Whole earth orbit is a demolition derby."

The bridge rose in the storm surge, groaning, metal on metal. The line of skulls stretched the full length of the bridge, shifting as the bridge shifted. Rakkim glanced back to where the guards had taken shelter.

"They don't come out here when the wind kicks up,"

said Jenkins. "Not since the north section collapsed last year. Evidently the builders never anticipated these new storms. They called it the Golden Gate in those days." He scratched the corroded railing with a fingertip, flicked it away. "It wasn't gold, of course. It was optimism." He looked at Rakkim. "You were the best student I ever had. Did I ever tell you that?"

"You tried to wash me out of the program. Kidd overruled you."

Jenkins shrugged. "You were gifted, but shadow warriors need to be empty inside so that the role can fill them. A void with a memory, that's the perfect shadow warrior." He squinted at Rakkim. "You were too free-spirited. I knew you'd be trouble."

Rakkim heard the flapping of wings, looked up . . . saw three dead men hanging from the bridge's superstructure, twisting in the wind. Seagulls beat their wings trying to maintain a grip on the men, peck-peck-pecking, but the storm made it difficult. The biggest gull screeched in frustration, settled back down on one man's stringy neck.

"Belt spies and saboteurs," explained Jenkins. "Guards caught them along the wharf."

"The Belt hasn't launched an offensive operation in years," said Rakkim. "Atlanta's got their hands full just trying to hold their country together, same as us."

"Guilty or innocent, the moral lesson remains the same," said Jenkins. "*Vigilance.*"

"What happened to you?" said Rakkim.

"A little of this, a little of that—"

Rakkim slapped him. A light slap, but so fast that Jenkins didn't see it coming.

Jenkins stumbled backward, caught himself from falling. He rubbed his cheek. "Yes . . . you're different, I see that now. You're the one who keeps his soul intact, not like the rest of us." He spat at Rakkim's feet. "Good luck."

Rakkim looked back toward the city. Searchlights lit the area around the wreckage of the old Transamerica pyramid, enormous cranes ringing the site. "The new mosque going up . . . biggest one I've ever seen."

"Biggest one in the world when it's completed." Pride edged Jenkins's voice. "Dwarf anything the heretics in Arabia or Indonesia have. It will seat over three hundred thousand believers someday. A million tons of lapis lazuli for the interior alone—"

"Where's the money coming from?"

"I've wondered about that myself," said Jenkins.

"The Old One?"

"I thought he was dead."

Rakkim looked past him.

Jenkins thumbed his prayer beads. "Ibn-Azziz has never mentioned the Old One's name, but he keeps his own counsel more and more these days, closeted away—"

"So, what *do* you know?"

Jenkins's free hand twitched toward the knife hidden in his sleeve, but he stopped himself. Saw Rakkim waiting for him to do something stupid. "I know things are changing, that's what I know," he said, the beads flowing through his fingers in an unending stream.

"Changing *how*?"

"Did you see all the rats in the city?" said Jenkins, struggling to hold his robe down in the wind. "Millions of them. I can hear them grinding their molars in the walls at night. Getting bolder too."

"I'm not interested in rats." Rakkim walked out along the bridge, and Jenkins hurried after him, skulls crackling underfoot. Twenty-seven thousand skulls lined the railings, supposed to be four or five times that number cobbling the bridge itself.

"Pay attention," said Jenkins, clawing at his arm. "First, ibn-Azziz had all the dogs killed, because dogs are un-Islamic. Fine. Then a pigeon shit on his head when he was coming back from prayers, so he had all the pigeons poisoned." Waves crashed against the bridge, but Jenkins didn't flinch. "Last year he had all the cats killed, don't ask me why. Now the city is swarming with rats and they're impossible to wipe out. Poison one and the rest learn, and pass the learning on, rat brain to rat brain."

"Maybe it's time to come home," Rakkim said.

"Are you here to relieve me? Is that it?" sputtered Jenkins, backing away. "I can tell you right now, you don't have what it takes to survive in this place."

"Don't worry, I can't wait to get out of here."

"Good, because you wouldn't last past morning prayers. Ibn-Azziz . . . he reads minds."

"The last transmission you tried sending to General Kidd," said Rakkim. "What did you want to tell him?"

"You keep thinking of the fire at the madrassa, don't you?" said Jenkins. "You're talking to me like we're old comrades, but all you see is those girls turning to smoke."

"What do *you* see?" Rakkim said softly.

"I see myself . . . an honorable Fedayeen doing his duty, no matter the cost."

"Then do your duty now and tell me the message you tried to send to General Kidd."

Jenkins flinched. "What's *happened* to you, Rikki?"

"Don't worry about me. Worry about yourself."

"You . . . you dare threaten me? I've penetrated ibn-Azziz's inner circle." Jenkins licked his lips. "I'm valuable . . . too valuable."

Rakkim's hand darted out, tugged at Jenkins's beard. "*Prove* it."

"S-Senator Chambers is working for the Grand Mullah, that's the message I sent to the General."

"Chambers is a *modern*," said Rakkim. "His wife drives a car. His daughter goes to university and bares her arms to the sun. Why would he align himself with ibn-Azziz?"

"Did I not teach you anything?" Jenkins cackled as the wind buffeted him. "It's the modern, the man without faith or future, who's the easiest to turn, the modern who hungers most for the fundamentalist's certainty. Freedom is a terrible burden, much too heavy for the weak man to bear."

Rakkim stared into the darkness.

Jenkins beckoned Rakkim closer. "The president . . . he's about to announce Chambers's appointment as secretary of defense. What do you think of that?"

Rakkim didn't believe it, but he kept silent.

"That's good information, isn't it?" said Jenkins. "Useful information. Oh, there have been costs . . . terrible costs to my staying here, but I'm performing a service—"

"Even if Chambers *is* ibn-Azziz's man . . . someone had to suggest to the president that he be appointed defense secretary," said Rakkim. "Someone the president listened to."

"Brandt is a weakling," said Jenkins. "The Republic deserves better."

"He's well-liked."

"Well-liked . . . a dangerous quality in a leader." Jenkins kicked a tiny skull aside, sent teeth flying. "Ibn-Azziz threw a shoe at the screen as we watched Brandt being inaugurated, called him pretty as a sodomite. Now though, he sees Brandt's weakness as a gift." The wind caught his robe, snapped it around him. "Last month, ibn-Azziz *informed* the president that he intends to build five hundred new mosques across the Republic, fundamentalist mosques with imams directly under his command. Practically dared him to refuse."

Rakkim kept silent. He hadn't heard anything about it.

"Your new president isn't the first to underestimate ibn-Azziz," said Jenkins, and Rakkim noted the *your* not the *our*. "Not the first, not the last . . . The former grand mullah made the same mistake. He used to tease ibn-Azziz for his youth and his asceticism, his vow of celibacy. The former grand mullah was brutal as a buzz saw, lusty and full-gutted, twice his size, but ibn-Azziz strangled him with his bare hands. I was there. I saw it with my own eyes," he said, the words dribbling out of him. "Ibn-Azziz was thirty years my junior, but he was the future, I could see that." He opened his robe, showed his protruding ribs . . . his lacework of scars. "I must have lost fifty pounds since that night . . . and I've done things, worse things than you saw tonight, but of the dozen of us who witnessed the murder, *I'm* the only one still alive."

"You've done well," Rakkim said soothingly. "You've done better than anyone could have expected, but now it's time—"

"It's the small sins that save you," counseled Jenkins, "*that's* how you survive when all around you are getting their heads sawed off. Ibn-Azziz hates tobacco. The Quran says nothing about it, but he hates it and that's good enough for most of them. Me, I'll sometimes smoke a cigarette before meeting with him. His nose wrinkles and he'll chastise me, sometimes . . . harshly, but it's a form of insurance. I don't try to be perfect. It's the perfect ones that attract suspicion. No, ibn-Azziz hates my tobacco addiction, but he knows a spy wouldn't draw attention to himself like that."

"I'll remember."

"Don't patronize me," sputtered Jenkins. "I know who you are. I know why you're really here." He backed up to the very end of the bridge where the concrete crumbled into the bay, and the steel beams twisted like rusty fingers.

"Take it easy," said Rakkim, following him.

Jenkins clung to the railing as the waves crashed. "Go . . . go ahead," he said, eyes wide. "Go ahead, kill me. That's why you've been sent, isn't it?" The cold spray drenched him. "I should be honored that Kidd sent an assassin—"

"There are no assassins anymore," Rakkim said gently. "Hardly any shadow warriors either. We're more trouble than we're worth. Haven't you heard?"

"No more assassins?" Jenkins cocked his head in disbelief.

"None."

"That . . . that's a mistake. Tell General Kidd we need men like that now more than ever."

"You tell him."

"You . . . you walk like an assassin. Do you realize that?"

Rakkim looked into the darkness. The hills in the distance

were shrouded in mist, the small towns across the bay long since abandoned.

"Nothing to be ashamed of . . . I wanted to be an assassin myself," said Jenkins. "You didn't know that, did you?"

Rakkim shook his head.

"Over eight hundred Fedayeen in my class at the academy and only two of us accepted into the assassin program." Jenkins's laugh was raw. "I thought I was a natural-born killer, but I didn't last a week. This other fellow, though, Darwin, I heard he completed the training without any problem at all, completed it so easily he scared his superiors. Afraid he might shrug off the leash and then where would we be?" He glared at Rakkim. "You and Darwin . . . you have the same walk."

"If you say so."

"About four years ago a police patrol found the body of a man in an abandoned church," said Jenkins. "Nothing unique about that. You'd be surprised where the dead turn up, but this man . . . he was all slashed up, blood *everywhere*, a regular slaughterhouse." A gust of wind caught him, sent him close to the edge. "Police thought it was a sadist at work, some serial killer, but I knew better . . . because I recognized the dead man. I hadn't seen Darwin since I washed out, but you don't forget a man like him. Even in death, his face had this mocking expression, like a particularly funny joke had been played on him."

Waves crashed against the bridge, the whole structure groaning. If Rakkim had been able to, he would have hidden Darwin's body that day, buried him under a mound of rubble in the church, anything to erase the assassin from the sight of man or God. Bleeding from a hundred cuts, Rakkim barely had the strength to walk, let alone cover the dead.

"Somebody drove a knife through Darwin's mouth and severed his brain stem," said Jenkins. "Nasty work. I had no idea who was capable of such a thing." The dim light from the stars didn't reach his eyes. "Then tonight, I saw you strolling ahead of me . . . even stepping on the dead, you hardly made a sound."

He lost his balance; bits of concrete crumbled into the water and he grabbed Rakkim's hand. "A predator's walk . . . it's subtle. I'm sure assassins aren't even aware of doing it, but shadow warriors, we notice everything, don't we?" His fingers dug into the back of Rakkim's hand. "What I . . . what I want to know, Rakkim . . . is how . . . how *you* killed an assassin?"

Rakkim pulled him to safety.

"Only Allah or another assassin can kill an assassin . . . that's what they say," hissed Jenkins, still hanging on to him. "So tell me . . . how did you do it?"

"Let me take you home," said Rakkim.

"Home?" Jenkins brayed. "Too late for that. Shadow warriors, the best of the best, that's what they called us. Look at me now. Look at *you.*" Jenkins picked up a skull from the railing, ran a thumb across one of the eye sockets. "You know, there's been times . . . times I've doubted the existence of God." He glanced up at Rakkim and his crooked grin matched the expression on the skull. "But there's never been a moment, not one single moment, when I doubted the existence of hell."

Rakkim knew exactly what he was talking about.

Jenkins cupped the skull behind one ear. "Go long!" He gave a little hop and passed it, a long ball back toward the city. The skull shattered on the roadway.

Rakkim didn't move.

"That . . . that's one of the things I miss the most about Seattle," Jenkins said softly. "A football game in Khomeini Stadium on a crisp autumn day, barbecued goat sandwiches . . . nothing better in the world. You still go to the games?"

"Sometimes. The Stallions are having a lousy season."

"Always next year." Jenkins's robe billowed in the wind. "What about the Zone? Do the Egyptian women still dance at the Orion Club?"

"It's called the Python Lounge now, but yeah, the Egyptians still dance."

"They used to darken their nipples with henna, but that . . . that was a long time ago."

"It's going to be daylight soon," said Rakkim. "Let me extract you. I'll take you home."

"Extract me? You make me sound like a rotting tooth." Jenkins shook his head. "Pity from an assassin . . ." He started back toward the city. "I *am* home."

CHAPTER 5

"What did you want to talk about?" said Sarah as they walked through the Catholic neighborhood, the streetlights out and never replaced.

"*Personal* stuff," said Leo. "Normally I'd ask Rakkim, but . . . he's not here."

"Okay . . . are you going to ask me?"

"Not yet," sniffed Leo. "I'm kind of still deciding."

People sat on their porches, smoking and talking, listening to music as Sarah and Leo strolled past. A couple of men waved to Leo. Dogs howled, or trotted along the broken sidewalks as though they belonged there. They did, at least in this sector. Muslims thought them unclean beasts, as dirty as pigs, but Christians loved their mutts. She heard laughter from inside the houses. A woman swung in a hammock, singing a modern version of an old blues melody, a paean to lost love. Christians never seemed to sleep, or worry that what they were doing was against God's law. They just lived. Anthony Colarusso, a good Catholic cop and one of Rakkim's closest friends, used to say if you were Catholic on a Saturday night, you'd never go to mosque again.

"Are you getting those headaches again?" Sarah said, stepping around a section of collapsed sidewalk. "Spider says he can hear you crying in the middle of the night."

"I'm *fine*. That's not it."

Last year Leo and Rakkim had gone on a mission into the Belt and barely made it back alive. Leo's arrogance and lack of social skills had been a constant problem, and his falling in love with a local girl, Leanne, only made things worse. Still, the kid was necessary equipment, that remarkable brain of his, at any rate. State-of-the-art cerebral cortex, but Spider and a team of underground neuroscientists had added a few nonfactory options. Leo was smarter than ever, and getting smarter all the time, but sometimes he was blinded by details and his naivete left him vulnerable.

Sarah could see homemade signal-jamming devices silhouetted on every rooftop, awkward contraptions of circuit boards and aluminum designed to block eavesdropping from the government. "Do any of those things actually work?"

"They work a lot better *now*," said Leo. "I gave a few suggestions to a couple of the brighter local kids, showed them how to tweak the grid."

The houses were bigger in this part of the district, three or four families sharing the space. A garden in every backyard, covered now with mulch to protect against the autumn frost. Cooking smells drifted from the kitchens, fried potatoes, green beans . . . bacon. Her stomach growled. She spotted a lookout hidden along the main access road leading to the rest of the city; a teenager in a hooded sweatshirt sporting night-vision goggles. Leo gave a hand signal as they passed, the teenager returning the sign.

"You made yourself at home here fast," said Sarah.

"I learned that from Rakkim." Leo sniffled, wiped his nose. "You should have seen him in the Belt. Some redneck would be fumbling for change to pay for cigarettes and Rakkim would toss a silver dollar onto the counter. Next thing you know, we're invited to dinner and hearing all about his job at the filling station and all the government people who've been stopping for gas the last few days."

They reached the base of an unused water tower covered in faded graffiti—SEAHAWKS and GO KANGS! and REPENT and LWHS CLASS OF 2009, crude drawings of frogs and a husky dog, dozens of hearts with initials in them. Leo eased into the shadows, looked around, then scrambled up the rusty metal ladder along one side. Sarah was stunned. Before he left for the Belt with Rakkim, Leo had been afraid of heights, afraid of cramped spaces, afraid of bugs and loud noises. She followed him up the ladder.

Leo waited for her at the top. Held out a hand.

She ignored the offer, pulled herself up onto the catwalk. She kept one hand on the metal railing and tried not to look down. It was windier up here. From this vantage point, Sarah could see the tail section of a jetliner sticking out of Elliott Bay, the result of a failed suicide attack on the city twenty years earlier by a renegade Christian sect. The wreckage had been left untouched as a reminder to the citizens to remain alert.

Leo surveyed the sky, head thrown back as he took in the security blimps ringing the city, a shifting grid of low-flying airships designed to shield the city from satellite surveillance and scramble the electronics of any attacker. "They made a mistake."

"Who did?" said Sarah.

"Whoever programmed the blimps." Leo pointed. "See? Northeast quadrant. They left a gap in the coverage."

"I'm sure it doesn't matter—"

"It's a *mistake*. Somebody didn't do a proper vector analysis. You don't see it, do you?"

"I don't." Sarah tickled him, made him squirm. "You must feel sorry for the rest of us."

"It's like being surrounded by sleepwalkers, but . . . sometimes I think maybe *you're* the lucky ones." Leo rubbed his forehead, caught himself. "I get so lonely."

"Have you spoken with Leanne?"

"Yeah, I have a secure channel set up."

"You're not lonely when you talk with *her*, are you?"

"That . . . that's what I wanted to talk with you about." More than ever, Leo looked like an enormous infant, smooth and soft, his features unformed. "Leanne . . . she says I sound different now."

"It's hard being apart," said Sarah. "Sometimes when Rikki comes home from a mission it takes a while for us to get back to where we were before he left. It doesn't mean we don't still love each other." She patted his hand. "Give Leanne a chance to adjust. You were only together for a few days."

"A few days was all *I* needed."

"Women need more."

"That's what Rakkim said." Leo watched the stars over the city, the blinking lights from airplanes making their approach, cataloging it all. "Rakkim . . . don't tell him, but he's my only friend. It's kind of stupid, because shadow warriors, their job is to make you like them . . . but even knowing that, I still think that we're friends."

"You *are* friends, Leo."

Leo blushed.

Sarah watched the stars. Wondered if Rakkim was watching them too.

"I don't think Leanne's father . . . I don't think Mr. Moseby likes me," said Leo. "Maybe I intimidate him. I do that to people."

"From what Rakkim's told me about him, I rather doubt that."

"I asked Leanne to marry me, but that didn't work out so great. She said she loves me, but she didn't want to rush things."

"Good for her. You've got time."

"What if we *don't?*" Leo's voice cracked. "What if those few days were all we had?"

"Then *act* like you've got forever. Be brave. Fake it if you have to."

"Fake it." Leo chewed it over. "I could do that." He cleared his throat. "Thank you."

"Glad I could help."

In the distance, the Grand Abdullah mosque dominated First Hill and the darkened fundamentalist district. Sarah turned away, preferred watching the ferries chugging across the water, their wake lit by moonlight.

"You ever think about leaving?" said Leo.

"No."

"Never? You're always talking about how we're falling apart."

"The Republic is being nibbled to death," said Sarah. "Aztlán wants the Southwest back, Canada wants the Great Lakes and the Mormon territories are already gone. China and India own half of our heavy industries, Russia floats our bonds. The Belt is in even worse shape. That's no reason to run away. We're weak because we're divided. The only way the two nations are going to survive is to become one nation again."

"Good luck with that." Leo spit over the railing. "Nothing wrong with running away. No more Republic, no more Belt, just grab Leanne and go. Start over someplace new. Someplace safe."

"There's no such place, Leo." Sarah looked across the bay, stared at the red warning lights blinking on the tail section of the downed plane. "So . . . do you think you can find that secure room in D.C. for me?"

"You don't give up."

"No. I don't."

"You want my help finding a piece of Jesus' cross. . . ." Leo massaged his gums with a forefinger. "You *do* remember Spider and I are Jewish, right?"

"So was Jesus."

Leo shrugged.

"Here's a story that may interest you—it certainly made me curious the first time I heard it," said Sarah. "Shortly after taking communion, on January 28, 814, the Emperor Charlemagne died and was buried in a cathedral in Germany. This was a man who had conquered most of Europe, and forcefully converted more people to Christianity than anyone before or since; the epitome of the holy warrior." She leaned closer to Leo. "Two hundred years later, Count Otto of Lomello secretly entered the cathedral shortly after midnight, accompanied only by the bishop and two of the count's trusted retainers. The bishop led them down a winding flight of stairs deep into the catacombs under the church, the four of them moving silently through the darkness, candles glinting on the bones stacked against the narrow passageway. After what seemed like hours, they finally broke through a false wall, and discovered the emperor's true resting place, a marble tomb sheathed in frost." She smiled. "So of course they pried open the door."

"And the tomb was empty," sneered Leo.

Sarah slowly shook her head. "No, Charlemagne was there, seated on a throne of gold, a crown on his head, but though his fine robes had rotted away . . . his flesh showed no sign of decay, his face so peaceful that he might as well have been asleep. The duke, a veteran of many wars, dropped his candle, the bishop muttering prayers as the darkness closed in."

Leo shivered. "You . . . you said it was cold in the tomb."

"Not that cold," said Sarah. "Clutched in the emperor's hand was a small, rough piece of wood. When the duke overcame his fear and pried the emperor's fingers away from it . . . the emperor crumbled to dust."

Leo stared at her. "That's . . . a good story, but people can say anything."

"The duke wrote it all down," said Sarah. "Wrote it in his own blood. I've read it myself. His Latin was atrocious, but I believed every word of it." Music drifted up from one of the nearby houses, and she nodded her head to the beat. "I read his account three years ago in a small monastery outside the city of Leipzig. The duke . . . the piece of the cross didn't do what he expected it to do. Not for him. The bishop committed suicide shortly after they violated the tomb, a mortal sin piled on mortal sin. The duke's retainers went mad. The duke, terrified, entered the monastery, handed over the piece of the cross to the abbot and wrote the story of the theft as a confession. He lived in a stone cell in the monastery for another forty years, and never spoke a word."

Leo looked out over the city, using its familiar geometry to ground himself. "So . . . okay, maybe there is a piece of the cross with magical powers, but that doesn't mean this . . . *zombie* found it under D.C."

Sarah took his hand. "The sacred relic stayed hidden away in the monastery for hundreds of years, until it was stolen around 1646, during the chaos of the Thirty Years War."

The night was quiet except for the sound of Leo's teeth chattering as they stood atop the tower. He watched her out of the corner of his eyes and she was beautiful, dark hair stark against her face, her expression totally aware, free and fearless.

"Rumors of the cross occur for the next hundred years," continued Sarah, still holding his hand in her warm grip. "A town cured of smallpox by a wandering tinsmith, a mountain village saved from an avalanche that roared all around it, a strange white light spotted in the hills of southern France at Easter. Some say it was finally brought to Louis XIV, that the cross was responsible for the grandeur and glory of Paris during his reign. If he truly had it, the relic didn't stay with him—it was gone by the time of the Revolution and Louis XVI's date with the guillotine, perhaps sold by the last king of France to pay his mounting debts." She released him, her voice softer now, like petting a cat. "The story I heard, the one I like best, is that Louis XVI lost the piece of the cross at cards to one of the visiting American patriots, Benjamin Franklin or Thomas Paine, and they brought it back to the Colonies." She looked at Leo. "The New Jerusalem, that's what they called the new nation. There's actually a coded reference to winning the cross in the Federalist Papers."

"You *really* think that piece of wood in D.C. is part of the true cross?" said Leo.

Sarah turned away from him, eyes half closed in the breeze. "Well, Leo, we're never going to know unless you find that room."

Leo hesitated, nodded. "I'll do my best. . . ."

"In case your best isn't good enough, I need you to contact Leanne's father on that secure channel of yours. Ask Moseby to leave for northern Virginia as soon as possible."

"You expect Mr. Moseby to wander around D.C.?"

"No, not yet," said Sarah. "I want him to go to zombie country and contact Eldon Harrison's wife. See if she knows anything.

I'll have a Fedayeen radiation suit waiting en route—no sense adding to his rad count before he goes into the city."

"I told you I'd locate the safe room. Just give me more time."

"*Leo.* Contact Moseby tonight. Please?"

"Sure." Leo squinted at the presidential palace. "That's odd." He pointed at the sky. "Look at the blimps. They've altered the aerial security configuration."

Sarah couldn't see anything different. "Maybe someone in authority just realized—"

"Hang on." Leo pressed a finger to one ear. Nodded. "Okay, Pop." He pulled a hand-link out of his pocket, flipped up the screen. "A squadron of Aztlán aircraft entered airspace over Nevada twenty minutes ago. Probably just a navigational mix-up . . ."

"It's a provocation, Leo, a reaction to the Aztlán oil minister's assassination in Miami this afternoon. They don't know who's responsible. Aztlán's probably doing the same thing over the Belt."

"What can we do about it?"

Sarah could see what Leo was talking about now—the blimps around the palace *had* shifted slightly. She started down the ladder, feet banging onto the steps in her haste.

"Wait!" said Leo.

"I have to get back to Michael."

"Wait up!"

She was on the ground now, walking fast, trying not to panic. The houses with their late-night music and laughter no longer seemed an indicator of the inhabitants' freedom, but of their ignorance. What had Leo called them? Sleepwalkers.

"Can you *please* slow down?" Leo called after her.

Sarah started running.

CHAPTER 6

Something was wrong, the Old One sensed it. He should have been pleased—earlier today, Lester Gravenholtz had killed the Aztlán oil minister, the first step in his plan to reshape the geopolitical landscape. In New Fallujah, ibn-Azziz's loyalty remained unquestioned, and with him, control of the Black Robes. Both the Republic and the Belt had fractious populations and weaklings governing them. The time for a strong man to appear was close at hand, and yet . . .

The Old One felt rested, but the excitement, the heat, the erotic tingle at his nerve ends was missing. Sex was always his first instinct after a session. *Always.* He tilted his chair to the upright position, took a few more unhurried breaths of pure oxygen before beckoning Massakar to remove the mask.

"Are you feeling better, Mahdi?" asked Massakar, his chief physician, a short Pakistani with tiny, delicate hands and bags under his eyes.

The Old One examined his reflection in the mirrored wall of the recovery room, tapped under his chin. His skin was taut, his eyes clear. His steel gray hair had regained its shine, and his upper lip had lost the indentations that so vexed him. He felt better after his rejuvenation treatment, better than he had felt in weeks, his blood cleansed of impurities, his lungs ionized, his system restored to its natural vigor by Massakar's technicians and their miraculous machines, may Allah be praised. He stood up, naked and unashamed before his own critical gaze. No, something was wrong.

After all these years, the Old One knew his body intimately; he sensed every heartbeat, every pulse, every sag and ripple in his flesh. . . . He stretched . . . and felt a slight heaviness in his limbs, a weariness. This is what dying feels like, thought the Old One, the first glimpse of the yawning abyss, a whisper that would slowly grow to a scream.

"Mahdi?" Massakar steepled his fingertips like a merchant fearful of losing a sale.

The Old One stared at Massakar.

Massakar lowered his eyes, trembling.

"What did you do to me?" asked the Old One, not raising his voice.

"My b-best, as always, master."

The Old One held out his hands. There was the faintest hint of yellow at the base of his cuticles. He plucked the thin skin on the back of his hand, released it . . . watched how long it took to smooth out. He looked up at Massakar. "Your treatments have not fully restored me."

"Yes . . . I know."

"Did you think I would not notice?"

"After last month's session, I thought . . . perhaps the instruments needed to be recalibrated." Massakar licked his thin lips. "But this time . . . I knew they were accurate."

"So my decline began *last* month?"

Massakar rubbed his small hands together as though washing them. "The decline only became statistically relevant last month. I first noticed certain . . . anomalies in the readings three months ago."

The Old One watched Massakar squirm. "What sort of anomalies?"

Massakar smoothed his white tunic. "A slight decline in liver function and renal output. A minute loss of cardiac elasticity."

"So replace my liver and kidneys, swap out this heart for a new one. You've done that before. What's different now?"

Massakar stiffened. "It's not . . . organ failure we're dealing with, Mahdi. It's a systemic breakdown. Deterioration at the *cellular* level. My skills are inadequate to reverse this. Perhaps another doctor, a better doctor—"

The old one waved him silent. "No, you are the best . . . as was your father before you, and your grandfather." He reached out, wiped away the doctor's tears. "I remember you when you were a child . . . and the other boys would tease you. You would cry even as you beat them, so fierce you were, and weeping all the time."

Massakar hung his head. "Forgive me, Mahdi."

The Old One stared straight ahead, trying to compose himself. It took every bit of his courage. The only sound in the room was the faint hum of the air-filtration unit. So this is how it ends, he thought, imagining his cells huffing and puffing like cartoon slaves building a pyramid, growing more fatigued by the moment, until finally . . . "How long?"

Massakar looked up, blinking. "Master?"

"How *long* do I have?"

"I . . . I can't—"

"Make an educated guess, *Doctor.*"

Massakar seemed to draw strength from being addressed by his professional title. "Three or four years, if the rate of decline continues uniformly. Less if there is a cascade effect on the major organs, which is . . . possible." He tugged at his lower lip. "Increasing your rejuvenation sessions to twice a month may help, but—"

"Thank you for your assessment."

Massakar fell to his knees, kissed the Old One's hand.

The Old One beckoned him to rise. "This information . . . it must be our secret. Not all of my subjects are as steadfast as you."

Massakar wiped his eyes. "Shall I send in the Abyssinian to dress you?"

"No, I think today . . . I shall dress myself." The Old One waited until Massakar backed out of the recovery room and closed the door behind him before slipping on his clothes. He took his time. Buttoning his white cotton shirt. Zipping his trousers, the gray summer wool English trousers from the cramped shop on Savile Road that smelled of pipe tobacco. Tucking in the shirt, his abdomen still firm. Slipping the titanium cuff links through the fabric with a faint sound, the click of the bezel. The silk necktie slid through his fingers as he tied a perfect Windsor knot, his thumb pressing a dimple. He pulled on his socks with their pattern of tiny clocks . . . ironic now. Wiggled his toes in his handmade leather shoes. Every sensation was suddenly heightened by Massakar's diagnosis. A blessing, he told himself. Allah has given me a blessing. First he gave me time. Then he gave me an ending. Yes, a great blessing.

He didn't believe that for an instant.

His reflection in the mirror showed a healthy, vigorous man in his sixties, although he was over 150. He was still almost six feet tall, his stature undiminished by the years. Smooth-shaven to allay suspicion. A strong, prominent nose. Dark eyes, alert as ever. Thin lips, a sign of cruelty, an elder in his tribe had noted long ago, but the Old One was not cruel, not at all. He was *clear*. He was certain. The elder was dust now, all of them dust.

The Old One stepped briskly through the door into an anteroom, and then through the private door into his suite . . . found Ibrahim, his eldest son and chief advisor, waiting. And Baby. The two of them glaring at each other.

Baby was twenty-three, slim and high-breasted, the poisonous flower of Southern womanhood. A daughter he had forgotten until a year ago, one of the many seeds planted across the earth, beautiful girls raised among the kaffirs in the Belt and Russia and China, raised among the faithful in Arabia and Europe. Most he never even saw, just occasionally read reports of their marriages to powerful men, and the steady stream of information they fed back to him. The power of the marital bed. Baby had shown up at his Miami compound last year without an invitation, along with a human killing machine named Lester Gravenholtz. Gravenholtz offered some unique possibilities, but it was Baby who was the true prize. No wonder Ibrahim hated her.

"Father," said Ibrahim, bowing.

"Father," said Baby, voice sultry with promise. Her dress

rustled around her long legs as she bowed, her honey blond hair falling onto her bare shoulders. She wore a simple, brightly colored silk dress cut high up one thigh in the contemporary Cuban style, the spoils of one of her many shopping trips with his concubines. She looked up at him as she rose, her mouth ripe and wanton as a plum.

Ibrahim straightened, taller than the Old One, hard and stern as a knotty stick. "I *told* this creature that you and I had private matters to discuss."

"You're up late, child," the Old One said to Baby. "It's almost dawn."

"I was restless," drawled Baby, hazel eyes playful. She walked slowly toward him, hips swaying. "Thought I'd come by and see if you wanted company."

"Her spies told her that I was on my way to see you," said Ibrahim. "She can't bear to think that I—"

"Her *spies*?" The Old One looked at Baby. "Barely a year in our company, and already she has cultivated a network of informants. What a remarkable woman."

Baby curtsied.

"I don't find her nearly as amusing as you do, Father," Ibrahim said tightly.

"You don't find anything amusing." The Old One flung open the double doors and stepped out onto the veranda of his penthouse on the fortieth floor of the Grande Hotel, Miami. One of his many corporations owned the hotel, the Old One keeping the top seven floors for himself and his retinue. "Leave me, both of you."

"But, Father," said Ibrahim, "we have to talk about—"

"Are you still here, boy?" Old One leaned against the pink marble railing, watching the Atlantic roll in. He stayed immobile until he heard the door to the suite close behind them, then allowed himself a small sigh. He slowly closed his fists lest they start to shake and undo his confidence. Best to survey the world that Allah had laid out for him, rather than linger on his own sudden mortality.

He stood there, marveling as the moonlight turned the peaks of the waves silver. Raised in the desert, he still found the ocean overwhelming in its beauty, the sea air clean and bracing. Ibrahim disapproved of his being outside, had ordered digital chaff generators built into the walls to prevent eavesdropping, and stationed heavily armed fishing boats offshore to protect him from missile attack. Foolishness. Well-intentioned, but foolishness just the same. *Anyone* could be killed. Ask Darwin. The Old One's expression twisted at the memory of his prized assassin, dead now over four years. Such a loss. Darwin specialized in killing those who could not be killed. The rich and powerful surrounded by bodyguards, politicians hidden away behind high walls and vast armies, protected by rings of elaborate technology. All had died at the Old One's command. Now Darwin too was dead, and the Old One could still not understand how it had happened.

The breeze shifted, brought the smell of ripe decay to the Old One's nostrils, as though some vast leviathan had been slain in the deep, and only now had risen to the surface, stinking in the moonlight.

CHAPTER 7

Just before dawn, barely an hour after he left the Bridge of Skulls, Rakkim approached the sentries on one of the main checkpoints out of New Fallujah. Jenkins might have given him up and issued an alert, but Rakkim didn't break stride as the sentries hefted their weapons, muttering to each other.

"I need a vehicle," Rakkim demanded, his green kaffiyeh flapping in the wind.

The lead sentry, a haggard man with a curling beard, bowed to him, pointed at a sedan nearby. "Take my car, *shahid*, and may Allah bless you on your path to martyrdom." The other sentries bowed, muttered their own blessings, afraid to meet his gaze.

Rakkim ignored them as he got into the car and drove off.

Shahid. Martyr for God. One who found eternal life through blowing himself to pieces, sending the infidel to hell as he himself ascended. *Shahid*, high praise in New Fallujah, praise wrapped in fear.

Rakkim was no *shahid*, but what was he? Jenkins had been right, Rakkim was no shadow warrior, not anymore. An assassin can only be killed by God or another assassin . . . that's what Jenkins had told him. So, how had Rakkim killed Darwin five years ago? How was such a thing possible? Rakkim had asked himself that question more times than he could count.

Darwin was the superior warrior, faster, more agile, unburdened by conscience, the greatest assassin the Fedayeen had ever turned out. It should have been Rakkim who died that day, bleeding from a hundred cuts as Darwin taunted him . . . until Rakkim threw his knife into Darwin's laughing mouth. An impossible throw but he had made it. He still saw Darwin's lips working around the hilt of the knife, trying to speak, his last words inaudible to anyone but God. That should have been the end of Darwin, but it seemed that both heaven and hell had rejected the master assassin.

Rakkim bumped down the road toward the second gated checkpoint, keeping his speed steady as the machine guns swiveled toward him. A huge security agent stood in the center of the road, one hand upraised. Rakkim kept driving. The man stepped aside at the last minute, shouted *"Allahu Akbar!"* The gate rose slowly, scraping the roof of Rakkim's car as he drove past.

For months after killing Darwin, Rakkim had felt . . . different. His reflexes were faster and his combat skills improved dramatically—he killed instinctively now, killed in ways he had no training in, and he took a pleasure in it that he never had before. Even his dreams had changed, like rummaging around in someone else's memories, and most unsettling of all, Sarah seemed even more attracted to him, their lovemaking raw and uninhibited.

Rakkim veered around a huge crater in the unlit road. A gigantic electrical tower canted in the distance, one of its supporting legs demolished, wires drooping. The hillsides around the city had been stripped bare of trees, houses bulldozed, businesses burned to the ground. The Grand Mullah had wanted everything around New Fallujah destroyed, all modern conveyances ruined, forcing the residents into the city, and under his control.

El Presidente Argusto, supreme ruler of the Aztlán Empire, strode across the command center of his hacienda, his silver-heeled boots clacking on the marble floor, one hand on the ornate hilt of his sword. He listened to the rhythmic echo of his footsteps, and it was all he could do to stop himself from drawing the sword and slashing at the air in frustration.

Hector Morales, his secretary of state, stood nearby, dressed all in black, head crested with a skullcap of blue-green hummingbird feathers, waiting to be recognized.

Argusto walked right past him. Let him wait.

Lean and graceful, Argusto was as vain as he was handsome, his beard a thin line running along his jaw, his dark hair carefully curled and oiled. He had trained to be a matador before becoming a pilot, and he still had an appreciation for pageantry, his clothes tailored to emphasize his lean waist and powerful physique. On days honoring Huitzilopochtli, the god of war, el presidente entered the Tenochtitlán arena and killed the fiercest black bull available. The applause from the crowd had sounded like thunder.

Morning light edged through the windows of the hacienda, dew glistening on the green lawns. His beloved jet interceptors flew guard overhead, left contrails in the dawn. As always, he wished he were flying, rather than forced to attend to matters of state.

Morales cleared his throat.

Argusto had been many things in his life: the youngest air ace in the war against the Yucatán, the youngest chief of staff of the Aztlán air force and now the youngest president of the nation, the conqueror who had annexed all of former Central America and the traditional lands of the north. More to come, *yanquis*, more to come. At Guadalupe Hidalgo, in 1848, Mexico had been forced to cede over one hundred million square miles of its land to the United States. The whole American Southwest offered to the *yanqui* invader on bended knee, turned over for the princely sum of $15 million. Insult added to injury. He tapped the hilt of his sword with his thumb. The payback had just begun.

Argusto listened to the roar of the jets overhead, inhaled the power of their passing. In seven years, he had sliced the army in half, while fully modernizing the air force, tripling the number of planes until his air command was second to none in the world. The army generals had complained bitterly, howling at the loss of their budgets and their men, but his vision had prevailed. Air power was Aztlán's destiny, particularly after nuclear weapons had been outlawed. Land armies were sloppy and killed too many people, but with their laser-targeted munitions his planes could cripple the infrastructure of any nation and leave the population intact. The Aztec empire had been built on slave labor. Aztlán, the reborn empire, would do the same.

First, though, this . . . atrocity in Miami had to be dealt with. His brother-in-law, the oil minister, slaughtered like a cow. The indignity to Argusto and the nation must be avenged. Venezuela was the most likely culprit, furious with Aztlán for doubling the tolls for their ships to traverse the Canal. Or perhaps Brazil was responsible, a veiled warning against Argusto's territorial ambitions.

Argusto's boot heels clicked along the floor as he turned the problem over in his mind. Sooner or later he would find out the guilty party, and then his great silvery birds would wreck vengeance from the sky. A grand day was coming.

Rakkim turned off his headlights, driving by starlight now, invisible to anyone who might be watching. He bounced along the winding road with nothing but the sound of the wind to keep him company. Being alone didn't stop him from listening for Darwin's voice, or looking to see him capering by the side of the road, but there was no one there . . . not this time.

Killing Darwin had changed him, but a mission to the Belt a year ago had made Rakkim realize to what degree he was no longer himself. Captured by some murderous hillbillies, Rakkim had been hauled off to a clapboard shanty, forced to drink moonshine laced with turpentine and handle snakes as a test of his faith. Bitten by a timber rattler, Rakkim writhed on the floor of the church, dying. In his hour of need, Darwin had appeared to him, mocking his weakness, contemptuous as ever.

Hey, dumbass. You just going to lie there and die?

"Leave me alone," Rakkim had said. "You're dead. I killed you."

I was playing with you and you got lucky. That'll teach me a lesson.

"What do you want?"

I want to be alive.

"I'd just kill you again."

Darwin smiled.

"What's so funny?"

You.

Rakkim watched the timber rattler that had bit him slide toward him across the wood floor. The snake stopped, triangular head flicking side to side, then retreated.

Rakkim felt himself drifting, barely able to keep his eyes open. "Go away. I got no time for ghosts."

Ghost? Oh, I'm a lot more than that. Darwin moved closer. *You don't look so good, Rikki.*

Rakkim tried to get to his feet. Sat back down.

Don't try and stand. Just relax and slow your heart down. You need time to metabolize the venom. Slower. You can do that, can't you?

"I don't need your help."

You need something. Darwin shook his head. *I still can't believe you killed me. It's embarrassing.*

"I killed two men in Seattle last month. Bodyguards for a Black Robe. Good fighters, ex-Fedayeen, and I killed them so fast . . . so very fast. I'm not even sure how I did it."

All that blood. Darwin's laugh sounded like wasps buzzing. *Kind of intoxicating, isn't it?*

"I'm not like you."

Don't worry. You're getting there.

It had been a year now and Rakkim hadn't seen Darwin again. Hadn't sensed his presence, not even in his nightmares. He still had Darwin's killing skills, but he was alone again inside his skin, and grateful for it. A brown rabbit darted across the road, practically ran under the wheels of the car before it scooted into the brush on the other side. Rakkim accelerated, happy to have avoided crushing it. That was something.

CHAPTER 8

The Old One stood on the balcony of his penthouse, wanting to burn the world to a cinder and scatter the ashes among the stars. The world and everyone in it. He could still hear his chief physician's lugubrious voice—*A systemic breakdown, master. Deterioration at the cellular level.* A death sentence was a death sentence, no matter how carefully it was worded. A death sentence for him but not for the world. Where was the justice in that? To die now, when he was so close to achieving everything he had worked for? What was Allah *thinking*?

Far up the coast, he could see waterspouts dancing opposite the casinos, man-made cyclones five and six hundred feet tall, with colored lights in their swirling arms. The tourists loved them, and so did the Old One. Not tonight, though. Tonight he loved nothing. He watched as the largest waterspout turned dark green, white and red, the colors of the Aztlán flag, an homage to the slain oil minister. The Aztlán Empire was gobbling up territory from Texas to Southern California, but Nueva Florida had wisely chosen neutrality, its strictly business mentality serving everyone's interests.

The tricolored waterspout rose higher and higher. Lester Gravenholtz had done a good job this afternoon; the brutality of its ambassador's murder had infuriated Aztlán almost as much as the assassination itself. Even so, the Old One wished Darwin had been here to do the job. Wishes, however, would not bring back Darwin. He watched the waterspouts spiral for ten minutes until they finally died down, leaving the surface of the water calm again, the colors bleeding into the deep. The darkness seemed bereft somehow.

The Old One shivered in the warm breeze off the ocean.

One got used to immortality. Took it for granted. Death, the fate of all other men, seemed a small, shabby thing, a distant memory. Until now. He amused himself with the thought that perhaps he should seek help from that backwoods faith healer Baby had told him about. Malcolm . . . Malcolm Crews, that was his name. Baby had inserted Crews into the Belt president's inner circle a few months ago. A brilliant move on her part. Ibrahim had been furious.

You would have thought the Old One would have grown tired of life, but if anything his hunger to live was more intense than when he was a youth. So much work left undone. He remembered the first whispers that he might be the Mahdi, the twelfth imam, the messiah chosen by Allah to unite all Muslims and establish a worldwide caliphate. The Old One initially resisted such speculation. The son of a wealthy sheik, educated at Oxford, he had no use for the burden of faith. Still, the whispers persisted, until finally he decided to visit the holy Iranian city of Qom.

Shiite pilgrims regularly journeyed to a well on the outskirts of the city, the place from which the twelfth imam was supposed to emerge during the last days. The Old One had visited the well after midnight, passing through a small village, feeling foolish, the site deserted except for a dozen of his most loyal retainers. He had peered into the blackness, whispered a prayer for guidance and then stumbled backward as Allah answered, spoke to him so clearly that even today he could still hear the echo of God's voice in his heart. As he stood there beside the well, dazed, a host of birds rushed out of the depths, a flock of white doves such as had never been seen before or since in that place. The birds wheeled above his head, their wings like frost in the moonlight, then just as suddenly they dropped to the ground at his feet, dead. The next day Archduke Franz Ferdinand of Austria was murdered in Sarajevo, precipitating the First World War, and the Old One was assured of his destiny.

In the years following, he had grown ever richer and more

powerful. Other men seemed dim and lazy by comparison, and he used their weakness against them, jerking them about as though they were suspended on strings. While those around him grew weary and gray, and his wives and children tumbled into the grave, the Old One continued. Time had slowed for him, and the Old One used all scientific means to increase his days. It had taken Massakar to remind him that though time had slowed for him, it had not stopped.

In the distance a wave-energy buoy bobbed on the water, warning lights flickering. There had been hundreds of them initially, the Cubans investing heavily in alternative energy. Almost 50 percent of Nueva Florida's electrical supply had come from the wave buoys . . . until the latest cycle of super-hurricanes had torn through, uprooting their land links and sending them hurtling far inland. The Cubans had shifted to solar power.

The Old One massaged his knuckles, wondering when he would start stiffening with the infirmities that troubled other men. Rage twisted through him again, rage and frustration . . . and doubt. Rage and frustration were to be expected, but doubt . . . to question his anointing was to question Allah's judgment and that was blasphemy. The Old One inhaled deeply, let the clean salt air fill him. Whether he had three years or three minutes, he would not falter.

Others had been rumored to be the *mahdi* over the course of history, sixty false prophets as predicted, the most successful of them gathering whole armies to their cause before their inevitable defeat, like that fool in the Sudan in the 1880s and Osama bin Laden a hundred years later. These imposters announced themselves with trumpets and declarations, turned themselves into targets for the infidels and then were surprised when they were destroyed. The Old One knew better. He might have hundreds of billions of euros in assets, thousands of men who would eagerly die for him, but against nations—against Christians and Jews and false Muslims—he had no choice but to use more delicate tactics: stealth, bribery, assassination—methods that required patience. The world was a vast, multilayered chessboard, and the Old One took years between moves. Perhaps he had been *too* patient, relying on his own false sense of immortality to achieve his aspirations.

He had spent twenty years engineering the rise of one of his many sons to a position of prominence in the Catholic Church, having favorable articles written about this young cardinal, eliminating rivals. When the man finally ascended to the papacy as Pius XIII, it turned out that his time in the Church had changed him. His son had truly become a devout Catholic, and proceeded to do everything he could to thwart the Old One's ambitions, jailing clerics loyal to the Old One, and dramatically increasing his security. The Old One's attempts to cajole him were rejected, as were his efforts to discredit him. When all else failed he summoned Darwin. A week later, Pius XIII was found lying peacefully in his bed at the Vatican, hands neatly folded in prayer, one staring eye red with blood. Dead of an aneurysm, according to a team of coroners. Darwin never did tell him how he had accomplished the feat. Now it was too late.

The Old One watched the stars reflected in the waves, let his gaze linger so that after a time he couldn't tell the heavens from the sea. . . . He whirled around, saw Baby standing just inside the doorway, a healthy young animal that had lost all fear of him. "I told you I wanted to be alone," he said quietly. "You disobeyed me."

"Yes, I did, Daddy."

"Where is Ibrahim?"

"Ibrahim is a good boy." Cold eyes, almost as cold as his own. "He does what he's told."

"Ibrahim has been by my side since he was born. I barely know you, girl."

"Ibrahim has been in your *shadow* since he was born, Daddy. I see things more clearly than he does . . . I can be more useful to you." Baby walked out beside him, leaned against the railing. "This thing you had Lester do today . . . killing the Mexican oil minister, it's fine and good, and Lord knows, Lester *needed* to kill somebody or there'd be no living with him, but I don't really see the purpose of it."

"I'm not used to explaining myself."

"That's because Ibrahim's too much of a fraidy cat to ask, but I can't really help unless I know your intentions, Daddy." Baby stroked the base of her throat. "So who's getting blamed for the killing, 'cause I know it's not going to be us?"

Us. The Old One looked past her, not wanting to be distracted. It had been a long time since he had shared more than bits and pieces of his plans with anyone, but Baby was right— even his inner circle was too intimidated by him to do more than acquiesce. By turns coquettish and crafty, she had improved his mood almost from the moment she arrived, and he had come to realize that even her seemingly idle suggestions were worth considering.

"Daddy?"

"The Belt president will be blamed," said the Old One. "Not immediately, of course, not directly. Aztlán has many enemies, but I'll make sure their suspicions eventually turn to the Belt."

"You looking to stir up border troubles or start a trade war?"

"It's a bit more subtle than that," said the Old One.

"Subtle? See, that's the problem, Daddy." Baby kicked off her shoes, vaulted onto the wide, flat marble railing, teetered slightly as a gust caught her skirt, the fabric boiling up around her. Forty stories above the earth she stretched out her arms, wiggled her pink perfect toes. "*Subtle's* just another word for *safe.*" She looked down at him, blond hair whipping across her face. "Daddy . . . it feels like everybody here's moving in slow motion, afraid to make a move. Well, I can't live like that. You may have all the time in the world, but I don't."

"Yes . . ." The Old One looked up into her eyes and the stars seemed to go out. "Having all the time in the world does change things, doesn't it?"

She hopped off the railing, stood before him, so close he almost took a step backward.

Baby breathed harder, a flush rising in her cheeks. "So what's *really* going on?"

The Old One watched her. There was a tautness to her, an eagerness, as though she were straining at an invisible leash. It made her incredibly attractive. He wished he could remember her mother, but he had only a vague recollection of a beautiful, pale-skinned girl with hair that smelled like pine soap. They hadn't had much time together, a few weeks . . . never enough time. A thousand years wouldn't have been enough and now he had so much less than that.

"*Please*, Daddy?"

"The murder of the oil minister is just the first step," said the Old One. "I intend to start a full-scale war with Aztlán, bullets and bombers and the rockets' red glare."

"Now you're talking." Baby clapped her hands in glee. "If you want a war, though, you better forget slow and steady. You need to jump-start a regular shitstorm . . . pardon my French."

"Yes, you may be right . . ." said the Old One. "It might be best to move forward my timetable . . . even at the cost of increasing the risk." Baby slipped her arm through his and the Old One suddenly could see her mother's excited face, the two of them locked in passion. "So . . . how would you suggest we start this shitstorm, as you so colorfully described it?"

"Well, FYI, blaming the Belt president for the murder of the oil minister is the wrong play," said Baby. "President Raynaud's popularity is thin as tissue paper. Aztlán demands his head on a stick, the senate's likely to give it to them. You want to set the Belt boiling, sic Aztlán on the *Colonel*. Folks in the Belt love him. Raynaud's just a vote whore. My husband's a certified hero with a chestful of medals. If Aztlán blames him for what Lester did, you're going to get your war sooner than later."

The Old One locked eyes with her. If it were possible for him to be afraid of a woman, she would be the one. Blood of his blood. "Thank you."

"You're welcome." Baby bit her lower lip. "I know what y'all are thinking. You're wondering if you underestimated me. Don't feel bad, men do it to me all the time."

"Yes . . . I imagine they do." The breeze kicked up off the ocean, moist and briny. He hadn't lived in the desert for well over a hundred years, but sometimes he still missed it. "Will the Colonel accept help from the Republic?"

"The Republic helping out the Belt?" said Baby.

"Would he?"

Baby pretended to be thinking about the question, but he knew she was really thinking about the rationale behind the question. "Well . . . there's plenty of bad feelings to go around, but he's a Christian. To forgive's divine."

"Good."

Baby moved closer. "So you're stirring up a war between Aztlán and the Belt, so the Republic can come riding to the rescue. You're going to a lot of trouble to get the Belt and the Republic to kiss and make up."

"I'm a peacemaker at heart."

Baby giggled. "Me too." She gave his arm a gentle squeeze. "You planning on putting the two pieces together again?"

The Old One shouldn't have been surprised, but he was. Ibrahim would have never understood; his faith would have blinded him to the possibility.

"Reunification's the only reason I can think of for you to do what you're doing." Baby didn't look at him. "Strange thing, though. You busted up the United States so you could put it back together again?"

"To reunite it under the banner of Allah, stronger than ever. A beacon to the faithful around the world, a call to initiate the caliphate."

"That's going to be a hard sell, Daddy. Ask Humpty Dumpty how that worked out."

"Desperation reminds even half brothers that they are brothers nonetheless."

"Yeah, nothing like a wolf scratching at the door to stop folks from squabbling." Baby glanced at him. "You got a big problem, though. From what I hear, even the Belt and the Republic together aren't strong enough to defeat Aztlán, not as long as the Mexican air armada can pound every one of our cities flat."

"Yes, that is a problem."

"I guess you're working on it, huh?"

The Old One didn't respond.

Baby swayed against him. "One thing I always wondered about. Why start your caliphate in the USA instead of some Muslim country? I mean . . . why not make it easy on yourself?"

"I *did* try to make it easy on myself." The Old One watched the stars on the water. "I placed the Shah of Iran back on the Peacock Throne, but that upstart Khomeini ruined things. Then the Saudi prince I had maneuvered to succeed King Fahd fell from favor. My contacts in the U.S. State Department convinced Benazir Bhutto to return to Pakistan, but the silly bitch got herself killed before I intended." He shook his head. "After fifty years of failure in the Muslim world, I decided the solution lay elsewhere."

"The Great Satan," said Baby, fingers on her head making devil horns.

The Old One laughed and for an instant he forgot all about Massakar's sad face and even sadder diagnosis.

"I like hearing you laugh, Daddy."

"What could have greater impact on the Muslim world than the collapse of their ancient enemy?" said the Old One as Baby's hair wafted across his face like angel wings. "I had already laid the groundwork—politicians and journalists, newsanchors and academics, they were all for sale, and the religious leaders sold themselves cheapest. Their whole culture was rotten, riddled with greed and filth. I merely helped things along." The tide splashed in, the waves stacking up in the moonlight. "However . . . it turned out that bringing down the Great Satan was easier than putting it back together again. I came close five years ago, but our friend Rakkim and his meddling wife made me postpone my plans." Clouds edged across the moon. "That's why Ibrahim is so cautious. Inevitability is a tenuous asset, not to be squandered. I can't afford another high-profile setback."

Baby kissed his cheek. "Well, you didn't have me beside you back then. Now, you do."

"Yes," said the Old One, the feel of her lips lingering. "Now, I do."

CHAPTER 9

Rakkim was hurrying home when he spotted Sarah and Michael getting on the monorail at Fremont, both of them dressed as modern Muslims, which made no sense. He had to run to catch up, just managed to slide through the door of the Catholics-only car behind them. He didn't even have time to sit down before the monorail left, the elevated train shooting rapidly across the capital. The Catholics-only car was half full at midmorning, service workers and young mothers, mostly, a few old people staring out the windows as they gnawed on fibrous vitamin bars.

He settled back in the hard plastic bench, kept one hand half over his face, as though deep in thought, watching Sarah and Michael through the smoked glass between the cars. The Muslim cars were more luxurious, the seats padded, the air lightly perfumed with the scent of vanilla, verses from the Quran inscribed on the walls in gold script. Only fundamentalist cars were legally forbidden to nonbelievers, with a Black Robe posted on the platform to make sure no infidels tried to enter. Even so, Catholics chose to be among their own kind. Sarah stared straight ahead, head high, but Michael gawked from side to side, even peered at Rakkim for a moment before being distracted by the fat man sitting opposite him tapping away on his handheld.

Rakkim still didn't understand why she was dressed as a modern, her forearms bare, her gauzy dress barely covering her knees. Moderns drew attention. Better to go out as a moderate Muslim—there were more moderates than any other group, and a head scarf and modest dress engendered anonymity. Fundamentalist attire offered near-total invisibility, faces and bodies completely obscured, but a fundamentalist woman on her own could be stopped by any passing Black Robe, asked to show written permission from a male family member. Better to go out as a moderate, or a Catholic, with their rugged, working-class clothes and practical shoes. Catholics dressed for flight. Sarah knew all this . . . so why was she dressed like a modern?

Sarah leaned over, said something to Michael, and the boy smiled. Rakkim ached to be with them. He had only been gone a couple weeks, but it seemed longer, and never more so than when he saw the two of them together, realized how self-contained they were. How little they seemed to need him.

It had been three days since he slipped out of New Fallujah, winding his way beyond the control of the Black Robes. He had changed clothes at a rest stop in Northern California, emerged as a Catholic day laborer and gotten onto a crowded bus to Seattle, standing for most of the trip as the bus stopped at every town along the way.

He should have contacted General Kidd as soon as he got off the bus at Seattle's downtown produce market, should have briefed Kidd on what he had learned in the fundamentalist stronghold; that was the protocol, but Rakkim had headed home instead, desperate to see Sarah and Michael, more shaken than he wanted to admit by what he had seen back in New Fallujah. He closed his eyes and saw the burning madrassa, heard the screams, fresh innocents flickering like candles. If a shadow warrior like Jenkins could lose his way and find a home on the Bridge of Skulls . . . what hope was there for Rakkim?

A shout from the other side of the car, an old woman pointing out the window. One of the large freeway overpasses below had collapsed, crushed cars scattered across the roadway. He turned, saw Michael with his face pressed against the glass as the monorail moved past the destruction.

"Might help if they actually put some cement in the concrete," muttered a man across the aisle, a skinny twenty-something in worn jeans and a Starbucks giveaway nylon jacket. "'Course, that would cost money." He held out a bright red can of Jihad Cola to Rakkim.

Rakkim didn't react.

The young man got up from his seat and sat down next to Rakkim. He offered the can of cola again, his cuticles rimmed with grease, his knuckles raw. "It's mostly vodka. Made it myself from potato peelings." He toasted Rakkim. "I'm Eddie Flynn."

Two schoolgirls nearby giggled, turned away, whispering.

Rakkim looked out the windows, watched the city pass by. "What's the occasion?"

"My big brother's just enlisted. Airborne Rangers." Flynn sucked at the cola can. "Now I've got the bedroom to myself. No more arguing over the holo or having to hurry through my shower before we run out of hot water." He clutched the can. "Aren't you going to tell me how proud I should be?"

"No."

"That's good, because I ain't proud. Stupid bastard'll probably get shipped out to the Arizona front to bake his balls. Mexicans don't get him, the scorpions will. I told him not to do it. . . ." Flynn wiped his nose, smeared snot across the back of his hand. "I said it ain't our country. If the Muslims want to fight the Mexicans, *let* them."

"Keep your voice down," said Rakkim.

"I got good grades, but you see me at university?" said Flynn. "No, I'm on my way to some shit job, just like you." He stared at his scuffed work boots. "School counselor told me if I wanted to convert, she could get me into the technical college." He looked up at Rakkim. "I told her to kiss my Catholic ass."

"Hail Mary, full of grace." Rakkim placed his fist against his chest, thumb curled inside, the sign of the Saint George rowdies, and the young man repeated the motion.

"I was *good* in chemistry," Flynn said, slurring his words. He took a swallow from the can of vodka, offered it again. "Try this and tell me I'm wrong."

"I believe you."

Flynn shrugged. "I guess you got someplace important to go.

Lucky you." He signed off, lurched over to the other side of the car and sat back beside the Catholic schoolgirls.

The train made five stops before Sarah and Michael got off at the House of Martyrs war museum in downtown Seattle. Sarah and Michael joined the crowd heading toward the war museum, as many working-class Catholics as Muslims among the visitors, as many locals paying respects as tourists seeing where their tax dollars went. Sarah held tightly to their son's hand. The breeze sent leaves skittering across the pavement, but the grounds of the museum were immaculate, swept daily, the grass neatly tended. Rakkim kept well behind them, altering his pace when need be, always keeping two or three people in his sight line. Even so, twice Michael turned around quickly, almost spotted him.

Rakkim took a side path, paralleled Sarah and Michael as they walked toward the entrance. He kept his head down, glancing occasionally toward them, but avoided staring. Michael's instincts were too sharp; Rakkim had already started training him.

The war museum was a modest, understated dome built beside the crumpled Space Needle, the old monument lying on its side, rusting in the weather. The exterior of the museum was surfaced with small tiles made by schoolchildren, each one inscribed with the name of a martyred soldier. New tiles were added every month, as new martyrs fell in defense of the nation. An honor guard of veterans in crisp full-dress uniforms stood at attention around the dome, hands clasped behind their backs. Veterans in wheelchairs flanked the entrances—every visitor, Catholic and Muslim, offered them blessings before entering, the veterans stoic and unresponsive as stones.

Rakkim noticed a tall, well-dressed modern man wave to Sarah, walk toward her. Rakkim increased his pace to intercept him. Michael, noticing the modern too, tugged at Sarah, but she kept walking.

The modern strode through the crowd and it parted, made way for the handsome man with the commanding air. Rakkim recognized him now—Robert Legault, the weekend newsreader for the national news show . . . and a former suitor of Sarah's, one of several Redbeard, her uncle and guardian, had selected for her approval. She had rejected Legault, rejected them all, rejected Redbeard's authority and his connections and married Rakkim. From what Rakkim knew, Sarah and Legault had never seen each other since their three chaperoned dates ten years earlier.

Rakkim stayed back, stayed in the crowd . . . watching.

Legault opened his arms as he approached Sarah and she nodded, pressed her palms together in greeting. Legault went to pat Michael on the head and Michael twisted away, didn't let him touch him.

Rakkim saw Sarah and Legault walk across the lawn together while Michael went ahead, turning around every few steps to check on them. They stopped on a rise above the war museum. He watched Sarah and Legault talk for ten minutes, until Michael tugged on Sarah's hand, and Legault bowed low, the gallant modern, and left the way he had come.

Sarah and Michael started toward the museum.

"Sarah!"

She turned, and both she and Michael ran toward him, the wind whipping her long brown hair; she stopped short as people stared.

Michael pulled at Rakkim's hands.

"Where did you come from?" said Sarah, closer now, barely able to contain herself. "I *missed* you." She touched his cheeks. "We'll have to flush out the collagen when we go home—I want to see your real face again."

"You don't like the new me? Some wives might prefer—"

"I prefer *you*."

Rakkim picked up Michael, reached out with his other hand to draw Sarah to him, squeezed her close. He buried his face in her hair, the three of them wrapped up while the crowd broke around them, clucking their disapproval. Leave it to a modern to marry a Catholic; probably did it to torment her poor parents. Rakkim clutched them even tighter.

"New Fallujah was that bad?" Sarah whispered in his ear.

Rakkim held her, unable to speak.

Women in black burqas walked past, cursed them, their voices muffled, calling Sarah a whore who would roast in hell along with her bastard.

Sarah gently disengaged from him, took Michael's hand, the three of them strolling toward the entrance of the war museum.

"Did I see you talking with someone?" said Rakkim. "I was pretty far away. . . ."

"Yes." Sarah touched her hair. "You'll never guess who I ran into. Robert Legault."

"He still doing the weather?"

"No, he's actually at the network now. Senior producer."

"I didn't like him," said Michael.

"I hope you gave Robert my regards," said Rakkim.

"Yes . . . of course."

Rakkim offered his blessing to the veterans stationed beside the entrance, while Sarah covered her head with a scarf she took from her purse and pushed down her sleeves.

The tone inside the war museum was hushed and respectful, the only sound the shuffle of feet across the marble floor and the buzz of soft voices. A baby cried and was quickly comforted. Taking photographs inside the House of Martyrs was forbidden. This was sacred ground, open to all, regardless of religion. The museum was never closed, never empty. Sarah said in the old days, before the transition, the graveyards for the nation's war dead had been overgrown and untended. Military parades had played to empty streets, or worse, the color guard had faced catcalls from those whose freedom had been paid for with others' blood. A terrible time for heroes.

"St. Louis, Kansas City, Youngstown," said Michael, pointing out the Midwest cities on the holographic battle display. Michael knew every one of them, could recount the names of the commanders and the outcome. The images scrolled past as they watched. Chicago, still smoldering. Detroit's auto works gutted. Denver. The St. Louis arch collapsed. Newark, the deepest penetration into the Islamic states by the Christian armies. Newark, fought for block by block, until Islamic reinforcements, most of them still in high school, had finally stopped the Belt advance. Bloody Newark. As many times as he had seen it, the scenes still made Rakkim tear up.

As always, there was a crowd around the display at the very center of the museum, the true heart of the memorial. The three of them waited their turn, hearing a steady murmur of *"Allahu Akbar, Allahu Akbar,"* over and over until they finally stood before the marble stand holding up a simple Arabic edition of the Quran. No bulletproof plastic or nitrogen-rich bubble was necessary to protect it. The book had been recovered from the ruins of Washington, D.C., found surrounded by broken glass and twisted girders, the holy relic untouched by the atomic blast, the cover pristine, its pages shiny and white.

Rakkim lowered his eyes. He kept seeing Sarah and Robert Legault . . . how the breeze caught her dress, the hem grazing Legault's leg.

They stayed a few moments, then moved on from the Quran, passed a group of men in traditional garb praying before a mural of the triumph of Newark, the turning point of the war. They stopped in front of a large photo taken at the armistice between the two nations, President Kingsley and the Belt president, Andrew Fullerton, shaking hands, both of them looking exhausted.

"I bet they were glad," whispered Michael.

Rakkim played with Michael's hair. *"Everyone* was glad."

Above the photo of the two presidents were two aerial shots of Washington, D.C. One photo portrayed a majestic city, filled with cars, monuments gleaming in the sun. The other photo, taken a day after the dirty bomb exploded, was one long expanse of rubble and twisted metal, the great monuments fallen, streets bubbled from the intense heat.

Rakkim hated both images, the one because it showed the glory that had been lost, the other because it immortalized the extent of the destruction. The Zionist betrayal, that's what the nuke attack on the capital had been called, the Israeli Mossad blamed for decapitating the previous regime. A lie. The great lie. The Jews weren't responsible, it was the Old One. Sarah had proved that. She had a mind that could follow the twists and turns of that evil bastard, a mind attuned to deception. Rakkim looked over at her, but, though she had seen them a thousand times, the photos of D.C. had her full attention.

"Can we go see the Defense of Detroit exhibit?" said Michael.

Sarah didn't move.

"Sarah?"

Sarah stayed looking up at the ruins, then finally wiped her eyes and walked away from the dead city, walking so quickly that Rakkim and Michael had to hurry to catch up.

CHAPTER 10

The Old One watched Gravenholtz from the command center of his pleasure yacht, watched the redheaded brute pace the hundred-year-old Tabriz in the main salon, undoubtedly aware that he was being observed but unable to hide his restlessness. A beast barely able to restrain itself carried a risk to its master, but the Old One had worked with beasts before. Back and forth Gravenholtz walked, but he avoided the large glass-bottomed area of the cabin offering a view of the ocean depths below.

It had been three days since Gravenholtz killed the oil minister, and the Old One had let him stew in a cabin belowdecks, without any contact or acknowledgment of what had occurred, letting time do the work for him, unsettling the creature, poking and prodding him like a sharpened stick through the bars of his cage. Patience was alien to Gravenholtz. Patience, the most useful of tools . . . but ever since his conversation with his personal physician, the Old One realized that there were limits to such virtues. Tickety-tock . . . that's what Darwin used to say, smiling, that most jovial assassin. Tickety-tock, tickety-tock. The Old One was not amused.

Baby stood beside him, resplendent in a flowery yellow sundress that bared her tanned shoulders and legs. She smelled of summer.

He could see desalinization plants a mile offshore through the main windows of the control center, dozens of them strung all along the coast, new ones being built all the time to keep up with the ever-increasing demand. On the outer decks sixty or so revelers danced in the late-afternoon sun, half naked most of them, bronzed and beautiful as they bumped to the afro-salsa beat. The Old One's white-jacketed aides roamed through the crowd carrying aloft silver trays of tiger prawns and octopus. The sweet life, which was the name of the Old One's yacht, *La Dolce Vita*, a sleek, 240-foot party boat flying a piña colada flag. The last place anyone would be looking for him.

In his white jacket and white linen trousers with gold piping, the Old One looked like a weekend commodore out for a cruise. The faux-nautical trappings were pure camouflage, as much a part of the charade as the music and the dancers. The World Court had cleared him of responsibility in the nuke attacks on the U.S. and Mecca, but he had learned caution over the years.

"Father?"

The Old One looked at Ibrahim, his oldest son and counselor.

Ibrahim tapped his earpiece. "John Moseby received a transmission two days ago from Seattle."

"Moseby is contacted regularly, is he not?" said the Old One. "I have other things to concern myself with."

"Moseby evidently left shortly after receiving the most recent one," said Ibrahim.

The Old One glared at him.

"Our . . . our men on the scene didn't realize Moseby's absence until moments ago," said Ibrahim.

"Moseby was a shadow warrior once upon a time . . . it should have been expected that he would retain his skills." The Old One pursed his lips. "Have our technicians been able to decipher the code Leo uses to communicate yet?"

"Sadly, no."

"A team of supposed computer experts defeated by one nineteen-year-old boy," said the Old One. "I should hire *him* and get rid of the rest of you."

"Father, the men who let Moseby slip away . . . shall I have them punished?"

"Why not have them continue to monitor Moseby's home?" interrupted Baby. "Allow them to redeem themselves, Daddy, they'll work themselves harder than ever."

"This is *not* your concern, woman," said Ibrahim.

"Leave the men in place, Ibrahim," said the Old One.

"Father—"

The Old One waved him away.

Baby waited until Ibrahim had left. "A weak man's always in a hurry to punish somebody, so he can show how tough he is." She stroked her throat. "Moseby's a family man, Daddy. He won't be gone long without wanting to talk to his wife and girl."

The Old One loved looking at her. She didn't even make the attempt to hide her ambition. "We're *all* family men, my dear."

Onscreen, Gravenholtz clawed a hand through his scraggly hair, ridiculous in his tourist clothes—madras shorts and a bright orange silk shirt decorated with images of old automobiles. The prosthetics he had worn to kill the oil minister had made him look only a bit more grotesque. Gravenholtz stared directly into the camera lens. Not the obvious one, but the camera inside a clear glass geometric sculpture. "You done playing games?"

The Old One looked at Baby. "*Are* we done?"

"It's time," said Baby. Ibrahim would have taken a moment to consider, to gather his thoughts so as not to embarrass himself. Not her. "Lester's hot enough to boil away the lies, but not so hot that somebody gets burned. Just right, I'd say."

"Hold this position, James," the Old One said to the captain, "a slow drift to appreciate the view." He offered Baby his arm and she immediately slipped her hand above his elbow. A few minutes later they strolled into the main salon. "Rested, are we, from our labors, Mr. Gravenholtz?"

"Okay, say it." Gravenholtz glared at them. "I freelanced the hit, and I ain't apologizing either. I'm supposed to open the door for your human bomb, and close it afterward? I look like a fucking doorman to—?" He jerked as a wallscreen flashed on, showed the Aztlán oil minister recoiling in shock. Even with the sound turned down, the minister's voice cracked, a cascade of Spanish pleading for his life as Gravenholtz's freckled hand grabbed his platinum necktie. The oil minister swatted at

Gravenholtz's huge hand, mouth twitching as blood ran from his eyes.

"No, Mr. Gravenholtz, you most certainly are *not* a doorman," said the Old One.

Gravenholtz seemed to vibrate slightly, set the silk shirt in motion, the cars seemingly to race across his broad chest. "How'd you get that footage?"

The Old One slipped off his loafers, walked barefoot across the intricate pale blue and gray carpet, slightly clenching his toes with every step, remembering the Persian girl who had woven it, a tall, beautiful girl with small breasts and eyes like fire. It had taken her two years of work, the Old One stopping by every few months when he passed through on business, drinking tea with her father while she labored over her loom in the corner, stealing glances at him when her father wasn't looking. The Old One had been young then, and when he took possession of the carpet he had taken the girl as his third wife, given her something better to do with those strong, nimble fingers than weave carpets. He swayed on the Tabriz, eyes half closed, remembering her aroma.

"I asked you a question," said Gravenholtz.

The Old One gazed at him. "Is that a demand, Mr. Gravenholtz?"

"Could you *please* tell me how you done that?" said Gravenholtz.

"I had a pinpoint camera installed in your right eye," said the Old One. "It transmitted—"

"When you do that?" The cars on Gravenholtz's chest raced faster.

"Do you remember our discussion of Sultan Murad and his janissaries the first time we met?" said the Old One.

"Yeah. You said this sultan didn't give a shit whether his guards were Muslims or not, he just cared that they were the best," said Gravenholtz.

"He cared that they were the best, but also that they were *loyal*," said the Old One.

"So I didn't follow the plan," said Gravenholtz. "Now what?"

"Oh, quite the contrary, you met all our expectations," said the Old One. "I wasn't sure what you would do, but Baby . . ." He soundlessly applauded his daughter as she curtsied. "Baby assured me that you would adapt the plan to your own . . . needs. She was quite confident that you would take the initiative, and so you did."

"So . . . you ain't mad?" said Gravenholtz.

The Old One walked over to the glass-bottom area. "Join me, Mr. Gravenholtz. Come on, no need to worry. It's quite safe."

Gravenholtz edged along the margins of the glass, keeping one foot on the carpet.

The morning sun sent shafts of light through the clear water, illuminating the cityscape below—Little Miami, the sunken city off the coast of Nueva Florida. A fake tableau, ten miles of illusion for the tourist trade peering into the abyss. The city was a perfect construct of South Beach at the turn of the century, bright pastel hotels and dance clubs and movie theaters, long lines of convertibles and Italian speedsters, all of it covered with starfish and barnacles, purple and red sea anemones waving in the currents. New Orleans had sunk into the Gulf, killing hundreds of thousands, and the best the idiots in the Belt could do with the site was declare it jinxed, off-limits for development. The Cubans, meanwhile, created a fake sunken city as an homage to the cocaine cowboys of yesteryear and drew free-spending visitors from all over the world. The Cubans were brilliant capitalists. Infidels destined to roast forever in hell, to be sure, but great and creative moneymakers.

The Old One watched schools of iridescent orange fish veer across the city, darting into the open windows and out again, a synchronized, hypnotic ballet. "You *really* should see this, Mr. Gravenholtz."

"I'll take your word for it," said Gravenholtz.

"I must insist, Mr. Gravenholtz."

"I told you before, call me Lester. Mr. Gravenholtz was my father, and if he was alive today, I'd kill him all over again."

"Come *here*, Lester."

Haltingly, careful as a fat man on thin ice, Gravenholtz stepped across the glass floor. A few feet away from the Old One, he glanced down, then turned away. Stared at Baby, a single bead of sweat rolling down from his left sideburn. "Ain't . . . ain't no big deal. I been to New Orleans. You seen one sunken city, you seen them all."

Baby tossed her soft hair. "It's all right, Lester honey." She picked up a compressed-air speargun, checked the balance.

"Yes, Lester *honey*," said the Old One, "it's all right."

"Watch yourself, pops," said Gravenholtz, his face the color of boiled pork. "Go ahead, whistle in your guards; let's see who's dead and who's alive afterwards."

Baby sighted down the speargun at Gravenholtz, tossed it aside. Shooting him with the speargun would have been as dangerous to the redhead as pelting him with a marshmallow.

The Old One observed a translucent jellyfish undulate past, the jellyfish a delicate, pulsing umbrella trailing acid tendrils. He plucked the fountain pen from the pocket of his white cotton shirt, looked up at Gravenholtz. "May I have your autograph?"

Gravenholtz wrinkled his brow.

"You must be a great and powerful man to speak to me in such a rude manner." The Old One held out the pen. "I'd like your autograph as a memento of our meeting."

Gravenholtz moved toward him, hands balling into fists.

The pen sprayed a stream of clear strings at Gravenholtz, the strings wrapping around his legs, tripping him, Gravenholtz's face slamming into the glass floor. He tried pulling himself up, but the Old One sprayed his torso now, the strings pinning his arms, tightening around him like a cocoon, tightening . . . tightening until he couldn't move. Gravenholtz lay there looking up at the Old One. "What . . . what did you . . . *do* to me?"

The Old One held up the pen. "An aerosol polymer with molecular memory. Heat activated. Amazing what they're coming up with in laboratories these days. I sometimes wish Allah had led me to a career in the sciences." He cupped an ear. "Did you say something?"

Gravenholtz's face puffed out as he tried to pull his hands free, but the strings only tightened further. "I . . . I didn't mean . . ." His voice was high-pitched and wheezy as the strings squeezed around his rib cage, compressing his lungs.

"I understand completely," said the Old One. "You're re-evaluating your comments. Perfectly understandable. It does hurt, does it not? Not so much the physical pain, but a man like you . . . it's the sense of helplessness that truly stings." He watched Gravenholtz flop about on the floor, sweat dotting his forehead. "A man such as you, serene in your brutality . . . yet here you are." He bent down on one knee, gently dabbed Gravenholtz's forehead with his handkerchief and tossed it aside. "I could just as easily have one of my servants wipe and diaper your ass and you couldn't do anything about it. Not. A. Thing."

Gravenholtz tried to bite at the strings, but couldn't reach. "Get . . . me . . . *out* of here."

"Patience, Lester. Patience and humility and obedience are the lessons I have to teach you. Obedience most of all." The Old One tossed the pen to Baby. "Go ahead, my dear."

Baby bent down, lightly circled the inside of Gravenholtz's left nostril with the tip of the pen as he tried in vain to squirm away.

"My daughter finds you entertaining, Lester. Amusing even, but she's dutiful and obedient above all else. Would you like to see what would happen if I ask her to shoot the snare string into your nasal passages?"

"No."

"Shhh, Lester," said Baby as she eased the pen deeper into Gravenholtz's nostril. "Don't you fret now," she cooed, pushing it in still deeper as he struggled, bound like a mummy.

"No!" said Gravenholtz, rolling against Baby. "Please. *Please.*"

"I think we've gotten Lester's attention," said the Old One. He watched as Baby slowly slid the pen free. The Old One chuckled, seeing her disappointment. The girl raised his spirits. He looked toward the geometric sculpture. "Yusef, come here."

A few moments later one of his aides entered the room, bowing, a slender young man in white shorts and shirt. He fell to his knees, pressed his forehead against the carpet, and the Old One thought again of the Iranian girl he had married so many years ago. He could remember everything about her from the downy hair at the base of her spine to her long toes . . . but he could no longer remember her name.

"How may I serve you, Mahdi?" said Yusef, his forehead still pressed against the carpet.

"Rise," said the Old One.

Yusef stood up, his eyes downcast as the Old One approached. He smiled as the Old One whispered in his ear. "Thank you, Mahdi."

After Yusef hurried away, the Old One walked back and stood over Gravenholtz. "It's important for you to learn your true place in the firmament, Lester. Important for you to appreciate exactly what your value is."

"Got it," gasped Gravenholtz.

Baby moved closer, gently stepped on his earlobe.

"I said I *got* it," shouted Gravenholtz as she ground his earlobe against the glass floor.

"I had a Fedayeen assassin named Darwin in my employ for many years." The Old One peered at the hotel they were passing over, a pink Moorish monstrosity with battlement walls and high turrets. Sand sharks floated over the swimming pool. Sea anemones waved from the tennis courts in a mosaic of bright colors. "Darwin was troublesome in his own way, very independent, with a mocking tone of voice that annoyed me greatly." He watched as a hammerhead shark slid along the bottom, restless, stirring up sand. "Yet, I tolerated Darwin's many indiscretions because he was so *wonderful* at what he did. It took my medical staff hours to determine the eleven spots on your body vulnerable to attack, the intersections where your subcutaneous plates need room to move. Darwin would have known in seconds, just from watching you walk. He'd have filleted you without even breathing hard." The hammerhead turned, circling closer. "A master assassin, that's who Darwin was, a perfect killing—" The hammerhead turned and shot upward with a powerful kick of its tail section, black eyes glaring at the Old One as it slammed full speed against the glass.

Gravenholtz screamed.

Baby lost her balance, laughed as her yellow sundress swirled around her.

The Old One's knees buckled, but he kept his footing as the hammerhead glided off into deeper water. "Are you feeling all right, Lester? Would you like something to calm yourself? A saucer of warm milk, perhaps?"

"*No.*"

"Stout fellow." The Old One glanced at Baby. "I wish you could have met Darwin, my dear. I think he would have been quite a match for you."

"Where's this Darwin you're so fucking in love with?" said Gravenholtz. "He's so good, why do you need me?"

"Darwin is dead," said the Old One.

"So I guess he's not such hot shit after all," said Gravenholtz.

"That's one explanation." The Old One beckoned to Baby. "Turn his head, my dear. I prefer not to touch him." He waited until Baby had forced Gravenholtz's head down, so he could look into the water. "Do you see him, Lester?"

Gravenholtz craned his neck. Jerked back.

Baby leaned closer.

Yusef, the Old One's young aide, sank slowly through the blue-green water, a weight belt around his waist. He bowed his head toward the Old One, trailing bubbles as he drifted down toward the pink hotel.

"Don't let yourself be burdened with thought, Lester," said the Old One, watching the young aide scattering fish in his descent. "No thoughts, no ego, no freelancing. Obedience is everything."

"Fuck," said Gravenholtz, watching the bubbles leak out of Yusef's mouth, each one smaller than the one before. "Fuck the *duck*."

"Baby and I will be doing a lot of traveling in the days ahead," the Old One said to Gravenholtz. "If you promise to be a good boy, we'll take you along with us."

"We're going to have us a grand time," said Baby. "Visiting some old friends and making new ones. Come on, Lester, don't be a stick in the mud."

Yusef's head flopped back as he plummeted through the blue water.

Gravenholtz turned away from the glass. He stared at Baby. "Hey, you know me, I'm always up for a party."

CHAPTER 11

Rakkim saw General Kidd and his son Amir at one of the outside tables of the Kit Kat Klub, the two men lounging in the late-afternoon sun, their long legs outstretched. The crowds that thronged the Zone gave them room, dropping their voices as they passed. A native-born Somali in his sixties, black as an anvil, Kidd commanded the Fedayeen, though his plain blue uniform was without rank, insignia or medals. Powerfully built, his cropped hair shot with gray, he radiated a dangerous calm. Amir was even taller, lean as a panther, his shaved head emphasizing his natural severity—he watched the crowd with undisguised contempt. As Kidd sipped his drink, he spotted Rakkim approaching and stood up.

"*Salaamu 'alaikum, sidi,*" said Rakkim, using the North African term of respect. He embraced General Kidd, saw Amir's jaw tighten.

"Abu Michael," said General Kidd, kissing Rakkim on both cheeks. *Abu Michael,* father of Michael, a Somali honorific reserved for friends and honored guests. "Peace be upon you."

Rakkim nodded at Amir. "*Salaamu 'alaikum.*" Amir returned the nod but not the blessing. Rakkim pretended not to notice.

"Sit," said Kidd, gesturing to an empty chair at their sidewalk table. "Make room, Amir."

Recorded music blared from inside the club, all bass and grind, some South African thump band popular on underground radio stations and joints in the Zone. Officially called the Christian Quarter, the Zone was a seedy section of the capital lined with nightclubs and game stores and unlicensed tech shops, a place of alcohol, music and dancing, where the cops were paid off and the Black Robes ignored. Loud and dirty, the Zone was a cultural safety valve, untamed, innovative and off the books, a moral free-fire area open to everyone—Christian and Muslim. After he retired from the Fedayeen, and before he married Sarah, Rakkim had lived here. He looked right at home in his casual, moderate attire: lightweight trousers and a soft wool checkerboard sweater in red and black, the sleeves concealing the Fedayeen knife adhered to his inner forearm.

"Your vacation went well?" Kidd tapped his index finger on the small static generator disguised as a cigarette lighter on the table. Between the ambient noise and the static generator, their conversation couldn't be monitored.

"Well enough," said Rakkim, noting how Kidd avoided specifics in Amir's presence.

A waitress appeared to take Rakkim's order, a busty young Catholic, her red hair in a corona of braids.

"Small khat infusion, please," said Rakkim, mirroring the general's own beverage, a sweetened concoction brewed from the leaves of a North African plant known for its stimulating and euphoric properties. As always, Amir drank only water. Fundamentalist Muslims considered khat an abomination, no better than alcohol, but Kidd was a traditionalist, a moderate who trusted Allah to judge what was right and wrong, not some pinched cleric with a soiled bag of his own sins hidden from view.

The waitress punched in Rakkim's request on her handslate, returned a few minutes later with his drink, touching his wrist as she set it down.

Kidd raised his glass, toasted him, but Amir made no move to join in. There had been bad blood between the two young men since Rakkim had inadvertently humiliated Amir a year ago—he had refused to spar with Amir, and when the younger man persisted, his knife thrust an inch from Rakkim's face, Rakkim had disarmed him, done it so easily that it surprised the both of them. Rakkim had attempted to mollify Amir's anger on several occasions without success, and Amir's subsequent rise to power had made the shame of his defeat even more acute.

The call to prayer echoed from the nearby Al-Zawahiri mosque, the muezzin's voice clear and undulating. *Come to prayer! Come to God!*

Amir glared at the people walking past, fun-seekers either oblivious to the call to prayer, or ignoring it. He caught the eye of a man in a gold and blue Christ the King High School jacket, the man so unnerved by Amir's expression that he stumbled over a crack in the sidewalk, hurried on. Amir had been acclaimed as the "Lion of Durango" for his exploits against the Mormons, and had personally safeguarded then-Senator Brandt and his family after the death of President Kingsley. Only twenty-six years old, Amir commanded the elite Fedayeen strike force defending the capital, and was expected to assume leadership of the Fedayeen when his father retired. It hadn't improved his disposition.

"I don't think Amir likes your choice of a meeting spot, *sidi*," said Rakkim.

Amir wrinkled his nose. "It stinks of vice and depravity."

Rakkim sniffed. "I think that's perfume."

"Are you mocking me?" Amir said softly.

"Fedayeen should feel free to announce their presence in any part of the city, Amir." Kidd eyed two young women swaying past, moderns with loose hair and university charm bracelets jingling with every step. "Did not the Prophet himself, all blessings upon him, embrace the range of delights this world had to offer without fear of being tainted?"

Amir started to stand. "Father . . . this is blasphemy," he sputtered.

Kidd gently pushed him back down. "If so, then Allah will take his vengeance upon me, and you need not concern yourself."

Amir spread his huge hands out on the table as though waiting for the earth to open up under them.

"Have you heard about our difficulty on the Southwest border?" Kidd said to Rakkim.

"Aztlán?" said Rakkim.

Kidd nodded. "A squadron of their attack jets entered our airspace three days ago . . ."

Rakkim inadvertently glanced toward the sky.

". . . the worst part," said Kidd, "was that they were over our territory for twenty minutes before they were picked up on our screens. We're not sure if they're utilizing some advanced stealth technology . . . or just our own incompetence."

"Or the Jews may have sabotaged our system," said Amir. "One way or the other, I'll get to the bottom of it."

"The president has appointed Amir to find out the cause of the breakdown," explained Kidd, his face devoid of emotion. "He's been given full command authority."

"Congratulations." Rakkim looked at Kidd. "You must be proud, *sidi*."

Amir stood up, bowed to his father. "I have a meeting with the president." He gave a curt nod to Rakkim and walked quickly away. People on the sidewalk moved out of his path.

Kidd downed his khat infusion, banged the glass down. "Now tell me, Abu Michael, what did you find out from our brother in New Fallujah?"

For the next ten minutes they talked, and when their glasses were refilled they kept talking, wiping their lips with the backs of their hands, laughing at things that weren't funny until the waitress walked away. Kidd dragged Rakkim's chair closer, the two of them bent over the table, so close that their faces almost touched.

"Senator Chambers working for ibn-Azziz? It makes no sense," said General Kidd. "The great liberal a pawn of the Black Robes?" He shook his head. "I don't believe it. Chambers's wife is a *Christian*."

"Which is why Chambers would be the last person we would suspect," said Rakkim. "There is a logic to it." A couple of moderns walked past, young businessmen, smooth and confident, and Rakkim thought about Robert Legault with Sarah this afternoon, the way they matched their pace across the grass. . . .

"Rakkim?" said Kidd. "I said, is Jenkins *sure* about Senator Chambers?"

Rakkim shrugged. "He told me the president is going to name Senator Chambers to be secretary of defense. Have you heard anything—?"

Kidd dropped his glass. Caught it before it hit the table. "Chambers . . . the senator is going to be appointed secretary of defense on the next full moon. The announcement won't be made for another few days." The planes of his cheekbones seemed even sharper as he leaned over the table. "Does Jenkins think the president is involved?"

"No. Ibn-Azziz considers the president an accommodating dupe, a man who's achieved his station by virtue of a good hair-cut and a bright smile."

Kidd's dark eyes betrayed no emotion. "Yes . . . one could see how he could form such an opinion."

"Jenkins . . . I know you've been comrades since the Great War," said Rakkim, "but I think he's lost his way."

"Lost his way? What is that, some shadow warrior mumbo-jumbo?" Kidd covered Rakkim's hand with his own, and it was as if they were in a private bubble, where the sights and sounds of the Zone were muted. "Jenkins's information is true or false. Jenkins is either a traitor or he's not."

"It's not that simple."

"It *is* that simple," said Kidd. "Six months ago, a shadow warrior operating in the Mormon territories *lost his way* and lured the tenth brigade into an LDS trap outside of Elko. Two thousand combat Fedayeen were annihilated. His brother warriors—"

"They weren't his brothers," Rakkim said. "Not anymore. The Mormons are his brothers now. A man lives in the territories long enough, and after a while, he isn't pretending. He might as well get baptized."

"Without loyalty all the training in the world is useless. *Worse* than useless," said Kidd. "That's why the president shut down the shadow warrior program. I argued against it, but he ignored my

counsel. All Fedayeen now are combat Fedayeen, with guide-
lines and boundaries and a chain of command."

"Then the president should have sent one of *them* to New
Fallujah."

"The president doesn't know anything about your mission."
Kidd squeezed his hand lightly, released him. "What about you,
Abu Michael? When you were on your missions in the Belt, did
you ever lose your way?"

Rakkim hesitated. Nodded. "The Belt is so seductive it's easy
to forget where you belong. That's why I retired. It hurts to be
lost. You go native because it's better to be wrong than to be lost."

"Yet you go on missions for me," Kidd said gently.

"I have a family now. They help me find my way back."

Kidd looked at the empty chair where Amir had been sitting.

"*Sidi*, we can't let Chambers become secretary of defense,"
said Rakkim. "Not until we know if he's working for ibn-Azziz."

"Ten days until the full moon . . . not much time to prove
something like that," said Kidd. "Asking State Security for help
is futile—they're slow and inept and porous. If Redbeard were
alive, he'd have a complete dossier on Chambers, every phone
call, every financial transaction, every prostitute he had visited."
He held up his empty glass to the waitress. "Redbeard wouldn't
have needed ten days to find out . . . but your mentor is in Paradise, probably teaching Allah a thing or two about keeping tabs
on His angels."

"I didn't think you liked him."

"He didn't like *me*. Blamed me for you joining the Fedayeen
instead of State Security."

"You had nothing to do with it."

"Well, Redbeard always looked for the invisible hand at
play—" Kidd stopped as the waitress set down fresh drinks,
waited until she left. "State Security requires a different mind-set
than Fedayeen, you know that better than I do. Redbeard was
deceptive even when he didn't need to be, always pitting people
against each other, but I respected him. In the early days it was

just he and I and President Kingsley. Hard times, dangerous times, but we were young and had high hopes . . . such high hopes it was almost a sin." He looked at Rakkim, his eyes warming. "He would have been proud of you."

"What . . . what if we get proof that Chambers is working for ibn-Azziz?" said Rakkim.

"Drink up."

Rakkim touched glasses with Kidd. "What do we do?"

Kidd swirled his drink, ice cubes clinking. "Why, we'll pray for guidance, as good Muslims would."

"We'll have to do better than that," said Rakkim.

CHAPTER 12

Jenkins shivered, pulled his heavy black robe around him.

Ibn-Azziz's personal apartment was an unheated stone cell deep beneath Alcatraz Island, a windowless room under the former prison where particularly troublesome prisoners had been housed a hundred years earlier. The walls were slick with moisture, mold sprouting in the crevices. The Grand Mullah could have lived in luxury, could have spent his nights in a sumptuous high-rise, cozy and warm. The dimly lit punishment cell suited him better.

"Are you *cold*, Imam Jenkins?" Ibn-Azziz lay on the rough stone bunk, wearing only a loincloth. His ribs protruded, his hair thinning and lifeless. He was twenty-six and looked forty years older. "Shall I have one of my men bring you a fur coat?"

Jenkins stood in the doorway, his frosty breath lingering in the air. "I'm fine."

"Perhaps some hot cocoa?"

"Yes, that would be wonderful," said Jenkins, playing along. "Marshmallows of course, and a plate of those chocolate chip cookies the Grand Mullah is renowned for."

"Indeed." Ibn-Azziz peered up at him. "I've gotten some troubling news." His voice was thin and reedy, but his eyes were hot coals. "Perhaps you could enlighten me."

Jenkins tasted fear. It seemed he was scared more and more lately. He should have gone with Rakkim, should have left when he had the chance. "I'll do my best."

"Your best . . . yes, I can always count on you to do your best." Ibn-Azziz nodded and one of his guards closed the iron door to the cell, the rusted hinges squeaking. Just the two of them now. As many times as he had been in here with ibn-Azziz, every time the door shut, Jenkins felt as though he were being buried alive. Ibn-Azziz sat up, flipped open a hand-viewer. "Come." He patted the bench next to him. "Sit beside me."

Jenkins sat. Ibn-Azziz smelled like wet newspapers.

The screen blinked on. A street scene, men shuffling forward in the dawn light, heads down. One of ibn-Azziz's long, yellow nails tapped the screen, freezing the image. Not a clear picture, but it was Rakkim, dressed as a laborer, his face partially obscured, streaked with grime. "This man . . . do you recognize him?"

Jenkins took his time, remembering what had happened to the last man ibn-Azziz believed to be a spy. The man had taken a week to die, howling the whole time. An innocent man . . . framed by Jenkins to cover his own tracks. "No."

"Take a good look."

Jenkins had been completely scanned before entering the cell. Even without a blade he might be able to kill ibn-Azziz . . . *might*. His fighting skills had atrophied, and anyway, there was no way to escape the guards outside. "I don't know him."

"He's Fedayeen," said ibn-Azziz. "Does that jog your memory?"

Jenkins shook his head. "I left the brotherhood a long time ago. If this one is truly Fedayeen—"

"*If?*" hissed ibn-Azziz.

"Who said this man is Fedayeen?" Jenkins said evenly.

"Our new perimeter cams picked him out of the crowd a week ago. Matched him from a database," said ibn-Azziz. "The picture is poor and he's altered his appearance from his days at the academy, but it's him. The old system wouldn't have matched him, but the new one uses more data points for comparison."

"I didn't know we had such capability."

"The upgraded system is only at a few locations. It's very expensive."

"Praise be to our mysterious benefactor." Jenkins shifted his weight. There was no comfortable position on the stone bunk. "What's the Fedayeen's name?"

"Rakkim Epps."

"Is he in custody?"

"No." A cockroach crawled across ibn-Azziz's leg but he ignored it. "The fools working perimeter security were slow to react, and by the time they realized they had a match, Epps had disappeared." He plucked the cockroach from his leg, brought it close to his face, the roach's legs wiggling wildly. "To make matters worse, they attempted to hide their failure, pretending the system had malfunctioned." He set the roach down gently on the floor, watched it scurry away. "I wanted to discuss their punishment with you."

"Of course."

"First, though, I wanted to talk with you about another matter." Ibn-Azziz looked up as the roach squeezed through a crack in the stone floor. "Four nights ago, a madrassa in the Polk district burned to the ground. Most of the girls, dressed for sleep, chose to die rather than have their immodesty displayed in front of men not of their own family. These righteous females burned bright and pure, but some of them . . . some chose to run away, half naked into the night." He stared at Jenkins and the air in the cell grew even colder. "Pray, tell me, imam, why you gave those *whores* absolution from their sin?"

Rakkim stood by the bedroom window, listening to the late-night call to prayer echoing across the rooftops of this Catholic neighborhood. Sometimes he heard the call and wished he were devout, wished he could lose himself in his faith, trusting in Allah to set things right, to reward the just and punish the wicked. Tonight, though, all he could think of was walking out of prayers in New Fallujah and seeing flames from the madrassa, a greasy glow over the buildings, burning its way into his heart. He heard Sarah get up, but didn't turn from the window.

"What's wrong?" Sarah pressed her hand against his chest. "Talk to me."

Rakkim looked at her standing there, naked in the moonlight. Her breasts were fuller now than before Michael was born, heavier. He was even more drawn to her ripeness.

"Did . . . did something happen between you and General Kidd?"

"You lied to me this afternoon."

Sarah didn't answer. Didn't compound the lie with another one. A small blessing . . . or just her knowing when to stay silent until she found out how much he knew.

"I was watching you this afternoon at the war museum," said Rakkim. "You didn't bump into Robert Legault by accident. You were there to meet him."

Sarah barely hesitated. "That's true."

"You lied to me."

"I was postponing telling you the truth."

Rakkim stared out the window. "Do you love him?"

"What? *Love* him? Rakkim . . . I've been in love with you since we were children."

"I know our history," Rakkim said. "I also know you lied about meeting an old boyfriend."

"Robert was never my boyfriend. He was *suitable*."

"And I wasn't."

"Redbeard was my uncle and my guardian; it was his responsibility to find me a suitable husband. You . . . you were a street urchin he brought home and trained to follow in his footsteps. He loved you, but—"

"That wasn't love."

"He *loved* you, Rikki. He loved you enough to treat you like his son. Loved you enough that he wanted you to take charge of State Security. His plans for you didn't include marrying his niece . . . but I didn't care. I stood up to him. I risked everything to . . ." Sarah shook him, the two of them so close that their naked bodies grazed. "Do you think I would bring Michael along if I was contemplating doing something immoral?"

"I don't know."

"Rikki, after all this time . . . don't you trust me?"

Rakkim looked into her eyes.

"Rikki . . . you have to answer."

"What *were* you doing there with him?" Rakkim ran his fingers through her hair, her neck soft under his touch. "It's a simple question. I'm sure there's a simple answer."

"You're not going to like it." Sarah took a deep breath. "Robert wants to do a three-hour TV special on Redbeard's life . . . not just a biography, but his effect on the nation, the difference that he made. Robert wants us to participate fully."

Rakkim shook his head. "You might as well send the Old One an invitation."

"Do you think he *needs* an invitation?"

"What's really going on, Sarah?"

"It's cold out here. Come back to bed and we'll talk about it."

"I can think better out here."

Sarah laughed. "God hates a coward, Rikki."

"God hates a fool too."

Sarah led him back to bed, the sheets still warm. She rested her head on his chest. "Aren't you tired of hiding from the Old One? Michael needs to start school."

"He's learning plenty. Between the two of us—"

"It's not just about us. We've always thought bigger than that."

"*You* have. Not me."

She sat up, the sheet falling away, and Rakkim couldn't take his eyes off her. "We have to get involved, Rikki. It was different when Kingsley was president, we had access, and Kingsley paid attention. Brandt, though . . . he's not listening to us, and according to what you found out in New Fallujah, the people he *is* listening to are determined to take the country back to the dark ages." She kissed him. "We can't afford to hide anymore."

Rakkim stroked her flank. "Why now?"

"What do you—?"

"Why does Legault want to do a special on Redbeard *now*? Why not last year or next year?"

Sarah shook out her hair. "Because I suggested it to him."

"That's what I thought."

"I'll take that as a compliment." Sarah slid on top of him. Her mother's tiny crucifix hung from a chain around her neck, bounced between her breasts as she rocked. "Five years of marriage and you're still jealous." She reached back, gripped him. "I feel like a newlywed."

Rakkim groaned. "You're a Catholic girl at heart."

"Well?" said ibn-Azziz. "Why did you absolve those schoolgirls from their sin?"

"At first I *was* content to let them burn," said Jenkins.

"Yet you changed your mind." Ibn-Azziz scratched his arms, gouged the flesh with his yellow nails, lips curling with pleasure. "So . . . my dear mullah, why did you disgrace yourself with mercy?"

"Mercy?" Jenkins's cackle echoed off the stone walls. "I spared the girls' lives, but it was only for the greater glory of Allah. Have you not noticed how often our jihadis fail in their attacks, killed before they can detonate their suicide belts?" He leaned closer to ibn-Azziz. "But who would stop a schoolgirl from entering a movie theater or a crowded mall? Such an innocent could go anywhere unchallenged. If there was mercy in my actions that night, then it was the mercy of allowing their death to *mean* something, rather than simply die for modesty."

Ibn-Azziz narrowed his eyes. "Modesty is a great virtue."

"Not so great as the smiting of our enemies."

"True." Blood trickled down the inside of ibn-Azziz's arms. "This idea . . . was it yours?"

Jenkins shook his head. "I wish that I could take the credit, but that would be a lie." Ibn-Azziz was trying to trap him. One of the police or another black robe had seen him talking with Rakkim at the fire—in the darkness, they hadn't recognized Rakkim as the man in the surveillance footage, but ibn-Azziz's suspicions had been aroused.

"Who deserves my gratitude?" said ibn-Azziz. "I am most generous, as you know."

"A man approached me after the girls had fled the burning madrassa," said Jenkins, "a jihadi on his way to paradise. He suggested that the girls, having already forfeited their souls, be given a chance to redeem themselves."

Ibn-Azziz tugged at his wispy beard.

"Schoolgirl jihadis, the youngest angels," said Jenkins. "We should wait, though, give them a couple more years, so their will becomes resolute . . . and so they can carry more explosives."

"Who was this jihadi who gave you such an idea?" said ibn-Azziz. "Tell me his name."

"He said his name was Tamar and he was on his way to Santa Barbara to send some Catholics to hell."

"Pity," said ibn-Azziz, immobile in the faint light, so emaciated that it looked like his body was collapsing in on him. "I would have liked to have met this man. Given him my blessing on his journey."

"I asked him to stay, but he was eager for his divine reward," said Jenkins, sensing that ibn-Azziz was still waiting for him to make a mistake. "He *did* allow me to take him to the Bridge of Skulls. He said it was his favorite place in the city, a monument to our triumph over perversity. He and I walked to the very end and prayed together."

Ibn-Azziz nodded. "Yes . . . you were observed with this jihadi by the guards at the bridge." He dipped a fingertip in his blood, added a tiny red fingerprint to the hundreds of other red marks on the wall. "It was a stormy night, they said. The bridge bucking and heaving so much that they were afraid to set foot on it. Yet . . . you did."

"Have you not told me that those who love God have nothing to fear?"

"*Inshallah,*" said ibn-Azziz.

"*Inshallah*," said Jenkins.

"Now then," said ibn-Azziz, showing his teeth, "what shall we do with the two men who let Rakkim Epps through the security cordon? The two who tried to cover up their incompetence."

"The Bridge of Skulls is hungry," said Jenkins, a chill starting up his spine. "We should feed it."

"Shall I accord you the honor?"

Jenkins inclined his head. "You are too kind."

CHAPTER 13

"I'm confused," Hussein said to Amir, as they sat cross-legged in the tree-shaded garden at the rear of Hussein's villa, the surrounding walls dotted with electronic chaff generators to prevent eavesdropping. A stocky white man with a pugnacious jaw and short gray hair, Hussein had lost his left arm in battle, the sleeve of his Fedayeen uniform folded back to his shoulder. Orange and yellow koi glided in the pond beside them, Hussein trailing the fingertips of his right hand in the water. "Your father sends Rakkim into New Fallujah and he tells you nothing. Yesterday, Rakkim gives your father an after-mission report and again, your father tells you nothing. So illuminate me, O Lion of Durango . . . is *Rakkim* General Kidd's spawn, or are you?"

"I don't need my father," said Amir, keeping his temper in check, refusing to take the bait. "I'll find out myself what Rakkim told him."

"Oh really?" said Hussein. "Will you ask the birds in the trees? Or perhaps . . ." He jerked his hand from the pond, clutching a dappled koi. Held it out to Amir. "Ask *him*. He's old and wise. Go ahead, ask him. No?" He kissed the wriggling fish on the lips and returned it to the water. "Don't make promises you can't keep."

"Then *you* tell me," demanded Amir. "What was Rakkim doing in New Fallujah?"

"I don't know either." Hussein wiped his hand, then leaned over the holographic display between them—thousands of red-plumed Roman Legionnaires caught between the two flanks of the Carthaginian cavalry, swords flailing as the horsemen attacked. "But I'm sure Rakkim wasn't there to go to mosque."

Known for his harsh criticism, Hussein had been one of the

great tacticians of the civil war, a Fedayeen commander second in skill only to his father. While General Kidd had found renown on the northern front, defeating the Belt forces in New Jersey, Pennsylvania and Ohio, Hussein had attacked the Belt from the west, driving the rebels out of New Mexico and Colorado, taking the fight into Texas and Oklahoma.

Hussein pointed at the holographic display. "As the Carthaginians charged through the trapped Romans, their enemy was so tightly packed together that Hannibal instructed his men to simply cut the hamstrings of the Romans and keep advancing—that way they could slaughter the crippled Legionnaires at their leisure once the battle was won." He looked at Amir. "The ultimate objective takes precedence over any individual player. You must not let yourself be distracted."

Amir nodded.

"Are you not troubled by your father keeping Rakkim's mission a secret from you?" Hussein waved a hand over the military reenactment of the Battle of Cannae, the soldiers dissolving into fine gray powder, the topography shifting from the trampled banks of the Aufidus River to a barren, gray landscape. Fedayeen armored strike troops were spread out, waiting to be deployed against the small city in the distance. Another wave of Hussein's hand and the holographic display changed to the dusty flatlands surrounding Amarillo, the heavy infantry of the Texas volunteers arrayed against the tanks of the Fedayeen Third Army. "It's almost as if he doesn't trust you."

"My father is teaching me the lessons of leadership," said Amir. "Trust no one more than is absolutely necessary. His caution is a compliment."

"Ah. A *compliment*." Hussein tugged down the jacket of his blue uniform. "How foolish of me not to recognize the accolade. You must be flattered."

"What is your point?"

"You need to see what is in front of your nose." Hussein curled two fingers and the Texas volunteers shifted into position along the western edge of the city. Drone surveillance aircraft drifted overhead, diaphanous as dragonflies. "Your father's not going to join us, you *know* that," he said, waving up antiaircraft batteries around the core of the city. "When the time comes, you're going to have to kill him."

Amir stiffened. "No."

"I remember your father in the early days. He looked like a king, moved like a king. None of us had the benefit of genetic boosters; we achieved what we did on strength and courage . . . and *faith*. We burned with belief and our faith sustained us more than food or drink. Your father should have acknowledged the Old One long ago. He had his chance twenty years ago, but turned it down. I suspect he will turn down the opportunity again. Blind loyalty, the Somali curse . . . it's going to be the death of him yet."

"I won't raise a hand against my father," said Amir. "Better the Old One asks me to kill Rakkim. I would, *gladly*."

"You might have some trouble with that, from what I've heard."

Amir felt his face grow hot. "Say the word and I will lay his head before you."

"An empty promise, I'm afraid. The Old One wants Rakkim left unharmed. It is your father who stands in our way." Hussein finger-flicked the Fedayeen forces into existence, spread them out into a pincer nearly circling the city, deliberately allowing an avenue of retreat toward the east. He kept his eyes on the display, making fine adjustments with his thumb and forefinger. "The question, Amir . . . the question is do you love your father more than your own salvation? At the end of days you will have to choose."

Amir remembered riding on his father's back as a child, feeling as though he were astride the world.

Hussein glanced up. "Don't trouble yourself. When the moment comes, you will act as Allah wills it." He nodded at the elaborate hologram. "The Fedayeen numbered five thousand arrayed against approximately twelve thousand Belt irregulars, tired and hungry men, but dug in and fighting on their own territory. So *tell* me, youngster, what would you do if you commanded these Fedayeen?"

Amir studied the hologram. Amarillo was a minor battle in Hussein's dash across Texas. He remembered studying it briefly at the academy . . . something about Hussein splitting his main force and sending the bulk of his men south toward San Antonio, a decision contrary to established military doctrine.

"What would you *do*?" demanded Hussein. "You don't have the luxury of time, so a siege or long bombardment is out of the question. The tanks are needed to support the attack on San Antonio, and you can't bypass the city and leave your forces subject to attack from the rear. What do you do, Amir?"

Amir leaned over the display, zooming in. The faces of the Fedayeen troops were in high relief, the sand on the treads of the Saladin tanks clearly evident. He gestured with his right hand and the city opened up, every major street revealed, every collapsed building and shattered overpass. "The enemy line is heavily reinforced . . . but static. Once it's cracked . . . or flanked, the city will be exposed and vulnerable to a blitzkrieg attack."

"Where would you make your assault?"

Amir examined the hologram, noting the access routes into the city, and the choke points where any Belt counterattack would bog down. A koi leaped out of the pond, landed with a splash, but Amir didn't react. He tapped a finger in the northeast quadrant where a new freeway system offered eight lanes into the heart of the city. "Here."

"Easy to get in," said Hussein, "but what happens when they slam the door after you?"

"My tanks would make short work—"

"Your tanks will sacrifice their mobility once they leave the main streets."

Amir reconsidered the problem. "This old irrigation canal is undefended. We can attack from the north as a diversion, then send the tank force up the canal and cut the city in half. Before they can shift their heavy weaponry we'll wipe them out."

"What if the enemy has mined the canal?"

"I'd send a reconnaissance team."

"If they were spotted, your element of surprise would be lost."

Amir slid a hand across his shaved head. "I'd take the chance."

Hussein patted his shoulder. "Boldness is a virtue in a warrior," he said, blue eyes flashing, "but in this case, your attack would have stalled. The canal *was* mined. The Belt commander was very good, well-schooled and disciplined."

There were some in the Fedayeen who thought that Hussein should have been appointed supreme commander of the Fedayeen, but Kidd's defense of Newark had galvanized the nation and, even more important, Kidd had the support of President Kingsley. Politically more astute, Kidd was gracious in victory, personally guaranteeing that captured rebels were humanely treated. By contrast, Hussein torched whole cities, poisoning water sources and showing no mercy. When Hussein was severely injured during the assault on Dallas, Kidd appointed his adjutant to take over the Third Army. The adjutant, unwilling to use the brutalities employed by Hussein, gave ground to the Texans' relentless counterattacks, retreating back to the border. Three months later, when Hussein was released from the hospital, the war was over.

Left with one arm, two prosthetic legs and the nation's highest military decoration, Hussein challenged the adjutant to a death match. In the chill of November, the two of them circled each other in the outdoor combat ring at the academy, went round and round, knives flashing as they waited for an opening. It was over within the first minute; Hussein eviscerated the adjutant, left him staring at his guts steaming on the sand.

There had been some grumbling at the manner of death, the adjutant deemed worthy of a heart strike rather than being gutted like a fish, but Kidd had stood quietly from the gallery, acknowledged Hussein as the victor and declared that Allah had spoken. Hussein served another ten years before retiring to his estate on Vashon, one of the small islands just offshore from Seattle. From time to time he tutored the best and brightest from the academy, schooling them in his own slashing techniques of attack and counterattack. Amir had been coming to his home for seven years now, ever since his first term at the academy. Amir's success against the Mormons last year was considered an adaptation of Hussein's feint and strike maneuvers against the Belt forces. It was only in the last year that Amir realized his education was secondary to his recruitment.

"How . . . how did you take Amarillo?" said Amir.

Hussein beckoned and his youngest wife appeared from the house bearing tea and sweet cakes, stuffed dates and dried apricots.

Amir watched her pour tea for them, head bowed, a soft smile on her face. Such tiny hands, and such long, slender fingers. She backed away and out of sight.

Hussein sipped his tea. "Do you find her lovely?"

"If she is lovely, it is for the glory of Allah and her husband," said Amir.

"A diplomatic answer." Hussein popped a date into his mouth. "There are times you are too much like your father."

"I respect you, Hussein," Amir said quietly, "but you should be careful not to underestimate me. I'm the only person who has the ear of both my father *and* the president. The Old One recognizes my value. You should do the same."

Hussein set his teacup down.

"Now tell me, how *did* you take the city?"

Hussein picked among the dried apricots. "I called for a meeting with the Belt commander. Offered to meet him on his own turf. Accompanied only by two officers, I approached the city in an open vehicle, passed through their lines staring straight ahead." He pointed at the display. "We met there . . . at a lovely

Catholic church. I'm sure the commander intended to unnerve me, but I was raised Catholic, did you know that?"

"No . . . I didn't."

"I was a good Irish Catholic with a bleeding crucifix tattooed on my left bicep," said Hussein. "I had it lasered off when I converted to the truth faith, but you could still see it . . . then Allah in his mercy chose to have it blown away with a rocket blast." He lifted the empty sleeve, let it drop. "A blessing. Now I can enter Paradise unsullied."

Amir watched the blue fabric ripple in the breeze. "Is that why you never had a prosthetic arm attached?"

"Seemed like the least I could do to show my gratitude." Hussein slowly chewed the apricot. "The rebels live-casted my meeting with their commander—Major Tom Muzilla, a tough old Texan with a wad of chaw in his cheek. We talked football and old movies and the way things used to be. The way things might be again, if politicians got their heads out of their asses and realized we were all Americans. He said he was in no hurry to fight with us, but if it was a battle we wanted, we best be prepared to die." Hussein looked at Amir. "I said I'd think about it. Said I was going to go back and pray for guidance. He said, 'Sir, take as much time as you need,' and we shook hands. His hands were rough as cactus, but it was a good, solid handshake."

Amir remembered his father's hands holding the glass of khat infusion this afternoon. When he was a child he felt he could curl up and go to sleep in the palm of his father's hand, sleep forever in safety and peace.

Hussein pointed to a spot near the eastern edge of the city. "That's the main natural gas delivery system. Guarded like it was Fort Knox. But here . . ." He tapped a point closer to the center. "And here, and here." More taps. "These are the primary intersections where all that gas feeds into the city . . . and those spots weren't guarded at all." He narrowed his eyes. "While most of Amarillo was watching their commander and me talk, I activated a squad I had sent into the city a couple of weeks earlier, and these men blew the gas feeds with incendiaries. Within ten minutes the whole city was ablaze, the streets filled with people on fire." He chewed, grinding away at the apricot, turning it to paste. "You could hear the screams from a mile away. Their security perimeter collapsed, volunteers throwing down their weapons in their haste to flee." He spit the apricot pit into the display, the hologram shimmering for an instant before regaining its structure. "Next morning the smoldering city smelled like bad barbecue, and we headed toward San Antonio to join up with the rest of our force."

"I . . . I never read anything about that," said Amir.

"It wasn't something that President Kingsley was proud of," said Hussein. "To be honest, it wasn't something I was proud of either. That Belt commander . . . he and I, we could have been friends if he wasn't an infidel dog." He glared at Amir. "You may have the ear of this coward they call the president, but never forget who put you in position to whisper your soothing words into his ear." He swept the holographic city into oblivion with a wave of his hand. "The secret of victory is to find the point of maximum vulnerability and then *strike*. No matter your feelings. No matter how much you respect the enemy. So when the moment comes for your father to choose sides, you best be ready to do what is required of you. If that means you have to kill him, then do it. Afterwards you can shed salty tears at his funeral like a good son."

CHAPTER 14

Spider curled in the armchair of his study, watching Sarah. The noise of the Catholic sector seeped through the security windows. "Have you told Rakkim what your zombie found in D.C.?"

"*Her* zombie?" Rakkim pulled the blanket up around Spider where it had slipped off. "Yeah, she showed me."

"Rakkim is . . . skeptical." Sarah looked at Leo. "Did you find where the safe room is?"

"Not exactly." Leo loudly blew his nose. His allergies had kicked in. Probably a dust storm in Tibet or somebody on Mars had a new kitten. "Not yet."

Spider dimmed the lights, the wallscreen flickering. "We cleaned up the original, increased the resolution."

The D.C. rubble bobbed onscreen, bones littering the sidewalk, the American flag in the gutter. A quick pan of the collapsed Capitol dome as the zombie gave his voice-over sales pitch, his breathing moist and heavy through the decon suit, boots kicking up cinders and dead newspapers. The cameraman's emaciated face was reflected for a moment in a sheet of glass, his sunken cheeks behind the plexi-hood, damp hair plastered across his scalp.

Static onscreen, then a dimly lit tunnel, the ceiling half collapsed, the zombie cursing as he squeezed his way through. His decon suit scraped against the sides as he scooted forward on his belly. *This . . . this here's something special.* The laser torch popped on and he started cutting away at the hatch to the access tunnel. Moments later a *clang* as the access hatch fell into darkness. Dust shimmered as the light from the camera poked through the opening.

The zombie grunted, tried to work his way through the

narrow opening. He stopped, panting. Tried again. Still too tight. *Gonna have to come back with a hand jack.* He swept the room: the wooden globe with the continents oddly shaped . . . a red rose in its vase . . . a couple of flintlock pistols . . . a yellowed document under armored glass. A man lay behind the desk, only his skeletal hand visible, sticking out of the sleeve of his blue suit.

The image wobbled as the zombie tried to squeeze into the room. A curse hissed into the darkness. The zombie turned the camera light on his arm, saw a tear in the shoulder of the decon suit. He slapped on a quick-patch, but the tear spread, the material weakened from years of toxic exposure. He looked into the camera, blinking, and even across time and space you could tell that he knew. *Sorry . . . I'm sorry.* His hand bumped the edge of the opening and he dropped the camera. The image bounced, stabilized for an instant, long enough to see the red rose on the desk collapse, petals shattering to dust. . . . The screen went black. Faint sound of the zombie sobbing before Spider stopped the recording.

"Why does he say he's sorry?" said Rakkim.

"It's a much clearer recording," said Sarah, "I just wish you could have located where—"

"Nobody can track a signal out of D.C.," said Rakkim. "The soup's too thick."

The wallscreen flared and the safe room was in sharp focus, the angle tilted.

"What . . . ?" said Sarah.

"Leo couldn't pinpoint the safe room," said Spider, "but Leo *did* succeed in walking back the signal sent to the zombie's Web site. We thought the camera had gone dead, but it's still operating. You missed it, Sarah, and so did we at first. It only broadcasts a five-second burst every twenty-four hours. Leo's managed to retrieve three of the bursts, spanning the last week. We've attached them on the main recording."

"Showtime," said Leo.

A flash of light illuminated the safe room. Low angle. More of the dead man visible now, his suit in rags, one shoe off . . . metacarpals gleaming through his tattered sock.

"There's no way you can triangulate the room's position from the signal?" said Sarah.

"Do you even know what that *means*?" said Leo.

"It wasn't possible, Sarah," soothed Spider. "We've been trying. The only way Leo was able to snatch the five-second bursts was because they had the same digital signature as the original data packet. What Leo did . . . it's really quite remarkable."

"Yeah, a little appreciation might be nice," said Leo.

"Something . . . something was different between the original recording and the five-second bursts," said Rakkim.

Spider froze the image. Turned to Leo. "I *told* you he would notice."

Leo rolled his eyes.

"What's different?" said Sarah.

The wallscreen jumped, the angle canted so that the desk looked as if it were about to fall over. "One of the things we were able to do when we cleaned up the image was to add a holographic component," said Spider, manipulating the remote. "Now we can see *everything* in the room."

Spider shifted the angle on the freeze frame . . . he ran across the smallest oil painting, the cleric's eyes cold and remote . . . the dueling pistols in their felt-lined box, each flake of rust highlighted on the striker . . . across the empty case . . . to the parchment under armored glass. The parchment was hard to read until Spider adjusted the focus . . . the parchment was an early draft of the Declaration of Independence, with a mention of "Our Lord and Savior Jesus Christ" that didn't appear in the final version.

The image onscreen shifted again, moved slowly over the skeletal man curled on the floor, one bony hand outstretched . . . past the hand . . . to what lay just out of reach, the small, flat piece of wood . . . dappled now with tiny white flowers.

"My God," Sarah said softly.

"Those flowers . . . they weren't there before," said Rakkim.

"No shit," said Leo.

"Are they *blooming*?" said Rakkim.

Spider nodded. "Rather interesting, wouldn't you say?"

"More than interesting, it's impossible," said Rakkim. "There's been nothing alive in D.C. for the last forty years. Even the cockroaches died."

"Blooming in total darkness," whispered Sarah, still watching the screen. "Eldon really did it. I didn't believe him. I thought he was just trying to get more money out of me."

Spider zoomed in on the piece of wood. The flowers were clearly rooted in the wood itself, a chunk of dark, pitted pine six or seven inches long, maybe four inches thick.

"Those are white anemones, according to the botanical index, by the way," said Spider. "A very archaic form of the modern flower."

Rakkim looked at Sarah.

"I told Eldon I was interested in something important." She reached out, grazed the flowers onscreen with her fingertips. "Not just historically significant, something that would get everyone's attention. That would change . . . everything." She trembled in the light from the wallscreen. "He'd been looking for two years, said he finally had a lead. Bigger than big, bigger than I could imagine, that's what he said."

"What is it?" said Rakkim.

"I . . . I could see the way things were going," said Sarah, lip quivering, unable to turn away from the screen. "Even . . . even before President Kingsley was killed it was clear that the whole country was unraveling."

Rakkim was beside her. "You've been saying that for as long as I've known you." He held her but she pulled away. "We're doing as well as the Belt."

"Exactly," said Sarah. "They're a failed nation just like we are, poor and weak."

"Here we go again," said Rakkim. "Reunification's a fine idea, as long as you get rid of all the people that go to sleep at night praying that God strikes the other side dead."

"There's not that many zealots," said Sarah, "they're just louder than the rest of us. We need something to bring us together, something greater than the things that divide us."

"Yeah, a bunch of posies on a chunk of wood are going to make us all love each other," snorted Leo. He dabbed at his nose with a tissue.

Spider zoomed in, the piece of wood filling the wall, a dull black stain in high relief.

"The cross?" Rakkim looked at Sarah. "Come *on*."

"You've heard the stories," said Sarah.

"Everyone in the Belt's heard the stories," said Rakkim. "Most of them believe it too; the secret behind the glory of the USA was that the founders were devout Christians, keepers of a piece of the true cross, the most sacred relic of all."

"Maybe it's true," said Sarah.

"Rikki, your people believe the black stone in the Kaaba in Mecca dates from the time of Adam and Eve," said Spider. "They consider it a source of great power."

"The black stone is *real*," said Rakkim.

"So is the cross." Sarah pointed at the screen. "Flowers, Rikki. Flowers blooming in a dead city . . ." Tears shimmered in her eyes, and Rakkim could see the blooms reflected in them. "People *need* symbols, something greater than their own lives. Remember . . . remember at the war museum last week? After the truce was signed, both sides sent search teams into the ruins of D.C. It was a suicide mission, but they had ten times the volunteers they needed. The men from the Republic found the immaculate Quran and put it in the museum . . . the team from the Belt brought out the statue of Abraham Lincoln, brought it out in pieces and reassembled it in Atlanta. It was a healing moment for both nations, a sense that they had done the right thing in fighting for their faith, but Rikki . . . Rikki, what would have happened if President Kingsley had given the Quran to the Belt, let them put it on display? And what if the Belt president had returned the honor, given us the statue of Lincoln?"

"Government isn't about religion or signs or symbols," said Rakkim. "It's about power and control and . . . *Tell* her, Spider."

"I gave up trying to tell Sarah anything a long time ago," said Spider.

"All this talk about a hunk of magic wood may get you all excited, but not me," said Leo. "What I want to know is where does it leave the Jews?"

"Where we always are, on the outside looking in and hoping for the best," said Spider. "Judaism is the wellspring for both Christianity and Islam. I'll leave it for others to decide if they've improved on the original source."

"It's a beautiful idea, Sarah, and I wish the world worked that way," said Rakkim, "but we don't even know where this . . . thing is."

"Not yet," said Sarah.

"Not yet." Rakkim looked around. "Have you thought that Leo might not be the only person who can walk back the data packet from the Web site?"

"I *am* the only one who could do it," sniffed Leo, a twist of tissue hanging from his nostril.

"No, you're not," said Rakkim. "You might be the smartest person in the world, but the second-smartest person will just need a little more time to do it."

"A *lot* more time," said Leo, the tissue jiggling with every word.

"This zombie . . . this Eldon, he had some powerful clients," said Rakkim. "Big money boys with the means to hire the best and the brightest. You might have plans to use the cross to bring the two nations together, Sarah, but I guarantee you, other people might have a completely different agenda."

Sarah kissed him. "Then we'll have to get busy, won't we?"

• • •

Ibrahim barged into the Old One's chambers after a perfunctory knock, out of breath, having hurried over from the communications offices. It was late and his father was leaving tomorrow morning, but this news couldn't wait. He started to speak, stopped when he saw Baby lounging on the couch. She wore a red silk robe, but one leg was up, wantonly exposing her bare flesh.

"What is it, my son?" said the Old One, seated across from Baby, his back to the wall.

"Father . . . I . . ."

The Old One gestured with his glass of chilled cider. "Out with it."

Ibrahim bit back his fury. To be addressed in such a manner, and in front of the slut . . . He bowed, certain that his face did not betray his emotions. "John Moseby just contacted his wife. It was a simple encryption this time."

Baby shifted position, the silk rustling. "If you were able to translate the message, it might be a ruse."

"It's *Leo's* encryption program we can't break," Ibrahim said. "Moseby doesn't have the same capability—"

"What did the man *say*?" snapped the Old One.

Ibrahim handed him a printout of the brief conversation. "The message itself is nothing. 'Sorry for leaving so abruptly, darling, but I promise to come back as soon as I can. Kiss Leanne for me, and know that I love you.' The message is nothing, Father, as I said, but it's where it was sent from that's of interest." Ibrahim let them wait for a few seconds. "Our men traced the call to somewhere in the zombie sector near Washington, D.C."

The Old One looked at Baby.

"Moseby is a finder," said Ibrahim. "He's doubtlessly been sent to retrieve something from the ruins."

"But y'all don't know what it is he's been sent after, do you?" said Baby.

"I think we can assume it was something very important, Father," said Ibrahim, ignoring her. "Otherwise why risk entering that cursed place?"

The Old One tapped his fingers together. "Do we have men in place?"

"They're already on their way," said Ibrahim.

"Have our men ask around," said the Old One. "See if any of the locals have had dealings with Moseby, or heard of any recent discoveries that might be of interest to us."

Ibrahim bowed.

"Baby and I will be leaving for the Belt later tonight," said the Old One. "See that you keep me apprised of any further news regarding Moseby?"

"Tonight?" said Ibrahim.

"Daddy and me are eager to hear a little of that old-time religion," said Baby, laughing. "If you're a good boy, maybe I'll bring you back a pecan nut log."

The Old One dismissed Ibrahim with a wave of his hand.

Flushed with rage, Ibrahim heard Baby's voice as he walked out the door.

"It's just like I told you, Daddy, Moseby's a family man. No way he wasn't going to talk with his sweetie."

Ibrahim kept walking. In spite of everything that had gone on before, all the things Baby had said and done to damage his standing with their father, it was at that precise moment that Ibrahim decided to kill her.

CHAPTER 15

Baby clapped along to the gospel choir as the Old One danced in the aisle of the gigantic tent, hands waving, praising the Lord along with the hundreds of other participants who had rushed from their seats to lurch and howl and talk in tongues like fucking idiots. She saw Gravenholtz watching her from one of the exits, red hair slicked back so he looked almost human. He tossed aside the white carnation he had been given at the door, barreled up to one of Crews's deacons and jabbed him with a forefinger.

In the pulpit, the minister Malcolm Crews dipped and capered, long legs flying to the beat, his image magnified by the TV cameras on the jumbo screens on the walls as well as beamed out to the rest of the Belt. She saw the Old One bump into an enormous black woman in a polka-dot dress, then grab her hand and swing her round and round, sweat rolling off both their cheeks in the Atlanta heat. Baby clapped along with the soaring vocals of the choir, grateful to be back in the Belt.

At the last minute Ibrahim had tried to talk the Old One out of leaving Nueva Florida last night, warning of crime or illness from the strange food, even suggesting that Baby planned to assassinate the Old One far from the protection of his loyal retainers. She had remained silent and when Ibrahim ran out of breath, the Old One had kissed him on both cheeks, thanked him for his concern and told him not to worry. *I journeyed alone into the teeth of our enemies before your mother was born . . . before your mother and grandmother drew their first breath. Am I less now than I was then?*

"Feel God's healing grace crackling through this temple! Feel God's power shake your bones and roil your blood!" shouted

Crews as he strode back and forth, his face all sharp angles, ax blades for cheekbones, a man always in motion, strutting and capering so that the cameras could barely keep up with him. "God's lightning gonna set you up, brothers and sisters, twist you up, juice you up!"

The Old One thumped and bumped along with the crowd, arms flailing, hair plastered to his forehead as he shouted "Praise Jesus!" to the heavens. Without his beard and with his hair dyed, he looked younger, and the stylish checkerboard suit wasn't much of a Sunday-go-to-meeting outfit, but more like something a wolf on the prowl might sport to sweep a girl off her feet. Ibrahim would positively *shit* if he saw him now.

Daddy had been acting *very* weird these last couple of weeks. He had always been steady, hardly showing any emotion at all, just watching things play out behind those cold dark eyes of his, but lately . . . he had been positively erratic—gloomy one day, just staring into space, and the next day, heck, the next *minute*, he was charging around, demanding everybody jump, acting like a man whose rent was about due and he didn't have money for the landlord. Now here he was in Atlanta, banging hips with strangers, sweating up a storm and seeming to have the time of his life.

It had been a year since Baby had fled the Belt. Miami was fun, but she had quickly grown restless. Eager to impress her father, she made use of her contacts in the Belt, gathering information, waiting for an opportunity. She didn't have to wait long.

Belt president Raynaud was derided for his upper-class accent and fake populism, but his wife, Jinx, flighty and beautiful, had charmed the nation with her honest smile and her small-town ways. Every time she changed her hairstyle the beauty parlors filled. Her only son's health problems made her even more beloved. It was when Baby got word that Malcolm Crews had resurfaced as a backwoods preacher in the Carolinas that she got excited. She had an eye for men she could use, always had— that's how she'd ended up married to the Colonel, a man in his sixties when she was still a teenager. It was nice being the wife of the Colonel, but what she was aiming at now was so far beyond that she could barely fathom it.

Malcolm Crews swayed to the music, eyes half closed, voice cracking, a tall, lanky scarecrow, veins on his neck standing out in the red and purple lights. "Do you *feel* it?" he called, looking right at Jinx. The first lady raised her hands over her head, swayed and almost fainted. Her bodyguards helped her out the private exit, out into the cool night air. Malcolm Crews barely noticed. The Man in Black, that's what they called him, preacher man in a shiny black suit and black string tie, his hair twisted into a dozen braids like Blackbeard the pirate. "Do you feeeeeeeeel it?" he shouted, finger pointing at the crowd, braids flying about him as he bobbled and twitched across the stage.

Baby felt it, all right. Must have been ninety degrees in that tent—her long dress clung to her, her skin spotted with perspiration. She lifted the back of her long hair, trying to cool off her neck. Not a breath of air in that tent, not a breeze in sight. Georgia in September was hotter than a pot of bubbling grits. She dabbed her forehead with a tissue and imagined having sex with that muscular young man two rows ahead of her, a big old boy with a milky white face and smooth cheeks.

If Baby had come a long way in the last year, so had Malcolm Crews. He led a ragtag army of end-times psychopaths once upon a time, an inbred mob Crews set loose to rape and pillage. They had terrorized the area for years before Crews bit off more than he could chew, gone up against the Colonel and that was that. His army annihilated, Crews and a small band of true believers melted away, and he took to preaching in the hill country, where his incandescent oratory quickly gained him a following. Wanted by the law for various atrocities, he moved constantly.

Six months ago, when Baby found out that Crews's traveling tent show had set up outside Atlanta, she talked to Janice Rae, wife of the president's chief speechwriter, and another of the Old

One's daughters. Baby told Janice Rae to bring the first lady and her son, Todd, to a prayer meeting. Then Baby contacted Crews. Give the man credit, he was open to possibilities and the risk didn't bother him a bit. *We're all going to hell anyway, why not enjoy the ride?* That's what he told Baby.

A few days later, in the middle of the service, little Todd, always sickly, had an asthma attack. His inhaler proved useless, as did the emergency injection Jinx Raynaud gave him. The child might have died, but Malcolm Crews laid hands on him, and moments later the boy pinked up and began breathing normally. Within a week, Crews had a full pardon from the president, and his revivals, which had appeared only on local television, went national. It quickly became the most popular show on TV.

"Cornpone Christianity, that's what the eggheads call my ministry." Crews leered in the spotlight. "Well, brothers and sisters, I was once a tenured professor, a Ph. of D. in American literature at Duke University. I was considered an intellectual, an educated man, a Brahmin in the high church of bullshit, and I'm here to tell you . . . I *love* cornpone. Can't get enough of it."

The crowd screamed their agreement.

The Old One caught Baby's eye from the aisle, gave her a wink, then the black woman put her hands on his waist and twirled him like a soda straw. He shook his finger in the air as he spun to the music, dancing as if it were playing just for him.

Baby was used to having to explain things to men, to lead them to the truth, but the Old One . . . she had barely started talking about her idea and he just *ran* with it. The Old One, it was like he had some huge puzzle he was putting together, and Crews was a piece he had been looking for, a piece he hadn't even known he was missing until Baby showed him. He had kissed her on the forehead, said she was a blessing from Allah, and Baby, who hadn't cried for real since she was a child, Baby had wept until her eyes bugged out.

Baby watched the Old One making his way back to her, still

shaking to the beat of the choir. He squeezed through the people who thronged the aisles, shouted "Amen!" and "Hallelujah!" his face glistening with sweat. She had never seen him look so happy.

"Look where we come to," said Crews, "look where this mighty nation, this new Jerusalem has ended up. Busted into pieces, coming apart at the seams. Don't blame the Muslims, *we* did it, brothers and sisters, we did it to ourselves. We trusted our ministers and pastors and they let us down. These supposed men of God sketched the line between good and evil with chalk instead of India ink, so when the wind kicked up, and the troubles came, that line got blown away. While we all stumbled around not sure what to do, the Muslims said, 'This is right and *this* is wrong.' " Most of the crowd nodded in agreement, but there were plenty who looked shocked.

The Old One looked at Baby.

"I gave Malcolm a few suggestions for his sermon," said Baby. "Spice it up a little."

Crews leaned over the pulpit. "So why should we be surprised that millions of good Christians tossed aside their Bibles and said, 'If Pastor Jones don't know if sodomites and fornicators got a ticket to heaven or not, if Pastor Smith don't know if killing babies in the womb is a sin or not, then I'm going someplace that *is* sure.' And they did. And that someplace was a mosque." He lowered his voice and the crowd went silent. "Well . . . this is one pastor who's going back to that old time religion, a right-and-wrong religion." He cupped an ear. "Who wants to come with me?"

"AMEN!" shouted the crowd. "AMEN!" People had rushed the stage, stood there below him, arms raised, the sick and the desperate, the lonely and the lost.

The Old One beat time with the music on his knees.

"Don't hate the Muslims," said Crews, looking out at the crowd. "They at least have the decency to believe their own good book. The ones you should be hating are the shilly-shallyers, the shuck-and-jive God hustlers who can't give you a straight answer if their life depends on it."

The people in the tent swayed back and forth.

Gravenholtz pushed his way down their row, sat beside the Old One. "I talked to one of the deacons. Peckerwood over there says he's Crews's driver. He didn't want to cooperate at first . . . but I convinced him to pass on the message to Crews you want to talk with him."

"Shhh," said the Old One.

"Some of you folks know my history," said Malcolm Crews, "my dark pages. I've done things that only Jesus Christ Himself could forgive. Evil things. Ugly things." He looked out over the crowd. "*Monstrous things.*" His teeth gleamed in the spotlight. "Yet . . . here I stand before you . . . pure as a newborn babe."

"Amen!" shouted a woman in the front row, and the cry was picked up and echoed across the room. "A-*men!*"

"I been washed clean, brothers and sisters. Washed clean as snow, clean as ice, clean as springwater." Crews capered onstage. "Washed in the blood of the lamb."

People sobbed, held their Bibles up in affirmation.

"Give me a fucking break," muttered Gravenholtz.

Black suit flapping, Crews skittered to the side of the stage where the maimed and the infirm had lined up. He jerked, slammed his right palm into the forehead of a white-haired lady—"*Heal!*" Knocked her backward into the waiting arms of his ushers.

If Baby didn't know better she would have believed it herself.

CHAPTER 16

"Congratulations, Anthony, that's great news," said Rakkim. "Marie must be thrilled."

"Yeah, well . . ." Colarusso took a bite from the hot dog, chewing with his mouth open as they walked down the busy downtown street. "She's happy he's marrying a Catholic, but she'd be a lot happier if Helen was Italian."

"When's the big day?"

"Couple of months." A gob of mustard hung on the side of his mouth. "They're in a hurry. I told him . . ." His tongue snaked out, grabbed the mustard. ". . . said you got your whole life to be married. What's the rush?" He folded the rest of the hot dog into his mouth, the crowd parting as they barreled down the sidewalk, giving way as much to Colarusso's bulk and aggressive posture as the gold chief-of-detectives shield on his suit jacket. The highest-ranking Catholic in the police department. "I told Anthony Junior to wait, but she's got a pair of Johanssons—"

"Pair of what?"

"Johanssons. Cans. *Funbags.* Jesus H., don't they teach you young guys anything?"

Rakkim smiled back at the three moderns waiting outside a coffee shop, businesswomen with high heels and blue streaks through their hair. "Well, mostly we pay attention to see what you old guys do and then we head in the opposite direction."

"You been married, what, five years? Might as well be five minutes. You'll find out." Colarusso wiped his mouth with the back of his hand. "I tried talking to Anthony Junior but he don't listen to me. Never has. *You* he listens to. No fucking justice."

"Not in this world."

"Not in the next one either, that'd be my guess." Colarusso

pushed a bit of hot dog bun back into his mouth with his pinkie, a drop of mustard falling onto the toe of his shoes. He wiped the offending stain off on the back of his trousers, kept walking.

"You find out anything for me, Anthony?"

Colarusso cut across the street to the park, Rakkim beside him, neither of them glancing at the traffic that screeched to a halt. A horn blared but Colarusso stopped that with a look, kept walking, finally sat down on a bench at the edge of the park. A good spot. One that offered a view of the lunchtime crowd eating on the grass and the passing sidewalk parade. Colarusso spread his arms across the back of the bench, enjoying the sun. "Did you know that Anthony Junior wants out of the Fedayeen?"

"Yeah. It's in the works. Should take another week for the approval to go through."

"You did that?"

Rakkim shrugged.

"Honorable discharge?"

"Man was cited twice for conspicuous bravery under fire, Anthony. What do you think?"

"You sure? His commander said no way they were letting him go before his seven-year commitment had been met. Said they invested too much money in his training."

"It's true. The genetic boosters alone cost close to a million dollars."

Colarusso belched into his fist. "Commander offered Anthony Junior another promotion. Said he could have his choice of posting. Gave him the God-and-country speech."

"It's a good speech. Works most of the time," said Rakkim, watching the people passing by the park. "Anthony Junior . . . is he sure?"

Colarusso nodded. Quiet now. Rakkim gave him time. "He said . . . he said he was done with it all. Just . . . *done*," Colarusso said finally. "I think something happened in that little town in Colorado during the last Mormon counterattack. He won't talk about it, but I think it turned things for him."

"Then it's time for him to pack it in." Rakkim watched a kid, a moderate Muslim, walk between two moderns engaged in conversation, the kid lightly bumping them, apologizing profusely. "That kid in the green silk jacket . . . he's good."

"What do you mean?"

"He pulled off a double play on those two moderns, which is a tough move, but what's really nice is afterwards he never changed his pace. Most boosters make a score like that, they tend to bolt."

Colarusso squinted after the kid. "Never a cop around when you need one, is there." He turned to Rakkim. "That was you once, right?"

"Right."

"Then you lifted Redbeard's wallet and he caught you."

"I was nine and I was overconfident."

"You're still overconfident," said Colarusso. "Redbeard must have liked that, though, bringing you home and everything." He dabbed at his upper lip with the handkerchief as Rakkim stayed silent. "Had to be a reason. Not like he thought a thief would be a good playmate for Sarah. Probably just wanted a son. Man needs a son."

"If that's what he wanted, he gave up on that idea soon enough. I think . . . maybe I was a project for him. See what he could teach me. What he could turn me into."

Colarusso laughed. "Well, fathers and sons . . . one way or the other, they always disappoint each other."

"I asked you a question before about Senator Chambers. Would it help if I bought you another hot dog? Maybe throw in a side of chili fries?"

"No." Colarusso patted his ample belly. "I'm watching my weight." He waited until a bus passed, the rumble of the diesel echoing. "Senator Chambers looks clean."

Rakkim tracked the security blimps drifting over the city, sunlight gleaming off their electronic arrays. "Looks?"

"Only thing that caught my eye was in the last eighteen

months, two of his longtime servants retired." Colarusso blew his nose into his napkin. "Both of them are dead now. One had a heart attack. One drove his car into a bridge abutment at a high rate of speed." He put away the handkerchief as the bus pulled away in a cloud of black smoke. "Wouldn't have thought anything of it . . . except you're asking questions."

"How old was the servant who had the heart attack?"

"Forty-seven. They say the good die young. Guess you and me, we'll live forever."

"You have the details?"

Colarusso slid a datastick into Rakkim's hand. "Full rundown on both of them. Any chance you'll tell me what this is all about?"

"Did you cover your tracks?"

"No, I been gobbling pretty-colored paint chips so now I'm retarded," said Colarusso.

"Sorry."

"You and Sarah got plans for tonight? Marie's planning on ruining a piece of meat and you're welcome to share."

"Can't do it. Sarah's dragging me to the university for a meet-and-greet."

"Sounds painful."

"You want to go in my place, I'll gladly eat Marie's food."

"Hard decision, but I'll pass." Colarusso scratched at a dried blob of something on his suit jacket. "I appreciate your help with Anthony Junior."

"He did his duty. If he thinks it's time to come home, then that's what he should do."

"He wants to be a cop. You believe that?"

Rakkim shook his hand, lost in Colarusso's mitt. "That's great."

"Yeah . . ." Colarusso beamed, lightly ran his fingers over his badge. "He said he likes the discipline and the camaraderie of the department, reminds him of why he applied to become Fedayeen. He said he wanted to do something that would help people, but he worried about the killing part. I told him most cops go their whole career and never draw their sidearm . . . and the ones that have to, well, *somebody's* got to stop the bad guys." He nudged Rakkim in the ribs. "Although I *did* tell him to forget that nonsense about helping people. That kind of talk will get him laughed off the force."

CHAPTER 17

"Quarterback of the Atlanta Rednecks used to live here," said Deshane, pointing at the house on the hill as they turned off the country road, the Cadillac lurching over the potholes.

They had been escorted to the car by one of Crews's deacons, but Deshane, clearly under orders, drifted far back from the other vehicles in the entourage. Gravenholtz had threatened the driver, but the Old One interceded, told him to settle back and enjoy the ride. They had been driving for almost an hour now, out past the outskirts of Atlanta and into the pinewoods. They hadn't seen headlights or taillights in twenty minutes.

Deshane beeped the horn and the heavy steel gates slowly slid back from the entrance to the mansion. He waved at the guards flanking the private drive.

The guards waved back, assault rifles slung awkwardly across their shoulders, whiskey bottles in their hands.

"Great fucking security you got here," muttered Gravenholtz from the front seat.

"They's just bored," said Deshane, a young black man with cornrows and sad eyes. "Pastor Crews said they can't have whores visit the guardhouse anymore. That didn't sit well."

"Yes, I can imagine," said the Old One, seated in the back with Baby. "Not really much for them to do out here, I imagine."

"Yes, sir," said Deshane. "Nearest neighbors about four miles away."

Baby rolled down the window, inhaled. "Honeysuckle. I missed that smell." There were no lights in view other than those from the house on the hill.

Deshane sniffed. "If you say so, ma'am."

"Oh, I do," said Baby, stretching out her feet as the wind blew through her hair. She wiggled her toes. "I most *definitely* say so."

"Have you been with Pastor Crews long?" asked the Old One.

"Just a couple months, sir," said Deshane. "The rest of the boys . . . they been with him lots longer."

"They End-Times Army?" said the Old One.

"I'm not really supposed to talk about that, sir," said Deshane. He slowly guided the Cadillac up the winding drive toward the main house.

Baby could hear music through the open window, getting louder as they approached the house, one of those ticky-tacky fake mansions that new money bought, with plaster columns out front and a high peaked roof—*Hollywood Southern Gothic*, the Colonel had called it once, disgusted. The mansion might have started out white but it needed a fresh coat of paint and half the front windows were broken.

Deshane pulled up in front, parked behind four other vehicles. He hopped out, opened the door for Baby, then ran around and let the Old One out. Started up the steep steps toward the door. "I'll leave you in the foyer and go see if Pastor Crews will see you now." He cleared his throat, looked around. "Probably best if you don't converse with the deacons. They . . . they can be a little prickly with strangers."

Gravenholtz kicked open the front door, knocked it half off its hinges.

Baby took the Old One's hand, the two of them strolling past the startled Deshane as though they were going to a cotillion.

The deacons in the living room looked up at Baby, snaggle-toothed louts with matted hair, black suits wrinkled. She didn't recognize any of them from the prayer service. They sprawled on couches that leaked stuffing, whiskey bottles in their hands. All of them were armed, pistols in their belts, rifles leaning against the walls. The room stank of dirt and tobacco, a sour, run-down odor like that of an old outhouse.

"I'll take it from here, Deshane, you scat now," said one of the deacons as he stood up, a hulking mountain man with a full gut and intelligent eyes.

"Y-yes, sir." Deshane backed away. He looked like he wanted to say something to Baby.

"Crews said company was coming, and I guess you're it." The mountain man glanced at Gravenholtz, then eyed Baby, taking his time. "My name is C.P."

"I'm Baby and these two gentlemen—"

"I don't give a shit about them," said C.P. A black dog rose from a pile of trash in the corner and padded closer, a huge mongrel with yellow eyes and a scarred muzzle. It growled at the Old One and C.P. kicked it, the dog skulking back to the corner. He snatched a mason jar from the lap of a man sleeping in a recliner. Offered it to Baby. "You want a pop? Fresh batch."

"No thanks," said Baby. "Moonshine makes me break out."

The deacon showed broken teeth. "No problem, sweetcheeks. I got me some cream I could rub on it."

Gravenholtz knocked C.P. against the wall so hard the plaster cracked. The other deacons jumped up, trained their weapons at Gravenholtz. Lester, God bless him, just stood there, massaging his crotch, daring them to do something, hoping they'd try.

Baby stepped forward, helped C.P. up, blood streaming down his scalp. "Just take us to Malcolm, before you get yourself in trouble. The rest of you boys go on about your business."

The deacons didn't lower their weapons.

"It's okay, fellas," said C.P., glaring at Gravenholtz. "No harm done. Me and this redheaded cocksucker will discuss the matter later." He wiped blood across his face with the back of his hand. "I'll let Malcolm know his guests done arrived."

"That's very cordial of you." The Old One kicked aside a half-eaten can of beef stew, the can rolling along the carpet, spinning out boiled carrots and mushy potatoes. "Tell him we're enjoying your wit and sparkling conversation, but we have business to attend to."

Baby watched C.P. stagger down the hall. The Colonel would have every one of these men scrubbed raw with pine tar soap and a bristle brush. Then he would have them clean the mansion from top to bottom, clean it so thoroughly that you could run your finger under a windowsill and not get it dirty.

C.P. knocked on the double doors at the end of the hall. Got a response and threw the doors open. He dabbed at his hair, wiped his bloody fingers on his pants. "Them city folks are waiting out here." He turned, beckoned.

Baby, the Old One and Gravenholtz walked down the hall and through the double doors.

Malcolm Crews stood with his back to them, stood facing a roaring fireplace, the room stifling. Thick red velvet curtains hung over the windows. Plush carpet underfoot. Overstuffed chairs and sofas had been pushed to the edges of the room, leaving a large empty space in the center. The walls were covered with Renaissance paintings in curlicue gilt frames, at least a dozen versions of the Madonna and Child. Most of them needed straightening. Whiskey bottles and money lay strewn across a desk that looked like it was built for some French king.

C.P. cleared his throat. "Pastor?"

"Close the door behind you as you leave, C.P.," Crews said gently.

"I can stay if you want," said C.P., one hand on the pistol stuffed into his belt.

"Go on now," said Crews, his back still to them. He waited until C.P. left, then turned. One of the burning logs in the fireplace collapsed in a cloud of sparks, the flames reflected off the walls and ceiling, framing him in fire.

"Well, Malcolm Crews, aren't you just the *cutest* thing," said Baby.

Crews stared at her, expressionless, his gaunt face crosshatched with wrinkles.

"I'm Albert Mesta," said the Old One, inclining his head.

"Sure you are, buddy," said Crews, hands on his hips. "You

don't look anything like your pictures, but I know who you are. I know who *all* of you are." He nodded at Gravenholtz. "I recognized this fella right off. Hard to hide a face like that."

"What makes you think I'd want to hide it?" growled Gravenholtz.

"Exactly," said Crews. "I say, *flaunt* the horror show."

"Sit down, Lester," said the Old One, seeing the look on Gravenholtz's face. "Baby and I have business with Mr. Crews."

Gravenholtz sank into one of the overstuffed chairs, the wood creaking under his weight. He tugged at his collar in the heat.

"You've certainly moved up in the world, Mr. Crews," said the Old One. "Last year at this time you were living in a muddy shack, attended by murderous cretins." He spread his hands. "Now look at you. You're living in a run-down mansion, attended by murderous cretins."

Baby laughed first, and the Old One and Crews joined in. Gravenholtz stayed silent.

"Nice suit you got there," Crews said to the Old One. "Little flashy but I like that."

"Indeed." The Old One fingered his checkerboard jacket, eyes lidded. "I'm feeling rather . . . wild these days."

"The Belt will do that to you." Crews dragged the sofa over, gallantly waited for Baby and the Old One to sit before he set himself down on the arm. "I guess I should thank you, seeing as how you helped me with the president's brat, little Todd . . . little *Turd*, that's what I call him." He raised his palm—"Heal!"—tried to strike Baby in the forehead, but she was too quick. "What was that stuff you had me put on my hand, anyway?"

"Contact *poison* for Janice Rae, contact antidote for you," said Baby.

"Janice Rae? That the first lady's girlfriend? Well, it did the job. Yes, indeedy." Crews looked from the Old One to Baby. "So . . . why did you do it?"

"Baby thought you might be useful," said the Old One.

"Useful?" Crews threw back his head. "I ain't *never* been called that before."

"Then no one's ever truly appreciated your gifts," said the Old One.

Crews hardened. "If I wanted to be jacked off, mister, I'd give the job to *her*."

"Sit down, Lester," the Old One said gently as Gravenholtz leapt out of his chair. "It was a metaphor, correct, Mr. Crews? Just a metaphor from a former professor of English."

Crews waited until Gravenholtz sat back down. "You're taking quite a chance coming here, mister. Lester there might be bad medicine where you come from, but my boys have handled worse."

"I rather doubt that," said the Old One.

Crews smoothed the lapels of his black suit—he looked like an enormous crow preening. "So what are you doing here?" He looked down his nose at the Old One. "You come to get saved?"

"No. I don't need saving," said the Old One. "Lester?" He didn't take his eyes off Crews. "Why don't you give us some privacy?"

"You sure?" said Gravenholtz.

"Go on, Lester," said the Old One. "Go play with the other boys."

Crews waited until Lester closed the door. "Can I get you folks something to drink? Got everything from corn liquor to twenty-year-old bourbon to soft drinks."

The Old One shook his head.

"I'm good," said Baby.

"Oh, you're more than good, lady," said Crews.

Loud sounds came from outside the door. Shouts and screams. Glass breaking.

"Nothing to worry about, Mr. Crews," said the Old One.

"Oh, I ain't worried," said Crews.

More screams. Gunshots. Rapid-fire.

"Poor Lester," said Crews. "My boys . . . I seen them do things you wouldn't believe human beings were capable of. . . ." He grinned. "But let's talk about *us*." He put his arm around Baby. "You look familiar, honeypie. Not just 'cause I used to see you on TV with the Colonel . . . we ever met before?"

Baby shrugged off his arm. "Malcolm Crews . . . you've hurt my feelings."

"I *have* met you before," said Crews. "I just can't . . ." He shook his head.

"I saw you in action when I was a girl," said Baby. "My mama took me to see you preach in a barn outside of Dawson. I was twelve at the time, and I thought you were really something, stalking across the floor like a ringmaster cracking a whip."

"*That's* right," said Crews.

"We were in the third row," said Baby. "You were looking at my mama during the whole sermon, and I didn't see a bit of the Lord in your eyes."

"Wasn't your mama I was looking at," said Crews. "I was sizing *you* up, sitting there in your Sunday best, Bible in your lap, fresh faced but already with back-door eyes. I remember looking at you and thinking I'd give you another year to marinate in your own juices. Old enough to bleed, you're old enough to butcher. I come back to Dawson a year later but you was nowhere in sight. Next time I saw you was on a news video, you and the Colonel getting married, but I didn't connect you with that sweet young thing." He stared into the fire for a moment, turned back to her. "I can still see the Colonel standing there in his dress uniform, stiff as a ramrod with you beside him holding a bouquet of wild-flowers. How old were you?"

"Just turned sixteen."

"Sixteen." Crews nodded. "You must about killed that old fart."

"You'd be *surprised*," said Baby.

The doors to the study creaked open and Gravenholtz walked in, a little out of breath, dragging C.P. by his hair.

Crews eased himself off the couch. Never said a word. Which was pretty impressive, if you asked Baby.

"Everything okay, Lester?" asked the Old One.

"Feel like I just took a good dump." Gravenholtz was bleeding from a dozen gunshot wounds, a flap of scalp over his ear hanging down. He hoisted C.P. up, and the man groaned. "He's the last one. What do you want me to do with him?"

The Old One glanced over to where Crews was edging toward a side door. "Don't go, Mr. Crews, we still have so much to discuss. Please?" He turned back to Gravenholtz. "You took care of all of them? Even the guards at the entrance?"

"I said so, didn't I?" said Gravenholtz.

"What *is* he?" said Crews. "Some kind of . . . robot or something."

"It's rather complicated," said the Old One. "Let's just say Lester is hard to kill."

CHAPTER 18

"I know what you're here for," said the history professor, wagging her finger at Rakkim. "You can't fool me."

"I can see that." Rakkim looked around the faculty annex trying to see Sarah. Probably fifty people there, arts and sciences instructors and their spouses. He spotted her on the far side of the room, near some trays of wilting vegetables. He waved but she was busy talking to a group of young women who clustered around her.

"Look at her," said the professor, standing too close. She patted her frizzy home perm. "She wants back in, doesn't she? Who can blame her?"

"Back in where?"

"Don't play innocent with me." The professor drank from her cracked teacup, sloshed some on his trousers, started to wipe it off. Another finger wag. "Don't get your hopes up. I may be Catholic, but I'm married . . . happily married."

"It's been good talking with you." Rakkim started to leave, but she blocked his path.

"She walks off the job five years ago, hardly a word to anyone," said the professor. "Now she suddenly shows up at the monthly tea and thinks she can get her old job back?"

"Sarah's not interested in her old job."

"She was always too good for us warhorses. Redbeard's niece. Youngest Ph.D." The professor's face reddened. "Famous for that book . . . which was not . . . *not* well researched. Popular, that's all she was."

Rakkim stepped around her, working his way through the crowd.

"Are you the husband?" asked an older man in a flared corduroy jacket. He smelled of the orange blossom incense burned at the Muhammad Ali mosque, one of the more prestigious modern mosques. "You're Sarah's husband, aren't you?" He stuck out his hand. "Dr. Ron Wallis, chairman of the history department."

Rakkim wanted to wipe his hand. "Hi, Ron, how are you?"

Wallis's expression revealed his desire to correct Rakkim, suggest Rakkim use his academic title, but he decided against it. "I'm fine, Mr. . . . ?"

"Epps. Rakkim Epps. I wish I had more time to talk, but—"

"Epps? Not short for Epstein, I hope." Wallis seemed pleased with himself. "Just kidding. Not that there would be a problem. I have nothing against Hebrews."

"I'm relieved."

"I take a certain pride in judging people on their own merits, regardless of—"

"Ron, I wish I had more time to talk with you, but I really need to speak with Sarah."

"I understand completely." Wallis pinched a deeper dimple into his green bow tie. "These academic affairs can be a little daunting to the . . . uninitiated."

"Daunted is exactly how I feel, Ron."

"Buck up," said Wallis. "No one here is any better than you, remember that. We just have certain intellectual credentials . . . areas of expertise." He gave a curt bow. "Remind Sarah my door is always open."

Rakkim started toward Sarah.

Sarah excused herself from the group of young women, put her hand on his arm. "Did Dr. Wallis tell you his door was always open?"

"Always open to *you*," said Rakkim. "I don't have the intellectual credentials."

"Poor baby," said Sarah, leading him to the group. "Ladies,

this is my husband, Rakkim. Rakkim, this is Emily, sociology, Carmella, Chinese history, and Satrice, American history."

Rakkim bowed.

The young women returned the bow, glanced over at Sarah as though for approval. Though they were only ten years or so younger than Sarah, they deferred to her as though she were the queen of the Nile.

"If you'll excuse me, ladies," said Sarah, "I want to pay my respects to Professor Hoffman." She trailed a hand across Rakkim's arm as she left.

"One-note Hoffman?" said Satrice.

"Be nice," said Emily.

Rakkim and the three women exchanged nods, looked around, saw both chaperones glaring at them from their elevated chairs. "I should probably go—"

"Don't mind those two vultures," said Satrice, a short, stocky woman drinking Jihad Cola straight from the bottle.

"*Satrice*," warned Emily.

"Chill out," said Satrice.

"Are you cold?" asked Rakkim. "I could get you a wrap."

Satrice had a beautiful laugh, warm and without a hint of mockery. "It's old time slang. 'Chill out' . . . it means relax."

"Satrice did her dissertation on twentieth-century American colloquialisms," said Carmella.

"True dat," said Satrice.

Carmella glanced at the chaperones, lowered her eyes. "I . . . I should mingle."

They watched her leave. "Finger-lickin' good," said Satrice.

Rakkim looked at her.

"It means she's chicken," said Satrice. "Ah . . . easily scared."

"It's so amazing to meet your wife," Emily said to Rakkim. "I was in high school when *How the West Was Really Won* first came out. It changed my life. I immediately knew I wanted to be a historian."

"They removed it from my school library," said Satrice,

"flagged it as a corrupter of morals." Her eyes sparkled. "We passed around our copy from girl to girl until it almost fell apart. We memorized whole chapters."

"Is it a little . . . intimidating to be married to someone so brave?" asked Emily.

"Sometimes," said Rakkim. "Sarah likes making trouble. It's one of the reasons I love her."

The two young women blushed. Satrice covered her reaction by taking a swig of cola, a smear of her bright red lipstick rimming the neck of the bottle.

How the West Was Really Won was the mainstream edition of Sarah's doctoral thesis, which theorized that while there were many factors in the shift of the USA from a secular nation to a moderate Muslim republic, the pivotal events took place in popular culture. Traditionalists were outraged, arguing that the book was sacrilegious for minimizing the role of prophecy and violent jihad. Without the intercession of her uncle, Redbeard, the book would have been burned and Sarah forbidden to ever publish again. As it was, the book became a best-seller that no one read in public.

" 'Though the jihadi attacks had little direct, long-term impact on the United States, the true importance of the 9/11 martyrdom was that it induced the former regime to overextend itself in fruitless military engagements around the world,' " said Satrice, reciting the prologue to Sarah's book from memory. " 'The political and economic consequences of this U.S. response were profound and long-lasting. After their failed attempt to create democracy in the Islamic homeworld, the Crusaders fled, grown weary of war, eager to return to their idle pursuits. This great retreat left the West no safer than before, but instead drained it of capital, manpower and, most important, will.

" 'When the U.S. troops trickled home from their wars of conquest, the former regime was confronted by a prolonged economic downturn, and a jobless recovery that only exacerbated the gap between rich and poor,' " continued Emily, as Satrice mouthed the words along with her. " 'Even the election in 2008 of a multiracial president named after the grandson of the Prophet (Peace Be Upon Him) could not prevent a cruel, godless capitalism from sending jobs overseas, where labor costs were cheaper, leaving millions at home unemployed, and embittered. Unlike in education in Muslim nations, God was not allowed to be spoken of in American schools, and the children and adults could draw no moral sustenance from a permissive culture that celebrated immorality and materialism.' "

People nearby stopped to listen, but Satrice and Emily paid them no mind.

" 'After the end of martial law, a new generation of pragmatic, modern American Muslim leaders stressed the importance of transforming the *popular* culture, as a means of affecting the larger population,' " said Satrice. " 'Thanks to the generous funding of the Kingdom, a twenty-four-hour Islamic television network offered programming geared to a young, non-Muslim American audience. This network featured innovative graphics, videos, and interviews with entertainers and sports stars who had converted to the true faith."

" 'The most important of these conversions was the public embrace of Islam by Jill Stanton at the Academy Awards, February seventh, 2013,' " continued Emily, the pulse at the base of her throat visible. " 'Jill Stanton gave her declaration of faith as she received the Academy Award for Best Actress. Her declaration coincided with her announcement of marriage to Mukumbe Otan, a devout Muslim, and center for the world champion Los Angeles Lakers. Within days, Shania X, the most popular country music recording star in the world, made her declaration of faith at the Grand Ole Opry. A week later, three major movie stars declared their submission to the faith, followed by the entire ensemble cast of a top-rated television series. These high-profile conversions created a cascade effect, and within months, thousands, then tens of thousands, then hundreds of thousands of young people were crowding the mosques and studying the holy Quran."

" 'The public declarations of Jill Stanton and Shania X were the tipping point for the spiritual renewal that' eventually led to the creation of the Islamic States of America,' " the young women said, reciting the words together. " 'The marriage of Jill Stanton and Mukumbe Otan, white and black, spoke to the transforming power of Islam over racism, the deepest wound of the West, which all their churches and technology could not stanch. Millions looked at them and wondered, if Islam could soothe the ache of racism, could it not feed the restless hunger of America's dispossessed? The answer was yes. Despite the nobility of our cause, violent jihad alone could never defeat the West. It was the "flowering rose" at the heart of Islam that gave us victory.' "

The two young women wiped their eyes. Several people nearby quietly applauded.

"I . . . we didn't mean to embarrass you," said Satrice.

"I'm not embarrassed," said Rakkim. "I'm proud of her."

"It was a pleasure to meet you . . . Rakkim," said Emily.

"Later, dude," said Satrice.

Rakkim saw Sarah seated beside a white-haired man in a shabby blue suit. She waved.

"El Presidente, *por favor*, this is a time for patience," said Hector Morales, secretary of state for the Aztlán empire.

"Why are you sweating, Hector?" Presidente Argusto turned to Morales. "Has the Belt president agreed to turn over this hillbilly colonel, or must I take matters into my own hands?"

"Excellency," Morales purred, "this situation presents a serious challenge to President Raynaud. The Colonel is beloved by the people of the Bible Belt—"

"Enough." Argusto strolled to the window of his office. Through the armored glass he could see all of Tenochtitlán spread out before him, the moon gleaming across the capital.

High-rises and office towers soared across the downtown area, airy confections of extruded polymers, connected by sky bridges and aerial trams. The lush gardens and ten-lane streets far below gave a feeling of imperial dignity. Dominating the city was the victory pyramid, sheathed in polished limestone brighter than the moon, an enormous structure three times the size of the Aztec pyramid of the sun. *His* pyramid. Half the world's supply of concrete and steel had gone into its five-year construction, along with lesser pyramids scattered across Aztlán. His enemies had accused him of bankrupting the nation, but Argusto's vision of melding the past with the present had prevailed. And silenced his enemies.

"I am just suggesting you be patient, Excellency."

"I *have* been patient. As you asked, Hector. I had our technicians recheck their findings. As you asked. I have even given you time to consult with the Belt president. *As you asked.*" He stared at the triptych mural, a mosaic twenty stories high spread across three buildings: a long line of captured enemies being led into ancient Tenochtitlán while the crowd cheered and threw flowers to their own victorious warriors. "At the economic summit Tuesday, we shall formally demand that the Belt turn over to us this rogue warlord."

"Such a public demand will create a firestorm in the Belt, Excellency. They are a people filled with pride."

"Then they will swallow their pride as we were once forced to do." Argusto didn't deign to look at the diplomat, preferring to stare out at the mountains beyond the city. "Leave me, Hector. Go debate someone."

It had taken days for Argusto's technical wizards to track a coded message sent from the oil minister's limo. A message sent by his brother-in-law's killer. A message sent to a warlord in the Belt. This man, this *colonel*, must be brought to justice, taken to Tenochtitlán and questioned as to the reasons for his actions. Then the man's heart would be torn out, offered to the gods in expiation of his sins. It must happen soon too, already Argusto sensed a certain . . . lack of respect among his enemies, domestic and foreign, a delight in noting his troubles.

Last night the Chinese ambassador had shamelessly flattered him at the state dinner, regaling the table with Argusto's many accomplishments, said the only comparable figure in history was Alexander the Great—and here the ambassador smirked—a military genius who without airpower had somehow conquered the known world. Argusto had nodded at the barbed compliment, raised a glass to toast the ambassador and said if Alexander had Aztlán's airpower, the ambassador would be speaking Greek and his rectum would be inflamed from doing his diplomatic duties. The silence had been delicious.

In the darkness beyond the mountains, Argusto saw a falling star streak across the sky. He didn't make a wish. A falling star was a failed star, a cinder burning in the atmosphere, and Argusto had no interest in failure.

CHAPTER 19

Gravenholtz stood just inside Crews's office, breathing hard, eyes wide. Blood spread across his white dress shirt, ran down his jacket, but he seemed unfazed, the gunshots from Crews's men unable to penetrate the flexible armor under his skin. Ferocious-looking wounds, painful too, but not life threatening.

Crews looked at C.P. flopped on the floor, then over at the Old One. "What . . . what are you doing this for?"

"Those boys of yours . . ." The Old One's checkerboard jacket seemed to shimmer in the light from the fireplace. "Murderous scum and toothless morons. Not at all the right image for what you're about to become, Mr. Crews."

"*About* to become?" said Crews.

"You've come a long way in the last six months," said the Old One. "Top-rated gospel show on TV, invitations to preach at the capital . . . are you satisfied?"

"No."

"Of course not," said the Old One. "One thing I've learned in a very long life, Mr. Crews, is that there's *never* enough."

"How about you tell Gravenholtz to put C.P. down?" said Crews. "Not like he's going anywhere."

"You're fond of him, aren't you?" said the Old One. "I could see that immediately."

"Well, I don't know about *fond*," said Crews. "C.P.'s been with me a long time."

"Very good," said the Old One. "I appreciate loyalty. Please, put him down, Lester."

Gravenholtz dropped C.P. onto the floor, then wandered over to the desk and picked up a spool of masking tape. He tore off a strip of tape and started pinning down the flap of skin on his scalp.

C.P. slowly rolled onto his hands and knees, gasping.

"Lester," said the Old One, "if you wouldn't mind, bring Mr. Crews one of those pistols."

"Why?" said Gravenholtz.

"Savor the mystery, Lester," said the Old One.

Baby started giggling.

"Do I amuse you, Baby?" said the Old One.

Baby nodded, still giggling.

"Mr. Crews, do you have *any* idea how long it's been since I've made anyone laugh?" The Old One beamed. "Let me tell you, it's a rare pleasure."

Gravenholtz handed Crews a revolver.

"Now, Mr. Crews," said the Old One, "if it's not too much to ask, I'd like you to shoot your old buddy C.P. in the head."

Crews hefted the pistol. "How about I blow *your* brains out?"

"Always a possibility, but I have faith in you, Mr. Crews," said the Old One. "A man of your ambition, your vision . . . there's no way you'll throw away this opportunity."

Baby saw the pen in the Old One's hand. The same silver fountain pen he had used to spray Gravenholtz, cocooning him in aerosol polymer. The Old One might have faith but he was no fool.

C.P. looked up at Crews. "Jesus, Malcolm . . . what are you thinking? *Kill* these people—" He grunted as Gravenholtz kicked him.

The Old One turned toward the doorway.

A man leaned against the jamb, a gangly fellow, his shirt soaked with blood. One arm dangled useless, but he propped a sawed-off shotgun against his hip with his good arm. His shattered jaw gave him an obscene grin, his face swollen like a pumpkin.

"Sit down, Deekins," said Crews, "take a load off before you hurt somebody."

The man in the doorway tried to speak, but his mouth wouldn't work. The shotgun wobbled in his grip as he tried to center it.

"*Lester?*" The Old One wagged a finger. "You said they were all dead."

Baby moved out of the line of fire.

"Do it, Deekins," said C.P., still sprawled on the floor. "Fuck you waitin' for?"

The man in the doorway fired as Gravenholtz stepped toward him, caught him in the chest; got off another shot before Gravenholtz snatched the shotgun from him.

Gravenholtz beat the man over the head with the shotgun, beat him onto the floor, flailing away at him even after his skull cracked.

"You can stop now, Lester," said the Old One.

Gravenholtz hit Deekins again. Threw the shotgun down.

"You never did tell me what you got planned for me," Crews said to the Old One, his voice calm. "This thing I'm supposed to *become*."

"That's the spirit," said the Old One.

"Daddy?" Baby crossed over to him, gingerly touched his cheek. "You got shot."

The Old One looked at the blood on her fingertips. Scowled at Gravenholtz.

"Just a scratch," said Gravenholtz. "What? That supposed to be *my* fault?"

"Yes, Lester, actually it is," said the Old One, as Baby dabbed at his cheek with a handkerchief. "Open a window, Mr. Crews, it's too warm in here." He waited until Crews complied. "Things are about to change, both in the Belt and in the Republic. I'm offering you a chance to be a part of those changes."

"I'm no Muslim, in case you haven't got the word," said Crews. "I'm born again."

"You're no more of a Christian than I am," said the Old One.

"I'm not going to argue." Crews checked the pistol, made

sure it was loaded. "Did you really nuke New York and Washington, D.C.?"

"Whatever I've done, I'm certain that God will forgive me," said the Old One. "As I'm sure God will forgive you."

"Mister, you're a lot more optimistic than I am," said Crews.

The Old One pointed at C.P. "Time to make a decision, Mr. Crews."

"These changes coming down the road," said Crews, scratching his chin with the muzzle of the pistol, "what exactly kind of a part am I going to have?"

"M-Malcolm?" wailed C.P.

"Don't you *get* it?" Baby said to Crews, stamping her feet. "We're bringing hard times to the Belt. Hard times to the Republic too. Nightmares and fever dreams, just the way you like it— don't pretend you don't, Malcolm Crews. Look at me! We're not here because you're some holy joe motherfucker patting babies and organizing fried chicken socials. I picked you because you smell smoke and reach for the gasoline, and my daddy and me, we're bringing hellfire to town."

Crews's eyes reflected the flames from the fireplace.

"Look at him, Daddy, his pecker's hard. Didn't I tell you?"

"She did, Mr. Crews. Indeed she did."

Crews tapped the side of his thigh with the pistol, expressionless.

"You been waiting for the end times, haven't you, Malcolm?" Baby spun slowly in the center of the room, her skirt fluttering out as she turned round and round like a wind-up ballerina on a music box. "Well, here it is, right in front of your nose. Boil, boil, trouble and toil . . ."

"I'm sure you remember your Bible, Mr. Crews," said the Old One. "John the Baptist was given the honor of announcing the coming of Jesus. It was he who first proclaimed him the Messiah."

"Well, you ain't Jesus and John the B. got his fucking head chopped off." Crews glanced at Baby. "Chopped off and put on a silver plate for Salome, the dancing girl."

Baby spun faster, laughing.

C.P. was almost to his feet, but Gravenholtz tripped him, sent him sprawling.

"We done yet?" said Gravenholtz.

"*Are* we done, Mr. Crews?" said the Old One.

Crews walked over to C.P.

"Hey!" said C.P., one hand raised. "Hey!"

"You remember Hecklenburg?" said Crews.

C.P.'s eyes darted. "That little town? S-sure."

"We hit them at dawn," said Crews. "It was late fall, but we got an early snow, and it crunched under our boots as we approached the houses? Snow coming down, big fat flakes in the early morning light . . . like it was raining blood."

C.P. nodded.

"Couple weeks before we found all these Halloween costumes in an abandoned warehouse, and the officers were wearing skeleton costumes, scampering across the snow like they were in some damned cartoon." Crews shook his head at the memory. "We start knocking down doors and the townspeople 'bout pissed themselves, screaming before the shooting even starts . . . but *you*, C.P., you crazy son of a bitch, you went one better." He glanced over at Baby. "Afterwards, we're checking for survivors, and I spot C.P. here wearing nothing but a purple wig and a gold lamé jockstrap, dragging a teenage girl down Main Street." He looked down at C.P. "Where in hell *did* you find a gold jockstrap?"

As C.P. smiled, Crews shot him in the face.

"C.P. . . . he was a good ol' boy," said Crews. "Always coming up with something to crack me up." He tossed down the gun. Looked over at the Old One. "You want to bring the whole place down around our ears, call forth fire and brimstone . . . you want to drown the world like a box of kittens, well, then, I'm your man, pops."

Baby winked at the Old One. "Told ya."

Gravenholtz nudged C.P.'s body with his shoe.

"This whole place is going to have to be scrubbed," said the Old One. "Bodies removed, buried someplace where they won't—"

"No . . . no. Let's leave everything as it is," said Crews. "I'll call a news conference, say we were attacked by end-times remnants angry at me for embracing the light."

"And you were saved by the grace of God," said Baby.

"Yeah, walked right through a storm of bullets untouched," said Crews. "Let's see John the Baptist try that."

"Throw away your black suits," said Baby. "Become the man in white . . . transformed."

The Old One stared at her. Nodded.

Gravenholtz snorted.

"Call your news conference first thing in the morning," said the Old One. "Sometime soon, Aztlán will formally charge the Colonel with ordering the assassination of their oil minister two weeks ago. I want you out there ahead of the story."

"What am I—?" said Crews.

"The politicians will equivocate, ask for time to go over the indictment, but not you," explained the Old One. "In the Colonel's hour of need you're going to stand by his side. Offer him your total support."

"The Colonel ain't gonna want *his* help," said Gravenholtz.

"Things are happening quite rapidly now, Mr. Crews," said the Old One, ignoring Gravenholtz. "I think you're going to enjoy yourself. Baby and I will be leaving shortly, but Lester's going to stay with you."

"You didn't say nothing about that to me," said Gravenholtz.

"There's a great deal I don't tell you, Lester. More than you can possibly imagine."

"Lester, honey, it's just for a little while." Baby stroked Gravenholtz's arm. "I bet you and Mr. Crews gonna be real good friends."

Gravenholtz pulled away.

"You want to know a secret?" Crews said softly. "Not all my

healing is fake. Oh, most of it is suggestion and reinforcement, no doubt, but sometimes . . . sometimes I feel something flowing from me into them, a heat pouring out from my hands and it . . . it *does* something to folks." He glanced at C.P. then back at the Old One. "I don't know why it happens, or how it happens, but sometimes I cure people, mister. Me, Malcolm Crews. I cure people and they stay cured. Arthritis, diabetes, heart trouble . . . I cured cancer a couple of times, cured it right out of them."

"This is a time of miracles, Mr. Crews," said the Old One.

Gravenholtz spit onto C.P.'s ruined face. "You're so good, let's see you raise that asshole from the dead."

CHAPTER 20

Rakkim knelt on one of the large, flat rocks in the water garden, picked a piece of broken glass out of the stream and put it in his pocket. The water garden had been Redbeard's favorite spot on his estate, a full acre of lush greenery under a clear, protective dome. Redbeard prayed here, planned and plotted here, taught Rakkim and Sarah the basics of statecraft and political survival here. He plucked another piece of glass from the stream.

Through a jagged gap in the shattered dome, Rakkim could see the villa where he and Sarah had grown up. Last year someone had driven a stolen car through the plasti-glass, tearing through several panels. The car had been hauled away but the break in the dome remained, along with another dozen breaches. No matter. The vegetation in the dome thrived, the bamboo actually growing through the holes in the roof in parts. He and Sarah and Michael had come here regularly, weeding the garden, cleaning out the streambeds, hauling away trash. Colarusso and his family joined them sometimes, picnicking among the yellow hibiscus blooms beside the waterfall. He picked another piece of glass out of the water. The late-afternoon sun slanted through the dome, bathing the lush greenery with soft, golden light. Cool mist from the waterfall floated across his face.

"I thought you'd be happy," said Sarah.

Rakkim took in the construction cranes around the villa, the workers gone for the day. "You should have told me."

"I wanted to surprise you . . . and I suspected how you'd react."

After years of vandalism and targeted attacks by followers of the Black Robes, Redbeard's villa was being renovated by the news network in conjunction with the planned retrospective of his life. The outer walls had been rebuilt, the main structure braced, and new landscaping designed. Sarah said Redbeard's office, smaller than most people expected, had already been fully restored. Evidently this was going to be the focus of the documentary, Sarah seated near the great man's desk, talking about his life and the effect he'd had on the fledgling republic.

"It's not the network's job to restore the villa," said Rakkim. "You and I would have gotten to it eventually. Look what we've done with the water garden."

"The villa was falling apart, Rikki."

"Maybe *that's* the lesson. A great man lived here. Slept fitfully here. Taught the people he cared about here . . . and when he was gone, when he died . . . it fell into ruin. Men who hated him in life burned it down, broke the windows, knocked over walls, but the things he did, the people he taught . . . they endured. Is that so bad?"

"We want to *inspire* people, Rikki." She leaned closer. "If we don't, somebody else will. Would you rather ibn-Azziz or the Old One captured people's imagination?"

Rakkim didn't answer.

"Redbeard's life is the story," said Sarah. "Head of State Security, never married, Redbeard devoted his life to protecting the nation from terrorist attacks during the early days of the Republic. His partnership with President Kingsley is seen as part of the golden era of the Republic. His peaceful death from a heart attack is part of his mystique, called to heaven by Allah with a whisper—"

"Okay, okay, enough," said Rakkim. "Just tell Legault to leave the water garden alone."

"I already have." Sarah took his hand. "Come on, I want to show you something."

Sarah led him out of the water garden, down one of the paths and into the rear of the villa, with its vaulted ceilings, marble floors, thick wood and etched glass.

"Nice to know that Legault has no fear of spending other people's money," said Rakkim.

"Hush." Sarah opened the door. "Well?"

Rakkim walked into the solarium. Stared at the clear blue water of the swimming pool.

"Not so bad, is it?" said Sarah, voice echoing. "Took them almost a week just to remove the debris people had thrown in. New filter, new aerator . . ."

"It's . . . just like when we were kids." Rakkim looked at her. "It's beautiful. I never expected . . ." He bent down, put a hand in the water. It was cool. Perfect.

Sarah kicked off her shoes, sat on the edge of the pool and dangled her legs in the water. "This morning Aztlán formally charged the Colonel with murdering their oil minister in Miami."

"I saw the live feed when I went out this morning," said Rakkim. "Thought Argusto was going to have a stroke."

"This is *serious*, Rikki. The three nations are in a precarious balance."

"Charging the Colonel doesn't even make sense—he's too far north to be worried about Aztlán's territorial ambitions. Besides, the Colonel doesn't have anyone who could pull off an operation like that."

"Aztlán seems to think he managed it." Sarah kicked her feet in the water, making waves. "They're demanding he be extradited to Tenochtitlán for trial."

"The Colonel's as popular as Elvis and he's got over eight thousand armed men backing him up, so I doubt he'll be enjoying that famous Aztlán hospitality anytime soon." Rakkim took off his clothes and dove into the water. He came up in the middle of the pool. "If President Raynaud had a brain he'd tell Aztlán to go fuck themselves—he'd have the whole country behind him. Might even get himself reelected."

Sarah watched him backstroking. " 'Go fuck yourself' isn't really a foreign policy. More of a . . . personal philosophy."

"I should have mentioned that last night at the faculty tea."

"You weren't too miserable, were you?"

"Time of my life. If my life was being stuck in a book." Rakkim beckoned. "Come on in."

Sarah shook her head.

"There are security guards on the access roads—this is as private as it gets. Come *on*."

Sarah looked around. Slowly unbuttoned her dress.

Rakkim whistled, beat at the water.

"*Stop* it," said Sarah.

Rakkim didn't.

Sarah finished undressing, neatly folded her clothes on the bench. Looked around again, then walked down the steps into the pool. Breaststroked toward Rakkim, trying to keep her hair dry. They embraced in the center of the pool, kicking to stay aloft. The afternoon sun turned the water droplets along her ear to gold beads.

"You'll have to thank Legault for me," said Rakkim.

"He wants you in the retrospective too."

"Not a chance."

"Such a shy boy."

Rakkim pressed his erection against her.

"Unhand me, sir," she ordered, her arms wrapped tightly around him, holding him close.

"Let's have another baby," Rakkim said softly.

"This isn't . . . this isn't the right time."

"When is the right time?"

Sarah shook her head.

They drifted apart. Rakkim floated on his back, staring up at the glass ceiling, the clouds floating overhead.

"I'm sorry," said Sarah, "it's just . . . there's so much going on right now."

"Yeah, I forgot how calm and simple things were when we had Michael."

"Don't be like that."

Rakkim closed his eyes and focused on the sensation of being in the pool again, the feel of the water. So many memories in that house . . . most of them good. Rakkim couldn't imagine what would have become of him if Redbeard hadn't taken him home that day, made him part of the family. He would have ended up in prison . . . or maybe working in the Zone, someplace where risk was rewarded, but he wouldn't have ended up here. With Sarah. He owed a lot to Redbeard.

"What are you thinking?" asked Sarah.

Rakkim opened his eyes. "How lucky I am."

"Me too." The birthmark between her breasts was just above the waterline. "Don't be mad at me."

"No . . . we've got time."

She squeezed out her hair.

"Who was that older man you were talking to at the faculty tea?"

"Karl Hoffman," said Sarah. "Professor Hoffman's one of the world's authorities on the subject of the true cross."

"I bet that's been a real career booster." He saw her expression. "Sorry."

Christians might believe that Jesus died on the cross, but Muslims didn't. The cross was a symbol of rebirth to Christians, but for Muslims it was just the vehicle of Jesus' deception and escape from the Romans. To them, Jesus was a great man, a prophet second in importance only to Muhammad, but he wasn't the Son of God.

"Professor Hoffman is very highly regarded internationally," said Sarah.

"Last night Satrice referred to him as Professor One Note."

Sarah splashed him. "Ask your friends in the Belt what the cross means to them."

"We're not in the Belt."

Sarah swam over to the end of the pool, sat on the steps, drying off in the last of the sun. "It always comes down to that. The Belt and the Republic. Christian and Muslim. We have to get beyond that, Rikki. Look at Spider, as Jewish as Moses, but *he's* helping me because he knows that reconciliation is best for everyone."

Rakkim strode over to her, sat beside her, feeling her heat. "You want me to go to D.C.? I'll do it. You want me to go to fucking Mars to find the Holy Grail or the Ark of the Covenant or any of that other junk from the Goldberg movies, fine, just say the word."

Sarah smiled. "Mars?"

"Well, maybe not quite that far." He kissed the water off her shoulder. "Just saying, if you want me to see what's really in that safe room . . ."

"I'll let you know." Sarah shook her hair out. "It's *Spielberg*, by the way. Goldberg was the political historian, Spielberg was the filmmaker."

Rakkim lightly pinched her nipple and she squealed, pushed him back into the water. He swam back, lay beside her, serious now. "I worry that maybe you're right. That we *don't* have time."

"For babies?"

"For anything," said Rakkim. "We walk around Seattle and everyone pretends to get along—maybe they avoid eye contact or curse you quietly, but we keep the peace. Even in the conservative districts, no one has been stoned to death in years for adultery or blasphemy. Then you go to New Fallujah . . . and you see what happens when fundamentalists take over."

"I know."

"You *don't* know. You might read about it, or see censored images on TV, but it's not the same as being there. I think about what Jenkins told me, all the new Black Robe mosques going up around the country, President Brandt backing down . . . Senator Chambers set to become secretary of defense. If that happens, ibn-Azziz will be able to do anything he wants. Him and his master, the Old One—"

"You don't know that Chambers is in the pocket of ibn-Azziz."

Rakkim rested his cheek against her belly. "No, but I'm going to find out."

"Redbeard had a technique . . . what did he call it?" Sarah

played with his hair. "The affirmation trap, that was it. Remember?"

Rakkim kissed her belly button. "No."

"I had stolen a bottle from his stash of Coca-Cola and he counted and found out . . . but he didn't know which one of us was responsible. He confronted us separately. I said I didn't know what he was talking about, but you . . . you took the blame."

"It was my fault for showing you where he kept them."

"He knew you well enough not to trust your admission of guilt, not when it came to me. So he never disagreed with you, just accepted the truth of what you were saying and took it to its logical conclusion. The simpler the better. In this case, it was just asking for your help in covering up your crime."

"Son of a bitch." Rakkim sat up. Importing Coca-Cola or anything else from the Belt had been a felony then; even Redbeard might have been charged if caught. "He asked me what I had done with the empty bottle, so he could dispose of it safely. He wasn't angry, he just said he wanted to protect us. We even talked about how good Coca-Cola tasted, how much better it was than Jihad Cola, how everyone drank it when he was a boy." He shook his head. "I tried to tell him that I had taken care of it, but he insisted on seeing the empty bottle. 'The whole household could be in jeopardy, Rikki. You, me, Sarah . . . we would all be equally guilty. You wouldn't want that to happen, would you?' " Rakkim looked at Sarah. "When I couldn't come up with the empty . . . he just patted me on the head and walked away. He didn't tell me the interrogation technique actually had a name."

"The affirmation trap. That's what Redbeard called it."

"Redbeard told you this? You were *five years old*. I was ten."

Sarah ran a finger down his spine, made him shiver. "I was smarter."

"Affirmation trap," said Rakkim. "I'll have to try that."

Sarah squeezed out her hair, water running down her shoulders. "It doesn't work on me."

"I wasn't planning on using it on you."

They were on their way back to the car, clothes still damp, when Sarah spoke again. "You said before that you felt like time was running out. You were right. That's why President Brandt and President Raynaud need to forge some kind of alliance."

"Good luck."

"The true cross can help bridge the gap," insisted Sarah. "People *need* symbols, Rikki. We're wired for it. Symbols are the most potent and direct language we have."

"Yeah, well, that's your specialty, not mine. Like I said, I'll go to D.C. I'll search for the true cross like some crusader on a mission from the pope. Just ask Spider and Leo if they can narrow the search. I'm not interested in sightseeing."

Sarah shook her head. "I already asked John Moseby to go."

Rakkim stopped. "When?"

"Leo contacted him on a secure link a few days ago. He's already on the way," said Sarah. "I know you think I should have asked you, but John's a *finder*. You said yourself he was the best. He's also a Christian."

"It's too dangerous."

"He's not going into D.C. Not yet, anyway. I sent him to talk with the wife of the zombie that found the safe room."

"I don't want John going into D.C. by himself, Sarah."

"He won't."

"You don't know Moseby."

CHAPTER 21

Senator Derrick Chambers slept with a night-light on. A small night-light in the shape of a sailboat, just like the one featured in his campaign ads—Chambers upright at the wheel, his sandy hair rippling in the sea breeze as he headed into the dawn. Captain Courageous. Rakkim switched the light off, the room almost completely dark now, except for a thin strand of moonlight that edged between the thick drapes. Plenty of light for Rakkim's Fedayeen eyes to see, but the senator would be blind. Terrible state for a man who needed a night-light.

Chambers sighed, turned over in bed. He was alone and Rakkim was grateful for that. The papers said his wife and children were in Hawaii while he attended to legislative matters, but there were always other possibilities. Not tonight, though.

Rakkim peeled back the hood of his stealth suit. Skintight, the material instantly mimicked any background color or pattern, rendering the wearer nearly invisible. The military used a slower version for night infiltrations, one that absorbed the infrared used by night-vision devices. Industrial spies and saboteurs used gadget-enhanced Chinese versions. Fedayeen assassins used the simplest-type stealth suit—no laser refraction, no sound-dampening capability, no auxiliary-light absorption. Anyone other than an assassin would get himself killed trying to get by with one. Rakkim had found it in a Level 6 security locker at the Fedayeen academy after he killed Darwin. It fit him perfectly.

He moved slowly across the room. Barely stirring the carpet. His heartbeat steady. He hovered over the senator, watching him breathe. He could count the hairs in his eyelashes in the darkness. He slipped out his knife, rested the flat of the blade across the man's lips.

The senator opened his eyes.

"Don't worry," said Rakkim.

The senator's eyes widened in the darkness.

"I'm going to remove the knife, but I want you to keep your voice down. I know the room is wired to alert your bodyguards if the sound level goes over ninety decibels, so we're going to have a nice conversation, you and I, like a couple of civilized gentlemen. Is that okay with you?"

The senator nodded.

Rakkim took the knife away.

"I can't see you," said the senator.

"It's all right, I can see you."

"What . . . what do you want?"

"Just what I said. A nice little conversation."

"May I sit up?"

"Sure." Rakkim waited until the senator shifted to an upright position, then sat down on the bed facing him. "Is that better?"

"Can I *please* put on a light?"

"I prefer the darkness."

"Yes, well, some of us don't have the advantage of night-vision goggles." Chambers cocked his head, listening. He was tall and handsome, lightly muscled, his chest waxed smooth in the modern style. "How . . . how did you get past my bodyguards?"

"That's my job, Senator. I'm good at my job, just as you're good at yours."

"What you're doing is a federal offense. Do you understand that?"

"Having a conversation is a crime? What a world we live in."

"Is it money . . . is that what you want?"

"You know better than that, Senator. I'm here at the request of a mutual friend."

"A friend?" The senator moistened his lips in the darkness. Squinted. "If a friend sent you, why won't you turn on a light?"

"I've always found that people speak more openly in the dark, and it's very important that we have an honest discussion,

Senator." Rakkim saw Chambers's hand stray toward the medallion around his neck. "Please don't do that. If you attempt to summon help, I might have to do something rash." He saw Chambers carefully place his hands back on top of the sheets. "Thank you, Senator."

"I . . . I take a certain pride in being a rational man," said Chambers. "I'm sure we can come to some kind of accommodation."

"I'm not interested in an accommodation, Senator. I'm simply here to get some answers."

"I don't . . . I don't understand."

"This is a very . . . precarious time for all of us." Rakkim watched the senator's erratic breathing, trying to get a read on him. "So much planning has gone into your appointment to secretary of defense—"

"How did you find out about that?"

"Please lower your voice."

"I *asked*—"

Chambers went silent as the tip of Rakkim's knife lifted his chin. "Are you capable of lowering your voice, Senator?"

"Yes," whispered Chambers, barely moving his lips.

Rakkim watched a single drop of blood run down the blade of his knife in the darkness. "Good." He removed the knife. "I know about your appointment because I work for the man who secured it for you."

Chambers dabbed at his chin with the sheet. "If you work for the president . . ."

Rakkim laughed softly. "Don't insult me, Senator. You know who I work for."

Chambers shook his head. "I don't . . . I truly don't."

Rakkim sighed, let the weariness fill the room. "Fine. You're a cautious man, and that's to be commended. Up to a point. As a cautious man you may be interested to know that someone has been looking into the deaths of those two aides of yours."

Chambers looked perplexed. Rakkim still couldn't tell if

Chambers was involved with the Old One, or if he was just the good modern that he seemed to be.

"Any idea who might be making those inquiries, Senator?"

"I assume State . . . State Security."

"It wasn't State Security."

"Well, then I don't know." Chambers started to speak, stopped himself for a moment. "Why should that concern me anyway? Sandor died of a heart attack. Alexander was killed in a car accident."

"I know how they died, Senator. I killed them."

"I . . . I beg your pardon?"

" 'I . . . I beg your pardon?' " mocked Rakkim. "I'm trying to help you, Senator, but you're making it difficult."

Chambers smoothed the sheets. "I really don't know what you want me to—"

"Who do you think is trying to derail your appointment?"

Chambers continued to smooth the sheets. "The Black Robes despise me. If I have any enemies, it would be ibn-Azziz."

Rakkim jabbed Chambers lightly on both sides of his chest, his hand moving so quickly that the second puncture was made before the senator gasped from the first one. "Ibn-Azziz is not your enemy. He's an errand boy, just like you." Rakkim watched a drop of blood form on each side of Chambers's chest, a second set of nipples, black and shiny as obsidian in the darkness.

"*Please* . . . I don't know what you want from me."

"I want to know if you have any loose ends you haven't told us about. Something that could become a problem if the wrong people discovered them."

Chambers stared into the darkness.

"You're going to have to help me," Rakkim said gently, "because I can't allow even a *potential* loose end to interfere with our master's plans."

"Who . . . ?"

"A great deal of effort has been put to bear for your

advancement," said Rakkim. "Now it's time for you to do something in return."

Chambers wiped at the blood on his chest.

"Senator . . ." Rakkim's voice was barely a whisper. "If you don't tell me what the loose end is, that means *you're* the loose end."

"Could . . . could you put on a light, please?"

"Not just yet."

Chambers dabbed his eyes. "There was a boy . . . one you don't know about. I had almost forgotten him myself . . . no, no, that's not true." He shook his head. "This is very difficult."

"Take your time, Senator. I've been told I'm a good listener."

Chambers laughed. "By *whom*? The men you're about to kill?"

"Tell me about this boy you had almost forgotten."

Chambers trembled, the sheets rustling against him. "His name was Louis. I cared very much for him. The others were just . . . diversions. They didn't even know my name. Louis, though, he was different. When the Black Robes scooped the others up, I stayed silent, but I didn't want anything to happen to Louis. I couldn't bear that . . . so I warned him." He looked around, trying to find Rakkim's face in the darkness. "I haven't seen him in years. I've had no contact of any kind."

"Please keep your voice down."

Chambers took a deep breath, exhaled slowly. "Louis cared for me very deeply. Tell the Old One that I *know* Louis would never do anything to hurt me."

"Unless?"

"Unless . . . it was absolutely necessary. Unless he had no other options. You shouldn't blame Louis, you should blame whoever backed him into a corner."

"Why don't you get dressed? We'll go someplace and discuss the matter."

"It might not have been Louis. It could have been my two

aides, Alexander . . . or Sandor." Chambers breathed so rapidly he was almost panting. "All those years they were in my employ, you would have thought there might have been some . . . some *discretion*. The more I think about it, I don't think Louis is responsible."

"Get dressed, Senator."

"I . . . I prefer to stay here."

"Get dressed."

Chambers's teeth chattered, *rat-a-tat-tat*, *rat-a-tat-tat*.

"Senator," Rakkim said softly. "Would it help if I turned on a light?"

CHAPTER 22

Malcolm Crews was on a tear. Dancing and prancing across the stage, jiggling like some retard stuck his dick in a light socket. Crowd loved it too, ate it up and asked for extra gravy. Made Gravenholtz want to walk down the pew squeezing their heads with both hands, pop their damn stupid noggins like green grapes.

"It's not enough that Aztlán invades our territorial waters in the Gulf and steals our oil," said Crews, his white suit flashing in the stage light, amplified voice booming off the walls of the great hall. "Not enough that they send troops splashing across the Rio Grande to claim our croplands. No, not nearly enough for these heathens." He shook his head in disbelief. "Now . . . now Aztlán's demanding we turn over Colonel Zachary Smitts to them! Turn over the last of our original warriors, the thorny bloom of the Belt. And for what? Because one of their oil ticks got himself killed in Nueva Florida." He shook his head. "Check the whorehouses and dope dens this oil tick frequented, don't come looking here for the guilty. Stay out of the Belt, Aztlán—*adios, muchacho*, Aztlán—this is the land of the free, the home of the God fearing, the one true God, you polytheistic cocksuckers!" He put a hand over his mouth in mock shock. "Did he say that? Did Pastor Crews really say that?" Hands on his hips now, face arrogantly thrust forward. "Oh sweet merciful heavens, and pass the biscuits, have I offended you, brothers and sisters?"

The crowd roared their approval, stamping their feet so hard that Gravenholtz thought they might bring the whole place down around their ears. The oil tick. That was a good one. He remembered the beaner oil minister looking at him from the back of the limo, talking about his poor fucked-up kid who needed somebody just as fucked up to hang out with. Gravenholtz had sat there, letting the man talk, trying to decide which one of the sentences qualified as his last words. *Are you lonely, Lester?* No, Gravenholtz had answered. It had been a lie, but he wanted to make the oil minister work for it. *My son has never had anyone to play with . . . no one who really wanted to play with him. Come live with him, Lester. You could have anything.* Anything? Gravenholtz answered, enjoying himself now, knowing what was coming.

"What's so funny, mister?"

Gravenholtz looked up.

A young woman stood there. Pretty girl in a frilly blue dress. White gloves and a gold crucifix bouncing between her little bitty tits. Light brown hair, turning up at the ends.

"Can you scoot over?" she said.

Gravenholtz scooted over, made room on the pew as Crews boomed away onstage in his shiny white suit, thrashing his arms overhead like he was summoning lightning.

She sat down in a rustle of blue fabric that spilled over on his leg. "Scuse me," she said, retrieving her skirt, her hand brushing against him. "You don't mind, do you?"

Gravenholtz shook his head, watching her eyes. Light blue, like her dress and . . . sweet. No, playful, like she was at a movie show.

She leaned closer, whispered in his ear. "I was going to sit further up, but I heard you laughing to yourself. I like a man who laughs in church. Too many serious folks make me want to run for the exits."

"Yeah . . . I like a good joke myself." Gravenholtz's throat was so tight he barely recognized his own voice.

"I could tell that right off." She smiled, her teeth white and a little crooked. "They say redheads got a good sense of humor."

A woman in the pew in front of them turned around, started to hush the young woman, but Gravenholtz caught her eye and she turned back around fast.

eas Aztlán, they got more gods than a blueridge retriever
cks." Crews stalked the stage, blindingly white, like a moon-
 on fire.

he crowd ate it up, but from where Gravenholtz sat it was
 much bullshit. Sure, Aztlán had brought back the Aztec
 the gods before the conquistadors came to town, but it
t like they had x-ed out Christianity. They just kind of
ed it all up together—Mary alongside that killer god wear-
lue hummingbird feathers, and the Virgin of Guadalupe
g a drum of human skin at the Easter parade. Religion was
out getting dumbasses to line up and sign up, making peo-
ay today for heaven tomorrow. Every time Crews shouted
God folk, the crowd amened—fucker was the best shit sales-
Gravenholtz had ever seen and that was saying something.
ews jabbed a finger at the front row and Karla Jean grabbed
enholtz's arm.

ztlán gods are dark gods. Gods that drown children. Gods
are travelers, hook 'em up and hang 'em high. Gods of fire
ods of mud, lizard gods and rabbit gods and scorpion gods
. but no Jesus Christ in Aztlán. Not a word. At least Mus-
evere Jesus. He may not be the son of God, to the folks in
public, but they sing his praises almost as loud as Muham-
himself. We got to remember who our real enemies are,
rs and sisters. We got to keep that thought in our hearts
inds. So when Aztlán says, 'Give us the Colonel,' well, I
e crowd in Jerusalem shouting for blood. I hear the crowd
ing to Pontius Pilate, 'Give us Jesus! Crucify him!' "
la Jean squeezed Gravenholtz's arm tighter.
ws shook his head. "Not this time. Not now. Not ever. Az-
nts to try the Colonel for his sins. They want to drag him
 capital city in chains. They want to bend him backwards
stone altar, tear his heart out and offer it to their gods.
utter gods." Crews listened to the people in the audience
and sobbing. "That's right, we won't let that happen. Not
e. Not this time."

The young woman stuck her tongue at the woman's back and
Gravenholtz laughed.

"There you go again," she said. "Oh my, where are my man-
ners?" She held out her hand, charm bracelet jingling. "I'm
Karla Jean Johnson."

Gravenholtz hesitated, placed his hand in hers. "Lester. Lester Gravenholtz."

"Pleased to make your acquaintance, Lester Gravenholtz,"
Karla said, giving his hand a soft squeeze before letting go.

"My hand's a little sweaty," said Gravenholtz. "Sorry."

"Just shows you're healthy," said Karla.

"Okay."

Karla Jean peered at him. "Gravenholtz? I know that name.
You were the Colonel's right-hand man, right? I seen you and
him on TV once."

Gravenholtz glanced around. "That was a while ago."

Karla Jean's eyes widened. "You're supposed to be dangerous.
Bad to the bone." She fanned herself with a stick fan showing
Jesus kneeling beside a white lamb. "Good thing we're in church
or I might fear for my safety."

Gravenholtz cleared his throat.

Karla Jean patted his arm, her charm bracelet tinkling. "If
Pastor Crews can turn away from Satan, I guess you can too."

Gravenholtz's face was hot. "Yes . . . if he can, so can I."

"Am I talking too much?"

Gravenholtz shook his head.

Karla Jean looked straight ahead now. "I haven't talked much
lately . . . maybe I'm making up for lost time." She glanced over
at him, then back at the stage. "I'm a widow. Almost two years
now. Longer than I was married. Figured it was time to get out,
be around people again. Said to myself, Karla Jean, wash your
face, put on a nice dress. . . ." She turned to him. "You want me
to move? If I'm embarrassing you—"

"No. Please, stay."

• • •

"Moseby, you're a welcome sight." The Colonel embraced him. "You should have given me more notice, I would have—"

"I didn't get much notice myself," said Moseby, walking beside the Colonel toward the armored jeep.

Moseby had taken the train up from New Orleans, awake most of the way, jostled and bumped as the *Charlie Daniels* chugged through the Belt on the deteriorating railbed. His wife, Annabelle, had protested his sudden departure, but Sarah had said time was critical. His daughter asked if he was going to meet Leo in Tennessee, acted as if she didn't believe him when he said no. Like he could stop the lovebirds even if he wanted to.

"I've got a vehicle you can take into the hill country tomorrow," said the Colonel. "Rugged beast, get you over and through just about anything. Got a map for you too, best one I could find, but you might want to—"

"Appreciate it, Colonel."

"You sure you don't want me to send a guide along? Got a corporal from that same general area."

"No, thanks."

"This corporal, he's a white man. Some of the hill folks, they never let loose of the old ways."

"I'll get by, sir."

"Of course. Besides, you don't really want company, do you?" The Colonel, a lanky autocrat in his mid-sixties, with long, graying hair to his shoulders, tugged down his gray uniform. Even walking down a country lane, he carried himself as though he were astride a stallion. "You and Rikki have too many secrets, if you ask me."

"My wife says the same thing, sir."

"Oh, I understand the need, it's just not my way." The Colonel drew himself erect. "I prefer things direct and out in the open."

"You would have made a good Fedayeen, sir, but you wouldn't have lasted five minutes in shadow warrior training."

"No . . . I expect not." The Colonel kept the pace. "Fought a

Fedayeen unit once on the Kentucky border. them ten to one, but they fought us to a stan away when we got more reinforcements. Good was craggy in the moonlight, his thick brows "Long time ago."

"Yes, sir."

"You glad you gave it up, Moseby? The Fe you had?"

"Very glad. I love the Belt, sir."

"Your wife and daughter . . . they're well?"

"I'm a lucky man."

The Colonel nodded. "Even luckier beca Some don't. Not until it's too late."

"Your wife . . . I haven't heard anything, wondering," said Moseby.

"Thank you for that. I . . . I didn't want to looked off into the woods surrounding them I'm foolish."

"Not at all, Colonel."

"No fool like an old fool." A vein along th throbbed. "After all she's done to me, the li humiliation . . . if Baby was to step out o now, I'd take her in my arms and I'd forgive I would."

The wind rustled through the trees as th leaving in a hurry.

The Colonel shook his head, and then the jeep, the door opening. "I hope you're h turkey this afternoon. Mean son of a bitch t and he went right for me."

"We've spent our time hating on the Mus ing any apologies for that, war is war, a to the death when the blood rises, but least the Muslims are one-God folk. Jus

"Not this time," repeated the crowd. "Not this time."

"Not this time," said Crews, voice rising. "Not this time!"

"Not this time!" shouted the crowd. "Not this time!"

Karla Jean released Gravenholtz's arm. Smoothed his sleeve. "I am *so* sorry, Lester. I must about cut off your circulation."

"No . . . I liked it. Made me feel like I was taking care of you."

Karla Jean nodded.

"After the sermon . . ." Gravenholtz cleared his throat. "Maybe you'd like to get a drink."

"I don't drink spirits."

"We could get something to eat then. If . . . if you want."

"I like ice cream."

Gravenholtz smiled. "So do I."

Karla Jean clung to him. "You should know . . . I'm not ready for anything boy-girl right now. You know . . . I just would like to go have some ice cream with you."

"Sure. Me too."

"I don't like being rushed."

"Me neither."

"I knew I could count on you. I knew it the first time I laid eyes on you." Karla Jean lowered her eyes. "I got a weakness for gingers. My husband . . . he was a redhead too."

Gravenholtz watched a single tear fall into her lap.

"I don't really feel much like ice cream," said Karla Jean. "You're not mad, are you?"

"No."

"I'm going to go home now." Karla Jean looked up at him. "You planning to be at the service day after tomorrow?"

"If you are," said Gravenholtz.

"I surely am. Maybe . . . we could go out for ice cream then."

"I don't want to push you."

Karla Jean looked into his eyes. "No . . . I'll be ready by then."

CHAPTER 23

"Your boy has fast reflexes," said General Kidd as Michael and a slightly bigger boy circled each other in the courtyard, sword-fighting with sticks. The sound of their battle echoed across the dirt, their bare feet kicking up dust. Mothers sat in the shade, tending to infants, laughing and gossiping—all were modestly dressed, their chadors banded with color, some with their faces veiled.

General Kidd and Rakkim sat cross-legged in the grass at the edge of the courtyard separated from the other men, watching the children's combat. Michael the only white face, smudged with dirt, intent as any of the others. The Somali section of the capital was clannish and heavily guarded, most of the men Fedayeen, always alert for outsiders. Rakkim was welcome here—the few times he attended mosque, he accompanied Kidd to the small, plain mosque at the center of the district.

"See?" Kidd pointed as Michael deftly parried the bigger boy's aggressive attack, always ahead of him. "See how he anticipates Shakur's movements? You've been teaching him."

"He's quick," said Rakkim, wary. Compliments came from Kidd's mouth as rarely as profanity.

"*Very* quick," affirmed Kidd. "He takes after you."

Michael feinted, drew the bigger boy off balance, speared him lightly in the chest. The boy cried out, not from pain, for it was but the briefest of contacts, but from surprise. The boy hung his head as the mothers applauded. Except for one tall, slender woman, whose white hijab perfectly framed her beautiful black face, making her beauty even more stark. She watched the boys without betraying any emotion.

Michael put his arm around the bigger boy, who shoved him

away. Michael pretended not to notice. He suddenly broke his fighting stick over one knee, squatted down and started poking at an anthill. The bigger boy hesitated, clutching his own stick, finally bent down beside him. Michael handed the boy the other half of his broken stick, and together they amused themselves with the ants.

"He's smart too," said Kidd as the bigger boy draped an arm over Michael. "*That* he gets from his mother."

Rakkim smiled. "It's true."

Kidd didn't smile. "Dangerous for a man to have a wife smarter than he is."

"I'll take the risk," said Rakkim.

"You need another wife," said Kidd. "At least one more. Three would be better."

"I can barely keep up with one," said Rakkim.

"I have a daughter, Irina," said Kidd. "She served us tea."

"She's very lovely," said Rakkim.

"She's fifteen and in good health," said Kidd. "She'd make you a good wife."

Rakkim looked into his large, liquid eyes. "*Sidi*, I'm honored, but—"

"A warrior needs more than one wife," said Kidd, "and I would be greatly pleased to make you part of my family."

"I feel like I am part of your family."

Kidd shook his head. "It is a matter of blood, Abu Michael." He took Rakkim's forearm, squeezed. "Your blood mixed with mine. It's *important*."

Rakkim stared at him. He was missing something. "Important . . . how?"

Kidd released him. Watched the two boys. They were playing tag now, dodging through the smaller children, whooping it up, but deftly avoiding contact with the toddlers.

"*Sidi*, what are you trying to tell me?"

"I have fourteen sons living," said Kidd, still watching the boys. "All warriors, but it will be Amir who will follow me in leading the Fedayeen. Amir may be challenged, but he is ferocious, widely renowned . . . and he has the respect of the president."

"When that time comes—and I'm in no hurry to see that day—when the time comes, may Allah grant Amir the wisdom to do what's best for the Fedayeen and the nation," said Rakkim.

"Amir is not suitable for the task." Kidd's eyes hadn't left the boys. "You know that as well as I do."

"He's young."

"His youth has nothing to do with it." Kidd half closed his eyes. "There is something wrong with him, there always *has* been. He is . . . a drum with a hairline crack, sound under most circumstances, but struck too hard . . ." He shook his head. Pointed at the two boys working at the anthill. "Shakur is Amir's oldest son. Amir loves him as he loves his own life. Even so, when Shakur's mother tells Amir that not only did another boy defeat him, but that it was *your* son who did it, Amir will beat him until he can't move."

"They're five years old."

"That won't matter to Amir," said Kidd. "All that matters is that Shakur and Michael fight again, and this time Shakur will have to win. If he doesn't . . . there is no telling what Amir will do to him."

"And all of this is because I snatched Amir's knife from him? I didn't mean to."

"There was no malice in your actions, I know that," said Kidd. "You did it because you wanted to stop Amir from escalating his demands to fight . . . and he would have done just that. He would have killed you that day if he could. You saved his life by taking away his knife, and that he will never forgive you for."

"Why does he hate me? I've done nothing."

"Amir is jealous of your skills . . . and there is another thing." Kidd touched his chest with his palm. "This other thing is *my* fault. Not yours." He raised his head, his profile stoic as he watched a toddler on the other side of the courtyard trying to walk, the child falling over and over, each time rising again. "Amir knows that I favor you over him. We have never spoken of it, but he can see."

Rakkim felt as if there were a warm egg in his throat.

"I want you to take over the Fedayeen when my time is over," said Kidd.

"That's impossible," said Rakkim.

"Not if I say so."

"A shadow warrior at the head of the Fedayeen?" Rakkim shook his head. "Most of the brothers distrust us."

"You are not a shadow warrior, not anymore," said Kidd. "Did you really think I couldn't see the change in you?"

"Then what am I, *sidi*? You tell me."

Kidd stayed so still that he could have been carved out of ebony. "I'm not sure. By Allah's grace and wisdom, I am not sure, but one thing I do know . . . you are the best one to lead the Fedayeen. The nation is in peril from within and without. If I falter . . . if I fall, you must be ready to take up the blade and carry on."

"You'll have a revolt within the ranks if that happens," said Rakkim.

"Your brother Fedayeen will rally around you soon enough . . . and those that don't . . . ?" Kidd shrugged.

"How will Amir tolerate the shame of being passed over? He's your *son*."

"The pain Amir will feel will also be shared by me," said Kidd. "You have only one son, Rikki. When you have more you will learn that you don't love them all equally. Mothers may love their children without limit or hesitation, but not so for men. Me . . . I may favor you to lead the Fedayeen, but I love Amir more than any of my sons."

"You'll break his heart."

"And break my own at the same time. I'd do it willingly to save the Republic."

"You think the Republic is at risk?"

"Ask Sarah," said Kidd.

Rakkim watched the dust clouds roll across the playground. "*Sidi?*"

"Yes."

"When we first sat down for tea and dates, Michael played with the other children. Shakur was not here. You whispered to your daughter when she served us . . . and a few minutes later Shakur joined in the games."

Kidd sipped his tea.

"You sent for the boy, didn't you?"

Kidd set down his teacup. "Michael needed a playmate close to his own age."

"You knew what would happen when the two boys started playing . . . knew where it would lead." Rakkim fought to keep the edge from his voice. "You set your grandson up for a beating, so that Amir and I would be forever at each other's throats."

"You were already at each other's throats, you just didn't want to admit it. Now you know." Kidd popped a papery date in his mouth, chewed lustily. "Interesting news this morning. The whole city is buzzing."

"Yes."

"A fortunate turn of events, wouldn't you say? Here you and I were concerned whether Senator Chambers was in thrall to the Old One, and now that problem has been resolved." Kidd smacked his lips, reached for another date. "Barely a week before his appointment as secretary of defense too."

Rakkim slurped his tea. "Allah works in mysterious ways."

"Allah? Perhaps." Kidd's large white teeth flashed in the sun. "I woke up for dawn prayers to find that Senator Chambers was caught staggering down the main street of the Zone, drunk and buck naked . . . the uncensored video is everywhere. *Everywhere.* You should have heard my wives giggling." He patted Rakkim on the shoulder. "Sad to say, in regard to the instrument of procreation and pleasure, Allah was not generous to that poor white man."

"Hung like a hamster," said Rakkim.

"Yea, verily."

The toddler learning to walk managed a dozen steps before falling over. He scrambled up, face scratched, clapping his hands with delight. Then he started walking again.

"Chambers has already resigned from the senate." Kidd licked his fingers clean. "Still . . . such humiliation seems a small price to pay for betraying his country. You should have killed him."

"I'm tired of killing."

Kidd toyed with another date, rolling it over his fingers.

"It comes too easy now. I barely have time to think and it's done."

Kidd tossed the date back into the bowl, wiped his hands. "You're tired of killing . . . but killing is not tired of you."

"What is *that*? Some Somali nursery rhyme?"

"Cool your anger, Abu Michael, I meant no insult," Kidd said gently. "Death walks beside you, that's all I'm saying."

"Oh, that makes me feel a *lot* better."

"Death walks beside you, but you are not his slave. Another man might have killed Chambers. *I* would have killed him." Kidd's eyes shone with humor. "Instead, the naked senator retires to his country estate . . . to spend more time with his family."

"*Sidi* . . . isn't that punishment enough?"

Kidd clapped him on the back, the other men craning their heads to see what was so funny. Kidd stretched out his long legs, rolled on his side facing Rakkim. "The president called me just after the news broke. Sounded like he was still half asleep. He asked me to recommend someone for secretary of defense. He seemed to be in quite a hurry."

"He should have done that the first time."

"You don't correct a president, Abu Michael, you merely compliment them on their wisdom in seeking your counsel." Kidd stroked his beard. "I suggested Joseph Vinh." He nodded to himself. "Vinh's merely adequate as a strategic thinker, but we served together in the Great War. I *trust* him. Right now, that's the most important thing."

"Putting Vinh up for defense secretary solves our immediate problem," said Rakkim, "but the bigger problem remains—who suggested Senator Chambers for the position? Who did the president trust enough to heed his counsel? *That's* the Old One's mole. That's who we need to find."

"Senator Nichols mentored the president when he first went into politics . . . they remain close," said Kidd, "and Jason Fletcher lavishly funded his campaigns . . . they still play golf at least once a month."

Michael and Shakur wandered off together, dragging their broken fighting sticks in the dirt. Michael suddenly raced ahead, Shakur giving chase.

"Love your children while they are young, Rakkim, hold them close," said Kidd, his eyes on the two boys, "because they grow up soon enough, and then . . . then they have no need of you."

CHAPTER 24

Mullah Jenkins saw one of ibn-Azziz's bodyguards slouched in the shadows at the south checkpoint leading out of the city, the man cleaning his fingernails with the tip of his knife while the regular patrol checked IDs. If it wasn't for Jenkins's enhanced night vision, he would have never spotted the man. The wind kicked up, a storm coming in fast. He turned into an alley and started running, his black robes flapping around him like bat wings. A member of ibn-Azziz's personal retinue at the south checkpoint, another one at the eastern checkpoint. Had to be a reason and Jenkins didn't like the answer he'd gotten.

He raced down the alley. Should have left with Rakkim when he had the chance. Should have left on his own *long* before then. He would have liked to convince himself that he stayed because he thought he had more work to do for General Kidd, but that wasn't it. He hadn't left that night because he was afraid Rakkim would kill him as soon as they were off the bridge. He could see it in Rakkim's eyes, a barely restrained moral outrage, a mixture of disappointment and disgust from his former pupil. Almost as great as the disgust Jenkins felt toward himself. He should have taken the risk and left with Rakkim. Even if Rakkim had killed him, that was better than falling into the hands of ibn-Azziz.

Something had gone wrong. Something to draw suspicion to him. Had he been too merciful? Yes . . . yes, the schoolgirls, the damn schoolgirls. He should have refused Rakkim's demand. Burned them all. Now, look at him, running for his life because Rakkim had a soft heart. The killer with a soft heart. Jenkins tried to laugh but couldn't summon the humor, his laughter as dried and atrophied as ibn-Azziz's mercy.

With late-night prayers finished, the streets were nearly deserted. No place to hide. His apartment was a death trap. He had an emergency refuge, a small room in an abandoned building near the old marina, but it was better to escape the city *now*, any way he could.

He forced himself to slow, head high, robe billowing around him, as befitting a cleric of his station. Ibn-Azziz had no reason to believe that Jenkins was aware of the danger he was in. The order to pick him up had probably been sent out only to the guards at the checkpoints. If that failed to snag him, a more general order would be sent out at first light, his image shown at every mosque during dawn prayers. Then no refuge would be safe. Nor would anyone risk angering ibn-Azziz to help him. All these years in New Fallujah, and there was no one he could call his friend, no one who would shelter him. The price of being a shadow warrior was that intimacy was a threat. You built your life on a construct of deceit, a house of lies that collapsed with the slightest pressure.

A door opened in the alley, and two men stepped out.

Jenkins froze, heart pounding.

The two men looked at him, fell to their knees. "Mercy . . . we ask mercy."

Jenkins saw that one of them had a lit cigarette in his hand. Doubtless they had slipped out of their lodgings to smoke in secret.

The man tossed his cigarette to the pavement, crushed it underfoot. The other stayed on his knees, head bowed.

Jenkins let them simmer in their sin for a few moments. Mercy too quickly given would be suspicious. He watched as they trembled before him, waiting for his decision.

"I know your names," Jenkins lied. "See that you double your donations at mosque tomorrow morning."

The man who had tossed his cigarette attempted to kiss the hem of Jenkins's robe.

Jenkins kicked, knocked him backward. He heard the door to

the alley slam, drew the hood of his robe tight around his face. As he was about to leave the alley, he heard a car approach and Jenkins shrank back, hugged the wall. A dark green car with two Black Robe enforcers inside drove past, though whether they were looking for him or for sinners, he wasn't sure.

He waited until the car's taillights disappeared before crossing the street. He headed toward the Bridge of Skulls. There was a small boat dock under the bridge, a dock available only to the Black Robe patrol units—the boats used to cruise the bay, looking for lights on after curfew or to intercept smugglers bringing in contraband. The storm would keep boats docked, and the guards huddled in their shacks. Taking one of the boats across the bay to safety would be dangerous in this weather, but the very risk made it less likely that ibn-Azziz would have the area under surveillance.

A long walk from here to the Bridge of Skulls, particularly if he stayed in the alleys and avoided the main streets. It could easily be dawn before he got there. He hurried on.

He started up one of the steep stairways toward the crest of the hill, taking the steps two at a time, holding up the edge of his robe so he didn't trip and split his skull. In the distance the new mosque loomed over the city; still only half completed, it dominated the skyline. The largest mosque in the world, seating three hundred thousand worshipers—ibn-Azziz said it would draw pilgrims from across the planet. Rakkim had wanted to know where the money to build it was coming from, which had gotten Jenkins thinking. Perhaps it had been his own discreet inquiries this last week that had roused ibn-Azziz's suspicions.

Not that he had found out anything concrete. Just that no government was involved, all donations came through individual foundations. What was most interesting to Jenkins was that the idea of the gigantic mosque didn't seem to emanate from ibn-Azziz, whose own ascetic nature rejected ostentation and grandeur. Persons unknown had presented the design for the mosque to him, suggesting that such a grand structure would not only honor Allah, but also shift the attention of the Muslim world from the decadent Arabian Peninsula to the pure Islam of New Fallujah.

A rat scurried across the steps and into the underbrush on the hillside. Jenkins slowed his pace slightly, his knees aching. The wind kept rising, swirling dead leaves around his ankles. The surrounding buildings were dark, although he sometimes heard the sound of a muffled radio from one of the apartments.

It started raining, not too heavy yet, but the slick steps were even more treacherous. He quickened his pace anyway.

More than the sheer enormity of the money donated for the mosque, it was the method of seducing ibn-Azziz that made him think the Old One might have been responsible. Money was irrelevant to ibn-Azziz, even faintly sordid. He was equally immune to love. At one time Jenkins thought ibn-Azziz craved power, but that wasn't the case. Power was simply a means by which ibn-Azziz brought people to Allah. *Someone*, though, had found his weakness.

Building the largest mosque in the world would have carried the taint of pride, but building the mosque to turn all eyes to the true Islam . . . that was precisely the kind of subtle vanity to which ibn-Azziz was susceptible. Such targeted temptation was a mark of the Old One, and setting up a spiritual counterweight to his enemies in the Middle East was a bonus. Jenkins had planned on sending another message to General Kidd, telling him of his suspicions about the Old One, but now such plans seemed as foolish as his decision to stay here.

Jenkins reached the top of the stairs, stopped to glance up and down the street before continuing. He was going to have to hurry to get to the boat dock before dawn prayers. The streets would be teeming with believers, his picture everywhere after that. He hung on to the railing. Placed a hand on his heart, trying to establish some sort of feedback link to slow himself down before his chest exploded. All the years here, all the close calls . . . yet here he was, panicked as a woman. One should get braver as one got older . . . there was less to lose. Why fear man taking what Allah would take soon enough? Easy to say when one believed in Allah. Paradise awaited the faithful. The problem was . . . he no longer believed.

The rain came down in sheets now, soaking through his robes. Thunder fumbled through the canyons of downtown. Jenkins looked around, walked calmly across the street, head high, then dashed through the alley. The rain was good for him, limiting visibility, making the city even darker. He ran on, drawing on the reserves of his energy, using his fear to fuel him, block after block, the boat ramp closer with every step.

Jenkins had been as good a Muslim as any when he first came to New Fallujah. Though the brutality of this brand of Islam had startled him at first, he had quickly risen in the leadership. Adaptability was the highest virtue of the shadow warriors, and he took pride in his ability to shed his personal morality for the greater good of the Fedayeen. "The grand atrocity," he had called it, but his years of cooperating with that atrocity had ground his soul down to a fine gray dust, and with it his belief in Allah. After all the heads he had added to the Bridge of Skulls, the slightest breeze would have been enough to blow away his soul, and there was always a storm brewing in this dead city.

He splashed through the puddles, blinking back the rain. His black robe was a leaden weight around him, and he was soaked to the skin, freezing, but he pressed on, legs pumping. Faster. Faster. It amazed him that his belief in the Fedayeen had outlasted his belief in Allah, but now . . . even that was fading. What had Rakkim said? *I don't give a fuck about my country. I'm here because of General Kidd.* Thunder crashed, momentarily deafening him. The young man would learn.

He huddled in the alley across from the street leading down to the boat ramp. He listened but there was no way to hear anything over the thunder and rain. No cars on the street. No lights in the windows. Bits of brightly colored paper swirled in the water streaming down the gutters—a birthday party somewhere, gaudy wrappings and bows . . . a sin among many sins, so many sins he could no longer keep track of them. He watched until the shiny bits of paper disappeared, then walked quickly across the street, into the shelter of the low buildings.

At the end of the alley, he saw the boats bobbing wildly against the dock. Suicide to try to navigate across the bay in this weather, madness to think he could reach the other side . . . Jenkins threw off his heavy black robe and started running. He could hardly wait to try.

He burst out of the alley, slid down the grassy slope toward the docks. As his feet touched the slats of the wooden dock, he saw movement out of the corner of his eye.

"What's your hurry, Mullah Jenkins?" cooed ibn-Azziz, the cleric bareheaded in the downpour, surrounded by bodyguards.

"There you are," said Jenkins, bowing. "I hoped to find you here."

"Hope is a honeyed word, is it not?" Ibn-Azziz turned to his retainers. "Our good mullah finds sweetness in our meeting."

The bodyguards fanned out around Jenkins.

Ibn-Azziz tapped his fingertips together. "What else do you hope, Mullah Jenkins?"

Jenkins took a step back, saw that his path was blocked by more of ibn-Azziz's men. Lightning cracked directly overhead. Jenkins jumped as did the bodyguards, but ibn-Azziz didn't flinch.

"You are shy, I understand." Ibn-Azziz waved his bodyguards back. "Is that better?"

Jenkins moved closer to the Grand Mullah, barely feeling the rain anymore.

"Good," said ibn-Azziz, a black-robed skeleton in the raging storm. "So *obedient*, Mullah Jenkins, I hardly recognize you."

Jenkins spread his arms wide, felt his Fedayeen knife against the inside of his forearm. "All your patience has finally paid off. You have tamed my defiant spirit."

"All blessings be to Allah, not my unworthy self." Ibn-Azziz cocked his head, water dripping off his nose. "Do you have something for me, Mullah Jenkins?" he mocked. "You look like a man with a surprise clutched to his heart."

Jenkins blinked the rain from his eyes, almost close enough now. The boats banged against the dock, louder and louder, the wind rising.

Ibn-Azziz cupped his ear. "I can't hear you." He beckoned. "Come closer, and share your wisdom."

Jenkins flicked the knife into his hand as he thrust forward, but ibn-Azziz was fast, so very fast, the blade slicing through the whirling black robe, but leaving ibn-Azziz untouched.

Ibn-Azziz danced out of reach as his bodyguards closed in on Jenkins.

Jenkins cut down one of the bodyguards, then another, trying to break through, but there were too many of them. He kept moving, looking for an opening, a way out. He carved another bodyguard with a flick of his wrist, wishing again that he had gone back to Seattle with Rakkim. He would have liked to see the Egyptian girls dance in the Zone one more time. He fought on. Behind him, he could hear ibn-Azziz praying, screeching away as thunder rolled across the city.

A hot stone rested inside Lieutenant Miguel Ortiz's belly. Getting hotter too as he led his men into the outskirts of Corpus Christi, their shadows enormous in the dawn light. They moved like devils through the underbrush, brown crickets fluttering before them as they crept silently toward the white church, crawling now, close enough that Ortiz could hear them singing, greeting the morning with hosannas.

This was not the first time Ortiz and his eight-man team had infiltrated the Belt. That's what Unit X commandos did. Just last month they had taken out a nest of pirates near Galveston, men who used speedboats to intercept Aztlán pleasure yachts cruising peacefully in the Gulf. Looters and rapists and murderers of innocent Mexicans. Texans with grudges were more dangerous than a swarm of fire ants. It had been a pleasure to creep up on the pirate hideout at dawn, the team's inflatables far down the beach. Sergeant Romo had taken out their single sentry, but it had been Ortiz himself who kicked open the door to the nest, firing his machine gun in short, accurate bursts. They had not left a single pirate alive. The team had sung folk songs on the way back to the mother ship. Today, though . . . he didn't imagine there would be singing.

As if hearing his thoughts, the congregation inside the church seemed to raise their voices, the very walls vibrating with the sound of their singing. *Up from the grave, He arose . . .* Ortiz knew the hymn. His grandmother sang it on Easter. It was more beautiful in Spanish. There were still plenty of people back home who went to church, prayed the rosary, but most young people worshiped the old religion, the ancient gods of Aztlán. So many gods . . . it was hard for Ortiz to keep track of them all.

Sergeant Romo looked at him and Ortiz gave a hand signal, watched as Romo took three men and circled around the church.

Ortiz was doing a terrible thing. The people inside the church were not pirates, or Lone Star rampagers who attacked peaceful Mexican fishing villages. They were innocent. Which would do them no good at all. He rested his cheek in the sand, still cool from the evening, and wondered if he really was going to do this thing.

A family raced up the steps to the church, a father, mother and two children in their Sunday best, hurrying, and Ortiz wished their car had broken down, wished a water main had burst and flooded the streets, wished for anything that would have delayed them five minutes. The door to the church opened, the hymn booming louder for a moment—*He arose a victor from the dark domain*—before it closed after the family.

Ortiz was aware of the rest of his men waiting for him to give the order. He nodded his head and the three men scuttled forward, placed their satchel charges and incendiaries around the walls, then quickly backed out. Sergeant Romo came around from the other side, placed a charge in front of the door, set the motion trigger.

The men had been quiet during the insertion, quietly checking and rechecking their gear. No boasts or jokes or talk of what they would do when they got home. They attended to business and avoided looking at him. He didn't blame them.

Sergeant Romo's men rejoined them, breathing hard, eager to get back to the boats.

The thin man had come to him two days ago. Ortiz had been drinking in a tavern when a man sat beside him, a thin man who spoke accented Spanish and drew the Unit X sign in the moisture on the bar. The man wiped away the sign, then said he had a mission for Ortiz and his team. Ortiz listened, demanded to know who the man *really* was. Said Tenochtitlán did not order the murder of women and children.

The Belt murders our oil minister, Miguel, and you expect us to do nothing? The man ordered another round of drinks for them. *Are you not a patriot?*

Ortiz had left the drink untouched on the bar, but he didn't walk away. Ortiz told the man he was a patriot, but not a butcher.

The man watched him in the mirror over the bar. Said authorization had already been sent. *Do your duty, Miguel.*

Yesterday the base commandant had called Ortiz in, said he had gotten orders, and transport would be provided to Ortiz and his team. The commandant didn't ask where they were going or what their mission was—he was used to Unit X operating on their own.

Ortiz raised a fist to Sergeant Romo and the team scurried back through the underbrush in twos, heading toward their rally point in the pine woods beyond the town. Ortiz was the last to leave, racing through the morning, casting aside all field discipline, scared that he would be left behind with what he had done.

The charges detonated as he reached the trees, a rapid sequence of explosions, the fireball rising into the sky. Ortiz stumbled forward, almost fell. He blinked back tears, and ordered his men forward to the boats.

CHAPTER 25

"I'll take them," said Leo.

The pale teenage chip jockey behind the armored glass rubbed his thumb and index finger together and Leo counted out $4,000 in hundreds, slipped them through the slot.

The chip jockey had the emotionless eyes of a crustacean, flat black eyes that should have been mounted on stalks. He lazily recounted the money, dragging out the process, then tucked the bills into his camouflage shorts. His long fingers placed the two new Chinese lithium chips into tiny glassine envelopes while his eyes did something else, maybe ran a salinization test or a plankton quality assessment. The chips slid out the one-way box onto the other side of the glass.

Leo rechecked the chips through a jeweler's loupe, nodded. "You got a demag case for these? Wouldn't want to scramble the configuration."

The chip jockey rubbed his thumb and forefinger together again.

Leo flipped him the finger, started for the door.

Rakkim waved to the chip jockey. "Good talking with you."

Leo jerked the door handle, but it didn't budge. He turned to the chip jockey. "Hey!"

The chip jockey picked his nose. Examined his fingertip. Pressed a button.

The heavy, metal-clad door hissed as the security bolts slid back into the door frame. Leo flung the door open, stepped out into the narrow alley, Rakkim right behind him. The door shut, the bolts slamming back in place.

Rakkim turned up the collar of his leather jacket against the light rain, but stayed put.

Every week it was the same thing. Leo asked Rakkim to come along on one of his buying expeditions in the Zone. The tech galleries along the lower level had the newest whizbang gear in the country, but they didn't open until after dark, and this part of the Zone was dangerous—even the police and tourists kept their distance. Leo pretended he wanted Rakkim along for company, and Rakkim pretended to believe him.

Every week they made the rounds, but they always ended up at this same chip shop, where the clerk reserved his best merchandise for Leo. Leo always bitched about the price or the condition, but the chip jockey didn't dicker. He didn't talk either. All these weeks and Rakkim had never heard the jockey utter a word. At the end of the transaction, Leo would ask for something. A demag case, a virus tracking number, a glass of water, something that should have been thrown in free after the money he had spent, and the chip jockey would demand to be paid, and Leo would always flip him off. Then Rakkim and Leo would go out for dinner. Rakkim would never understand brainiacs.

Leo zipped his jacket all the way up, not eager to step out into the rain. "I still wish you'd come with me to Las Vegas," said Leo. "We'd have fun."

"Yeah, you, me, a conference full of math whizzes, what could be better?" said Rakkim.

"Being invited to deliver a paper in front of the International Pure Math Symposium is a real honor," said Leo. "Just thought you might want to be there to see it."

"You said they invited Spider."

Leo sniffed. "What's your point?"

"They didn't ask *you* to deliver an address," teased Rakkim. "They asked your father."

"My father is too sick to travel. Besides . . . he'd be the first to tell you I've far surpassed him." Leo started down the alley.

Rakkim grabbed Leo by the shoulder, pulled him back.

"*What?* Oh."

Two men stood at each end of the alley, the four of them

strolling toward them, jaunty as sailors home on leave. One was Kissell, a near-giant that Rakkim had seen a few days ago—Senator Chambers's chief bodyguard, a clean-shaven thug with tiny eyes and a soft gut. The other three he had only heard about, identical triplets, Black Robe enforcers working out of the Hassan Nasrallah mosque, three slender sadists given carte blanche to keep the faithful in line.

Rakkim's knife slid into his hand.

Leo banged on the chip jockey's door. "Hey! Open up!" The cameras over the door swiveled, took in the approaching men. Leo kicked at the armored door. "Let us in!"

The lights went out in the store.

"Son of a *bitch*!" screamed Leo.

"You looking for work?" Rakkim said to the bodyguard. "I hear the Kit Kat Klub is hiring toilet swabbers. I could put in a good word for you."

"Keep talking," said Kissell.

"I didn't think the senator recognized me," said Rakkim. "That's what I get for going easy on him."

"Chambers didn't have any idea who you were." Kissell had a small voice for such a big man, almost a squeak, as though all that flesh had compressed the sound. "It's Grand Mullah ibn-Azziz who told me your name. He's a little upset. Come along, I'll take you to New Fallujah—you can offer your apologies in person."

If ibn-Azziz had tagged him for exposing Senator Chambers, then Jenkins had given him up. "No, thanks. I get carsick."

"It wasn't really a request," said Kissell.

The triplets unslung shock whips from under their raincoats, slender three-foot flails that could shred flesh.

"Careful, fellas," said Rakkim. "You don't want to hurt yourselves."

Two burly workmen started down the alley from the main street, stopped when they saw what was going on, then turned and fled.

"What do we do, Rakkim?" whispered Leo.

"Move aside and let this tourist pass, Kissell," said Rakkim. "We'll discuss things in private. No reason to complicate—"

"No," hissed Leo.

"Go on, Leo," Rakkim said quietly, "I'll catch up with you later."

"I . . . I c-can help," sputtered Leo. He bent down, clawing at one of the paving stones, trying to dislodge it, but his fingers slipped on the wet surface and he went sprawling.

The triplets laughed, their whips coiling and uncoiling as they moved closer.

"Help!" Leo scrambled to his feet, shouting to the nearby stores. "*Help!*"

No answer.

Rakkim pushed Leo into a small alcove, the doorway to a boarded-up holo shop, then took up a position in front of him. "Be ready to run . . . and don't look back."

"What am I, a baby?" said Leo.

Rakkim watched the triplets approach, taking their time. Sparks crackled from their whips. He felt calm. Eye of the hurricane. Waiting around as the storm clouds rolled in and no way to avoid it. He stepped out into the alley, eager to get started.

The triplets fanned out, wolf-packing.

Rakkim tap-danced for them, got a smile from one of the triplets, the one with the scar under his right eye. A winner. He pointed at scarface. "You get to die first."

Scarface's smile disappeared. Eyes hot now. He moved ahead of his two brothers.

Rakkim advanced in a half crouch. He kept his left arm up to protect his face, his right hand held the knife close—*like a bouquet of roses for your mama*, that's what his blade instructor at the academy used to say.

A shock whip flicked, missed, not even close. Another one right behind, slightly closer, but scarface held off, closing in. Another snap of the whip. Another. They thought they were herding him, but he moved right where he wanted to be, waiting for an opening. He lunged at scarface, retreated across the wet stones.

CRACK.

Rakkim flinched, the whip snapping an inch from his face, sparks crackling.

Scarface cawed.

Rakkim dodged right, just out of reach of the other two, feinted as the whips cracked around him, then charged scarface as he moved in to catch Rakkim from behind. The man's eyes widened as Rakkim slipped by him, driving the blade into his chest with a twist as he passed. In and out, fast but not fast enough. Rakkim bit his lips shut as a whip caught him across the back—the leather jacket offered some protection, but the pain wobbled his legs as he scuttled out of reach.

Scarface stayed standing, stayed there as the drizzle drifted down on his vacant expression, then fell to his knees, still holding the whip. Fell forward, sparks shooting out from under him.

Rakkim smelled burned hair in the rain.

One of the other triplets bent over scarface, tenderly turned him over. Blood spread over the stones. He looked up at Rakkim. "Fuck ibn-Azziz. I'm bringing you back in pieces."

Rakkim laughed. "Did you rehearse that line before you left for the office?"

"Relax, Jerry," said the other one. "Killing him isn't going to bring back Jimmy."

Jerry stood up. "Shut up, Johnny."

Rakkim hooted. "Jimmy, Johnny and Jerry? What are you, the three blind mice?"

"*Do* something," ordered Kissell, rain dripping off his nose.

Leo dashed from the alcove, blew past the bodyguard, splashing down the alley.

"Let him go," said Kissell. "This is the one we were sent for."

The two remaining triplets moved in, whips snaking, reckless now. Rakkim darted from side to side, stayed away from any solid strikes, but the glancing blows cut through his jacket and seared his flesh.

Rakkim charged, feinted at the last minute, came in low and caught one of the triplets behind the knee, sliced his femoral artery. The man fell screaming in the alley. His brother rushed Rakkim.

Rakkim backed up, stumbled on a patch of uneven stones and fell.

The last triplet charged, his whip biting into Rakkim, slashing his arm, his chest, just missed his face, so close the sparks burned his cheek.

The wounded triplet lay curled up holding his leg, bleeding out onto the stones.

Kissell kicked the dying triplet in the back. "Get *up!*" He went to kick him again when the third triplet's whip snaked out, wrapped around his neck, Kissell's eyes bulging.

The last triplet jerked his whip and Kissell's head went flying off his shoulders, bounced down the alley.

Rakkim tried to dodge as the last triplet came at him, but his legs were numb, his movements slow. Water streamed down his face as the triplet stood in front of him, whip sizzling. He flicked the whip, the tip grazing Rakkim's chin, a perfectly controlled cut.

"I'm going to burn off your ears first," said the last triplet. "Then your nose . . . your hands, your feet. I'll deliver you alive, but you're going to wish you were dead."

"Talk, talk, talk." Rakkim wiped rain from his eyes, blood too. He raised a crooked arm to protect his face, holding his blade close. "Go ahead . . . do something stupid."

The last triplet eased toward Rakkim, the whip sparking.

Rakkim had to force himself to maintain his grip on the blade. He blinked, saw movement behind the triplet, heard footsteps splashing.

The last triplet turned and was hit full in the face with a paving stone. Knocked backward, he lay unmoving, skull crushed.

Leo stood over the last triplet, breathing hard.

"You . . . you throw like a girl." Rakkim laughed, as his legs gave out, sent him sprawling. "Leo . . ." He held his hand out. "Help me up."

Leo stared down at the dead triplet.

"*Leo?*"

Leo looked like he was about to cry. "I . . . I never killed anyone before."

"Well . . . you picked a good time to start." Rakkim lay back on the cold stones. Rainwater eddied around his head.

CHAPTER 26

Lester Gravenholtz stared straight ahead as Malcolm Crews strutted across the stage of the grand amphitheater in Atlanta, posturing for the TV cameras. Crews was sermonizing his balls off, but Gravenholtz barely noticed, concentrating instead on not looking around for Karla Jean again. He about had a crick in his neck as it was. Enough was enough. You'd think no pretty girl had ever looked at him twice without being paid . . . which was pretty much the case, except for Baby, which was a whole nother story.

Gravenholtz shifted in the pew. Up until Baby gave him the look, he had been loyal to the Colonel, his strong right arm, and even if the Colonel held him back sometimes, gave him a talking to when Gravenholtz wanted to lay waste to the countryside, well, that was just the Colonel's gentility, his sense of Southern honor. No harm in that. The Colonel was fair and square, when most men in his position would have taken what they wanted with both hands. Besides, there were always plenty of badasses even the Colonel thought deserved killing, so Gravenholtz had plenty of room to work out his aggressions. Yeah, it had been some good times before Gravenholtz took up with Baby.

Gravenholtz glanced around . . . no Karla Jean. Fuck her. *Fuck* her.

Not that Baby hadn't been worth ruining his life over. He groaned thinking of her, and the old lady next to him scooted away from him. Seeing Baby in the morning light, those creamy curves . . . the sweetness of every inch of her . . . and that dirty mind . . . that had been what really sold him. He balled up the tract the ushers handed out, threw it on the floor. Over and done with. He might as well have been a tissue she blew her nose in,

f here." She had a shy smile, like she hadn't shown it to any-
n a long time. "I want you to take me home."
ravenholtz stood up, his ears burning.

Moseby slipped back into the truck, shut the door. Sweat
down his forehead, the faceplate of his radiation suit fogged
. He could see the Washington Monument through the
dshield, the white limestone gleaming in the sunshine, but
gerously canted. Still standing, though. They built things
ng back then.

He had tried talking with the zombies living on the outskirts
D.C. when he first arrived, tried to bribe them for maps that
arted the hot spots, but they were wary, seeing him for what he
s, an outsider looking for treasure they viewed as their own.
ing black didn't help either; those who talked with him didn't
ake his hand or invite him into their homes. Instead, they took
s money and gave him bad information and bad maps. After
ly three days of stumbling into unmarked hot spots, he had
ceeded his recommended roentgen count, was well into the
nger zone. Every minute he stayed here now risked further
liation poisoning.

He wished he could talk to Annabelle. Just hear her voice . . .
laugh.

Moseby cleared his throat, tasted metal. He plugged his suit
the truck's electrical system, turned up the air-conditioning.
suit was fine, but the truck he had borrowed from the
onel wasn't up to the job, its shielding stopgap and the air-
tion system inadequate. His own fault for cutting corners
of haste. Sarah had pleaded with him to wait to begin his
h, but Moseby had been fired up when she told him what
ould be looking for.

he cross . . . a piece of the cross where Jesus had been cru-
, a piece of the cross upon which he had shed his blood.
by had been a devout Muslim once . . . he had become an
more devout Christian since falling in love with Annabelle.

then tossed away. Oh, she acted like things were temporary, like any day now she'd show up in his bed and put him through his paces, but he knew better. He wasn't a fucking moron.

"I've been asked to tone down my rhetoric," said Crews, voice low, as though imparting a secret to the crowd and the millions watching him on television. "I've been advised, 'Pastor Crews, you best tone down your condemnation of Aztlán. Leave such things to the politicians, Pastor Crews, and tend to matters of God.'" The lights flashed off his pure white suit as he strode across the stage. "I've been told to tone down my defense of the Colonel, told to leave this good man to the tender mercies of those who know more than I do about"—he spat the word—"geopolitics." He stood under the hot lights, arms outstretched, martyred, slowly shaking his head. "And brothers and sisters to that I say . . ."

The crowd leaned forward.

"I say, God damn the politicians."

People in the crowd jumped to their feet, applauding.

"God damn the appeasers."

More people stood, raised their hands over their heads.

"God damn those who attempt to silence your pastor."

The crowd thundered their approval.

Crews was talking dangerous stuff. Last night Jinx Raynaud, the president's wife, had Crews perform a private healing on her son, warning him afterward that her husband wanted Crews to quit stirring the people up against Aztlán, give him time to work things out with the Mexicans. Crews told her he answered to God Almighty, not man.

You ask Gravenholtz, Crews didn't answer to God or man, but his approval ratings were over 70 percent and rising, which was a lot more than the president could say. It was just like Baby had predicted. The Old One was probably ready to buy her a solid gold island in the South Seas. Lot of good it did Graven-holtz. His job was to keep an eye on Crews, make sure he didn't go off track, and wait for the Old One to give him something important to do. Anything was better than this . . . sitting here night after night while the whole country went nuts for Malcolm Crews. The man in white. What a fucking joke.

The crowd finally sat down, let out a collective sigh. Crews wiped the sweat from his face with a white silk handkerchief, bent down and gave it to a little girl at the edge of the stage. You'd have thought he'd cured her cancer the way the crowd reacted.

Gravenholtz had to force himself not to look around again for Karla Jean. Man had to hang on to his pride. She said she'd be here tonight, but that was just a lie. Some excuse to get away from him. He felt his face blister up thinking about her. There had been some moments there when he actually thought she was interested in him. Not 'cause she wanted something from him, or because she was scared of him, but because she *saw* something in him . . . something nobody else did. Shit, something even he didn't really believe was there. Instead, she was just like the others. His hands twitched. Somebody was going to get hurt tonight. Somebody who had no idea what was coming his way.

A light touch on his shoulder. "Is this seat taken?"

Gravenholtz looked up into Karla Jean's eyes. "You're late."

"I . . . I was afraid."

"Afraid of what?"

"Are you going to scoot over, Lester? Or you want me to stand out here forever?"

Gravenholtz made room for her. Inhaled her perfume as she sat down, her long hair brushing against him. "Afraid of *what*? You got a problem with somebody, you let me—"

"*You're* the problem, Lester."

"Me?"

Karla Jean rested her hands in her lap, nestled among the folds of her pale yellow dress like a pair of white doves. She kept her eyes down. "I have feelings for you. First time . . . first time since my husband died. It's a little overwhelming."

Gravenholtz placed one of his hands over ___ out ___ completely.

"I don't want to be hurt," said Karla Jean.

"I'd never hurt you," said Gravenholtz.

"Men always say that."

"*I'm* saying that. I won't ever hurt you, and I w___ else hurt you either."

Karla Jean looked deep into his eyes. Leaned o___ cheek on his shoulder.

Gravenholtz felt a sense of peace that he had n___ fore. There had never been a moment like that wit___ a moment that he wasn't boiling over. Karla Jean s___ hand and he could hardly breathe.

"If I agreed to stay silent, who would talk about t___ burned to the ground in Corpus Christi?" asked Crew___ the president or the opposition leaders do more than p___ vice to this atrocity in the city named the body of Chris___

"No!" shouted the crowd, as Crews's image loome___ feet high on the Jumbotron.

"Two hundred and forty-seven good Christians incin___ a Sunday morning and yet the Aztlán ambassador is s___ to the White House for coffee and biscuits."

The United Nations had sent a peace envoy to A___ to work things out between the president and the Az___ sador.

"Two hundred and forty-seven men, women a___ roasted alive while they prayed to God, and now . . ___ says, hey, it's not our fault. It wasn't a sanctioned m___ even though a team of Aztlán commandos carried ___ stalked the boards, hands flying. "Not our fault, ___ was a single rogue officer. One bad apple."

People wept, shouted for vengeance, stamping ___

"Anyone here believe that? Anyone here ___ Anyone?"

Karla Jean leaned close to Gravenholtz. "L___

The chance to actually find a piece of the true cross in the dead city, to bring it forth into the sunlight . . . Sarah didn't have to convince him.

Moseby leaned back in his seat as the truck's electrical system boosted his suit's air-conditioning. A breeze blew scraps of paper down the street, tumbling end over end like ghosts. He was never going to get this place out of his mind.

Exploring the sunken city of New Orleans should have prepared him for anything. He had dived among the dead in the French Quarter and the surrounding districts for years, sometimes pushing them aside to gain entrance to a hotel or storefront, dead fingers waving . . . but this place . . . D.C. spooked him. The waters that had covered New Orleans on one dark night provided a screen for the emotions somehow; the soft green light, the brightly colored fish and sprouting sea grass gave a certain continuity. The dead of New Orleans rested among *living* things. Here . . . the grand buildings lay unchanged, frozen at the moment of destruction. There was no life in D.C. The dead were alone.

Last night Moseby had sat in his truck, exhausted, breathing in the stink of his self-contained suit. He had dozed off for a few minutes, awoke disoriented, the monuments gleaming in the moonlight, perfect as a tourist snapshot, and Moseby had wanted to tear off his suit and wander the empty boulevard, go wading in the Tidal Basin and wash himself clean. He had actually reached for the toggle switches on his suit before he caught himself, and the recognition of what he had almost done shook him, made him put the truck in gear and peel off down the street. He raced along for a dozen blocks, knocking smaller vehicles aside, before he regained control of himself.

Moseby sat up. Checked his gauges. Started the engine, the noise and vibration reassuring somehow. He needed to get out of here *now*. Get out of this suit. He'd have to contact Sarah, risky or not, and tell her he had rushed things. Maybe she could find some way to get him a better vehicle, fully shielded, maybe get him some better maps too. Knowing her, she was probably already working on it. The cross was worth dying for, definitely, but Moseby had to stay alive long enough to find it first.

"Thanks for parking down the street," whispered Karla Jean as they stood on the doorstep of her small house. "I've got nosy neighbors."

Gravenholtz glanced around. Hardly any lights on in the surrounding houses. No one on the street. The grass in the yards was overgrown, bikes rusting in the weeds.

Karla Jean unlocked the door, hand trembling. "I . . . I feel like such a whore."

Gravenholtz stepped inside after her, closed the door. It smelled clean . . . like she did. Just a single light on in the tiny kitchen. One room, a cast-iron bed in the corner. Wildflowers stuck in a cut-down Coke bottle on the nightstand. Photo-holo display facing the bed, switched off now.

"Do you think this is wrong, Lester? I don't want to ruin things between us."

"No . . . what we're doing is right. We don't gain nothing by waiting."

"That's . . . that's what I told myself." She stood on her tiptoes to kiss him.

Her lips were soft against him, and Gravenholtz felt like he was twelve years old again, inexperienced, uncertain and scared at the wonder of it all. He put his arms around her, surprised at how slender she was, her body taut against him.

"We . . . we don't have to hurry," he gasped. "Been a while for me."

"I can't believe that. A man like you . . ."

"No, been a *long* while since I was with anyone like you. Maybe even never."

"You're just flattering me, Lester Gravenholtz, and you don't have to—"

"I mean it."

Karla Jean stared at him in the dim light. "I believe you." She touched his face with her small, slender hands, felt him flinch. "What is it?"

"I don't like you eyeballing me . . . I'm ugly."

She slapped his chest. "You most certainly are not."

Gravenholtz shook his head. "I got a face like a pig's ass."

"You're strong-looking. *Determined.* Not like the weaklings and pretty boys I see every day. You're a man who knows what he wants and is not about to let anyone stop him. What woman wouldn't be attracted to that?"

Gravenholtz nodded, not trusting himself to speak.

"You want a drink?" said Karla Jean. "I got beer . . . bourbon—"

"Do *you* need a drink?"

"No." Her eyes were certain. "No, Lester, I don't."

"Me neither."

She kissed him again, lightly brushed her lips against his, and there was nothing else in the world but her at this moment, no one but the two of them in this little house on the edge of town, no past, no future . . . just now.

Karla Jean stepped away from him, trailing a hand across him as she moved away, as though she couldn't bear to part. "Take off your clothes," she said softly.

Gravenholtz blinked.

She unbuttoned the top button of her dress. "Please?"

Gravenholtz tried to speak. It was easier with a hooker. You paid them and did what you wanted and then you left. Even easier when you raped a random woman . . . not because you didn't have to pay—Gravenholtz didn't care about money—but the passion of the act . . . their rage and disgust made it better. This, though . . . when you cared about the woman, when she cared about you . . . there was *so* much to lose.

"Please, Lester." Her fingers toyed with the next button. "I have to see you. Really see you." Her lower lip trembled. "My parts . . . my female parts are tiny as the rest of me. I got to make sure you don't hurt me."

"I told you . . . I'd die before I hurt you."

Karla Jean sat on the bed. "I won't ask you again."

Gravenholtz kicked off his boots. Peeled off his pants and underwear, left them in a heap. He pulled off his shirt without unbuttoning it, stood there before her naked. He was breathing so hard you would have thought he had run a race.

Karla Jean stared at him from the bed.

"What? You look surprised."

"I am a little." Karla Jean pulled a pistol out from under her pillow. Centered it on his chest. "I thought you'd have on some bulletproof vest or something. I heard you been shot a hundred times and never died. Everyone said you had some kind of . . . special protection." She pulled back the hammer of the gun. "I guess you left it at home tonight."

Gravenholtz covered his penis with both hands.

"I couldn't believe it when I saw you in church. I thought, Just maybe there *is* a God."

She switched on the photo display with a remote. An image appeared of Karla Jean in a white wedding dress, a skinny young man in a badly fitting suit beside her. The young man was looking at her with the same expression Gravenholtz had got when he'd thought about Karla Jean these last few days—like how did he get so lucky? And maybe . . . maybe everything that had gone before could change now. Karla Jean and the young man were dancing inside a small church now, round and round, dizzy with a secret joy.

"You recognize him now?" said Karla Jean.

"Should I?"

"I guess you killed too many men to remember them all. Well, I remember him. His name was Bryce Lee Johnson and you killed him three years ago outside of Harrisburg. He was a gunsmith, traveling the back roads to save money so we could start a family. Way I heard it, you wanted his personal weapon, the one he used to show off the quality of his work, and he didn't want to sell it. So you snapped his neck like a chicken bone and tossed him aside."

Gravenholtz still didn't remember him, but he remembered the gun, a beautiful .41-caliber Colt with an etched barrel, silver inlays and a soft trigger pull.

The pistol never wavered. "It's coming back to you now, isn't it?"

"Karla Jean . . . I'm sorry about your husband."

"I bet you are."

"Shooting me won't bring him back. If you can forgive me, maybe the two of us—"

"The two of us?" She stepped closer, snarling. "The *two* of us?" She fired the pistol and he staggered backward, feeling like he had been punched in the heart. She advanced, fired again and again and again, each shot knocking the breath out of him, the house echoing with the sound.

She fired again, just inches from him, and Gravenholtz saw her gasp, put her hand to her neck. In the dimness, something black was leaking through her fingers.

"Karla Jean?"

She wobbled, sat down heavily.

Gravenholtz bent down beside her, moved her hand and clamped his own over the wound. A bullet fragment had ricocheted off his subdural body armor and nicked her carotid artery.

She clutched at his bloody shirt. "Why . . . why didn't you die?"

"Don't talk." Gravenholtz tried to apply pressure on the artery, but his hand was slippery.

"I *shot* you. You should . . . you should be dead."

"You didn't know what you were doing. You were just angry, that's all."

Her eyes looked sleepy.

"Please . . . please don't go," said Gravenholtz, losing his grip on her neck. Her body jerked, blood spurting. "I . . . I forgive you, Karla Jean."

She turned her head away.

Gravenholtz thought she was trying to avoid looking at him, then realized she didn't even know he was there anymore. She was trying to get one last glimpse of her husband.

CHAPTER 27

Rakkim gritted his teeth as Marie Colarusso cleaned his wounds. He lay on a white sheet covering the sofa in their living room, his leather jacket in bloody tatters on the floor. "It's not as bad as it looks."

"It's bad enough." Marie, a middle-aged woman with a doughy middle and gray roots showing in her reddish hair, reached for a piece of fresh gauze. "I'm so tired of tough guys."

"You're lucky Leo called me," said Colarusso, his uniform unbuttoned. "Got me on my private number . . ." The chief of detectives glanced at Leo. "Someday you're going to have to tell me how you did that."

"You wouldn't understand," said Leo.

Colarusso belched into his meaty fist. "He always like this?" he said to Rakkim.

"Pretty much," said Rakkim. "You should have seen him in the Belt. Half the folks thought he was retarded, the other half wanted to hit him with something."

"Sit still," ordered Marie, bending over the gash in his side. She tenderly dabbed at the wound. "Big brave Fedayeen," she snorted.

"You keep up this attitude, I'm not bringing you any more of my business, Marie," said Rakkim.

"Figured I better bring you here instead of a hospital," said Colarusso. "Too many questions, and too much paperwork there. Four dead men, one with his head cut clean off . . ." He shook his head. "Never a cop around when you need one."

"Thanks, Anthony," said Rakkim.

"What about me?" said Leo. "I saved your life."

Rakkim winced, shifted slightly on the couch. "Thank you, Leo."

"You're welcome." Leo grinned. "I could get used to this hero stuff."

Colarusso rolled his eyes. "Kid brains a miscreant and wants a medal."

"You told me the triplets were as dangerous as anybody in the city," said Marie, still bent over Rakkim. "You said they were implicated in dozens of murders."

"Well . . . yes," said Colarusso.

"Killed even Fedayeen, that's what you said." Marie sprayed antibiotic on the open cuts.

Colarusso pretended not to hear.

"So that would indicate to me that if this young man wants a medal for *braining* one of the triplets, he certainly deserves one." Marie pursed her lips. "Anthony?"

Colarusso walked over to where Leo waited. He moistened his thumb, quickly made the sign of the cross on Leo's forehead. "Happy now?"

"*No.*" Leo wiped his forehead. "That's disgusting. What *is* it with you people?"

"Who's hungry?" Maryellen, one of the Colarusso girls, stood in the doorway with a plate of sandwiches. She was curvy like her mother, with pale white skin and sandy hair. "I made the roast beef with horseradish, just like you asked for, Leo."

Leo took three of them.

"A healthy appetite is a sign of virility," said Marie.

"Don't get any ideas, Marie," said Colarusso.

Marie checked Rakkim's body, crisscrossed with welts and cuts. "I still think you should let me stitch you up. Some of those are *deep.*"

"Just the zip clamps are fine," said Rakkim. "They'll close up by tomorrow."

Marie shook her head. "Anthony Junior heals overnight too. Now, at least. Those Fedayeen injections . . . I worry about what they'll do to him in twenty or thirty years. Give him cancer or something."

"Don't worry, most Fedayeen don't live that long," said Rakkim.

"Well, I'm glad Anthony Junior is done with it," huffed Marie. "I thought having a Fedayeen in the family would bring more suitors for the girls, but—"

"*Mother*," said Maryellen.

"I'm . . . I'm engaged, Mrs. Colarusso." Leo looked at Maryellen. "Sorry."

"No skin off my nose." Maryellen set down the plate of sandwiches with a clatter.

Leo watched her hips as she left.

"Did you call Sarah?" asked Rakkim.

"She's on her way now, her and the boy," said Colarusso.

Rakkim sat up on the sofa, held his side. "It's *late*, Anthony."

"You try talking Sarah out of something she wants to do," said Colarusso. "I sent an unmarked car for them. The detective's a good Catholic, knows to keep his trap shut. I'll take you all back home when you're ready to travel."

"I'm ready now," said Rakkim.

Marie gathered up her first aid supplies. "I'll leave you men to your shop talk. Leo, if you want to come into the kitchen, Maryellen's got a fresh cherry pie just aching to be cut."

Amir looked up from the holographic re-creation of the sweeping cavalry attack of the Northern Alliance fighters and U.S. Special Forces that had crushed the Taliban in 2001. "Are you going to tell me what is gnawing at you?"

Hussein glared at him, unmoving in the evening.

Amir went back to the battle display, repositioning the Allied forces, light infantry, armed with swords and rifles. As always, his attention was drawn to American CIA agent Mike Spann, who fought on horseback beside the Northern Alliance as they charged dug-in Taliban equipped with Russian T-55 tanks and mortars. Amir watched as the Taliban forces fled, leaving their weapons behind. Spann was a kaffir, but he was a warrior above all else, a warrior who had died in battle for what he believed in, died in combat against great odds, and Amir admired him.

"You were right, Amir. Something does eat at me." Hussein sat cross-legged in the garden at the rear of his villa, an iron-haired Fedayeen, one of the heroes of the war against the Belt. The empty left sleeve of his uniform was folded back to his shoulder, his posture rigid. "I have painful news."

The holographic display disappeared with a wave of Amir's hand.

"Your father . . . your father has made a secret recording to be released only in the event of his death," said Hussein. "The Old One used all his wiles to get a copy."

Amir waited. For Hussein, the most merciless of the early Fedayeen commanders, to be so shaken . . .

"Yes." Hussein turned his gaze on the orange and yellow koi gliding slowly back and forth in the pond beside them. Metallic green flies darted across the surface of the water. He looked at Amir. "Your father has passed you over."

Amir didn't react. He already knew the answer but he asked the question anyway. "Who has my father favored over me?"

"Rakkim."

Amir nodded.

"So much for your hope that you can convince your father to join us."

Amir felt the ache in his heart radiating out to the rest of him.

"You know what you're going to have to do, sooner or later." Hussein gripped his shoulder, squeezed. "I'm sorry."

Amir looked past Hussein, past the high walls of his villa, past the years. . . . He was a child again, no more than five or six, walking beside his father, and everyone they passed lowered their eyes, blessed his father, feared him. Amir had slipped his hand into his father's as they walked, taking in his strength, promising himself that he would be just like him when he grew up. His father had seemed so tall in those days, his skin a deep black, pure black, his voice like thunder—Amir had grown even taller than his father, but in his mind he was always reaching up for his father's hand.

"Amir? Have you not been listening?" said Hussein. "I said, the Old One says you must take action to minimize the damage of your father's last request."

"Tell our master not to worry," said Amir. "I'll gladly kill Rakkim."

"No," said Hussein. "That has been expressly forbidden."

"Does our master *also* favor Rakkim over me?"

"Lower your voice," said Hussein. "I am not privy to our master's deepest thoughts, I am only telling you what he has told me. He wants Rakkim alive."

"Then what am I to do?"

"Your father's statement is a *request* for his successor, and a request only." Hussein snatched a fly out of the air with his good hand, shook it back and forth in his fist. "Trust me, young one, the dead do not have nearly the authority they think." He released the fly, tossed it toward the pond, the insect disoriented, its flight erratic. A golden koi leaped high and snapped it up.

Colarusso watched Leo follow Marie out, then sat down on the sofa next to Rakkim. "Interesting playmates you got, troop. Leo said it was ibn-Azziz sent the triplets, which is bad enough, but I recognized the fella got his head chopped off—that's Senator Chambers's bodyguard."

"Ibn-Azziz had his heart set on Chambers being defense secretary," said Rakkim, "but it's the Old One who's pulling the strings."

"You know that for sure?"

"Chambers told me."

"I bet that was an interesting conversation," said Colarusso.

"It would have been more interesting if Chambers knew who suggested his name to the president," said Rakkim.

"President gets lots of advice," said Colarusso.

"He only listened to one person in this case," said Rakkim.

"You're certain Chambers didn't know?" said Colarusso.

"I'm certain."

"Yeah, got to believe a man with his pecker in the wind . . ." Colarusso pressed his finger to his earlobe, listening. "When?" He nodded. "Who's on-scene?" He looked at Rakkim. "Keep me posted. I'll expect a full report in the morning." He released the com-link set to his ear. "Senator Chambers was found dead at his country house an hour ago. Looks like suicide, which is bullshit, of course."

"What about his family?"

"They're safe. On holiday, according to the servants. Grand Canyon." Colarusso picked at a tooth with his pinkie nail, wiped it on his necktie. "Always wanted to go to the Grand Canyon. Probably should do it sooner rather than later, before it's part of Aztlán."

Rakkim heard a car coming down the street.

A few seconds later, Colarusso heard it too. He glanced at the security screen above the fireplace, saw a car pull up out front.

"Thanks again, Anthony."

"No problem, troop." Colarusso watched Sarah and a plain-clothes cop walking up the front drive, Sarah carrying Michael in her arms. "How soon until you leave for New Fallujah?"

"You can read minds now?"

Colarusso shrugged. "Just basic police work. You can't kill the Old One; you don't even know where he is. So you'll have to settle for killing ibn-Azziz, right?" He lumbered to the front door. "Besides, maybe ibn-Azziz knows who put the bug in the president's ear." He looked at Rakkim. "So, when are you leaving?"

"Tomorrow."

Colarusso opened the door. "Sarah, come on in. You look beautiful. Who's that big boy with you?"

CHAPTER 28

The Old One had a cold. He sat in an oceanside cabana in Miami, watching the young couple playing on the sand with their toddler, and he hated them for their smooth, healthy pinkness. He wanted to drown the three of them in the shallows, hold their heads under while they thrashed, hold them under until their mouths stopped moving.

The Old One sneezed. The *worst* possible time to catch something. Ibrahim would be waiting for him inside the suite, wanting to watch the festivities in the Gulf with him, but the Old One didn't want to move. He wrapped his thick terry-cloth robe around himself, pulled the hood lower. The sun beat down on the cabana as he shivered, feeling ice form in his marrow. For the first time in decades, the Old One was sick . . . and the sickness was a sign of the change that had befallen him.

When his personal physician had first told him that he was dying, the Old One had been stoic at first, then oddly elated, toying with his newfound mortality, the delicious friction of risk. It didn't last. He felt every passing day, every waning moment as a subtraction, a loss. After all these years to finally be this close to success, and have it taken from him . . .

The Old One coughed, set off a rattling in his chest. He gently touched his cheek, felt the roughness where the shotgun blast at Malcolm Crews's mansion had scorched his skin. That pimply kaffir had almost killed him, ended his life in that overheated, run-down mansion with flies buzzing against the screens and garbage strewn on the lawn. So close to death . . . as though Allah had taunted him, given him a reminder of the muddy end men came to. The Old One tasted mucus in his mouth, a slimy lozenge that disgusted him.

The toddler in her frilly yellow bathing suit frolicked along the tideline, splashing as the waves trickled toward her. Her hair was as yellow as her bathing suit, a mass of tight curls like a sunflower. Her whole life lay before her, all those endless possibilities, while the Old One's life was winding down. Every breath she took, every joyous coo and tumble, was an insult to him.

The Old One rubbed his arms, trying to bring the blood to the surface, to get warm. It didn't help. He had caught the cold right after the near miss at Crews's mansion. The Old One had risked death before, dozens of times, but this was different. None of those other brushes with death had frightened him. If anything they had affirmed his identity as Allah's chosen one, the Mahdi. All gone now. Catching a cold, a *common* cold, was just a harbinger of things to come. Worse was on the way, age and infirmity riding toward him across the sands, a pale rider urging his mount on, faster, faster, faster. The Old One felt his cells slowly breaking down, toxins building up, his luck running out.

A dozen high-altitude helicopters hovered to the south, sculpting clouds with their ion beams. Beachcombers pointed and the Old One watched too—part of the appeal of cloud sculpting was not just the skill of the pilots, but trying to figure out what was being created. Words and symbols were easy, but this was much more ambitious. A day with barely any breeze helped, but still, there was an enormous amount of clouds being put to use. The helicopters zipped about, working in tandem, faster now, the object slowly taking shape. Color was added, the seeded particles activated in various parts of the cloud, a vast black cloud with silver and red streaks . . . all of it in slow motion as the helicopters dipped and soared around it.

The Old One turned, hearing the Ethiopian girl turn over in the bed at the rear of the cabana. A bare breast peeked out of the sheets as she dozed, languid in the heat, beads of perspiration on her forehead. Her mouth opened slightly and he knew that were he to kiss her, she would taste like honey. He had warmed himself with her before, clung to her, let her share her heat with him . . . but she had not stirred him, and though soaked with sweat, his own chill had prevailed. He watched her sleep until he lost track of time, imagining himself inside her, warm and safe . . . forever young.

His earpiece tingled, doubtless Ibrahim eagerly awaiting the events in the Gulf. The Old One plucked it out of his ear, threw it into the corner.

He huddled in his robe, tried to take comfort in the fact that Malcolm Crews was doing well in the Belt, even better than Baby had anticipated. The Old One and she watched Crews's television show every day, critiquing his performance, gauging the reactions of the crowd, both in the audience and across the Belt. Crews knew how to speak the lingo of the Belt, not just the proper words and phrases, but more important, the *emotional* language, the hopes and fears of that mass of unbelievers. Crews would be crucial to the mass conversion that was coming, preparing the ground for the Old One.

Ibrahim watched Crews only when the Old One insisted. Jealous of Baby usurping his role as chief advisor, Ibrahim dismissed the idea of converting the Christians, claimed it was impossible other than through brute force. The Old One knew better. The threat of the sword worked wonders among atheists, weaklings who believed only in this day, this moment, but Christians were *faithful*. They had merely embraced a false faith. They had confused Jesus for God. Once shown the true face of Allah, they would become his most loyal and ferocious followers. The path to the Caliphate started in the former United States, and the Belt citizens would be his shock troops to convert the rest of the world.

The Old One fought back a cough. Yes, he had ample reason to be pleased. Things were moving rapidly now, hurried on by his own increasing desperation. Today's action in the Gulf would be a big step. Credit Ibrahim with the planning and execution of the action, as he would rightly be the first to claim.

The Old One coughed, kept coughing until there were tears

in his eyes. Oh, the loss of Senator Chambers's defense appointment had been vexing, and he didn't need that pinched ascetic ibn-Azziz to tell him Rakkim was responsible. Idiot, who *else* could it be? The method of Chambers's undoing, parading him naked through the streets . . . The Old One smiled. Most men would simply have murdered Chambers, but Rakkim . . . the youngster loved his little jokes, and the Old One appreciated playfulness now more than ever. That was one of the reasons he had been so drawn to Baby. She was competent and creative and cold-blooded . . . but, even more, the girl *enjoyed* herself, which was more than he could say for Ibrahim, always fussing and worrying.

He closed his eyes, swallowed the bile brought up by his coughing spasm. Yes, there were many reasons to give thanks to Allah, but still . . . after all his efforts, all the many years, the Old One was not going to live to see the final resolution of his plans. That would fall to Ibrahim, or Baby, or someone else Allah deemed more worthy to carry the Caliphate forward. The Old One's triumph left a bitter taste.

Applause interrupted his reverie. The young family stood on the sand looking up, clapping their hands wildly.

The Old One didn't know how much time had elapsed, but the cloud sculpture was finished, at least enough of it for the beachcombers to recognize what it was: the new Brazilian luxury car, the Rio D. The black cloud car was long and sleek, with silver chrome trim, red and leather inside, green accents, a perfect simulation, and there . . . The Old One leaned forward, staring. The wheels of the Rio D were actually *moving*, going round and round over the deep blue sea. He was tempted to wake the Ethiopian girl and show her, but better she slept on. Perhaps later he would have use for her.

The Old One heard footsteps, turned and saw Ibrahim run up to the entrance to the cabana, stopping before the one-way security curtain. He wore a dark three-piece suit and lace-up shoes.

"F-F-Father."

The Old One shivered, returned his attention to the young family. The little girl was dragging a pail behind her . . . one of the waves caught her, filled the pail, the weight of it knocking her over. Her father pulled her into his arms, the little girl crouping up seawater.

"*Father?* It is nearly time."

The Old One opened the security curtain and Ibrahim scurried inside.

Ibrahim looked at the blank wallscreen. "You're not watching?"

The Old One shivered, covered it with a stretch. It would not do to show weakness in front of Ibrahim. "Go ahead."

Ibrahim rushed over, switched on the screen. He scrolled through the remote until the image of a packed ballroom came on, people dancing.

"Is the signal properly banked?" said the Old One.

"No need for security masking, Father," said Ibrahim, the screen showing a vast display of cut fruit, lobster and fresh fish, mounds of caviar and a whole suckling pig with an apple in its filthy mouth. "The signal is beamed from the Aztlán Board of Tourism channel, millions of people are watching."

"What's the name of the liner? The *Yucatán Queen?*"

"*Yucatán Princess*, Father."

"You vetted the crew of the speedboats? Made sure the registration is in order?"

"*Yes*, Father. I have attended to everything. Have I ever disappointed—?"

"Knockety-knock!"

The Old One turned, saw Baby standing outside the security curtain in a pale green sundress.

"Send her *away*, Father."

The Old One touched a button and Baby strolled inside, her bare feet bringing in sand. Her toes were painted bright pink, like the inside of a conch shell.

Baby glanced at the screen. "What are you boys up to?"

"It's none of your concern," said Ibrahim.

"Ibrahim has instituted a mission in the Gulf," said the Old One. "It's about to come to fruition."

Baby stared at the screen, saw a remote shot of the luxury liner churning across a flat blue sea, happy people on deck waving to the camera. "That's real pretty, but it doesn't seem like all that much, to me."

"I'm sure it doesn't," said Ibrahim.

The Ethiopian girl raised herself up on one elbow, rubbed her eyes.

"Go back to sleep," said the Old One, addressing her in her native tongue.

The Ethiopian girl rolled over, the sheet slipping down around her hips, already snoring.

"You don't look so good, Daddy," said Baby. "You okay?"

"I'm fine."

"Well, I got something here that's gonna make you feel a whole lot better." Baby held up a thumb drive to the Old One. "Let me turn that thing off, and I'll show—"

"Don't you *dare*, woman," Ibrahim said quietly.

"Wait your turn, Baby," said the Old One. "Besides, I think you're going to enjoy the show that Ibrahim has prepared for us."

"For *you*, Father," said Ibrahim. "My efforts are all on your behalf."

Baby dragged a chair next to the Old One, sat down beside him as the tourism channel showed people gambling in the luxury liner's casino, bent over the roulette and craps tables. She looked at Ibrahim, sniffed. "Least you could do is serve popcorn."

CHAPTER 29

Mustafa bin-Siq leaned against the railing of the *Yucatán Princess*, watching the sunset over the Gulf, the water so warm you expected the sun to sizzle as it settled in. A poetic image for an engineer who wrote poetry and painted watercolors in his spare time, which, alas, there had been little of lately. Through the deck vibrations, he felt the port engine labor slightly, then smooth out. First assistant engineer Zapato should look into that, make a few adjustments to the fuel flow . . . bin-Siq stopped himself, half closed his eyes. No, there would be no need for that now.

"Hey, Paulo, can I get you some coffee?"

Bin-Siq jerked. He usually had this spot on the upper deck by himself, the passengers congregating on the lower decks where the bars and discos were.

The steward shifted, the gold buttons on his white jacket catching the sunset. "Didn't mean to startle you . . . sir."

Juan . . . that was the steward's name. Juan Tesca, a young man from Sinaloa, who always had his head in a book when he wasn't working. "Not your fault. I was just thinking."

The *Yucatán Princess* was one of a string of small Aztlán cruise liners that regularly sailed the Mexican Gulf Coast, with stops in Tampico, Havana, St. Petersburg, New Orleans and Matamoros. When the second assistant engineer got sick in Havana, as the Old One had planned, bin-Siq had presented his credentials and been hired. For the duration of the voyage, he was Paulo Maradona, an Argentinean engineer between ships.

"Nice, huh?" said the steward, nodding at the sunset. "Private too, I like that. You hear about tomorrow?"

"No."

"Captain called off the stop at New Orleans," said the steward. "Said it was too dangerous considering the noise the Belt's making about that church bombing in Texas. Lot of the passengers were plenty pissed off. They were hoping to dive the ruins, maybe come back with a hood ornament from a Cadillac or a string of Mardi Gras beads. They're talking about demanding a refund."

"Not our problem, is it?"

"Guess not."

Bin-Siq glanced at his watch. "You probably should get back to your duties."

"So . . . yes or no?" said the steward.

"Yes or no *what*?"

"Can I get you some coffee?"

"No . . . no, thank you."

"I guess you don't want to be kept awake."

Bin-Siq smiled. "I intend to sleep like a baby, no matter what."

"Iron constitution, huh? Okay, I can see you want to be left alone. Adios, Paulo."

"Adios, Juan." Bin-Siq watched the young man descend the metal stairs, and thought of the cubist painting by that Frenchman, "Nude Descending a Spiral Staircase," where the kinetic movement of the nude woman was captured in one static image. The painting was, of course, un-Islamic, but he admired it nonetheless, the mechanical sensuality, so cold and austere and elegant.

Bin-Siq turned back to the sea. Engineering had in some ways been a poor career choice, but the Old One evidently had need of a marine engineer, and that was that. Not that such a thing had ever been articulated to him by the Old One; he had only met the Mahdi once, as a boy of ten, treasuring the memory of the man's even gaze resting upon him. Not a word passed between them. Twenty years later, his time to serve had arrived.

Three weeks ago he had gotten a call while on a freighter en route to Manila, a voice saying at the first port he was to leave for Havana and wait. Bin-Siq had not hesitated. There was no one to say good-bye to. He had lived a quiet life at sea, a life of solitary prayer, biding his time with his work and his books . . . and his watercolors. Like Juan, the steward, he too found solace in the quiet of the printed page, avoiding the clamor of the holos, and the crudeness of conversation with his fellow sailors. So he had gone to Havana and done as the voice on the phone had directed him. He had waited.

Spider lay on a lounge chair on the flat roof of his house, bare-chested, basking in the sun. Sarah sat on a chair beside him.

"Why would Moseby do such a foolish thing?" said Spider.

"He's a *finder*," said Sarah, shading her eyes with her hand. "He spent a few days questioning the locals in zombie country, got nowhere and decided to go into D.C. and look for the cross himself. I should have known he'd do something like that."

"It's not your fault," said Spider.

"I sent him on the mission," said Sarah.

"And he *chose* to go," said Spider, eyes closed, his chest and shoulders covered with silky gray hair. "Are you so all-powerful that no one can refuse your requests?"

"I wish," said Sarah.

Spider didn't react. "What's Moseby's condition?"

"Mild radiation poisoning, from what I can determine. He's taking the standard drug regime to reduce the effects, but—"

"Was there a malfunction in his rad suit?"

"No. Evidently one of the zombies gave him a map of the city with the hot spots mislabeled."

"That was to be expected." Spider sighed in the heat, his eyes still closed.

"Rakkim's going to have to go help him," said Sarah.

"You always intended to do that. Do you think me a fool?"

"Yes, but . . . I had hoped that Leo might have narrowed the search grid first."

Spider opened one eye, stared at her. "Tell Moseby to stay where he is. Tell him to *wait*. Give Leo more time. As soon as he comes back from Las Vegas—"

"You're letting him go?"

"Leo . . . Leo is beyond restraint. Smart as he is, he still seeks the approval of supposed wise men. The opportunity to address the International Pure Math Symposium is just too tempting. I told him he'll be disappointed, but he has to find out for himself."

"How is he getting there?"

"Oh, you know Leo." Spider tickled his hairy belly, his white skin pink now. "He hacked into the national travel database, created a fake history for himself—he'll pass through border control at the airport without a second look." He turned his face to the sun. "Mullah Cushing may have a more difficult time on his next trip abroad. Leo made some . . . additions to the mullah's security profile." He smiled again. "Evidently the good mullah is suspected of having a hidden pocket in his small intestine where he hides datachips for his Jewish overlords."

Sarah looked across the city. Defense blimps floated thickly around the presidential palace, the Fedayeen on high alert, but daily life went on in the capital as always. The monorail ran on time, the freeways were crowded and *Temptations of a Young Muslim* was still the most popular television show.

"You're not going to wait for Leo to come back, are you?" said Spider.

"We can't wait."

"Do you really want Rakkim barreling around D.C. with no idea where he's going?"

"Moseby might not be able to get a straight answer out of the zombies, but Rikki has a different way of asking questions," said Sarah. "He can get at the truth just talking and skipping rocks into a lake. I've seen him do it."

Spider rose up on one elbow. "I hope you know what you're doing."

Sarah closed her eyes. She refused to show her own doubts to Spider or anyone else.

In spite of all his spiritual preparations, there had been a moment of doubt as bin-Siq boarded the *Yucatán Princess*, a moment when he wondered what would have happened if he had turned and walked away, lost himself in the city, the maze of flesh . . . but bin-Siq had done his duty. Soon he would earn the blessings of Allah.

The sun had sunk lower when he saw the first dot on the horizon, first one then another, coming straight out of the setting sun. The lookouts on the com deck would be blinking behind their binoculars. Bin-Siq felt a delicious anticipation from the soles of his feet to the crown of his head, an effervescence, like bubbles rising through cold, clear water.

He leaned forward over the railing as the dots slowly neared, his fingers tapping on the railing in delight. Such a long time to have waited. There had been times lying in his bunk, surrounded by tons of steel and infidels, that he had almost smothered in doubt, but he had stayed true. He had remained faithful. Now . . .

Two speedboats . . . moving very fast . . . He squinted . . . could it be? Yes . . . bin-Siq clapped his hands in delight. The boats each towed a water-skier behind them, the tow ropes invisible . . . it looked as though the skiers were carried forward by wings of desire.

The *Yucatán Princess* made a minor course correction, and the speedboats kept pace.

In the sunset, the Gulf seemed ablaze, the two boats shooting across the flames toward the cruise liner. Down below, bin-Siq could see the tourists crowding the rail, pointing at the approaching speedboats. Their voices rose, excited, not in any way concerned—they were ten miles from land, the Belt a mere shadow in the distance. Surely this was some entertainment the company had planned for them, some small compensation for the cancellation of their New Orleans dive.

The captain's voice boomed over the loudspeakers, warning off the boats both in Spanish and in English.

One of the water-skiers waved and the crowd on deck cheered.

The captain would be on the radio now, alerting his superiors in Puerto Madero, asking for guidance.

Bin-Siq inhaled deeply, drew in the clean salt air. He felt himself growing lighter and more diaphanous by the moment. Were Juan here he could look right through him now.

The .50-caliber machine guns on the foredeck opened up, fired a warning burst near one of the boats. The crowd of tourists went silent for a moment . . . then cheered even louder.

The two speedboats came directly at the *Yucatán Princess* now, full speed. The water-skiers each unfurled the flag of the Belt, the banners snapping in the reddening glow.

The crowd lowered their voices, retreated back from the rail, hurrying inside.

The machine guns fired. Tore up the water. The crew were unused to anything other than simulations, and the speedboats zigzagged now, made themselves hard targets.

Bin-Siq had shaved his head before boarding the *Yucatán Princess* in Havana. This morning he had shaved his body completely, made himself presentable to enter Paradise.

The speedboats closed in, engines roaring. Close enough now that bin-Siq could almost make out faces. He wondered how long those men had waited to hear the call from the Old One, telling them their time had come.

The machine guns swept across the water, intersected one of the boats.

The explosion rocked the *Yucatán Princess*, sent debris from the speedboat skyward.

Screams echoed from below and bin-Siq himself cried out.

Each of the speedboats was packed with TNT, enough to

cripple the *Yucatán Princess* but not sink her. Any more weight would have made the boats sluggish. No, the job of sinking the *Yucatán Princess* was left to bin-Siq. His luggage contained fifty pounds of plastic explosive. On his shift early this morning, he had formed the explosive between the bulkhead and the main fuel tanks, then attached a radio receiver to the detonator.

The other speedboat hurtled forward, aimed directly midship.

Bin-Siq took the small transmitter out of his pocket.

The machine gun fired frantically at the remaining speedboat, which was less than fifty yards away now, scudding over the waves.

The Belt speedboats would be blamed for the destruction of the *Yucatán Princess*; any investigation would identify the men responsible and doubtless there would be some connection to the authorities in Atlanta.

Bin-Siq held the detonator as the speedboat roared ever closer. He thought of his watercolors carefully taped to the wall of his cabin—seascapes, birds in flight, sunrise on the waves and a storm on the horizon. He didn't have much talent but he loved the softness of the images, the gentle gradations of color. They soothed him in the long years of waiting. Sad to think that all his work would be lost now.

The second speedboat crashed into the *Yucatán Princess*, the explosion knocking bin-Siq down. He quickly stood up, the ship listing as the captain's voice came over the loudspeaker, reassuring the passengers.

As bin-Siq pressed the detonator he gave thanks to Allah and hoped that he would be able to paint watercolors in Paradise.

CHAPTER 30

The Old One swept Baby up in his arms, swung her around the cabana, her hair streaming out, the two of them giggling like children. Ibrahim glowered nearby, the wallscreen behind him frozen on the piece of the cross dotted with flowers. The Old One finally put Baby down, heart pounding, all trace of his cold but a memory. He had never realized how much he loved life until he had been faced with dying. Now . . . now Allah had graced him with a miracle, a most unforeseen reprieve from the claws of death.

"Oh, *Daddy*." Baby fanned herself with her palm, breasts heaving in the green sundress. "Oh my, that was something."

"I fail to see the significance of this . . . this piece of wood, Father," said Ibrahim. "Rather than celebrate a useless relic, you should be reveling in our triumph with the *Yucatán Princess*." He switched channels, the screen showing a dozen news helicopters hovering over the debris field clotting the Gulf. "See, every network in the world is covering what I did . . . what *we* did."

"Yes, yes, my son, a job well done," said the Old One. "I'm very proud of you."

Ibrahim remained defiant. "I just do not understand your . . . *excitement* over this thing." He glanced at Baby. "I can understand such behavior from her. She has lived among the infidel too long, but *you* . . ."

Baby switched the screen back to the piece of the cross. "Look at it, Ibrahim, this is what Sarah sent Moseby after. Daddy had our whole tech unit working on it for weeks now, and they finally captured the transmission the zombie sent from D.C."

"I'll send my blessing to them," said the Old One. "This is indeed a great—"

"This is *foolishness*," spat Ibrahim.

"Foolishness?" the Old One said softly. "Do you think me growing feebleminded in my dotage?"

Ibrahim shook his head.

"Perhaps you think I need a keeper," said the Old One. "A loyal son who will guide my halting steps?"

Ibrahim gestured at the screen. "Father . . ."

"Reunification will take a leap of faith by the Belt," said the Old One. "A trust that there's room in Paradise for all of us. With the cross of their savior in our hands—"

"The cross is a *lie*," said Ibrahim.

"Not where I come from," said Baby.

"Listen to her, Ibrahim. She speaks the truth," said the Old One. "Besides, has it not been said that Jesus Himself will appear to join the Mahdi in the final battle?"

"I don't see Jesus, I see a piece of *wood*," said Ibrahim, "no better than some curio from a tourist shop. Father, this female has bewitched you."

"*Enough.*" The Old One patted Ibrahim on the cheek. "Congratulations on your success with the *Yucatán Princess*, a flawlessly executed operation. All of Aztlán will be enraged, none more so than Presidente Argusto. Our moment of triumph approaches, my son, now go, make arrangements for my departure. I'm curious to see how Las Vegas has changed in my absence."

Ibrahim stalked out the door of the cabana.

The Old One watched him go, his good spirits tinged with regret. Ibrahim had served him well for many years. All things must pass, he told himself, then thought of the cross lying somewhere in D.C., and reminded himself that dust need not be *his* fate. Ibrahim's problem was that he was a modern man, steeped in facts and logic. A man who dismissed sacred relics as mere superstition. The Old One knew better. A piece of the cross would give legitimacy to the Old One's rule, just as he told Ibrahim . . . but that wasn't the root of his excitement.

One of his great-grandsons, Joshua, had been a cardinal posted to the Vatican, part of the pope's inner circle. The boy had told him a story once, a story about a piece of the true cross kept in a vault under St. Peter's Cathedral, one of several pieces that had survived the centuries. One piece had been sent to Czar Peter of Russia, and disappeared before the death of Czar Nicholas in 1917. Another piece had been stolen from a monastery in France and was presumed lost at sea aboard the *Titanic*. Another piece was rumored to have been carried back to the thirteen colonies by Benjamin Franklin, an unbeliever himself—a piece that had been secreted in the capital of the new nation after the revolution, symbolizing their covenant with God.

The Old One stared at the wallscreen, so elated he could barely breathe. He didn't care about Christians and their covenants, but Joshua had told him stories about the piece of the cross at the Vatican, stories of miracles performed by its touch, of water turned to wine and the sick healed. And one story . . . of a dying pope restored to youthful vigor, a dying pope who lived another forty years and brought the Church to its greatest glory. A story. Joshua, for all his prominence, had never seen the piece of the cross hidden in St. Peter's, but he had not doubted its existence or its power. Now . . . the Old One basked in the sight of flowers blooming on the wallscreen. Now, he too had no doubts.

"Daddy?" said Baby. "I didn't mean to cause problems between you and Ibrahim."

"Was the Colonel so easily fooled by your protestations of innocence?" said the Old One.

"Yes, sir, he was," she drawled.

The Old One wanted to dance with her again, cut loose the bonds of mortality with the scent of her. "Those kisses of yours must have addled his brain."

"I think they worked on another part of his anatomy, Daddy."

The Old One roared at her wantonness, the strength it took to speak to him like that.

Baby indicated the cross on the wallscreen. "What are we going to do about this?"

"About *what*, my dear?"

Baby stamped her feet in mock annoyance. "Daddy, don't tease me. I heard about a piece of the cross tucked away somewhere in D.C. since I was a little girl. Heard all kinds of tall tales about it. Least I always thought they were tall tales." She pointed at the screen. "If the cross can grow flowers in that foul place . . . there's no telling what it could do." She slipped her arm in his. "I mean, having the folks in the Belt jabbering in tongues is all well and good for *you*, Daddy, but me . . . I might want to live forever myself."

The Old One didn't react. Not a twitch or a blink betrayed him, but he wondered if Ibrahim wasn't right after all, that Baby *was* a witch, able to read minds.

"Living forever, that's not a bad thing, is it, Daddy?"

"Allah promises the gift of eternal life to all believers, my child."

Baby squeezed his arm. "Yeah, Daddy, but I don't want to have to *die* to find out."

The Old One switched the screen back to the sunken *Yucatán Princess*. The camera focused on various items designed for maximum emotional impact: a child's sneaker decorated with red hearts, a smoldering life preserver, a party hat with streamers and sequins. All well and good, anything to turn the temperature up in Aztlán. Argusto was going to have to retaliate in some truly *grand* fashion now.

Baby watched the rescue boats search for survivors. "Kind of sad, isn't it?"

The Old One switched back to the cross, the flowers tiny but perfectly formed. "Someday we'll have to go on hajj together."

"Me?" Baby shook her head. "I want radiation poisoning, I'll go to D.C."

"The nuke that went off in Mecca was much smaller than the ones that detonated in New York and Washington, D.C.," said the Old One. "I was very clear about that. The idea was to blame the attacks on the Israeli Mossad, not ruin the holiest shrine in Islam."

"Didn't work out quite like you planned, did it?"

"Nothing ever works out as planned, my dear. Only weaklings and atheists let that stop them. One adapts, one regroups, one *continues.*"

"I was just making a point." Baby lightly squeezed his arm. "What are you doing in Las Vegas, anyway? I'd like to come along, if it's okay."

"I have other plans for you." The Old One pointed at the cross. "I want you to go back to the Belt. Link up with Mr. Gravenholtz, and bring that back to me. Do whatever you need to, but bring it to me."

"Daddy . . . like you said, D.C. is lots worse than Mecca," Baby said. "Besides, how do you expect Lester and I are going to find it?"

"You don't have to find it, that's Mr. Moseby's job. *He's* the finder. You merely have to . . ." The Old One snatched at the air. ". . . take it from him after he's fetched it." He kissed the crown of her head. "Mr. Moseby's a family man, just as you said. He'll be eager to call his wife if he's successful, and when he does, my men will be listening. Go to the Belt. I'll let you know where he is when the time comes."

"I've got a better idea," said Baby. "Don't give me that look, Daddy, it's just that I know some people who keep me up to date on the Colonel. Dowdy housewives that I said had pretty ankles, or menfolk who watch dirty movies of me in their mind." She tossed her hair. "Anyway, one of the mechanics in the motor pool saw Moseby with the Colonel about a week ago. Mechanic said the Colonel came to him and wanted him to fix up one of the heavy-duty trucks, put in some lead shielding, install an air filter, trick out the transmission. Didn't take a genius to figure out somebody was going into D.C. Mechanic was surprised when the Colonel and Moseby woke him up in the middle of the night, asked him to explain how to operate all the special things he had done to the truck."

"You think Moseby will come back to the Colonel's with the cross?"

"He can't leave D.C. to the north or west; too much radiation," said Baby. "Coming back the way he came makes more sense. Besides, he might need help."

"So you intend to join Gravenholtz and wait someplace near the Colonel until—"

"Hell's bells, no. Can you imagine me laying low in some motel with Lester, watching wrestling matches and the hunting channel on TV?" Baby shook her head. "No, I'll find something else to keep Lester busy."

"What are you going to do?" asked the Old One.

Baby saw her reflection in every shiny surface of the room. "Me . . . I'm going home to my loving husband."

"You think the Colonel will take you back?"

"Look at me, Daddy." Baby slowly turned, gave him a good look. "Wouldn't you?"

CHAPTER 31

Jenkins lifted his head away from the steel support beam of the Bridge of Skulls. "I . . . I thought that had to be you," he croaked.

"You saw me?" said Rakkim.

"Saw what you *did*." Jenkins's mouth sagged, half his lower lip torn away. One of his eye sockets was empty. "I might not have the night vision you do . . . but I see well enough. You killed . . . you killed the big one . . . *entirely* too quickly for my taste."

Rakkim glanced back toward the end of the Bridge of Skulls—the four dead sentries propped up in a semblance of duty along the railing. "I'm on a tight schedule."

"The big one . . . Salim . . . he likes . . ." Jenkins licked his cracked lips. "Likes looking up at me while he drinks soda pop, pouring out what he doesn't finish . . ." He gasped as Rakkim took a bottle of Jihad Cola out of his jacket.

"Next time I'll kill him slower, okay?" Rakkim slowly gave him a drink, cupping his hand under Jenkins's chin.

"You do that."

Rakkim sat on one of the rusted girders that formed the superstructure, perched there twenty feet above the bridge deck, right beside where Mullah Jenkins had been pinned to the main girder, steel bolts driven into his thighs and shoulders and hands. The gulls had been working on him for the last week, torn chunks of flesh from him, pecked out one of his eyes and near-missed the other. Dried blood crusted the girder.

"I don't think I can free you," said Rakkim.

Jenkins fixed him with his one remaining eye. "*Sure* you can."

Rakkim hesitated.

Jenkins's good eye fluttered. "Five days I've been stuck up

here. Wind and fog and cold and heat . . . and when the sun comes up, the gulls start in again. Five days, no food, no water but the rain. Fedayeen tough . . . it's a curse sometimes." He opened his mouth and Rakkim dribbled in more cola. "What . . . what made you come back for me?"

"I didn't come back for you. I came back to kill ibn-Azziz."

"Ah." Jenkins's head sagged forward. It took an effort to pull it back. "So General Kidd finally decided to cut out the cancer."

"*I* decided. General Kidd doesn't know anything about it."

"Oh . . . *my*, you really have slipped the leash, haven't you?"

The bridge groaned as the tide rushed in.

"Were . . . were we ever friends?" Jenkins wheezed. "I can't remember."

"No. We weren't friends." Rakkim tried to give him another drink but Jenkins turned away. "We were brothers."

"I wasn't sure. I've been having such dreams these last few days . . . such beautiful dreams . . ." Jenkins looked past Rakkim, looked out toward the far shore, beyond the reach of the Black Robes. "I slipped my leash too. Slipped clean away and didn't even know it until it was too late. Couldn't find my way back if I tried."

"Where does ibn-Azziz—?"

"You should be careful, Rakkim."

"I'll be careful."

"Everyone says that . . . but we all make mistakes." Jenkins didn't take his eye off the distant shore, its outlines obscured, shrouded in mist. "We fool ourselves. The best of us . . . the best and the brightest, we're the easiest to fool." He started to cry. "I *told* him, Rakkim. I told ibn-Azziz it was you who ruined things with Senator Chambers."

"It's all right."

Jenkins sobbed softly in the night, tears running down his cheeks, even the ruined eye socket glistening. "He had his men . . . they did things to me, Rakkim—" He lunged forward, half pulled himself free of the spikes. "I was *glad* you ruined

Senator Chambers. Even when they hurt me, I was glad. You made ibn-Azziz so angry. . . ."

"Did he ever tell you who suggested the president appoint Chambers secretary of defense? The president would never have listened to ibn-Azziz."

Jenkins shook his head. "I don't think he knows. Did I . . . did I tell you ibn-Azziz belongs to the Old One?"

"Chambers already told me." Rakkim gently wiped away Jenkins's tears. "You did well. No one could ask more of you."

"Yes, that's why I'm pinned up here being pecked to pieces—because I'm such an inspiring success story." Laughing hurt, but Jenkins tried it anyway. "Before . . . you started to ask me . . . you wanted to know where ibn-Azziz sleeps."

"If you know."

"*Of course* I know. There hasn't been a day since ibn-Azziz became Grand Mullah that I haven't thought of killing him. I just . . . I just never did it." The breeze made him shiver, the bridge creaking. "Thinking of it, and doing it . . . they're not the same." His head lolled to one side. "It's not going to be easy to kill him. I don't care how good you are."

"Help me then. Tell me where he sleeps."

"Do you believe in God?"

"Yeah . . . sure," said Rakkim.

"Then you *need* help," Jenkins said. The bridge shifted, bones clattering around them. "Come closer."

Rakkim bent over him, straining to hear.

Jenkins forced himself to speak. "That's all," he said afterward, voice papery now. "I got no more left."

Rakkim bowed his head toward his teacher.

"Don't forget your part of the bargain." Jenkins looked toward the far shore. "I don't want to know when it's coming. Surprise me. Like it's my . . . like it's my birthday."

Rakkim's blade was already in his hand.

"I used to believe in God too," said Jenkins, still facing the dim hills in the distance. "Now, though . . . I hope there's no God. Nothing and nobody there. Me . . . I'd rather slide into the darkness and never wake up than be judged on what I've done here."

"God will understand."

Jenkins shook his head, still watching the distant shore. "Not the God I heard about."

"Maybe you heard wrong. Maybe God forgives."

Jenkins snorted. "You spent too much time in the Belt."

Rakkim drove the blade into Jenkins's heart in the middle of the man's laugh. Prayed to God to forgive them both.

Rakkim pulled ibn-Azziz's head out of the ancient porcelain toilet, the Grand Mullah collapsing onto the floor, sputtering, coughing up great gouts of filthy water. For twenty minutes Rakkim had brought him to the brink of death and back again, and for twenty minutes ibn-Azziz had refused to name his contact in Seattle who had promoted Senator Chambers for defense secretary. Twenty minutes . . . Rakkim had never heard of anyone lasting more than five in such circumstances without giving up anyone and everything.

"Go ahead, *kill* me," taunted ibn-Azziz through clenched teeth. Rakkim had broken his nose slamming his face into the toilet—blood streamed down the Grand Mullah's bony face, his eyes flaring with hate. "Kill me, you kaffir scum. I'll be in Paradise—"

Rakkim backhanded him, sent him sprawling onto the wet stone floor. "No room in Paradise for you, boy wonder. Not while the ovens of hell need shit to fire them."

Ibn-Azziz struggled to get to his knees, water still running from his nostrils.

Rakkim's earpiece vibrated—Sarah leaving him an encrypted message. She must have boosted the signal to reach him this far underground, which meant it was important, but right now, he had things to take care of. In the corridor, Rakkim could see two of ibn-Azziz's guards, dead, like the other six he had killed getting down here. A cramped cell deep under the main prison, torn from the raw rock and reserved for the worst of the worst, and ibn-Azziz had made it his home.

"Come on," said ibn-Azziz, breathing hard. Water dripped from his scraggly beard. "You're not giving up that easy, are you?"

There was a shift change in less than an hour. Plenty of time to escape. Not nearly enough time to get ibn-Azziz to tell what he knew.

Ibn-Azziz held up his trembling hands. "Break my fingers . . . perhaps that will make me talk." He wriggled his fingers. "*Do* it."

Nothing on the walls. No mattress. Just the toilet and a tiny cold-water sink. Condensation dotted the ceiling. "You ever think of redecorating?" said Rakkim. "Maybe put in a nice rug . . . or one of those free-standing fireplaces—"

"Shall I take you to see Jenkins?" said ibn-Azziz, still on his knees, enjoying the discomfort. "He's got a lovely perch on the Bridge of Skulls."

"I've already talked with him. He's out of your reach now."

"He . . . *betrayed* you, did he tell you that?" Ibn-Azziz spat out one of his teeth, sent it bouncing across the stone floor. "He gave up your name as though offering me a sweet."

"He told me."

Ibn-Azziz tried to hide his surprise.

"I told him it didn't matter. It just gave me an excuse to kill you. I should have done it sooner, but I didn't have time to study your habits. Jenkins helped me out on that."

"Do I appear frightened?" Ibn-Azziz wiped his nose, his torso crisscrossed with old scars. "Do you think death scares me?"

"No . . . I don't think it does. Not yet."

"Not *yet*? Do you intend to school me in fear?" Ibn-Azziz asked. "I *bring* pain, I do not feel it."

"You bring a *lot* of pain too. I've seen your handiwork."

Ibn-Azziz held his head high. "This world is a sewer, a vast cesspool fouled with sin and depravity. The people are beasts, rutting and sweating, abandoning Allah—"

"You need to get out more."

Ibn-Azziz launched himself at Rakkim, but Rakkim tripped him, knocked him back down, his head hitting so hard the sound echoed.

"You might want to put some ice on that," said Rakkim.

Ibn-Azziz rolled over.

"You're going to be a real disappointment to the Old One."

"Don't even speak his name."

"Yeah, it is a little pompous. 'The Old One.' Ooooh, I can feel my nutsack clench." Rakkim squinted. "You got a little bit of toilet paper on your forehead."

Ibn-Azziz tore at his forehead for the nonexistent speck of tissue.

"That old bastard probably had high hopes for you," said Rakkim, "and now . . . well, not to be cruel or anything, but *look* at yourself."

"My . . . my master will understand my failings. . . ."

Rakkim shook his head. "I've met him. He's not the understanding type." He checked his watch. "The rest of the mullahs consider the Old One an apostate, so when you're killed he won't have the Black Robes to back him up. That's going to upset him."

"My master has conquered death, he does not require the Black Robes' support." Ibn-Azziz pulled himself up, legs rubbery. "The Mahdi stands astride history."

"I'm going to kill him too, by the way. Gonna gut him like a feeder pig, as they say in the Belt. You . . . you're just the appetizer."

Ibn-Azziz laughed, sprayed a mist of blood. "Are you death?"

"Just an amazing facsimile." Rakkim lowered his voice. "Here's something to think about as you squat in hell. Before I kill the Old One, I'm going to tell him that you helped me find him. I'm going to tell him—"

"*Liar!*"

"I'm going to tell him you pissed yourself you were so eager to give him up."

Ibn-Azziz moved quicker than Rakkim would have believed, got his hands around Rakkim's throat, those yellowed nails digging in.

Rakkim looked into ibn-Azziz's eyes, and he could see the man's soul compressed into an oily black knot, smelled the stink of the Grand Mullah's breath and let him continue.

Ibn-Azziz clawed at Rakkim.

Rakkim gently placed his thumbs under ibn-Azziz's chin, pushed his head back. "Are you afraid yet?" he whispered, ibn-Azziz's fingers so tight around his throat he could barely speak.

Ibn-Azziz hung on.

Holding ibn-Azziz's head back with one hand, Rakkim drove the fingertips of his other hand into a spot just under the jaw. Not too hard a blow—that would have killed ibn-Azziz outright—but just enough to fracture the hyoid bone. The move yet another souvenir from Darwin, a particularly cruel assassin killing technique. Rakkim had no idea how he had learned the maneuver—perhaps something else that had passed between him and Darwin at the moment of the assassin's death. Rakkim dropped his hands to his sides, no longer worried about being strangled.

Ibn-Azziz tried breathing through his nose, his grip already weakening.

"How about now?" whispered Rakkim. "Afraid yet?"

Fear bloomed in ibn-Azziz's eyes, took root as he struggled. He released his grip on Rakkim's throat, frantic now.

Fracturing the hyoid bone caused the tissues to swell, pinching off the air passage—the more ibn-Azziz struggled, the more constricted his throat became. Ibn-Azziz had toughed out nearly being drowned in the toilet, had actually seemed to grow stronger, but this situation was infinitely worse. The very ferocity that had allowed him to laugh in Rakkim's face worked against him now, his rage narrowing down his airway with every beat of his heart. No pain, no glory, just the gathering darkness.

Rakkim watched ibn-Azziz flopping on the floor, watched as the panic overtook him, ibn-Azziz feeling his dreams dying, his memories dying . . . and at the end, he watched as ibn-Azziz's soul flared like a horsefly in a furnace, leaving only ashes.

Rakkim walked out of the cell. Soon as he got clear, he would check Sarah's message. See what was so important.

CHAPTER 32

Rakkim heard Moseby before he saw him, heard him throwing up and spotted him bent over beside the landing gear of a F-37 Marauder, a tall, well-muscled black man, his short hair sprinkled with gray. Moseby was wiping his mouth as Rakkim approached out of the shadows, making plenty of noise so somebody didn't get hurt. The silhouettes of dozens of other jets loomed around them in the moonlight, fighters mostly, but a few gigantic stealth B-7s too, their jagged fuselages giving them the appearance of gigantic bats. Three days after killing ibn-Azziz, Rakkim was on the other side of the country and he still hadn't slept.

Moseby threw up again.

"You get some bad oysters?" said Rakkim.

"No oysters in this part of Virginia," said Moseby, a little wobbly.

"Radioactive oysters. What's the matter, you weren't monitoring yourself?"

"Got a couple hundred Rs, no big deal."

"Sarah's pissed off. You weren't supposed to go into the city without me. She asked you just to talk with—"

"The zombie's wife didn't want to talk to me, and I wasn't about to wait around until you showed up," said Moseby. "I had an idea where to look based on the download."

Rakkim embraced him, felt Moseby tremble. "You look like shit, John."

"I overstayed my welcome, that's all. D.C.'s nasty."

"Your suit didn't protect you?"

"The truck I got from the Colonel was useless . . . and I didn't have enough air filters," said Moseby. "You have to switch them out three times more often than the regs say."

"I've got plenty of filters coming in anytime now." Rakkim glanced up at the night sky, saw just stars and the ridges surrounding the abandoned airbase. "You want to be medevaced out? At least get a transfusion?"

Moseby took a swallow from his canteen, rinsed his mouth out and spit. "I'm fine."

"Let's walk," said Rakkim, keeping a clear view of the western approaches to the airfield. "Spider and Leo managed to narrow down the search area for the safe room. We're still looking for a needle in a haystack, but it's a smaller haystack."

The planes stretched for miles, lined up haphazardly on the landing strips, spilling over onto the weed-choked fields. The former LeMay Air Force Base was just another aircraft graveyard now. Most of the Belt's air force had been destroyed on the ground, their avionics fried by a directed satellite surge from the Islamic Republic. At least it was *supposed* to be directed. In reality the surge had blown microchips and computer components from sea to shining sea, leaving dead planes from both sides on runways, and sending a rain of commercial and military aircraft spiraling to earth. The lucky pilots managed to land at bases like LeMay, where the control towers still marginally functioned. The rest crashed into farmland and cities, fireballed across the night, their last radio transmissions fuck-fuck-*fuck*. Many of the commercial planes had been retrofitted, but the military jets' sophisticated hardware had been irreplaceable, and they had been mothballed where they landed, allowed to rust and rot.

Rakkim looked around as they strolled down one of the runways, crickets screeching in the damp air. Weeds grew through cracks in the concrete. "Never seen so many planes in one spot."

"Maxwell, outside of Montgomery, is even more crowded," said Moseby. "Must be a couple hundred planes there, half of them nose-down in the dirt where the pilots blew the landing 'cause their instruments were cooked."

"Why haven't the planes been looted? They seem relatively untouched. No graffiti—"

"It's the Belt," said Moseby. "People love the military. Folks think it's just a matter of time before somebody comes along, fixes the planes and off they go, into the wild blue yonder."

"Must be nice to believe in fairy tales," said Rakkim.

"Nice to have faith," said Moseby.

Rakkim didn't want to argue. "How was D.C.? Bad as they say?"

"Bad enough." Moseby stopped for a moment, put his hands on his knees until the dizziness passed. "Not as many bones as I expected. Must have something to do with the radiation . . . or the chemical clouds. Plenty of skeletons, don't get me wrong, but I've seen worse in New Orleans." He straightened. "It was the buildings in D.C. that got to me. All those landmarks, looking just like they did before the blast, all that clean white marble . . ." He shook his head.

The two of them walked past clumps of sleek fighters, their canopies cracked from the sun, tires rotted off. A gigantic C-57 cargo plane lay crumpled in the grass, one wing torn off, the fuselage still blackened from the crash landing forty years ago. One of the control towers had collapsed into a pile of concrete blocks. Another had been obliterated by a light bomber that overshot the runway.

"The Colonel's worried about you," said Rakkim.

"You saw him?"

"Woke him up in the middle of the night—"

"You love doing that, don't you? Shaking people out of a sweet dream."

"You know me, John, I'm a man of simple pleasures." Rakkim could see Moseby remembering his own wake-up seventeen years ago, Rakkim's blade against his throat. Sent to kill him for going rogue, Rakkim had seen Moseby's pregnant wife beside him and backed off, disappeared into the night.

"How's Sarah and the boy?" said Moseby.

"They're fine. I can hardly keep up with either of them. How is your family?"

"Annabelle's concerned. Leanne?" Moseby sighed. "All she thinks about is that boy."

"Leo's a good kid."

"Then let *your* daughter marry him."

"I don't have a daughter."

"Exactly," said Moseby.

Rakkim smiled. "He hasn't got sense to come in out of the rain, but Leo's smart. So smart even Spider doesn't understand half of what the kid's talking about."

"Just what I need, a son-in-law who's smarter than God and useless as tits on a bull."

Rakkim stopped under the protection of the twisted tail section of a crashed jet. "These people of yours bringing the vehicle . . . you trust them?"

"Corbett's a percentage player." Moseby patted the flechette auto-pistol on his hip. A high-body-count weapon. "I trust *this* to keep him honest."

Rakkim pulled the starlight scope out of his denim jacket, handed it over. "Give him this then. Wouldn't want him to think he has a hidden advantage."

Moseby hefted the German-made scope. "Where did you get it?"

"Guy in a crashed F-77 interceptor had it attached to a sniper rifle. Must have been out squirrel hunting. I had to explain to him that you can't hunt varmints with a night scope. Not sporting."

Moseby tucked away the starlight scope. "You kill him?"

"Just revoked his hunting license. He's sleeping off the shame of it. Heck of a nice rifle."

"I'm slipping." Moseby turned, looked toward the far hill. "They're coming."

Rakkim had already heard the engines. They had time. He lightly touched the undamaged section of the jet—the USAF insignia looked new. "Must have been quite a sight in the old days seeing these things in formation over the cities. Sky pilots, I think they called them." He ran his fingertips over the insignia. Gave him chills. Just like Sarah said, there was magic in the idea of that nation, the greatest power on earth for a while. Who didn't wonder what it would be like for those days to come again? Re-unification . . .

"They relied too much on airpower," said Moseby. "All the countries did. Now that nuclear weapons are outlawed, wars are won in the dirt."

"*Now* they are."

After the satellite surge destroyed the air forces of both the Republic and the Belt, other nations redesigned their own systems, spending billions to buffer their avionics from electro-magnetic discharges. It had worked until the Chechen Alliance attacked Russia, hacking into the Russian military command center. In ten minutes the Russian air force was destroyed by the Chechen abort virus—those planes in the air fell to earth like dead sparrows, and those on the ground were locked down and useless. The virus spread rapidly from the Russian command center to every nation with which it had reciprocal relations. The Chechens didn't care, they had no air force to speak of, but within an hour, airpower had ceased to be the dominant military strategy.

It took years for the major nations to rebuild their fleets, yet again. Since modern aircraft were utterly dependent on their computer systems, the choice was made to delink their air wings from command and control centers. While this squadron-based structure was inefficient, it prevented the whole air defense system from being destroyed by an enemy virus. Like Moseby said, wars were won in the dirt. Until a year ago.

Last year, the Nigerians had developed a supposedly unhack-able command and control center, the Kabilla-9, which allowed the tactical coordination of all air units. Frightfully expensive, its purchase considered a provocative act, the Kabilla-9 had so far only been bought by the expansionist regimes of Ukraine, Brazil and the Aztlán Empire.

"They're getting closer." Moseby took a deep breath. "You have the credit chip?"

Rakkim handed the chip over. He could see sweat beaded across Moseby's forehead.

Moseby looked west, saw headlights coming through the trees. "Do you want to . . . ?" Rakkim was gone. Moseby stepped out onto the tarmac, waited for Corbett. He didn't have to wait long.

The two vehicles burst out from the trees, the one in the lead a large van with traction tires, riding low on its shocks, the other an old Cadillac limo with the roof sawed off. Corbett waved from the passenger seat of the limo.

Moseby unslung the flechette auto-pistol, his finger on the trigger.

The two vehicles skidded to a stop, sent up a cloud of dust that billowed across Moseby. "Sorry about that." Corbett swatted the driver. "Big Mike likes to make a big entrance."

"No problem," said Moseby, caught in the glare of the headlights.

Corbett jumped out, a short, skinny cracker with thinning hair, one cheek puffed out with chaw. He stalked toward Moseby, bib overalls barely reaching the tops of his cowboy boots.

Big Mike stayed behind the wheel, engine running. He fired up a cigar, peering at Moseby through a blue haze.

Corbett shook hands with him. "You got the funds?"

"Let me see the war wagon," said Moseby.

Corbett led him over to the van, banged on the hood. Both front doors opened, and two men stepped out. They leaned against the front wheel wells, arms crossed. "Four-wheel drive, of course. Armored all over, including the floorboards. Puncture-proof tires. Lead-foil paneling and leaded glass all around, cuts down radiation by ninety percent. You want to have kids someday, you should still wear a rad-suit, which I can supply."

"I've got my own," said Moseby, peering inside the van.

Corbett spit tobacco juice. "Good for you." He pointed at the large air compressor on the roof. "My own design, and proud of it too. Close to a sealed system, but even if there's a leak, you're going to have a constant one hundred and ten percent air pressure inside, so nothing out is coming in. You're going to appreciate that when you get to D.C., 'cause there's some nasty shit there you don't want to breathe." He turned up the interior lights. "You sure you want to go into the city by yourself? It's no pleasure cruise, I'll tell you that."

"I don't like company."

"Yeah, I had a cousin like that," said Corbett. "Regular hermit, he was, although you ask me, he just didn't trust his fellow man."

"What else this thing have?"

"All business, okay, that's fine with me," said Corbett. "Got roentgen counters inside and out, so you know when you're approaching a hot spot. D.C.'s not the same all over. That rad counter starts pinging faster than a twenty-dollar mouth whore, you *scoot*." He grinned at Moseby. "I want you back as a repeat customer."

"You said there was a decontamination area," said Moseby.

"In the back," said Corbett, beckoning.

Moseby whipped around as one of the men stepped away from the wheel well. "Tell these two to stay where they are."

"Easy now," Corbett said to Moseby. "We're all friends here." He spit again. "Boys, you stay put. Don't want Mr. Moseby to get his bowels in an uproar and shoot one of you." He looked at Moseby. "Happy now?"

Moseby kept his finger on the trigger.

Corbett opened the back door. Showed off the compartment inside. "This is what you're really paying for. Specially designed for treasure hunting, not sightseeing. See . . . you sit down on the jumpseat, close the door and press this button here." He pointed. "See it? Takes sixty seconds to cycle out the dust and air, pipe in fresh. That way you don't track radiation or toxins into the main compartment when you come and go. Pretty nifty, huh?"

"Yeah."

Corbett put his hands on his hips. Made him look like a banty rooster. "Most folks are more impressed."

"I thought this was the first one you made," said Moseby.

Corbett licked his dry lips. "Right. You . . . you're the first person who's had the money to pay for it. Most folks just kick the tires and say they'll come back later . . . but they never do." He wiped a line of brown spit that had run down his chin. "So, you got the funds?"

Moseby pulled out the chip Rakkim had given him.

"Good." Corbett handed him a remote credit tablet. Waited while Moseby slid the chip through. Checked the transaction. Nodded. "Congratulations. You're the proud owner of a grade-A war wagon, Mr. Moseby." He shook hands, held on.

Moseby tried to free himself.

Corbett looked toward the crashed F-77 interceptor, still squeezing Moseby's hand. "*Do it. What are you waiting for?*"

Moseby jerked free. Tossed Corbett the starlight scope. "I think this belongs to you."

Corbett dropped the scope, backed away. He turned and started running.

The two men pushed off from the van, reaching into their jackets. One pulled a revolver as his head exploded. The other almost got a shot off before he was knocked off his feet, brains everywhere. Big Mike jumped out of the limo, shotgun firing wildly before being brought down by a controlled burst from Moseby's flechette auto-pistol, the tiny, jagged projectiles almost cutting him in half.

Corbett dashed among the abandoned planes, seeking out the shadows, zigging and zagging through the night. He kept low, shifting his speed until he was out of sight.

Moseby checked the dead, put away his weapon. He looked

up just as Corbett burst from the brush at the top of the ridge, running flat out. Corbett spun around at the same instant Moseby heard the gunshot, fell facedown in the moonlight. Another head shot. "That wasn't necessary," said Moseby.

Rakkim emerged from the darkness, the sniper rifle slung over his shoulders. "Sure, it was."

CHAPTER 33

Baby saw the jeep stop atop the next hill over, faced it, assuming that the Colonel was watching her through some high-res binoculars. She had chosen this spot with care, a gentle slope overlooking the river, a few trees for shade but not enough to hide anyone. She wanted the Colonel to see that she was all alone. She sat on a blanket, a wicker picnic basket nearby—the Colonel was old-fashioned, which she had always found endearing, a sign that he didn't feel he had to keep up. Last thing she would do was show up with a liquid-nitrogen-cooled basket and an instant sweet-tea maker.

The breeze off the river below wafted her hair around her shoulders and she let her head fall back, reveling in the sensation. Oh, she was aware of the effect her actions had on the Colonel. The place under the trees was seductive and cool, the wildflowers fragrant. She loved the Belt. Miami was beautiful, but the days were too hot and the nights were humid. Air-conditioning was harsh on her skin, drying it, and her hair suffered too. No, all things considered, the Belt was best.

The Colonel must have seen enough, the jeep starting up, moving slowly over the surrounding hills toward her.

Baby leaned back, stretched her legs out as she watched the Colonel approach. A black ant crawled slowly up and down the folds of the blanket until it reached her bare leg. It hesitated, feelers twitching, then stepped onto her calf. She reached down, pinched the ant flat and tossed it aside, her eyes never leaving the jeep.

She wondered where Gravenholtz was. Two days ago, she sent him off to zombie country with some money and that bad attitude of his. Honey and vinegar to get the locals to give up

what they knew about Moseby. Not that they'd tell him anything . . . and even if they did, Lester wasn't about to go into
D.C. No, he'd drive around, getting lost and too dumb to admit
he didn't belong there. She hadn't told him about the piece of
the cross, of course. Just said to wait until Moseby showed up and
bring him and whatever he was carrying back to Atlanta. By the
time Lester finally gave up, Baby would be in Seattle, handing
over the cross to her daddy and telling him just what she wanted
as a token of his appreciation. *How about the* world, *Daddy?*

The jeep pulled up nearby and the Colonel got out, wearing the informal gray uniform that emphasized the width of his
shoulders. He strolled over, taking his time, still handsome in
spite of the years, carrying himself like a king.

The greatest hero of the war, the savior of the Belt, they
called him. He could have been president, it had been offered
to him on a platter, but he turned it down, went back to the Tennessee hills. It was only when the central government dissolved
into a stew of greed and ineptitude that the Colonel had raised
an army to protect his territory from bandits and renegades. His
old comrades left everything to join him, brought their guns and
their sons. The Colonel became the most powerful warlord in
the Belt, independent of Atlanta politics and politicians, a free
man in a free land. Twenty-five years later he controlled most of
Tennessee. Crime was rare and quickly punished; taxes were low
and he still retreated to his farm every winter, walking his fallow
fields and reading the Bible.

Baby stood up. "I wasn't sure you were going to come, Zachary."

The Colonel looked at her, his eyes cool and blue.

"I wouldn't have blamed you." Baby felt the sun through the
trees, her clothes warm against her. "I wouldn't blame you no
matter what you did to me."

"I've been shot three times," said the Colonel, a faint quaver
in his voice. "You've seen my scars. Doc pulled a 30.06 round
out of me at Blitheville. We took so many casualties, he had run

out of morphine, but he went ahead and did it, saved my life. Thought if I could survive *that* pain I could handle anything . . . but you leaving me . . . it hurt worse."

Tears ran down Baby's cheeks. "I . . . know."

"I got your message last night," said the Colonel. "Didn't sleep at all afterwards. Just laid there in bed trying to decide what to do." He reached out, wiped away the tear clinging to the corner of her mouth. "The bed . . . our bed . . . it's been empty since you left. Must have been a hundred times I promised myself I'd get rid of it, burn it to ashes, put a bullet in it . . . but I never could." He blinked back tears of his own. "Your smell still lingers . . . doesn't make any sense . . . been a whole year and then some, but there's times I turn over in the middle of the night, and I'd swear you're there."

Baby took his hand, held it to her cheek. "I am *so* sorry."

"No fool like an old fool, that's what they say."

"You're not the fool, Zachary. I am. I was so young when we got married, young and in love, but I never really had a chance to stretch my wings."

"Where's Lester?"

She had been ready for the question, but she didn't answer right away. "Does it matter?"

"It matters."

Baby smoothed down her dress. "It's not about Lester. It's about you and me. Lester . . . he's not worth a pinch of dirt."

"I heard stories . . . he was spotted in Atlanta not too long ago."

"I wouldn't know. I walked out on him a week after we stole your helicopter."

"Did . . . did he force you to steal it? To go away with him?"

"You think Lester Gravenholtz could make me do *anything*?" Baby gave him her best pout. "I know I hurt you terrible, but that's no reason to insult me."

The Colonel toyed with a smile. It looked like he was out of practice.

"I'm sorry," said Baby. "I don't expect you to ever forgive me for what I've done, but I wanted to see you face to face, let you know how sorry I am for everything."

The Colonel stared at her. He had looked at her the same way on their wedding day at that little church in the wildwood. Calm and steady before the preacher, the Colonel in his dress uniform with the silver buttons, standing there evaluating the situation, trying to put aside his emotions and see what was right in front of him.

Probably the exact same way he had approached one of the great battles of the civil war, Memphis or Nashville or Owensburg Wood, the Colonel assaying the risks and rewards, recognizing the inevitable casualties, the dead and dying, pain spread like a shroud across those he cared about. At the end of the day, the Colonel had led his men into combat, fearless as the bullets flew like rain, ordering them into certain death for the greater good, the band of brothers rent and bloodied, but charging forward just the same, until their enemies dissolved like mist in the dawn. The Colonel had never misread a battlefield or misjudged a strategic option, but he had misread Baby on their wedding day and he misread her now.

"What's in the picnic basket?" asked the Colonel.

"Who wants to know?"

The Colonel's eyes took her in. "The man who loves you," he said so softly she thought it was the wind in the trees.

Baby took his hand, pulled him onto the blanket, his knees popping. She opened the picnic basket. "Well . . ." She tapped a finger on her cheek. "I've got iced tea, lemonade, chicken sandwiches and red potato salad, pickled green beans, corn muffins—"

"You make the muffins?"

"Don't be silly," said Baby.

The Colonel helped her set out the food on the blanket.

"I did make the chocolate chip cookies myself," said Baby, putting the plate of cookies in front of them.

"Always liked your cookies," said the Colonel, taking the biggest one. "I *did* look for you after you left. I had people on the lookout all over the Belt."

"I wasn't in the Belt. I was in Miami."

The Colonel pushed aside a wisp of his long gray hair, covering his disappointment. "I've never been to Miami. Heard it's nice."

"Not near as nice as Tennessee."

"Big hotels and people from all over the world splashing around in the ocean," said the Colonel. "They say the water is warm. Say you can stay in it all day and not get a chill."

"Like Grandma's bathwater," said Baby. "I'd rather swim in one of our mountain lakes, where you come out covered in goose bumps, so alive your whole body's tingling."

"Takes a while for a person to decide what they like best, I guess," said the Colonel. "Some folks never do decide. Always changing their mind, back and forth."

Baby poured him a glass of lemonade. "I'm not going to change my mind, Zachary. That's not why I came back."

The Colonel sipped his lemonade, winced. She always made it too sweet for him.

"Zachary? I'm here now, but I'm not staying. I just wanted you to know it wasn't you that was at fault."

The Colonel wiped his lips. "Married people have troubles once in a while—anyone who tells you different has never been to the altar."

"You . . . you're not listening."

"I heard everything I need to," said the Colonel. "You're here now, that's all that matters. From the first moment I saw you, the very first moment, that's all I ever wanted."

Baby played with his fingers, aware of his yellowed nails. She watched the river flow past, on its way to God only knew where, and couldn't wait to get moving herself. Soon as she was done with her business here, she'd hightail it back to the Old One. Ibrahim would already be busy poisoning things behind her back. She was going to have to take care of that boy once and for all. Have to do it careful, though.

"Just sitting here with you . . . never thought it would happen again," said the Colonel.

"Hush now," said Baby. "Let's just enjoy what we got."

Gravenholtz should be making the rounds of zombie territory by now. Two days after she left him and he was probably still grumbling about her going back to the Colonel and why did *he* always get the dirty jobs?

Well, we all do what we're good at, Lester, honey, she had told him, standing there with the sun shining through her clothes.

I thought we could have a little vacation, just the two of us, Lester had persisted. *Who's gonna know? Shit, I'm not afraid of the Old One.*

I am, Baby had said. It was a lie. Kind of.

Baby unwrapped a chicken sandwich, handed it to the Colonel. "I put a few mint leaves in there, just the way you like it." She put a hand on his knee. "You're too good for me."

"I know." The Colonel took a big bite of the sandwich. "Maybe I'll let you dirty me up a little bit tonight. I am still your husband, aren't I?"

"You're still my husband," said Baby.

CHAPTER 34

The Old One stood behind Leo, who was playing all six hands at a twenty-one table at the Gilded Lily, the biggest casino on the Las Vegas strip. Gigantic tropical flowers bloomed from hydroponic tanks along the walls, orchids and lilies the size of basketballs, their delicate petals wiggling in the air currents. The Old One wriggled his nose at their heavy fragrance. Leo was just as Baby had described him, big and soft and pale as an infant, his eyes fixed on something just out of range, something no one but he could see.

Leo looked up at the Old One, went back to his cards. No reason anyone would recognize the Old One—he had always maintained a shield of privacy, was almost never photographed, but just in case, he had shaved his beard, lightened his skin and blued his eyes. He wore the shimmering, oversized silk suit of a modern European businessman.

The dealer showed a jack, a good card. Leo split a pair of eights anyway. Stood pat on a twelve, two fourteens and doubled-down on a ten.

The bored dealer actually raised an eyebrow, then turned over his hole card. A six, for a total of sixteen. House rules, he had to hit on sixteen or less. He slid a card out of the shoe: a queen. Busted. He paid off all six of Leo's bets.

Leo added the chips to his already huge pile, then glanced behind him. "I'm going to have the table tied up until I take a cab to the airport." He placed a hundred-dollar chip in front of each of the six table positions. "Three hours, seventeen minutes."

The Old One pulled out a chair, sat down. "That's plenty of time for us to talk, Leo."

The dealer dealt two cards facedown to each of Leo's

positions. Dealt two cards to himself, one faceup, one facedown. His up card was a king.

"How do you know my name?" said Leo.

"What are you going to do, sir?" said the dealer.

Leo continued to bet against all good sense, hitting on sixteen, seventeen sometimes, splitting sixes . . . and he kept winning.

The pit boss wandered over, a bulky man with the face of a bulldog.

"I can't figure him out," the dealer said to the pit boss.

"It's a system," said Leo.

"You're a card counter," said the pit boss.

"That's not illegal, is it?" said Leo.

"No . . . not illegal." The pit boss looked at the dealer. "Are you using a fifty-deck shoe?" When the dealer nodded the pit boss smiled at Leo. "Good luck with your system."

Leo watched the pit boss lumber away. Covered each of his spots with a thousand-dollar chip. He won four of the six. Won five of the next six. "You never did tell me how you knew my name," Leo said, stacking his chips.

The Old One stuck out his hand. "Harry Voigt, Harry Voigt Investments. Geneva, Shanghai, Nairobi."

Leo didn't take the hand. He put down a five-dollar chip, the minimum bet, at each of his positions. Lost all of them when the dealer made twenty.

"I heard you read your paper at the Pure Math Symposium," said the Old One.

"Did you come by to laugh at me in person?" said Leo.

"I came to apologize for the way you were treated."

"Place your bets, sir," said the dealer.

"May I buy you a drink?" said the Old One. "You don't need to prove anything at this table, and if it's money you're interested in . . . I'll be happy to pay for your time."

"Place your *bets*, sir."

Leo stood up, stuffed his chips into the pockets of his sport coat and followed the Old One into the lounge. They sat at a booth in the corner.

"You have no idea what a pleasure it is to meet you," said the Old One.

"Yeah . . . well, it would be if anybody understood my paper," sniffed Leo. "Nothing like being the smartest one in the room and having everyone think you're an asshole."

"They *were* hostile," said the Old One. "I think they were expecting your father."

"My father's brilliant, but he'd be the first one to tell you he can't keep up with me."

"Beyond the Poincaré Conjecture: An Exploration of the Fourth-Dimensional Spheroid." The Old One shook his head. "I had no idea what you were talking about, but I was certain that you did. It was your certainty that intrigued me . . . and the fact that the other mathematicians in the room felt so threatened by you. I decided you might be operating at a much higher level than they were . . . or you might be the unlettered buffoon they seemed to think you were." He looked at Leo. "May I order for the both of us?"

"I don't drink alcohol."

"Then I won't either." The Old One tapped the table-screen. "I've ordered a couple of Brain Fizzes. I think you'll like it. Cerebral stimulators in a base of fruit essence."

"So what are you, some kind of math groupie?" said Leo.

The Old One laughed. "I came to the conference with a rather complex problem to solve. None of the other speakers were able to solve it. I thought you might like a chance."

The waitress delivered the two Brain Fizzes. Leo tentatively took a sip. "Ummm." He drank half of it. Wiped his mouth with the back of his hand.

"I'm glad you like it," said the Old One, taking a swallow. "There's a pleasant euphoric quality to it also, which is always welcome."

Leo finished his. Tapped out an order for a couple of refills. "What kind of problem?"

The Old One activated the privacy screen on the table, the clatter of the room instantly lowered to a whisper. "I don't know if it's in your area of expertise—"

"I don't have an *area*," said Leo. "Everything is my expertise."

"How fortunate for you."

"You would think so," said Leo, "but you'd be wrong." He leaned over the table. "You ever hear that expression, 'too smart for his own good'? Well, that's me."

"I don't think it's possible to be too smart," said the Old One.

"You've never spent any time in the Belt, have you?" said Leo.

"No . . . I can't say that I have. Dangerous place, from what I've heard."

Leo puffed up slightly. "You got to stay on your toes, that's for sure."

"You've *been* there?"

The waitress brought two more Brain Fizzes.

"I haven't just been there, I've traveled all over it," said Leo. "Almost got myself killed a couple times . . ." He hooked a pinkie into the blue foam of the drink, licked it clean.

"I'm very impressed, Leo. You did this alone?"

Leo shrugged. "I had company. Man named Rakkim. Used to be Fedayeen."

"This Rakkim was your bodyguard?"

"More like . . ." Leo took a long drink of the Brain Fizz. "More like my sidekick."

"You're a man of many talents, Leo." The Old One shook his head. "I hope it doesn't embarrass you if I say I'm a bit in awe of you."

Leo blushed.

"Being treated so shabbily at the conference . . . it must have been very disappointing."

"Their loss."

The Old One toasted him. "Are you married?"

"I'm engaged."

"Congratulations. Who's the lady?"

Leo started to speak, stopped himself.

"I see," said the Old One. "Caution is a virtue, Leo. I'm a bit of a romantic, that's why I asked. A strange characteristic for a businessman, I know." He pulled at his chin where his beard used to be. "I lost my wife, Helen, last year . . . still haven't gotten over it."

"Sorry to hear that."

"We never had children." The Old One stared into his drink. "Your father is a very lucky man. Having you as a son . . . well, he must be very proud."

"Not after he finds out I got laughed off the stage."

"Not everyone was laughing. *I* certainly wasn't. You'd be telling the truth if you said that the theory you presented drew mixed responses. No harm in that."

"I guess so."

The Old One handed Leo a computational tablet. "Here's the problem I wanted to show you. I sent it to several of the other speakers a month ago, but they were all stumped."

"Is that supposed to intimidate me? Because I'm not like anyone else." Leo drank the rest of his Brain Fizz. Reached over and snagged the Old One's untouched second drink. Tapped out another order as he stared at the computational tablet.

"If it helps, Dr. Cheverton suggested that the answer involved some sort of algorithmic transformation."

"The day I need a suggestion from Cheverton is the day I'll open a vein," said Leo, still looking at the problem.

The Old One laughed. Dr. Cheverton, whose research facility was underwritten by one of the Old One's shell corporations, had led the chorus of disapproval of Leo's presentation, the personal tone of his attacks encouraging others. "I enjoy your sense of humor."

Leo brightened. "You think so? Most people . . ."

"Most people don't appreciate you, Leo. That's obvious. I

want you to know something. Whether or not you're capable of solving the problem, I admire you."

Leo looked away for a moment, then turned back to the Old One. "You never told me why you want this problem solved."

"My company controls assets worth over one hundred billion Swiss francs. For safety's sake, the financial data is currently scattered in various encrypted accounts, so if one account is compromised—"

"And you want to combine them into one account with encryption you can trust."

"Yes," said the Old One. "It would greatly improve efficiency."

"So you had somebody devise an encryption program."

"Not somebody. A *team* of somebodies. The very best men in the field." The Old One indicated the computational tablet. "Took them years to come up with this oscillating program that shifts at regular intervals—"

"How often?"

"Every three hours."

"Smart."

"I spent seven million dollars renting the use of the linked computers at the Chinese Science Institute," said the Old One. "They took five days to solve—"

"At which point it had already shifted forty times," said Leo.

The Old One didn't answer, annoyed at being interrupted.

"So you thought you'd try it out on the best minds in the world, see if human creativity could defeat the encryption when computer power couldn't." Leo sniffed. "You wasted your time with dolts like Dr. Cheverton."

"Am I wasting my time with you, Leo?"

"Come back in an hour. Go on, shoo."

Seething, the Old One gritted out a smile and left. When he returned in an hour, Leo was eating a hot fudge sundae covered in whipped cream and maraschino cherries. An empty sundae dish was pushed to one side. The Old One sat down. "Any luck?"

Leo spooned in ice cream. "No such thing as luck." Hot fudge dripped from his full lips.

"Did you solve it?"

"Not really a solving situation." Leo bit into a maraschino cherry, squirted red juice across the table onto the back of the Old One's hand. "That's why even the linked computers couldn't answer the problem until it was ancient history." His spoon dredged out more hot sauce. "You have to *anticipate* the solution. Leapfrog it." He waved the dripping spoon at the Old One. "It's intuitive as much as inferential. Need a human being for that." He grinned. "Of course, I'm probably the only human being in the world who could do it, so maybe there *is* such a thing as luck. I mean, if my father had come here instead of me, you'd still be thinking it couldn't be done."

"You *did* it?"

"Thirty-seven minutes. Would have been faster, but I had to go to the bathroom."

The Old One blotted cherry juice off the back of his hand with a napkin.

"So your team is going to have to come up with something a little tougher to crack," said Leo, slurping ice cream. "Either that or reset the system every five minutes."

"We can't do that. There are certain . . . other considerations."

Leo shrugged.

"I'm very impressed," said the Old One. "I hope we can get together in Seattle."

"Really?" The spoon banged against the side of the sundae dish as Leo got the last of the chocolate sauce. "You're coming to Seattle?"

"I've got business there, and I intend to pay you for your work."

Leo licked the spoon. "Maybe you could meet my father. He's an amazing individual."

"Oh, I'd like that *very* much," said the Old One.

CHAPTER 35

"That was *good*," said Baby. "That's what I've been missing."

The Colonel lay beside her, breathing heavily, one hand resting on her bare thigh. Moonlight squeezed through the pulled curtains of their bedroom, turning the darkness cool and gray.

Baby threw a leg over him. "You're trapped now."

"I know," sighed the Colonel.

They were in the summer cabin, part of a hidden encampment protected by the surrounding mountains and two hundred of the Colonel's best troops. This time of year, the Colonel would usually be set up in one of the small towns, or back at the farm, but since Aztlán had accused him of assassinating their oil minister, he had chosen the security of the summer cabin. Baby had only been here a few times before, remembered it mostly for the wildflowers that seemed to spring up overnight, and making love in the deafening thunderstorms.

Baby picked up their wedding photo off the nightstand. "I look so young."

"You're *still* young."

"My mama wanted me to wait, but I was sixteen, I knew my own mind." Baby replaced the photo on the nightstand. "You made me happy. Don't ever forget that."

"I missed you." The Colonel stroked her back, made her shiver. "I didn't know how much until this moment."

"I hardly thought about you at all," said Baby, enjoying the look on his face. "Didn't even watch news about the Belt the whole time I was in Nueva Florida." She lowered her voice so he had to strain to hear. "I tried to put everything out of my mind. Start over. I wanted to be a new person . . . but no matter what I did, I was just me." She tugged at his chest hair. "Now that I'm here beside you again . . . feels like I've never been gone."

"Hard to believe everything that's happened since you left." The Colonel lay propped up on the pillows. "A year ago Malcolm Crews sent his band of dopeheads and maniacs up against me . . . today, he's the loudest voice defending me against Aztlán."

"I've seen him all over the tube ever since I came back," said Baby. "He's respectable now. *More* than respectable. He's the Man in White. How did *that* happen?"

"Damned if I know."

Baby let the silence gather in the twilight, let it coil around itself, tighter and tighter. "When are you going to ask me?"

"Ask you what?"

"Don't be like that. You got to have questions you want to ask me. Why I did it, and what I did afterwards, and was I unfaithful, and who—"

"You're here, that's all that matters."

"That just means you don't want to know."

"That's right, I don't want to know," said the Colonel. "Man goes looking for trouble, trouble's got a habit of following the scent right back to him."

"Okay," said Baby. "But if you ever—"

"I won't."

Baby slid her hand along the sheet, handled his man parts. She had almost forgotten the heft of him. Old man with a big pecker . . . deduct twenty years for that. "I'm not staying, Zachary. I don't want you to get your hopes up."

The Colonel sighed as she lightly squeezed him.

"I been wanting to ask you . . . whatever happened to John Moseby?" Baby felt him tense. "Last I saw of him he was half dead with the bends or something from diving in that underground lake. I just hoped he pulled through. You told me Fedayeen were tough—"

"Moseby survived."

"Praise the Lord." Baby released him, stared at the cracks in the ceiling. "It wasn't you, in case you're wondering. And it definitely wasn't Lester Gravenholtz, who I left two days later, thank you very much. You were a good husband, the very best—"

"Baby . . ."

"I went from my mama's house to your house. Never was on my own for a minute. I needed to find out what that was like, and Miami sounded strange and exciting."

"I understand. I wish I didn't, but I do," said the Colonel. "Were you still in Nueva Florida when the oil minister was murdered?"

"Oh my, yes," said Baby, feeling the warmth run down her neck to the tops of her breasts. "Awful thing. The things they showed on the news, 'bout to turn my stomach."

"I saw the footage too. The look of the body, the rage of the killer . . . reminded me of the kind of thing Lester was capable of."

Baby covered her mouth. "I thought the exact same thing, but was afraid to bring it up. You think we should contact the Aztlán embassy in Atlanta?"

The Colonel chuckled. "I doubt that Aztlán would put much weight in anything you or I have to say. Even if they did, they'd probably assume Lester was still in my employ."

"I was just trying to help." Baby curled up beside him, the Colonel hard as knotty hickory. "Maybe you should warn Rakkim. Lester had a huge hate-on for him. Not just for cutting up on him, but for the way Rikki looked at me. Lester gets his feelings hurt, there's no fixing it."

"If Lester was going to come after Rakkim, he would have done it before now."

"I guess so." Baby's hand snaked across the Colonel's belly. "It's just . . . just that killing the oil minister was the first we heard of Lester in a year. Maybe he was hurt and now he's well, and back doing what he likes best." She sat up, her body like marble in the moonlight. "You were the only one could keep Lester in line once he got the killing taste . . . heck, even you had trouble holding him back."

The Colonel watched her and for a moment Baby was afraid she had moved too fast. He nodded, and her doubts evaporated.

"You can tell Rikki yourself," said the Colonel.

"Can you reach him in the Republic?"

"I don't have to," said the Colonel. "He should be back here sometime in the next week."

"Rikki's in the Belt?" Baby hid her pleasure. This changed *everything*. "Is that why you said you weren't worried about Aztlán?"

The Colonel pulled her back to him. "Rikki's not here to help me. He's . . . looking at property around Gatlinburg. Tensions been easing between us and the Republic, and you know Rikki, he loves the Belt. I told him it's a good place to raise a family."

Baby tugged at the gray hairs on his chest. The Colonel was lying about Rikki looking at property. Rikki was here to help Moseby find the cross, she was sure of it. She had come here to steal the cross from Moseby and bring it to her daddy, but this new development was even better. Daddy had a real thing about Rakkim. All he talked about some nights, the two of them standing out on the balcony looking at the stars. Said Rikki was unique, a pivot point that he could use to move the earth itself. Didn't want him killed. Didn't even want him taken prisoner, if it could be helped. Just wanted to talk with him. No force. No threats. Said threats wouldn't work with Rikki anyway. Just wanted to give him a chance to see the light. Another chance.

Evidently they had talked once before, four or five years ago. Daddy had offered Rikki anything, and Rikki turned him down flat. The refusal, of course, had just made Daddy want him more. Baby had played that same game with men all her life, but Rikki, it was no game to him. Still, Daddy wasn't about to give up. If Baby strolled back into Daddy's suite bringing a piece of the cross *and* Rikki . . . well, let's just say Ibrahim would be lucky to end up as an attendant in a West Virginia outhouse.

"Baby?"

"I'm sorry . . . I was just thinking how happy I am," said Baby.

"You know . . . Lester had reason to be jealous," said the Colonel. "I saw the way Rikki looked at you too."

"*Hush* now. Rikki . . . he's just got those eyes, like some kind of hawk," said Baby. "Rikki doesn't miss anything. I could see how you might mistake that for interest, though." She looked at him the same as she did when she told him "I do" in that little church. "You got no reason to be jealous of anyone. I'm in your bed."

"*Now.*"

"I deserve that." Baby lowered her head. "I don't blame you one bit. You want to send me away, just—"

"I want you to stay," said the Colonel. "I want you to stay forever, if you've a mind to. And if I wake up tomorrow and you're gone again . . . then I'm still the luckiest man on earth to have spent one night with you."

Baby rested her head on his chest, felt his heart pounding and knew that it belonged to her.

CHAPTER 36

The woman who answered the door wore a bad wig atop her wrinkled face, a shapeless blue cotton dress hanging on her bony frame.

"Mrs. Harrison," started Moseby, "I'm John—"

"I remember you. . . ." The woman chewed her lip, revealed her few remaining teeth. "We talked a while ago . . . you were driving one of the Colonel's trucks."

"Couple weeks ago, yes, ma'am," said Moseby.

"Couple weeks? Seemed longer." She peered at Moseby. "You got a touch of it, didn't you?"

"Ma'am?"

"D.C. fever," said the woman. "I can see it in your eyes. Told you not to go there. No place for an outsider." She looked at Rakkim. "That your owner?"

"No, ma'am," said Moseby. "I'm not indentured. This is my friend Rikki."

"Good morning, Mrs. Harrison," said Rakkim. "Pleasure to meet you."

"I bet," said the woman. "What do you boys want?"

"Can we come in, Mrs. Harrison?" said Rakkim. "I'd like to talk to you. My wife, Sarah, had dealings with your late husband."

"You're *Sarah's* husband? That girl in Muslim country? Come on in. Make sure you wipe your feet." She shuffled into the house, feet slapping on the wood floor. "Darryl! We got company." She waved at a sagging sofa. "Sit yourselves down, I'll fetch you boys something to drink."

A man walked from a side room, skinny as the woman, equally toothless, his hair in patches on his scalp.

"The white boy's Sarah's husband," Mrs. Harrison shouted from the kitchen.

"Pleased to make your acquaintance," said Darryl, pumping Rakkim's hand. He hesitated, did the same for Moseby. "Howdy."

Mrs. Harrison emerged from the kitchen carrying two bottles of Coca-Cola between the fingers of her left hand, a bottle opener in the other. Rakkim saw Darryl's eyes widen at the bounty. She popped the tops, passed the bottles to Rakkim and Moseby. "Didn't figure you boys would cotton to cold well water," she cackled. "Go ahead, drink up."

"What about you?" said Rakkim.

"Darryl and I aren't thirsty," said Mrs. Harrison.

"No . . . no, we ain't," said Darryl.

"I want you to know," Mrs. Harrison said to Moseby, "the reason I didn't invite you into the house last time wasn't 'cause of your skin color. We're not racists in this family, not like some I could mention." Darryl nodded. "Just that my brother-in-law here was away, and it wouldn't be right for a woman alone to have a strange man in the house."

Moseby sipped his Coca-Cola. "No offense taken."

"Where were you, Darryl?" said Rakkim.

"Away." Darryl didn't take his eyes off the pop bottle in Rakkim's hand.

"Your wife has been a good friend to this family," Mrs. Harrison said to Rakkim. "She bought things from my husband for years, big things and little things, always paid top dollar. Asked about his health too. Only one who ever did. Are you a historian too?"

"No, not me." Rakkim took a long drink, the coldness and carbonation numbing his tongue, trickling down his dry throat. Nothing like it. He looked around the living room, surprised at the cleanliness and relative opulence of the surroundings. Hand-crafted furniture, a hutch filled with china, wallscreen TV. Even a piano in one corner. He checked the rad counter on his wrist—relatively low radiation count too. Credit the new-looking air scrubber on the roof. He looked at Darryl. "I'm not that thirsty and I'd hate to see the bubbles go to waste. Would you mind sharing this with me?"

Darryl glanced at his sister. "Okay . . . that would be good. No sense wasting."

Rakkim handed the bottle over.

Darryl started to snatch it, forced himself to slow down.

"Rikki and I are going back into the city, ma'am," said Moseby.

"That's foolish," said Mrs. Harrison. "You're going to poison yourself."

"We've got a better vehicle this time," said Moseby.

"I noticed," said Mrs. Harrison. "Seems like I saw a man named Corbett driving a van just like it."

"We bought it from Corbett," said Rakkim.

"That so?" Mrs. Harrison massaged her gums with a forefinger. "Well, you might have paid him, but the Corbett I know would sooner give up his balls than that war wagon."

"He's got no need for the van now," said Rakkim. "Or his balls."

"Glad to hear it." Mrs. Harrison examined her forefinger. "Honest . . . like your wife, that's saying something, but you still don't know where you're going, and the war wagon's not going to change that," she said. "Couple of outsiders driving around the city thinking treasure's going to call out to them."

Rakkim walked over to the family photographs that lined one whole wall. Photographs, not holograms, some of them ancient black-and-whites too. Poor folk in their Sunday best, kids behind the wheels of trucks, hard-eyed men and suspicious women, two young men in homemade rad-suits pretending to hold up the Washington Monument.

"That's me and Eldon on our first trip into the city together," said Darryl, standing beside him. "We hammered out an FBI insignia from inside a federal building a day later. Sold it for almost eight hundred dollars. Would have got twice that much but we chipped it."

"*You* chipped it," said Mrs. Harrison.

Rakkim checked out a grainy snapshot of a tired young man with a cigarette dangling from his lip, an automatic rifle slung in front of him. His jungle camouflage uniform blended in with the dense green foliage around him. A medal under glass was on the wall next to him. "Who's the soldier?"

Darryl stood beside him. "That's Eldon Harrison the first," he said, his gums whistling slightly. "Our great-grandpa. We got an Eldon in every generation since. My brother was the fourth in the line."

"Looks like he saw clear to the other side," said Rakkim. "That's a Silver Star."

"Yup. They don't give those out in cereal boxes."

"Where was that photo taken?"

"Vietnam. First war we ever lost. Not the last, though." Darryl sipped the Coca-Cola, offered it to Rakkim.

"You finish it," said Rakkim.

"Obliged," said Darryl, as fixed on the photo as Rakkim. "He was killed in action eighteen days after that picture was taken. A real hero. The best of us. Never even got to see Eldon Harrison Junior."

"I'm sorry," said Rakkim.

Darryl nodded.

"You had any more time to think about what we talked about, ma'am?" said Moseby.

Mrs. Harrison sat across from him, knees pressed together. "I've tried my best, but I can't come up with anything else. I'd tell you if I could."

"I know that," said Moseby. "It's just that sometimes things that you don't think are important turn out to be."

"I made Eldon three fried eggs the morning he left for the city and there was a spot of blood in one of the yolks," said Mrs. Harrison, her hands in her lap like they didn't even belong to her. "Just the tiniest spot of blood, but that's bad luck. I was going to throw them all out, start fresh, but Eldon told me I was crazy to waste good food." She blinked back tears. "That was the last meal I ever cooked for my husband. You'd think what I cooked or didn't cook wasn't important, but I think of that fried egg sizzling away in a dab of bacon grease, and I see that spot of blood . . . and . . . and I just want to die."

Darryl looked over at his sister-in-law, then at Rakkim. Shrugged.

Rakkim stared at another photo, a wedding photo, the young couple holding hands, grinning shyly at the camera. The slender bride seemed lost in the folds of her wedding gown, the groom stiff. He squinted at the date on the bottom.

Darryl tapped the glass over the photo. "That was a happy day. God, me and Eldon got so drunk the night before I didn't think he was going to make it through the ceremony."

"I didn't have any doubts," Mrs. Harrison said. "He knew what I had waiting for him that night. Both of us sixteen and raring to go."

"He was happy, Bernice." Darryl took a swallow of Coca-Cola. "No matter how bad things got, he was happy. Made me jealous, I'll tell you the truth."

Rakkim stared at the date on the wedding photo. If they were sixteen when they got married, Mrs. Harrison was only thirty-six. She looked like she was in her sixties.

"Do you love your wife, Rikki?" said Mrs. Harrison.

"Yes, ma'am, I do."

"You have children?" said Mrs. Harrison.

"A son."

The mister and I had nine," said Mrs. Harrison. "Three of them alive and well, praise God."

Rakkim pointed to another photo, three children in neat blue school uniforms with white piping on the sleeves and trousers. "Is this them?"

Mrs. Harrison rose from her chair, crossed over to him. Moseby followed her.

"That's my angels." Mrs. Harrison tapped the biggest child.

"That's Eldon the fifth." Tapped the girl. "That's Evelyn." Tapped the smaller boy. "And that little dickens is Zachary. Named him after the Colonel, greatest man who ever lived after Jesus Christ and Eldon the first."

"Nice-looking children," said Rakkim. It was the truth. They looked radiant.

"They're at the Bush Academy in Ottawa, Canada," said Mrs. Harrison. "Your wife got them a full scholarship. I guess you didn't know that."

"No, ma'am . . . I didn't," said Rakkim.

"Cost a pretty penny to go to that school," said Darryl. "All those rich kids . . . they're never going to want to come back here."

"I hope they don't," said Mrs. Harrison. "I most definitely hope they don't."

Rakkim couldn't take his eyes off the holo of the three children. "They . . . they look like they fit right in to that fancy school."

"You seen them a year ago, you wouldn't a' said that," said Darryl.

"They had the usual problems . . . usual for around here," said Mrs. Harrison. "Then my husband made a big find about a year ago. Everything changed after that."

"Eldon was always the lucky one," said Darryl.

Mrs. Harrison blushed, turned to Rakkim. "With the money we got from his big strike we were able to send the children to the clinic in Montreal. Bought them new kidneys, new pituitary glands, complete blood wash, of course. I visited them in the hospital afterwards and hardly recognized them. They were as fresh and beautiful as the day they were born."

"What did your husband find in the city?" said Moseby.

Mrs. Harrison shook her head. "I let the mister take care of business, and he let me take care of the home. Worked out pretty well all these years."

"He never told me either," said Darryl. "His own brother. Said it was none of my concern."

"He never brought this treasure home?" said Moseby.

"No," said Mrs. Harrison. "I guessed it was too big to carry."

"And too valuable to share," said Darryl.

"Why don't you take the Coca-Cola and go back to your room," said Mrs. Harrison. "Go on now." She waited until Darryl left. "He's not a bad man. Just always thought he got hind tit."

"Did your husband ever tell you what he was looking for on that last trip?" said Moseby.

"I *told* you, he kept his business to himself," said Mrs. Harrison.

"We know he made several trips for Sarah, before he found what she wanted," said Rakkim, looking over the other photos, trying to imagine the man who would leave all this and go into the dead city, time after time, even as his children sickened and died, even as he was eaten up with death. The sense of history and place that held them here . . . Rakkim didn't have it. Neither did Moseby; he had left the Republic and the Fedayeen for love and never looked back.

"He must have at least told you what he saw along the way . . . some building, some landmark," said Moseby. "We just want to know where to start looking, Mrs. Harrison."

"I'd help you boys if I could," she said. "Your wife . . . she's been a blessing to our family," she said to Rakkim. "She done things for us we could never repay. Getting the kids into the Bush Academy, that wouldn't have happened without her. So, you'll have to believe me when I tell you, when the mister left that last morning . . . all he said was he was going somewhere bound to break his heart."

"The whole city makes me want to cry," said Moseby.

"That's *you*, and your outland ways, bawlin' over a stubbed toe or a runover kitten," said Mrs. Harrison. "My husband was made of stronger stuff. We lost our first three babies . . . I never seen him shed a tear when he broke ground for their graves, just cursed the earth for taking them. I can't imagine what it would take to break his heart, but that's where he said he was going."

If burying your children didn't break your heart, Rakkim didn't know what would . . . but Eldon Harrison had found it in D.C. Rakkim stared at the soldier in the jungle. Eldon Harrison the first. The best of them, Darryl had said. The noble dead. He took a deep breath, then walked over to Mrs. Harrison, embraced her, and she was all sharp bones and startled femininity. "Thank you for all your help, ma'am."

Mrs. Harrison nodded. "You give our love to your wife."

They were almost at the war wagon before Moseby spoke. "Why are we leaving?"

Rakkim turned and waved to Mrs. Harrison, who stood on the porch watching them. She didn't wave back, instead turned and went back inside. "She told us enough," said Rakkim. "I think I know where the safe room is."

CHAPTER 37

"Look, Mama, Elvis is shaking," said Steve, mimicking the King's movements.

Betty Grassley looked up and Steve was right, the cloud sculpture of Elvis was moving his hips, a cloud sculpture of the young Elvis, slim and sexy in rolled blue jeans and a dark shirt, floating five thousand feet above Graceland, the light breeze animating him.

Steve shook his hips like Elvis, the fake sideburns he had bought in the gift shop curling slightly from his pink cheeks. The black pompadour was his own. He wore his favorite jumpsuit, the red, white and blue bicentennial version that Elvis had worn for the first time at the Charlotte Coliseum, March 26, 1976. Steve had been born on March 26, and Betty considered it a sign from God.

Two blue-haired ladies beamed as Steve shimmied. "He's got the moves," one said.

"He's nine years old and consecrated in the blood," said Betty. "Elvis lullabies were the only thing that put him right to sleep."

"Amen," said the two ladies.

Betty sat down on one of the many benches in the Meditation Garden while Steve stared up at the sculpture in the clear blue Memphis sky. Her feet hurt. She waitressed six days a week, and on the seventh day she went to Graceland. There was a beautiful limestone chapel on the grounds, but that was booked up for years with weddings. No, she considered the whole thirteen-acre site to be one big church, and the Meditation Garden was where she liked to pray. Steve liked the Jungle Room and the two lions beside the main gate, but there was nothing like sitting here in the open air, smelling the blooming jasmine. Most of the tourists stayed in the Heartbreak Hotel across the street; they congregated around the crypts where Elvis's mama and daddy, Gladys and Vernon, were buried, but she preferred this spot, the most tranquil place in the garden.

She quietly slipped off her shoes, massaged her arches as she listened to Elvis singing "How Great Thou Art," one of her favorite hymns.

Presidente Argusto guided his JX light bomber into a vast, puffy white cumulus cloud over southern Tennessee. He glanced at the display on his windscreen, noted his precise position, accelerating now, leaving his two wingmen behind. This was to be his mission, and his alone. *Mano a mano*, a killing stroke to avenge the insults visited on him and Aztlán, a harsh lesson but a necessary one. The murder of his oil minister had been bad enough, but now these Belt peons had blown apart an Aztlán cruise ship, killing almost everyone on board. The Aztlán people demanded vengeance and Argusto was more than happy to oblige.

He delighted at the centrifugal pressure as he banked sharply—even in his G-suit he could feel his chest pressing toward his spine as the JX surged forward. Magnificent aircraft. Chinese stealth design, Swiss avionics, Aztlán laser-guided missiles. Invisible, fast and deadly.

They had left from the El Paso airfield, he and his wingmen, headed off across the Gulf as though on a normal training mission. Fifty miles off New Orleans they had dropped into stealth mode, depending on the mission control center outside Tenochtitlán to take the helm and zigzag them through the overlapping maze of Belt radar installations. If he wanted, the digital display on his windscreen would reveal the current position of every plane in the Aztlán air armada, and mission control could deploy each of them as needed.

The integrated control system was a force multiplier—Argusto's tactics against the Central American Union had been brilliant, but it had been the Nigerian integrated system that allowed him to destroy the enemy's air defenses within the first twenty minutes of the war. Not that Argusto feared being intercepted by the decrepit Belt fighters, or even the new Russian antiaircraft missile systems President Raynaud had installed around key sites. The JX could take care of itself. It was the *surprise* that mattered to Argusto. Let the Belt peons realize that at any moment, day or night, their world could be set ablaze. Let them understand their position in the new world order.

Argusto blasted out of the cottony cumulus cloud, the cockpit nearly silent, only the faint whoosh of air rushing past as he headed into the deep blue sky. From the ground the plane would be a flash of light, a flare of sunlight.

Morales had been appalled when Argusto informed him what he intended. The secretary of state begged him to reconsider, saying the attack would inflame the Belt beyond all reason. What did he call it? "A gross overreaction," *mio presidente. Por favor, por favor.* Argusto had expected such a reaction from Morales; it was the response of his air marshal, Bettencourt, that had surprised him. Bettencourt counseled against the presidente himself leading the attack, arguing that he was too valuable to the empire, his loss in combat disastrous to the nation. Argusto had heard the marshal out, then asked him a simple question: *Do you doubt the superiority of your aircraft, or do you doubt the skill of your presidente?* Bettencourt had stepped back from the precipice and saluted.

Radar confirmed Graceland seventeen miles away. What Morales hadn't appreciated was that it was precisely because of Graceland's spiritual and cultural significance that it had to be taken out. Kill the heroes and you kill the soul of a nation. Twelve miles. The vibration surrounding him was pure music, a symphony of power overwhelming everything in its path. Five miles. He shot directly into a rockabilly Elvis cloud sculpture floating above the shrine, slightly roiling the interior. Two miles.

He burst into the sunlight, bathed in glory, the tears of Huitzilo-pochtli, god of the sun, god of war. At the peak of his accelera-tion, Argusto released the bomb . . . the egg of death.

Steve arched his back slightly, the nine-year-old a little confused as he watched the cloud sculpture. "Mama?"

Last week Betty's best customer had given her two tickets to the special prayer service that Pastor Malcolm Crews led on the south lawn. She and Steve had shown up at dawn, shown up in their Sunday best, and the line stretched for a half mile. Even Jinx Raynaud, the first lady, was there. Although she didn't have to wait in line, of course. It even looked to Betty like the first lady had spotted Steve's white jumpsuit and smiled, but she couldn't be sure.

The service, on the anniversary of Elvis's death, was focused on resurrection and renewal. Pastor Crews stalked the stage, white suit gleaming in the August sunshine. He said Elvis wasn't dead, but was seated at the right hand of God, up there with all the saints, a Tennessee boy made good. One of God's favorites. *God loves us all*, Pastor Crews said, *but who could blame him for loving Elvis just a little bit more than the rest of us?* The crowd laughed, applauded so hard it sounded like a thunderstorm on Judgment Day. He had preached for five hours straight, people fainting, people talking in tongues, people jerk-dancing in the aisles while the ushers tried to calm them down.

Betty had bought Steve a Hawaiian Punch snow cone; he made a mess of it on his white jumpsuit, but she didn't care. The stains would wash out, that's what she always told herself. Pastor Crews said this was a time of great tribulation, *the big show, brothers and sisters, the moment when the chosen will be separated. God's lambs will enter into heaven and the goats will be slaughtered. . . . There's gonna be barbecue in heaven*, Crews had shouted, *best barbecue you ever ate*, and the crowd roared with laughter.

Steve swiveled his hips, the white cape of his jumpsuit

swaying with him as he played an invisible guitar. Sometimes, when she looked at him, Betty could see the King himself, reborn. He suddenly stopped playing, his hands falling to his sides as he looked up.

Today is August sixteen, brothers and sisters, Crews had said at the sermon last week. *The unbelievers will tell you that Elvis died on this day, but we know better, don't we?* Shouts of agreement. Testifying. *Elvis could no more die than you or I,* said Crews. *He's merely gone ahead, to set a place at the table for us.* The band kicked in with "Are You Lonesome Tonight" and the whole crowd sang along, Pastor Crews too. *Resurrection Day,* he kept saying, *it's a comin', can't you feel it, brothers and sisters?*

Betty could certainly feel a change coming, and not a minute too soon. She was tired. Not just tired of working the long hours, and hardly enough time for Steve, she was tired of the news, bad news added to bad news, layoffs and payoffs, and damn Aztlán beating at the door, heathens demanding land that God gave to the Belt. Those Muslims in the Republic were looking less like the Antichrist, and more like kinfolk all the time. Just like Pastor Crews said.

A group of tourists stood staring at the sky, Atlanta people from the fancy-pants look of them. One of them pointed, jabbing his finger. You'd think they had never seen a cloud sculpture before. Not that Graceland's Elvis wasn't better than anything they had in the big city, but still, they should have some respect. This wasn't some tourist trap. This was where Elvis had lived and died, where he rested his weary head when the world got too heavy for him. This was hallowed ground.

Betty tried to slip her shoes back on, but her feet had swollen. She wiggled her toes in the cool grass, enjoying the sensation. She liked to imagine Elvis walking on this grass, this very same grass, barefoot, just like her, 'cause Lord knows, he carried his own burdens, that man did. She wiped her eyes, grateful to be here in this blessed spot, thanking God for this moment.

"Mama?" Steve pointed at the sky. "Mama, what's happening?"

Something . . . something had busted out of Elvis's chest, stirring the cloud sculpture beyond its ability to maintain itself. Betty shielded her eyes with her hand.

Steve scampered beside her, held on to her hip. "What . . . what is it?"

Betty squinted up at the sky. Yes . . . she could make it out now. An airplane. Someone was going to be in big trouble for disturbing Elvis. . . . She sucked in a breath as the plane released a silvery egg. No, not an egg.

People walked quickly from the Meditation Garden, started running.

"Mama?"

"Hush, now." Betty picked Steve up in her arms, felt him warm against her, hair smelling sweet with his boy sweat. "It's all right. Everything's fine."

Steve craned his head, trying to get a better look at the plane, but Betty kept him turned away, gently bouncing him like she did when he was a baby. Lord, that boy could eat.

He put his arms around her neck. "What is it?"

"Nothing." She ran her hand through his hair, the bomb hurtling right toward them, so close now she could practically read the serial number on the devilish thing. "I just love you, child, that's all."

CHAPTER 38

Rakkim accelerated onto the sidewalk; the reinforced front end of the van shoved aside a wrecked car, sent it slewing back into the street.

"You could slow down, wind your way through the cars," said Moseby. "You pop a gasket, or burn out the transmission, game over."

Rakkim drove on, tires crunching over broken glass where the storefronts had blown out from the shock wave of the suitcase nuke. Thirty years later and the glass still glittered like diamonds in the morning sun. The van did what it had been built for—the seals kept the radiation level inside low enough that they didn't need to wear the helmets of their rad-suits, and the air scrubbers kept things breathable. Outside . . . nothing could fix outside.

"I already checked that area, by the way," said Moseby. "I checked the whole ellipse."

Rakkim downshifted, the puncture-proof tires rolling over a flattened sedan. Other scavengers had come this way, Pennsylvania Avenue a regular zombie thoroughfare. It had been late afternoon when they left the Harrison house—they had driven to the outskirts of D.C., checked the rad-detector until they found a relatively cool spot among a grove of stunted trees and parked, waited for daylight. Moseby had slept, his breathing erratic, but Rakkim stayed awake, making sure they hadn't been followed. The city had been completely dark except for a dim glow near the Capitol building.

"I hope you're right," said Moseby. "Doesn't seem much to go on, though."

"You saw the photos of Eldon the first in Vietnam. He's their bright and shining star," said Rakkim. "Like you said, the whole city is a heartbreaker, but for that family, for Eldon in particular, it's the Wall that's going to make him ache." The van hit a pothole, but he maintained control. "I've seen pictures of the Vietnam Memorial . . . that long expanse of black granite would wring tears from a stone." He slowed . . . stopped, the engine rumbling, the air compressor banging away on the roof.

Moseby didn't ask why Rakkim had stopped. He had done the same thing on his first trip into D.C.

Rakkim stared out the leaded windshield. Most of the major buildings in the city looked untouched, but the suitcase nuke must have gone off near Pennsylvania Avenue because the White House wasn't white anymore. Paint scorched. Windows melted. The iron picket fence surrounding the mansion twisted from the heat of the blast. Rakkim finally put the van in gear, drove on. He had no idea how long they had been there.

Moseby coughed into his fist. "Two more blocks . . . make a right onto Ninth and then another right onto Constitution."

"How are you feeling?"

"I've been worse," said Moseby.

Rakkim could see the Washington Monument tilted but still standing, which Sarah would probably find deeply symbolic. Give her the chance she'd put the image on the new money once the country was reunited.

"Watch out." Moseby pointed. "Zombies dug a tank trap just past that bench. See it?"

Rakkim guided the van over the curb and onto the grass, circling around the tank trap. Somebody had gone to a lot of work, digging a trench across the street then covering it up with painted cardboard. Any vehicle speeding down the road would bust an axle for sure. He drove back onto the street. "I didn't know zombies scavenged each other."

"They don't," said Moseby. "The tank traps are more to stake a claim, warn others off." He blotted his face with a forearm. "Same thing happens in New Orleans. You dive the French

Quarter, you spend more time watching out for hook lines than moray eels."

Rakkim glanced at the sniper rifle on the floor between them. "I saw lights on the other side of the Capitol building last night."

"They were working that site when I was here too. They saw me, but kept their distance. Most zombies don't go looking for trouble. It's dangerous enough just *being* here." Moseby rested his hand on the butt of his flechette pistol. "They don't usually work nights, though. Too easy to trip and cut your suit on a piece of rebar. If they're going twenty-four/seven . . . they might have found something good." He checked the rear screen. "Could be bad luck for us. If they found something valuable, they'll be nervous about company." He looked down the side streets. "This van isn't going to help things. Mrs. Harrison recognized it. Zombies might too."

"They think we're Corbett and his boys, they might keep their distance," said Rakkim.

"They think we're Corbett and his boys, they might feel they have to take us out before we steal whatever they've found."

Rakkim accelerated.

Moseby hung on as they bounced along, Rakkim changing lanes, driving up on the sidewalk, anything to avoid a pattern and make them an easy target. They passed the Jefferson Memorial . . . the Lincoln Memorial, empty now, Lincoln moved in pieces to a place of honor in Atlanta. Moseby steeled himself as they drove up the National Mall and approached the Wall. He had told Rakkim that he had gone over the site, but in truth his exploration had been cursory. It was just too grim—that expanse of heroes, their names etched in black granite with no one to read them, none but the dead.

Rakkim drove on to what was left of the lawn, the armored van sinking slightly. He pressed the accelerator, the four-by-four digging in, as he continued down a winding slope and finally parked. The van was hidden now as much as possible. He turned off the engine, looked at Moseby and slipped on the hood of his rad-suit, put on his gloves while Moseby did the same. Rakkim slipped the small, radiation-proof container for the cross into a side pocket of his suit, then the two of them eased into the back of the van. It was a tight fit, but they managed to squeeze into the decontamination area, then sealed the inner door, opened the outer. Rakkim was first out, stepped onto the ground as though he were landing on the moon. The sound of his own breathing unnerved him.

"Relax," said Moseby. "Most of the suits the zombies use allow in five or six times the rads. Just breathe slowly. You don't want to burn through your air filters too fast."

Rakkim walked past him, drawn to the wall that gleamed in the sun. He stood there staring, the names superimposed on his own reflection, seemingly part of him now. Moseby stared too. All those names . . . Rakkim never knew any of them, all of them dead seventy or eighty years, but they were warriors, just like he was. It was telling, somehow, that the zombies, who had no compunction about hammering off pieces of the Capitol or the Supreme Court or the White House itself—not one of them had ever tried to sell a chunk of the Wall. There would have been buyers too, there were always buyers, but no zombie would do the dirty work.

"We should go, Rikki," said Moseby, his voice muffled.

"I know," said Rakkim, not moving. A few minutes later he placed a hand on the cool granite, said a silent prayer for the men who died in service to their country.

Then they started looking, each taking a different direction around the Wall, keeping their eyes out for any irregularities, any sign of recent activity, a bit of torn rad-suit, a hidden door, a smudge on the Wall itself. They crossed paths after two hours, started another circuit, expanding their area of interest.

It was late afternoon, the sun slanting through the petrified trees, before Rakkim spotted an indentation in the ground where rainwater had collected. The spot was along an inconspicuous outbuilding, where the old government stored mementoes left by mourners at the Wall. Not much of an indentation, but when he stuck a gloved finger in the water, it was deeper at one point than another, as though someone in a hurry had stepped there. He pressed himself against the side, sighted along the outbuilding . . . and saw an edge, a lip where the facing didn't fit properly. He looked under the facing, made sure there wasn't a nail or anything sharp, and lifted. A small section slid up, revealing a narrow escape tunnel leading down into the darkness. Someone had burned off the steel hatch to the tunnel with a laser torch.

"John . . . ? *John!*"

Rakkim was standing there when Moseby ran over. Moseby patted him on the back. "You've got the makings of a real finder." He took out a small digital camera, held it at arm's length toward himself. "My name is John Moseby. I'm a deep-water Baptist, Church of the Redeemer, Sumner, Louisiana." He turned the camera on Rakkim. Waited. "Rakkim?"

"I . . . I'm Rakkim Epps. Fedayeen. I'm Muslim . . . but I don't have a regular mosque. Except maybe the Horn of Africa mosque I attend sometimes with General Kidd."

Moseby stopped the camera. "What's wrong? You claustrophobic?"

Rakkim couldn't take his eyes off the darkness. "Evidently." He slipped into the tunnel headfirst, inching forward on his hands and knees, his shoulders brushing the sides. The flashlight helped.

"You all right?"

Rakkim was breathing so fast his face mask fogged up, the respirator unable to keep up. He closed his eyes, slowed his heart rate, waited until his mask cleared and then continued. He could hear Moseby enter the tunnel behind him, narrating their descent for the camera as they continued. Sarah wanted complete documentation to show the world what they had found. He couldn't wait to get back out into the open air.

Up ahead the flashlight showed where the zombie had cut

the interior steel hatch away, the safe room beyond. He could also see the raw edge of the opening that had snagged the zombie's suit. "We're almost there," said Rakkim, fumbling out his own laser torch. "I just want to clean up the edge."

"Careful."

Rakkim popped on the torch, flinched at the sudden bright light. Took just a few sweeps to smooth out the jagged metal. A few minutes more for it to cool. He slowly eased himself through the opening, dropped onto the floor of the safe room. "I'm in."

Moseby peeked through the opening. Lit up the room with his camera, panning from one side to the other. He was bigger than Rakkim, but somehow entered the room gracefully, barely making a sound. "This room was first discovered by a brave man named Eldon Harrison. Mr. Harrison gave his life trying to recover what was hidden away in this sacred place. Both Rakkim and I, and all Americans, honor his memory."

Rakkim leaned against the heavy desk, panting. He hadn't heard the word *Americans* used outside of a historical context within his lifetime. He walked around the desk, his footsteps raising a fine dust. The piece of cross lay on the floor, barely eight inches long, just outside the reach of the skeletal dead man who had come to fetch it. There were even more flowers on the wood now. He bent down, gingerly touched a blossom, half expecting it to shatter, but it bent and then sprung back.

Moseby moved into position, still filming. "As you can see, what we think is a piece of the true cross has sprouted in the toxic air of this city, sprouted in total darkness. I don't know why this has happened now, but maybe because its healing powers are needed now more than ever." He glanced at Rakkim, still keeping the camera on the cross.

"As a Muslim I don't attach the same religious significance to the cross as Christians," said Rakkim, "but seeing it covered in flowers . . . it's amazing."

"It's a *miracle*," said Moseby. "I don't care what you believe, this is a miracle."

Moseby stopped the camera, put it away, then fell to his knees. Bent his head in prayer while Rakkim looked away.

When Moseby was done praying, Rakkim laid the piece of the cross in the small, white pine box it had originally been stored in, careful not to crush the flowers, then slid the box into a rad-proof pouch. Moseby filmed the whole procedure.

"Anything else—?"

"Shhh." Rakkim moved toward the entrance to the crawl space, listening. He heard whispered voices echoing. Then the sound of something bouncing against the metal walls of the crawl space. "Down!"

Rakkim dived behind the desk, the pouch with the cross under him. Moseby moved a little slower, the concussion from the explosion blasting him against the wall.

Baby saw the Colonel in his dress uniform as she walked from the barn and knew he had gotten the call from Malcolm Crews. She swatted dust out of her jeans. "What is it?"

"I have to leave for Atlanta," said the Colonel.

"What happened, Zachary?"

"Graceland happened," said the Colonel. "Aztlán crossed a line, now the whole country's raging for war."

"You're not?"

"I've seen war."

"Then why go? It's the army's job anyway, not yours. General Paulson—"

"Paulson's lost the confidence of the officer corps," said the Colonel, standing stiff as a saber, "and President Raynaud's useless. He's ready to resign, go back to Leesburg and breed bulldogs." He looked past her. "Never liked bulldogs myself, but I have to admit, the president's got an eye for bloodlines."

"I don't want you to go."

The Colonel kissed her, but it was the kiss of a man already gone. "I just got a call from Malcolm Crews. Man's crazier than a shithouse rat, but he defended me when Aztlán was calling for my head, defended me at great risk to himself. Crews says he's got twenty million listeners who think it's time for me to step forward, including half the generals and the first lady herself."

"What you're doing . . . some folks might call it treason."

"There is that," admitted the Colonel, "but then, that's what the British said about George Washington." He tugged at his jacket. The Congressional Medal of Honor bobbed around his neck. "If it comes down to it, I'll choose treason over abandoning my duty."

He looked at her with such regret that she feared he was going to change his mind and stay. It had taken her ten minutes to convince Crews to call the Colonel and tell him to get his ass to Atlanta—preacherman was getting used to doing things his own way.

"I leave for Atlanta in an hour," said the Colonel. "Taking the men here with me. The rest will be following shortly. I've made arrangements for you to take refuge in Canada."

Baby stamped her foot. "I'm not leaving. You think you're the only one gets to be brave? I'll wait here until Rikki and Moseby come back from D.C. Those two boys may need a hot meal and a cold beer."

"More likely they'll need a doctor."

The Colonel kissed her, holding her so tight she felt the silver buttons of his jacket pressing against her, and she kissed him back just as passionately, wishing she really were a simple girl, with simple dreams and simple desires. A girl like that could be happy with the Colonel.

Ears still ringing from the explosion, Rakkim stood up, wobbly, disoriented from the shock wave. Dust and reinforced concrete drifted from the crawl space. He shone his flashlight into the opening. Saw the tunnel collapsed at the first bend, the metal blackened. His face mask was misted with blood. He felt the weight of the earth on his chest. Could . . . could have been worse, though. Whatever it was, a grenade, percussion round . . .

it had gone off too soon. Or maybe the zombies who had sent it down the crawl space knew just what they were doing—seal the place up but not destroy anything valuable in it. Come back at their leisure, reopen the tunnel and see what they could see.

"The cross okay?" gasped Moseby.

"Fine." His legs still rubbery, Rakkim walked over to where Moseby slumped against the wall. "How about you?"

"I'll make it." Moseby checked the camera. Nodded.

Rakkim examined Moseby's suit, hands trembling as he held the flashlight, taking his time. No tears, no breaks, no loss of integrity. Then he had Moseby do the same thing for him. Good news all around. After they changed out their air filters, Moseby looked up the tunnel, shook his head. "How's the claustrophobia?"

"Thanks for reminding me." Rakkim stepped over the skeleton near the doorway. The reinforced door was jammed, but there was room for him to squeeze out. A long hall ran down the full length of the building. The flashlight still had plenty of power . . . but it seemed dimmer, lost in the expanse of flat gray paint.

Moseby joined him in the hallway, limping.

"I may convert to Christianity," said Rakkim as they trudged down the hall. He hefted the pouch with the piece of the cross. "This thing's already bringing us good luck. Like you said, it's a miracle."

CHAPTER 39

The Montgomery Farms milk truck hit a pothole, Rakkim's head whipping forward. Third time in the last half hour. Driving too fast, Rikki. He stayed off the brakes anyway, looked over at Moseby curled in the passenger seat. "John?" Dust swirled in through the seams in the doors and floorboards, radioactive dust and probably worse. "*John!*"

Moseby lifted his head. "I'm alive."

"Good," said Rakkim. "Go back to sleep."

Moseby slumped back down.

It had taken Rakkim and Moseby all night to find their way out of the safe room in the Vietnam War Memorial depository, most of the exits blocked, the darkness stifling. They had walked for miles, backtracking, lost in a maze of corridors and stairwells. He was grateful to be in the sunlight now, grateful for the toxic breeze that blew around them—better to die outside, better to die anywhere than die underground.

Rakkim checked the rearview. An actual mirror not a screen. Milk truck must be thirty years old. One of those jury-rigged zombie jobs that offered only transportation, not protection. No wonder the zombies they had stolen it from hadn't chased them far. Figured the truck would kill them anyway.

Last night, there had been a point when they had found themselves at yet another dead end, a point where Rakkim had almost given up. His light had fallen down a grating, and Moseby had turned his own light off while they rested, wanting to conserve the batteries. Rakkim had felt himself starting to panic, unable to breathe, certain that the ventilation system in his suit was malfunctioning. Moseby must have heard him gasping, because he suddenly reached out, put the flashlight in Rakkim's hand, told him not to turn it on, just know he could if he needed to. The panic attack dissolved. A few minutes later, still in total darkness, Rakkim gave him the flashlight back and they continued.

It had been Moseby who finally figured out that the way out was counterintuitive—they had to go deeper underground to find the passage that led them up again to the outside. When they finally crawled out the emergency exit, the sun was just coming up, a hot red ball over the marble monuments of the dead capital.

After Moseby had filmed the two of them, he bowed his head for a moment, then looked up at Rakkim. "You don't pray anymore?"

"God and I have decided to ignore each other. It's for the best." Rakkim had stopped, his glib relief at being outside dissipating.

The van was gone.

"We got . . . what we came for," said Moseby, coughing up a pale pink mist. "We could try walking out."

Rakkim held up his machine pistol. "Or we could get the van back."

Another pothole disturbed his reverie, Rakkim lurching forward as he put one hand out to keep Moseby from hitting the dash. Moseby slept on as Rakkim carefully drove around stalled cars and a motorcycle with melted tires. The van would have rolled right over the obstacles, but they hadn't gotten the van back and the milk truck's transmission slipped in and out of gear.

Rakkim checked his rad-meter. Might as well roll down the windows for the protection the truck gave. Useless piece of shit, but it was still better than walking. Most of the spare air filters for their suits had been in the van; they wouldn't have survived the hike. As it was . . . midafternoon and they were almost out of the city. Maybe another five or ten miles before the radiation level dropped appreciably. A couple hours after that and they'd be back at the Colonel's place. Get Moseby into the field hospital the Colonel had set up.

Moseby groaned in his sleep.

No way to care for him. Couldn't open up his suit and stitch him up without him getting a fatal dose of radiation. He was just going to have to hang on until Rakkim could get him help. Rakkim accelerated, the truck's engine protesting, revving way too high.

They had found their van at the site behind the Capitol building, the zombies working on something at the rear of the building, over a dozen of them going at it with jackhammers and laser torches, filling a large flatbed truck with bits of marble . . . marble heads . . . presidents, probably, or senators who hadn't gotten caught. They circled around the site, approached from the north where the zombies would least expect it.

One of the zombies was taking a torch to the rear compartment of their van, trying to fix the seals that they had ruined breaking into it. Guy didn't even have a homemade rad-suit, just a rubbery face mask like painters used. Rakkim closed within twenty yards of the van, Moseby a few steps behind, the two of them leapfrogging closer and closer, until they took cover behind an abandoned taxicab. A briefcase was still in the backseat of the taxi. Looked like alligator.

As Moseby sprinted to the van, he slipped on some loose rocks, twisted an ankle. He didn't make much noise, but the zombies stopped jackhammering at that moment, and one of them turned, saw Moseby. Everybody had a gun, of course.

Rakkim shot three of them, then raced to help Moseby, bullets splintering the pavement around them. Moseby got hit just before Rakkim reached him, pitching forward. Rakkim knelt beside Moseby, slowly sweeping the machine pistol across the site.

Three of the zombies scurried over to protect the van, set up a fire perimeter.

Rakkim had no choice but to retreat, providing cover fire as Moseby limped ahead of him. Moseby got hit again, spun around but didn't fall. Rakkim carried him to the first zombie vehicle he saw. The milk truck. *Montgomery Farms, Home of*

Contented Cows. Piece of shit truck with useless radiation shielding and no air filters. He drove off, the zombies pocking it with gunshots. He stopped a few blocks later, slapped a couple of pressure bandages on Moseby's wounds, sealing the holes in the suit at the same time.

Rakkim drove on the shoulder of the road now, bypassing the line of abandoned cars alongside the Marriott Hotel, its ragged front awning flapping like a flag.

"You're a lousy driver," said Moseby, his voice raspy.

"Glad you're awake. Time to change your air filter."

"You take it," wheezed Moseby.

"I just changed mine." Rakkim fished the last air filter out of his side pocket, replaced the one on Moseby's suit ventilator. He examined the used one, filthy, three stages beyond *replace.* Tossed it aside. His own was in the same condition.

"You . . . you *sure?*" Moseby breathed deeper with the new one installed. "I thought we only had one filter left."

"You miscounted. I replaced mine about a mile back."

"You're not pulling some dumbass stunt, are you?" said Moseby.

"I look like a hero?" said Rakkim.

"You look like a guy who should have left me back there," said Moseby.

"If I did that, who would get me out the next time a building collapses on me?" said Rakkim.

Moseby breathed easier with the fresh filter, his face mask clearing. His eyes fluttered.

"Get some rest," said Rakkim. "I'll wake you when we stop for burgers and fries."

"Milkshake." Moseby yawned. "I want a vanilla milkshake too."

The melonhead on the front porch thought he was a big man with that assault rifle slung in front of him, covering Gravenholtz as he pushed open the gate.

"That's far enough," said the zombie, a skinny geezer, his face raw and scaly like a steam burn. "God, mister, you're an ugly son of a bitch."

"You're not very neighborly," said Gravenholtz, his hand still on the gate.

"You ain't my neighbor," said the zombie.

"I don't want trouble." Gravenholtz knew he should smile or something, but he just couldn't be bothered. He'd been knocking on doors in Shitville for two days without success; fucking zombies all had the same suspicious attitude. No faith in their fellow man. Which Gravenholtz fully justified by kicking their brains out, but that wasn't really the point. None of them knew anything, which pissed him off even more. He checked his rad-counter. Good thing he didn't intend having kids. So much for Baby telling him he didn't need a rad-suit, and *Where am I supposed to get one on short notice, Lester honey?*

"You don't want trouble," said the zombie. "What *do* you want?"

"Just got a few questions to ask you."

"First the black, and now you." The zombie leveled the assault rifle at Gravenholtz's midsection. "I'm getting tired of you outlanders with your questions."

"Don't blame you," said Gravenholtz, pleased that he had finally found someone that had met Moseby. He walked on through the gate, stopped at the edge of the porch. "All these interruptions must cut into your jacking-off time." The zombie didn't react. For all Gravenholtz knew he had hit it right about the jacking-off time.

"You got money?" said the zombie. "I take cash or credit chips."

"Sure, I got plenty of money."

"The black give me two hundred dollars to tell him if I knew where Eldon was working the city," said the zombie. "I told him a bunch of bullshit and kept the money." He curled his finger around the trigger of the assault rifle. "How about you empty your pockets and we'll see how much bullshit you bought yourself?"

"Yes, sir," said Gravenholtz, his hands in the air. "Please don't shoot me."

The zombie jabbed the barrel of the rifle at him. "Hurry up. Price of bullshit is going up every minute."

Gravenholtz reached into his pocket, pulled out an ivory credit chip with a platinum edge. Saw the zombie's eyes widen. Gravenholtz stepped forward onto the front steps, held out the chip, trembling . . . dropped it.

The zombie's eyes dipped toward the falling chip for a second.

Gravenholtz grabbed the barrel of the assault rifle, swung it and slammed it into the zombie's knee, brought him down, howling. Gravenholtz beat the other knee with the rifle, the zombie screaming, gave him another few whacks for that "ugly son of a bitch" crack. Normally Gravenholtz would use his fists to break somebody up, it was more satisfying, but he didn't like the idea of touching the zombie with his bare hands.

"Jeez, mister, jeez . . ." blubbered the zombie as he flopped on the porch. "What did I ever do to you?"

Gravenholtz sat on the steps. Lit a cigarette. He thought of Karla Jean. He thought about her since she died. Since she tried to kill him. Strange he didn't hold it against her. Made him even sadder that she was gone. Woman like that, holding a grudge against him all that time . . . that was a woman worth loving. He just wished he had a chance to change her mind. Might have made a difference. He sure as shit wouldn't be sitting here with this toothless fuck.

"Mister?"

Gravenholtz blew a smoke ring over the zombie's head. Like a halo. Made him laugh.

"Mister, *please*."

"You said the other fella who came around here . . . the black . . . you said he asked about a man named Eldon."

Gravenholtz puffed out another smoke ring. "I want you to tell me where this Eldon lives. You can do that, can't you?" He put the cigarette out on the zombie's bare wrist, listened to him shriek. "But no bullshit. You don't even want to *think* about telling me anything but the gospel truth."

The front axle snapped on a smooth downhill stretch of mountain road, no reason for it, just gave out, and Rakkim fought the wheel trying to keep from ramming through the flimsy guardrail before bringing the milk truck to a stop.

Moseby struggled upright, his clothes soaked in sweat. "Are we there yet?"

"Almost." Rakkim set the emergency brake, helped Moseby out. They had gotten rid of their rad-suits about an hour ago, Rakkim balling them up and burying them so no one would find them and get contaminated. The truck itself was still hot, but the air filters in their suits were blocked, and asphyxiation was a more immediate danger. Blood from Moseby's wounds oozed from under the pressure bandages.

Moseby leaned against the milk truck, a smiling cow painted on the side. "How far?"

Rakkim coughed. "A few more miles."

"How few?"

"Quit asking so many questions." Rakkim squinted in the late-afternoon sun. "We're almost there. Hop on my back, I'll carry you halfway."

"Just get me a walking stick and try to keep up," said Moseby.

By the time Rakkim came back with a suitable stick, Moseby was lying in the road, passed out. Rakkim dragged him into some shade, then got back into the milk truck, put it into neutral and released the brake. He watched as the truck picked up speed, wobbling, then crashed through the guardrail and into the woods below. No one in their right mind would attempt to salvage it, but there were plenty of people not in their right mind. The world was full of them, more produced every minute.

Moseby opened his eyes, his face veiled with dust. "I'm tired."

"I'm hot, I'm thirsty," said Rakkim, sitting down beside him, shoulder to shoulder. "And I've got a boo-boo on my hand from driving."

Moseby laughed, coughed up a bubble of blood. His face turned serious. "I want to see it, Rikki."

"You already saw—"

"I want to touch it," said Moseby.

Rakkim pulled out the rad-proof pouch, slid out the bleached-pine box.

Moseby opened the box. Stared at the piece of the cross. The flowers swayed in the breeze. He ran his fingers across the rough wood, eyes closed now.

Rakkim waited for some sudden transformation, but Moseby looked as worn and beaten as before, blood crusted on his shirt.

Moseby opened his eyes. "Thank you." He closed the box. Rakkim started to put the box into the pouch, but Moseby stopped him. "No need for that. Hardly any radiation to the box at all. None on the cross."

"I know."

"Then leave it *out*," said Moseby. "Accept the miracle."

Rakkim tossed the pouch away, too tired to argue. He stood up. Offered Moseby his hand.

"I'm just going to stay here a—"

Rakkim lifted him up, threw him over his shoulder and started walking. Moseby groaned softly with every step.

"You just don't listen," said Moseby.

"I know." Rakkim staggered slightly, kicking up pebbles. "It's a character flaw."

"If something happens," said Moseby. "You know . . ."

"I'm not telling Annabelle your last words or anything," said Rakkim. "*You* tell her when you show up on her doorstep. That woman scares me."

CHAPTER 40

Rakkim floated on his back in a warm sea . . . buoyant as a jel-lyfish, drifting on the tide, arms trailing. He thought of Sarah, reached for her, but she wasn't there. He couldn't remember where she was. Misplaced her. Or she had lost him . . . he forgot which. He tried calling her name, thought somehow she might hear him . . . come join him. It wasn't far. He was right over . . . the bridge . . . the mountain . . . just around the bend. He called louder now, his throat aching with the effort. If you can't be smart, you might as well be persistent, that's what Redbeard had said, Rakkim barely ten, new to Redbeard's house, trying to understand the rules so he could break them and still survive. *Persistence. Never quit, Rikki. No one can beat you if you don't quit.* So many lessons from Redbeard, but that was Rakkim's favorite. He called out to Sarah again, his voice weaker now . . . wondered what lessons she had learned from Redbeard. Her uncle. Blood of his blood, something Redbeard never allowed him to forget.

The sun was warmer. Closer too. Rakkim reached out, tried to bring it to him, use the sun to boil away the water so he could walk on dry land again. Walk home to Sarah. The sun smiled at him, a face forming slowly . . . a woman's face . . . Sarah. He tried saying her name but he didn't recog-nize the words that came out. She lightly touched his hair, her fingers cool against his skin. Sarah . . . He said her name again.

"You better get your eyes checked, darlin'," said Baby, leaning over him, her light hair brushing against the sheets.

Rakkim flinched.

"Well . . . nice seeing you too," said Baby.

Rakkim looked around. He was in a hospital bed, one of a dozen in the whitewashed room. All of them empty, except for one near the window, the patient's face half hidden by an oxygen mask, tubes in his arms. "M-Moseby?"

"He's still alive, which is saying something." Baby looked even more beautiful than he remembered, a little tired, maybe, but her skin was smooth, her mouth ripe. She wore tight jeans and a man's dress shirt with the top two buttons undone. Pistol on her hip, one of the slim automatics that Belt gunsmiths specialized in. "Doc, can you come over here?" she called, not taking her eyes off him.

Rakkim saw his Fedayeen knife on the stand beside the bed, a single piece of razored carbon polymer imbued with his own DNA. He picked it up, flipped it end over end. "Where's Gravenholtz?"

"He's not here, that's all that matters." Baby watched as he pressed the knife against the inside of his right forearm, the knife melding to his flesh. "Doc said he couldn't understand how that knife sticks to you without a scabbard."

The doctor ambled over, a paunchy man with a clipped mustache and a frayed white jacket. The V between the index and middle fingers of his left hand was yellow from nicotine. "The sleeper awakes. You're a very lucky man, Mr. Epps. If Corporal Hitchens hadn't found you two on the road—"

"I want to talk with the Colonel," Rakkim said to the doctor.

"I'd lose that tone of voice." The doctor plucked a bit of tobacco off his lower lip, flicked it onto the floor. "The Colonel and just about everyone else have gone to Atlanta, so you can thank the lady here for tending you night and day. We're short-handed and Baby bathed you, saw to your medications, changed your IVs, and anything else I asked."

Rakkim sat up in bed, head spinning. "Why . . . why are they gone?"

"Easy." The doctor smoothed his mustache. "You got a touch of D.C. syndrome."

"Aztlán bombed Graceland last week," said Baby. "Colonel's gone to Atlanta to organize the counterattack."

"We're attacking *Aztlán*? How long have we been here?" said Rakkim.

"Three days," said Baby. "Doc completely changed out your blood, pumped you full of chelating minerals to hoover up the radiation."

The doctor pulled a pack of cigarettes out of his jacket pocket, glanced at Baby. "I'm taking a smoke break. Call me if you need help."

"How's Moseby doing?" Rakkim called after him.

"He's progressing," the doctor said, not bothering to turn around as he pushed open the door and stepped out into the twilight, a cigarette already in his mouth.

"What exactly does 'he's progressing' mean?"

Baby lowered her eyes. "Moseby . . . he needs to get to a real hospital, but we can't do that until he stabilizes. Fact is, doc's surprised he's even alive. Gunshots compromised his rad-suit. Fedayeen or no Fedayeen, he should have been dead five times over from infection and unknown contaminants floating around in D.C."

"Moseby's tough."

"Yeah, well . . . that's one explanation," said Baby.

"What's that mean?"

"It can wait."

Rakkim swung his legs over the side of the bed, tore the IV out and started toward Moseby. Baby put her arm around him, supporting him as he walked, and he didn't stop her. She smelled too good, and he was afraid he'd fall over without her. He sat on the edge of Moseby's bed. "Hey, big man. You looked like you could use some company."

Moseby stared up at the ceiling, the machine beside him making steady clicking sounds. Oxygen hissed from the large tank nearby.

Rakkim took Moseby's hand. Squeezed. Felt Moseby weakly

squeeze back. "I'm going to get some fresh air, John, but I'll be back. Don't you run off now."

Moseby blinked rapidly.

Rakkim walked outside, Baby beside him. "Surprised seeing you here. Last I saw of you, you were waving good-bye as the helicopter took off."

"I made a mistake," said Baby. "You may hold it against me, but the Colonel forgives me, that's all that matters."

"I'd like to have been there for *that* homecoming," said Rakkim, standing on his own now. "Nothing like the wayward wife on bended knee . . ."

"You can be a very nasty person, Rakkim Epps."

"You have no idea." Rakkim walked across the grass, taking deep breaths. The site was nearly deserted, just a sentry at the north end of camp, scanning the nearby woods.

Baby touched a finger to her ear. "Is that you?"

Rakkim looked back at her.

"He's right here, Zachary, suspicious as ever." Baby removed the phone clip from her ear, handed it to Rakkim. It was warm against his ear.

"How are you, Rikki?" said the Colonel.

"Fine . . . just fine, sir," said Rakkim. "Moseby took a couple of slugs in zombie country. Doc patched him up, but I need to get him to a better facility. Mecklenburg, maybe."

"The roads are bad," said the Colonel. "Don't rush things."

"I was surprised, sir, to see Baby here," said Rakkim, his voice neutral.

"Temporary, I'm afraid," said the Colonel. "She's made that clear. Honesty hurts like a bitch, Rikki, but what else do we have?"

"Sorry to hear that, Colonel," said Rakkim, staring at Baby. He had figured that she would string the Colonel along until she could get something out of him.

"My own damn fault," said the Colonel. "Man my age marrying a girl of sixteen. What did I expect?"

"Are you going to be in Atlanta long?" said Rakkim.

"I'm not sure," said the Colonel. "Somebody needs to teach Aztlán a lesson, and people here think I'm the man for the task." He said something to whoever was with him. "I've got to go. Glad you're doing well and give my best to Moseby. Could you let me talk with Baby again?"

Rakkim handed her back the phone clip.

Baby listened. "I love you too, Zachary. You take care of yourself, hear?" She air-kissed the phone, switched it off. "Are you hungry for solid food?"

"A little." Rakkim jerked. He had forgotten . . . "Where are my things?"

"What you're looking for is under Moseby's bed," said Baby.

Rakkim watched her.

"I looked inside the little box, what did you think I'd do? Way you hung on to it even while you were passed out . . . figured it had to be important." Baby hooked her fingertips into the front pockets of her jeans. "It's safe, no one's messed with it."

"You put it under John's bed."

"Thought it might do him some good having it close. Help him heal."

Rakkim walked quickly back to the field hospital.

"Of course, why trust me? I only stayed around so I could steal it once you were feeling better." Baby kept pace with him all the way inside the building and over to Moseby. She bent down, reached under the bed, and the seat of her jeans was worn smooth and shiny. It bothered him that he noticed. She dragged out an old footlocker, flipped it open, and he saw the bleached-pine box.

Rakkim opened the box. The piece of the cross was inside, nestled in the red velvet lining, flowers blooming. He looked at her. "How . . . how did you know?"

"You think I'm an idiot?"

"No, I don't think that at all."

"I knew what it was even before I looked at that thumb

recording you made," said Baby. "I heard about the true cross in D.C. my whole life," she said, playing with her hair, "but I never heard a thing about flowers on it."

Rakkim lightly touched the tiny flowers. Barely larger than a pinhead, but perfect in every way.

"I did the same thing myself. Hard not to touch beautiful things . . . make them part of you." Baby bent forward over the box. "Don't know what kind of flowers they are, but they sure smell good." She inhaled, holding on to his leg to brace herself. "Smells like some kind of spring day when I was a kid, and everything was new . . . and good."

Rakkim closed the box. Held on to it.

"Up to you what you do with it, but I'd put it back where it was," said Baby.

"You really think it's helped him?"

"Rikki . . . I don't know, I truly don't. Might have been just good doctorin' or that Fedayeen bounce-back, but he should be in the cold, cold ground by now and he's not."

Rakkim put the box back in the footlocker, pushed it under Moseby's bed. If she wanted to steal it, she would have already done it and been long gone.

The two of them watched Moseby sleep, his breathing rough.

"One thing I thought was interesting," said Baby, slipping her arm through his. "The pine box, and the cross itself . . . they're not radioactive. Hardly moved the rad-counter at all."

"Moseby noticed that too."

Baby's eyes were a deep blue, the color of the sea that he had been floating on before he woke up. "That's kind of strange, don't you think, considering all the years it's been in that terrible place." Her eyes warmed on him and he felt dizzy. "Guess God can do anything he sets his mind to."

CHAPTER 41

"This is nice, isn't it?" said Baby.

Rakkim watched the sun just starting to set over the mountains, streaking the snow with rivulets of orange and red. Baby sat beside him on a rocky outcropping overlooking the valley below.

"You're looking a lot better today," said Baby. "Told you a long walk was what you needed."

Rakkim watched hawks floating above the valley, predators, always on high alert—had to appreciate a creature that knew what it was doing. Yesterday, he had sent a confirmation message to Sarah, a single word—*Yes*—but with the chaff in the atmosphere kicking up, there was no way to know if the satellite transmission had been received. He didn't expect a response anyway. The Belt had gone into lockdown mode after Graceland was hit. No way anyone was going to extract him and Moseby. Rakkim would have to get Moseby home by himself, then bring the cross back to Seattle. No telling when Moseby would be well enough to travel to a real hospital.

"Fine, don't talk," said Baby, her knees tucked up, wearing those same tight jeans and a fresh dress shirt with the sleeves rolled. "I don't know why you act so mean to me."

"Because I know you."

"You *think* you know me."

Rakkim glanced at her. The sunset was reflected in her eyes.

"You don't think people can change?" said Baby.

"Some people."

"But not me?" Baby's lower lip quivered. "Why not me?"

Rakkim watched the fire in her eyes. "I just wonder why you came back. I wonder what you want from the Colonel."

"What if I came back because I felt bad for the way I treated him?" said Baby. "What if I wanted to try and set things right between us, because I cared about him?"

Rakkim forced himself to look away. Concentrating instead on the dark clouds forming toward the northeast, storm clouds building up. He imagined it already raining in D.C., the zombies still toiling away as the rain sluiced down the gutters.

"You never made a mistake? You never tried to clean up the mess you made?"

Rakkim looked back at her. It was hard not to. Hard not just to watch her . . . the way she moved, the way she sat, the way the sunlight eased across her skin. The Colonel never had a chance. Most men didn't. "I've tried," he admitted.

"I guess you're a special case then," said Baby. "Not a bit like me."

She hadn't done anything to make him suspect her motives. Not this time anyway. He had been as surprised as the Colonel when she skipped out with Gravenholtz. Just as surprised to see her back here. The worst thing, though . . . the absolute worst was he was glad to see her. Half dead, feeling her cool hand on his forehead as he blinked his way back to consciousness, then seeing her face . . . before he remembered all the reasons he had to worry, he had been happy to see her. More than happy. The way he felt, it was as if she'd come back for him, not the Colonel.

"I'm not so bad, am I?" said Baby. "For a moment just now you almost liked me, didn't you?"

"Yeah, but I caught myself."

"I wish you didn't think you had to do that." The temperature was dropping, a cool wind rolling down the mountains, sending Baby's hair billowing around her shoulders. A brown rabbit zigzagged across the field toward its burrow, and Baby wrapped her arms around herself. "First time we met, I could see you were attracted to me. I felt the same way about you. Not like we'd have done anything about it, but there's nothing wrong with what goes on inside our heads. Not like God reads minds or anything."

"He better not, or we're all fucked forever."

Baby laughed and it was clear and warm and honest, just the two of them alone in the middle of nowhere.

"We should go back," said Rakkim. "I want to check on Moseby."

"You *did* like me when we first met, didn't you?" said Baby.

"Just a little," said Rakkim.

"I could tell." Baby rubbed at the goose bumps covering her bare arms, then kissed him. A short kiss, but she was the one who pulled away, and the taste of her lingered in his mouth. "I'm sorry, Rikki . . ." She blushed. "I didn't mean to do that."

"No harm done." Rakkim said it, but he didn't believe it. "We'll let it be our little secret." Stupid thing to say. He hadn't meant to say it . . . just like she hadn't meant to kiss him. Baby was the last person he should be sharing a secret with. He started back to the field hospital before he said something else he would regret.

She caught up with him, walked with him down the winding, stony path, neither of them talking, wrapped in a prickly embarrassment . . . the nervous edge of desire. A Belt joke, one he had heard in every filling station in the Appalachians: What's three things'll turn your head inside out faster than fresh moonshine? Mountain air, mountain water, mountain girls. It wasn't particularly funny, but it was true.

"I wasn't honest with you before," said Baby, watching where she stepped. "I didn't come back to make things right by the Colonel. I decided that after the fact."

Rakkim kept walking.

"I came back in case you found that piece of the cross you were looking for," said Baby. "The Old One sent me and Lester to fetch it for him."

Rakkim stopped.

"I don't like lying to you," said Baby.

"We all do things we don't like," said Rakkim.

"Don't get all high and mighty with me. I don't want the cross."

Rakkim grabbed her arm. "Where's Gravenholtz?"

"I sent him on a wild goose chase into zombie country." Baby jerked away from him. "Hope he *dies* there. Him and the Old One can go fuck themselves." She started back down the mountain. "You can *all* go fuck yourselves."

Neither of them said a word as they slowly descended the mountain. He thought of Baby every step he took. Wondered what she had been doing with the Old One for the last year, and why she had decided now to free herself from him. *You don't think people can change?* She didn't have to tell Rakkim the truth, but she had. She could have grabbed the piece of the cross anytime in the three days she had tended to him, but she hadn't. *You never tried to clean up the mess you made?*

Gunshots echoed from down below and Rakkim started running, careening down the path, sliding on loose gravel. So much for Baby sending Gravenholtz on a wild goose chase. Three or four times he almost skidded into the brush, but he stayed upright, kept running. He could hear Baby far behind him, trying to keep up, but he didn't look back. It took a half hour to get back to camp and by then it was too late. It had probably been too late when he first heard the gunshots.

Rakkim stopped at the edge of camp, just inside the shelter of the trees. The sentry at the north end of camp lay in a heap. The other sentry lay near the field hospital, his skull crushed. The door to the hospital hung off one hinge, creaking back and forth in the breeze. Rakkim approached the hospital from its blind side, the side without windows, flattened himself beside the open door, listening. Heard nothing but the faint electrical ping from the machine monitoring Moseby. He glanced through the doorway. Saw the doctor sitting in the chair beside Moseby's bed, his head half twisted off. Saw Moseby too. Saw everything. Rakkim slipped through the door, blade in his hand.

"Was wondering if you were ever getting back." Gravenholtz lay in an empty bed on the other side of Moseby's, his head propped up with three pillows, red hair spiked out as if he were an enormous porcupine. For some reason, he wore a white surgical gown that was too small for him, the seams popping. He swigged from a bottle of grape Nehi. "I was about to come looking, but figured you'd turn up eventually."

Moseby groaned, the sheet pulled up around his neck. His hands and feet were bound to the rails, his mouth wrapped in adhesive tape.

"You look tired, Rikki." Gravenholtz chugged the Nehi. "Baby must be wearing you out."

"Baby's not here."

Gravenholtz belched. "Just once I wish somebody would tell me the fucking truth the first time I asked." He threw the bottle, hit the doctor, and the doctor's body slid off the chair and onto the floor. "Doc tried to tell me you and Baby had left for Atlanta yesterday, but I knew you wouldn't leave your good buddy here." The bed creaked as he got up and stood over Moseby. "He was no help either. I was nice to him too. Gave him a good-conduct medal and everything."

Rakkim could see Eldon Harrison's Silver Star driven deep into Moseby's chest, the sheet soaked with blood. Baby had told him the truth about the wild goose chase—it had been Harrison's wife who had told Gravenholtz where they might be.

"I could hardly believe it when that zombie bitch told me *you* were with Moseby. My lucky day." Gravenholtz tore the medal out of Moseby's chest and Moseby shuddered, his screams muffled by the adhesive tape. "Here, you might as well take it." He tossed the Silver Star at Rakkim's feet. "You look like a hero."

Rakkim looked into Moseby's panicked eyes. "It's okay, John. I'm going to kill him."

Gravenholtz pulled a pair of latex gloves out of the pocket of his surgical gown, waved them at Rakkim. "You're ready for your exam? No telling what we're going to find."

"Lester Gravenholtz, what in the *world* are you doing here?" Baby stood in the doorway, tapping her foot.

"Here's somebody else likes to lie to me," said Gravenholtz, his expression a mix of lust and rage. "Big joke, huh, having me spend the last week talking to retards and monsters."

Rakkim eased closer.

"You best leave right this minute, Lester," said Baby, walking right over to him, fearless. "Go on, git. Rikki and I have business to take care of."

"Business, huh?" Gravenholtz humped an imaginary woman. "*This* kind of business?" He saw her put her hand on the pistol sticking out of her jeans. "You going to shoot me?"

Baby shook her head. "Wouldn't do any good."

Gravenholtz's smile was ugly as a raw wound. "See, she didn't say she didn't *want* to, she just said it wouldn't do any good." He put on one of the gloves, his huge hand shredding it. "Where's that piece of the cross?" He shook off the ruined glove. "You look surprised, Baby. How long did you think you could keep me in the dark?"

Baby didn't answer.

"Ibrahim told me what you were really here for," said Gravenholtz. "I don't think he likes you very much."

"There is no piece of the cross," said Baby. "None that Rikki and Moseby could find anyway."

Gravenholtz grabbed Baby's head, pulled it back so she was looking up at him. "Where is it?"

Baby slapped at him. "Let me *go*."

"Tell me where it is and I'll take you with me." Gravenholtz bent her head back even farther, her long neck straining as she struggled to stay upright. "You won't have to worry about anything. You know you've always been able to sweet-talk me."

Rakkim darted in, slashed Gravenholtz along the shoulder, blood dappling his surgical gown. He backed up as Gravenholtz released Baby, trying to lead the redhead toward the center of the room.

Baby hurried over to Moseby, clawed at the straps, trying to free him.

Gravenholtz turned away from Rakkim, kicked the hospital

bed, and sent it skidding into the wall. The impact whiplashed Moseby, his head flopping. Gravenholtz stared at the footlocker that had been hidden under the bed. Baby grabbed for the footlocker but he batted her aside. He looked at Rakkim. "Well, well, well . . ."

Rakkim charged Gravenholtz, shifted his blade from hand to hand, stabbed the redhead again and again, trying to keep him off balance, but something was wrong. Either Gravenholtz was faster than he remembered, or Rakkim was still weakened by his time in D.C., because Gravenholtz kept narrowing the space between them. Even worse, though Rakkim had an intuitive awareness of the seams between Gravenholtz's subdural armor, his knife thrusts were late, missing by millimeters, the blade merely slicing the skin. Blood ran from a dozen spots on Gravenholtz's torso and legs, but he was unhurt.

"That's the best you got?" demanded Gravenholtz, face flushed with exploded capillaries. "What's *happened* to you, boy?" He glanced at Baby. "You sure you want to throw in with this—" Gravenholtz gasped as Rakkim drove his blade deep into his side, right through the thin spot between two plates. Cursing, he retreated, blood spurting.

"Where are you going?" Rakkim taunted, jabbed him again. And again. "Stick around, I've got something for you." He danced forward on the balls of his feet, came in low, but slid in a patch of blood, one leg going out from under him.

Gravenholtz punched Rakkim as he scrambled up.

The blow barely grazed Rakkim's jaw but his whole face went numb. He slashed away at Gravenholtz, trying to clear his vision. The redhead hit him again and the wind rushed out of Rakkim, staggering him.

Gravenholtz advanced, grinning, a big white slab of meat with piggy eyes, leaking blood all over himself—it might have been sweat for all he cared. "Don't die so easy—"

Rakkim slashed him across the knuckles, slashed him to the bone and Gravenholtz howled.

"Lester!" Baby shouted, trying to get between them. Bravest thing Rakkim had ever seen. "Lester, you were told not to hurt him!"

As Gravenholtz started to knock her aside, Rakkim drove his knife into the soft tissue under the redhead's chin, the blade shearing up, splitting his tongue and embedding in the roof of his mouth.

Gravenholtz screamed, hammered him in the ribs, the knife tearing free as Rakkim sprawled onto the floor, unmoving. Gravenholtz looked down at him, blood streaming from the gash in his mouth, then shuffled over to the footlocker and threw it open. He carefully lifted the lid of the small pine box, looked at Baby. "This is it?" he said, voice slurred. He plucked one of the tiny white flowers, sniffed it and tossed it aside. "You *got* to be shitting me."

"Take it and go," said Baby. "Just leave us be."

A bubble of blood popped at the side of Gravenholtz's mouth.

"Don't go." Rakkim got to his feet, wobbly. "Stick around."

Gravenholtz nodded, blood running down his neck. "That's the spirit." The flap of skin under his chin jiggled with every wheezing breath.

Rakkim circled. A few more minutes and maybe Gravenholtz would start choking on his own blood. A few more minutes and maybe Rakkim would get another chance to hurt him, really hurt him.

Gravenholtz closed the pine box, tucked it away in his pants pocket. He never took his eyes off Rakkim. Not for an instant. "Let's . . . let's you and me play some more, Rikki."

A *whoooooosh* of deep blue flame flashed between them, and they both jerked back.

Baby stood beside Moseby's oxygen tank. She had wheeled it over, unhooked the outlet from the metal tube and lit the pure oxygen, turned it into a giant blowtorch. "I told you, Lester, get on out of here."

Gravenholtz shook his head. "Not till I—" He howled as the

flames licked toward him, singeing away one of his eyebrows.

"Go *on!*" Baby rolled the oxygen tank closer, the flame three feet long now. "I don't care what kind of armor you got, I'll roast you like a marshmallow."

"I believe . . . I believe you would," said Gravenholtz.

"That's the smartest thing you said all day," said Baby.

"Okay," said Gravenholtz, backing toward the door. "I got what I come after."

"What's your hurry?" said Rakkim, trying to hide the pain it took to breathe.

"Look at the tough guy." Gravenholtz spit blood on the floor at Rikki's feet. "You break way too easy. Lucky for you the old man wants you kept alive."

"You're making a mess all over yourself," gasped Rakkim. "Better start wearing a bib."

Gravenholtz started toward him, but the blue flame shot out again and he pulled away.

Rakkim let him go. Not that he had much choice. He rested his hands on his knees until his vision cleared. When he was able to stand, Baby had already turned off the oxygen tank and was bent over Moseby, who lay twisted across the hospital bed. She was crying, clutching Moseby's hand and calling his name.

Rakkim limped over to the bed. Moseby stared at the ceiling, eyes frozen, his jaw slightly agape. Like he was surprised at what he was seeing.

"I *hate* Lester," said Baby, tears running down her face. "I know . . . I know where he's going. When we find him . . . when we find him, Rikki, I want you to kill him."

"It's a promise." Rakkim closed Moseby's eyes with a gentle sweep of his hand.

CHAPTER 42

Rakkim took the curve, had to hit the brakes when he saw the line of cars backed up on the four-lane highway, the cute little muscle in his jaw twitching. He and Baby were on their way to Atlanta after leaving the Colonel's camp. It should have been a day's drive, but war fever was in the air, the roads clogged, airports shut down. Gravenholtz had disappeared on his way back to Nueva Florida—Baby hoped he was having the same trouble they were. If they could reach Atlanta, the Colonel might be able to put them on a diplomatic flight into Miami. They could get there before Lester.

"Told you we should have taken the swing-around outside of Pemberton," said Baby, one foot hanging out the rolled-down window. He had been stealing glances at her for the last five miles. Wasn't a man alive who didn't admire a barefoot girl.

Rakkim craned his neck, trying to see how far the backup extended. He inched past an overpass with REMEMBER GRACELAND! painted in six-foot-high red letters.

Ever since Aztlán bombed Graceland last week, getting even was all anybody talked about. President Raynaud urged diplomacy, but Malcolm Crews's sermons carried more weight, and Crews wanted war. Stuck in traffic last night, she and Rakkim had watched Crews on the dashboard TV. After the choir sang "Onward Christian Soldiers," Crews had announced a special guest. When the Colonel stepped through the curtain, the applause was so loud that the speakers almost blew. Car horns blared up and down the highway. She wished Daddy was able to hear the horns, just so he could appreciate what she had done for him. It had been *her* idea to pin the blame for killing the oil minister on Zachary instead of President Raynaud. Having Aztlán go after him had united the Belt, just like she said. Credit where credit is due, Daddy.

The Colonel's private army was now over one hundred thousand men and rising daily as new recruits poured in. Word was Zachary was planning to deploy toward the southern border, picking up support as he went. The Belt president had threatened him with treason, but quickly retracted it; many of his own forces had already defected. With the airports closed to civilians, and the roads clogged with military vehicles, they made slow progress toward the Nueva Florida border.

Red taillights stretched into the distance. Rakkim whipped out of his lane and onto the narrow shoulder. Backed up and drove the wrong way, accelerating as the side of the car brushed against the guardrail, giving off a shower of sparks.

"Rikki, you got to be the only man in the world smiles as he's about to crash and burn."

"That's not it," said Rakkim. "I was thinking of you turning that glorified blowtorch on Gravenholtz. Pretty brave thing to do, Baby."

"You were pretty brave yourself, mister," said Baby. "Lester about pulled the hair out of my head—I was just glad you were there to stop him." She pushed her sunglasses back onto her forehead. "Seems to me like we're a good team."

Rakkim drove across the median and onto the other side of the freeway.

Baby wiggled her pink toes out the window. Rakkim hadn't disagreed with her. She was making progress with him.

They had been on the road for almost two days, Baby occasionally dozing while Rakkim drove. Yesterday she had insisted they stop at a motel so she could take a shower. She hoped he would agree to spend the night, but he was insistent, said he'd leave her if she didn't hurry. She didn't argue, just took a long shower at their motel room, washed her hair twice, warm conditioned it too while he paced around the parking lot. She wanted to dry her hair in the sun, see how he liked that, but that would have been pushing things. Time enough for that later. He might act tough, but the way she carried on over Moseby dying had softened him toward her. Rikki was weakening by the mile.

"You want a Coca-Cola?" said Baby.

Rakkim held out his hand.

Baby pulled a Coke out of the six-pack on the floor, tapped the frost button twice. Sweat formed on the glass bottle as she twisted off the cap. "Say please."

"Please."

"Say pretty please with whipped cream and a cherry on top."

Rakkim snatched the bottle out of her hand, accelerating toward the swing-around.

For a man in a hurry, Rakkim had spent way too much time at the Colonel's camp taking care of the dead first. Like the dead cared.

After Lester took off, Rakkim had gathered up the Colonel's massacred soldiers, put them and their IDs into sleeping bags and laid them in the walk-in freezer off the mess hall. He had asked her if she wanted to say a prayer, which she didn't, but she did. After that, Rakkim had carefully cleaned Moseby's body, wrapped him in a white sheet and carried him to the top of a hill overlooking the valley. The last light of the sunset turned everything to beaten gold, as Rakkim dug the grave. He had stopped twice, gasping in the night air, not so much from hurting . . . more from the sadness of the thing.

Baby picked a couple of small yellow wildflowers, laid them on the grave, and after Rakkim said some Muslim prayer, she sang "I Got a Home in Gloryland." She had a beautiful voice, and what the hell. She liked Moseby too, as far as that sort of thing went.

"What are you thinking about?" said Rakkim, his eyes on the road.

"Just . . . that I used to imagine how nice it would be to go on a long drive with you," said Baby. "Now here we are."

"This isn't a drive," said Rakkim.

"You think I don't know that?" said Baby. "You think you're the only one's got a heavy heart? Sometimes you just have to make the best of things."

"Sorry . . . I'm just trying to get used to you sitting beside me." Rakkim looked at her. "Why didn't you just grab the piece of the cross when I was unconscious? Instead you took care of me."

"It's . . . it's complicated."

"I've got time."

"Let's just say . . . maybe I'm not as bad as you think I am."

"Maybe." Rakkim pretended to flinch as she pretended to punch him. They drove on, back the way they had come. "The Old One's a Muslim. Did he ever tell you why he wanted a piece of the cross?"

"You're a Muslim. Why do *you* want it?"

"It's complicated."

"You got that right." Baby rested her hand on his leg. Waited for him to tell her to move it . . . but he didn't.

"How did the Old One look before you left?" said Rakkim.

"I don't know." Baby tried to keep her voice light, as though she had never considered the question before. She wondered how long Rakkim had been turning the idea over in his mind, before asking. "He looks old, but healthy. Like the Colonel." She patted his leg. "Except the Old One's got this strange energy about him. He stays up all night sometimes, doesn't seem to get tired. Why?"

Rakkim glanced over at her. "Most Christians think the cross has healing powers. Isn't that why you put it under Moseby's hospital bed?"

"I figured it couldn't hurt."

"So maybe that's why the Old One wants it."

"He's a Muslim," said Baby. "He doesn't believe in the crucifixion."

"Maybe *he* figured it couldn't hurt either."

Baby looked out the window. She knew where Rikki was headed. No wonder she was so attracted to him. A man that smart was dangerous, but once you put him in his place, once you trained him . . . well, then you really had something.

"The Old One told me once he was over a hundred and fifty years old," said Rakkim, driving with one hand on the wheel. "I didn't believe it, but he's been around for a long time. Maybe he's finally feeling his age."

"I *did* notice something different before I left," said Baby. "His doctor, Massakar . . . he doesn't look the Old One in the eye anymore. Like he feels guilty about something."

It was true too. That's what had made Baby suspect the real reason for the Old One's interest in retrieving the cross. Daddy might tell her and Ibrahim it was all about reunification, but she knew the man had gotten some bad news from his doctor and was ready to believe in anything that might turn things around. Baby knew better. She had held the piece of wood in her hand for two hours waiting to feel something. Might as well have been holding a dead branch for all the good it did.

"There you go," said Rakkim, pleased with himself. "Piece of the cross . . . well, you can see how he might be tempted."

"I *could* see that," said Baby, like she had never considered it before. "Time is the only thing even money can't buy."

"Exactly." Rakkim watched her. "He would have given you anything for it."

"You ever think maybe I didn't *want* anything from him?"

"You worked for him in Miami."

"I didn't have a choice back in Miami." Baby played with her hair. "That old bastard can pound sand up his ass for all I care."

Rakkim laughed. First time she had seen him let loose since they buried Moseby.

"There was another reason I couldn't do it." Baby lowered her eyes. "You know how I feel about you."

Rakkim drove for a while before speaking and she let the silence tighten around them. "I'm married," he said at last.

"Man like you is only at home out on the edge with the other wild things," said Baby. "You got no business being married."

"Tell that to my wife."

"I just might do that."

Rakkim glanced over at her, then back at the road.

"You *can't* be serious, Amir," the president said, taking the snap from his brother-in-law. He stepped back, tall and graceful, his hair perfectly tousled.

"Completely serious," said Amir, easily faking out his coverage as he went for a pass.

General Kidd sidled to his right, blocking the two rushers coming in from that side—the president's nephew and older brother—giving Brandt time to launch a pass to Amir.

"Peter!" called Amir, dashing down the sideline, ten steps ahead of his pursuer.

Peter. Amir actually referred to President Brandt by his first name. Yes, they were in the presidential compound, and yes, it was a family barbecue and touch football game, but Kidd would have sooner cut off his thumbs than address the president in such a fashion. Yet the president didn't seem to mind. They weren't that far apart in age, and Brandt reveled in the informality between him and the young Fedayeen hero.

The president threw a high, tight spiral that dropped right into Amir's outstretched fingertips. He crossed the chalked goal line, held the football overhead in triumph.

Amir's wives applauded from where they sat on the lawn with their children, the only women at the barbecue in burqas. Three of Kidd's wives also applauded, young and fashionable in their iridescent chadors. Fatima, his oldest wife, was home with a migraine. She always had a migraine when they were invited for barbecue and football at the president's residence. How he longed for such a headache.

The president and Amir high-fived each other, mocking the inability of the other team to stop their relentless scoring. Forty-eight to six. An embarrassment for all concerned. As the only two Fedayeen present, fairness dictated that they be placed on separate teams, but the president wouldn't hear of it. A weak man who needed to win. When the first lady announced that the food was ready, Kidd gave thanks to Allah for His mercy.

The first lady, her sisters, and the general's wives served the men: corn on the cob, potato salad, hamburgers and barbecued goat. The first lady herself poured the general a tall glass of lemonade, blessed him as she handed it over. After all the men were served, the children were called. The president, Amir and General Kidd sat on a blanket laid out under one of the many trees in the compound. The president's older brother started to join them, but the president waved him away. General Kidd sat down across from the president, wondering what was so important.

The president nibbled at a grilled chicken kebab. "What do you think of Amir's idea?"

Kidd tore a strip of barbecued goat, eating with his fingers. "What idea is that?"

The president looked at Amir.

"I've not mentioned the strategic initiative to my father yet," said Amir.

Kidd chewed slowly, grinding the meat with his strong white teeth. "I'm waiting."

"I've suggested to Peter that he address the nation shortly," said Amir. "An address not just to our nation, but to the Belt. We'd have to contact the authorities in the Belt first, of course, ask them to drop their static generators, as would we, but that's easily done."

"What would you have the president say?" asked Kidd.

Amir glanced at the president, then back at his father. "I'd like him to make a formal declaration of support for the Belt against Aztlán. An affirmation that we were a united country at one time, and that though now divided, we remain united in spirit."

"United in spirit?" said Kidd.

Amir squirmed slightly. "Yes."

"I have no problem with the phrase as a rhetorical device," said the president, "but the political repercussions are enormous."

"*You* think we're united in spirit with the Belt?" Kidd said to Amir. "Since when?"

"Since it became necessary," said Amir. "Aztlán is a ravening beast. We keep tossing it bits of our territory to keep it at bay, but all we're really doing is stoking its appetite."

Kidd licked his fingers. The boy was right, but the idea of aligning with the Belt . . . that didn't come from him. Kidd had fought the Belt, seen the brave and the dead on both sides. He rejected Belt theology but he respected Christians. Good fighters. Passionate as any Somali. He would rather spend time with a Mississippi Baptist than a prissy modern any day. Not Amir. He despised Christians. Considered them blasphemers and idolaters, fit only for conversion or death. So who had this idea come from?

"What do you think, General?" asked the president.

"I think it's a good long-range strategy," said Kidd. "We currently have over fifty percent of our military tied down along the border with the Belt."

"Exactly," said Amir. "A declaration of unity allows both nations to shift their forces against Aztlán, the true enemy."

"National unity should be pursued *quietly*, through diplomatic channels," said Kidd, "not out in the open for all to see. That way, both nations can gradually redeploy their forces, building trust over a few years, and keeping Aztlán unaware of our intentions."

"That's exactly what I was thinking," said the president.

"Father, you're too cautious," said Amir. "Argusto does not suffer the same affliction."

Kidd's eyes flashed.

"We need to act immediately," said Amir. "These are dangerous times."

"What do you know about dangerous times?" snapped Kidd.

Amir stared back at him, the planes of his cheeks sharp and shiny as obsidian.

"We're just having an innocent discussion on a sunny day,"

said the president, stretching out his long legs. "No harm in that. As my two chief military advisors, I welcome such talk. It's . . . *stimulating.*"

Kidd stared at the president. This was the first time he was aware that Amir's advice was considered equal to his own.

"The goat is tasty, isn't it?" said the president.

"Publicly supporting the Belt will give Aztlán an excuse to take action against us, which is just what Argusto wants," explained Kidd. "Our ground forces may be superior, but Aztlán controls the air. We go to war, they win."

Amir didn't react, didn't lower his eyes, just kept staring at his father.

The president tossed aside his sandwich. "Who wants to pass the ball around?"

Amir slowly stood up. Bowed to his father.

Kidd watched the two of them trot off to the center of the field. He wished Rakkim were here. More and more lately he wished Rakkim were beside him.

The president tossed the football from one hand to the other, squinting in the sun. "Your father is right, Amir. We're in no position to take on Aztlán. They own the skies."

Amir snatched the ball away from the president. "What if they didn't?"

CHAPTER 43

"Y'all want a refill, hon?"

"Thanks," said Rakkim, as the waitress filled his coffee cup and started down the counter.

"How about me?" demanded Baby. "What, am I invisible?"

The waitress ignored her, chatting with a hefty farmer with tattooed forearms. A game show played on the TV over the counter, a photo of the young, swivel-hipped Elvis on one corner of the screen, *Never Forget* superimposed.

Rakkim dropped a twenty-dollar bill into the REBUILD GRACE-LAND canister on the counter. "I don't think she likes you."

"If I was a bubblebutt like her, I wouldn't like me either," said Baby.

Their progress toward Atlanta was still slow, and their calls to the Colonel hadn't gone through. Aztlán was jamming most communications in the Belt.

A trio of rough-looking men walked through the front door, automatic rifles slung over their shoulders. What with the mobilization, restaurants and markets had abandoned their gun-check policy and just let people be. With everybody armed, things tended to stay polite. As long as folks weren't too drunk. One of the men noticed Baby, nudged the others. They tripped over their own feet twice on their way to a booth.

"Where you folks headed?" said the waitress, sliding a plate of grits and eggs in front of Rakkim.

"Atlanta," said Rakkim. "They say ninety-five is closed, but we're hoping to find an alternate route. If you got any suggestions . . ."

Baby gripped Rakkim's upper arm, cocked her head at the

waitress. "It's our honeymoon. What with the war coming we didn't want to wait another minute."

Rakkim tried to shrug her off, but she held on.

"I thought me and the mister was about to set the sheets on fire last night," said Baby.

"My Gerald and I were the same way," said the waitress. "Wait until you have kids."

"Oh, I bet you and your husband still rock and roll," said Baby.

The waitress smiled as she topped off Baby's coffee. "We do all right."

"Knock that kind of talk off," said Rakkim after the waitress had left.

"Everybody likes lovebirds," said Baby. "Maybe she asks around to see if anybody saw Lester."

"I already asked," said Rakkim. "Nobody's seen him or the truck he boosted from the Colonel." He stretched. Definitely feeling better, the effects of his radiation exposure minimal now. "Gravenholtz might have changed rides."

"Like I said, we'll catch him in Miami." Baby watched herself in the mirror behind the counter, touched her cheek. "Look at my complexion. Sleeping in the car is ruining me."

Rakkim glanced at her, then went back to his grits. He spent too much time looking at her as it was. She knew it too. "How is it you think you can crack the Old One's security?"

Baby leaned closer. "You think shadow warriors are the only ones know how to make friends?" she whispered. "The Old One's got all kinds of people working for him, and most of them like nothing better than impressing a pretty girl with what they know." She reached over and scooped up some of his grits with her fork.

"If you're hungry, why didn't you order something?" said Rakkim.

"I like eating yours better," said Baby, sucking on the tines of the fork. "I know I said I wanted you to kill Lester when we catch up with him . . . I just hope you're up to it."

Rakkim stabbed at his sunny-side-up eggs, the yolk running across his plate.

"I didn't mean that the way it sounded."

"Sure you did."

"It's a bad habit of mine, I'd be the first to admit it." Baby rested her head on his shoulder. "Seems like I always got to be testing a man."

Rakkim shrugged her away.

Baby smacked the counter with her hand. Heads turned but she ignored them. "Jesus, Rikki, I was just playing."

"Maybe I don't want to play. You ever think of that?"

"Maybe you need some damn rest. *You* ever think of that? It's been days. . . ."

The waitress came by again with the coffeepot. "Everything okay?"

Rakkim waved her off. "Just a little lovers' spat."

"I been asking around about alternate roads for you two honeymooners," said the waitress. "So far, looks like you're out of luck, but I'll keep trying."

Baby waited until the waitress moved away. "That was sweet what you said, Rikki."

"Don't get excited. I didn't want to draw any more attention than we already have."

"A *lovers'* spat." Baby tapped her nails on the Formica counter. "Seems to me you could have come up with some other phrase to deflect attention. That's interesting, don't you think . . . you choosing to say that?"

Rakkim put his coffee down as LIVE SPECIAL REPORT bannered across the TV. The camera showed Seattle, panned across the cityscape. He heard boos and curses as the Grand Caliph mosque appeared, then the camera cut to President Brandt standing behind a podium in his private office. Somebody turned the sound up. The picture quality was crisp—the usual signal jamming between the two nations halted for the broadcast.

". . . welcome you all, citizens of the Belt as well as the Republic," said Brandt. "These are momentous times . . . challenging times, calling for anything but business as usual."

"What's going on?" said Baby.

The camera pulled back and Rakkim was startled to see the president flanked by General Kidd on one side and Amir on the other. The president usually chose to dominate the stage. For Kidd to be there implied state of national emergency, since Brandt, who had no military experience, needed the presence of the general to reassure the country. Kidd's erect posture and serene confidence did just that. But why was Amir there? *Kidd* represented the Fedayeen. If anything, the chairman of the joint chiefs should have been present to affirm the support of the army.

"Recent events, and in particular the brutal attack on Graceland, have forced me to conclude that a state of war exists between the Belt and Aztlán," intoned the president.

The diner was silent, only the sound of sizzling bacon interrupting the stillness.

"While Aztlán bombs innocent civilians in Tennessee, the government of Tenochtitlán also pressures the Republic for our territory and our natural resources," said the president.

Rakkim paid no attention to the president, drawn instead to Kidd and Amir. Kidd remained impassive, eyes straight ahead, but Amir betrayed a certain . . . eagerness.

"Citizens of the Belt and the Republic, I say to you . . ." The president's eyes darted toward Amir for a second, then back to the camera. "I say to you, *my fellow countrymen*, that this state of affairs cannot be allowed to stand."

"What the *fuck* did he just call us?" asked the farmer with the tattooed forearms.

"Shhhh," said someone else.

"We've had our difficulties, both Belt and Republic," said the president, "but like the great Abraham Lincoln once said . . . if we don't hang together, we'll hang separately."

That last line was a masterstroke. Lincoln was the patron saint of the Belt, even more revered than Elvis himself. For a moment Rakkim wondered if Sarah had worked on the speech for the president. Wondered if she had secretly begun advising him, the way she had counseled President Kingsley. The theme of reconciliation was exactly what she had been talking about for years now. Rakkim kept expecting someone in the diner to yell out an obscenity, or demand the TV be turned to another station, but no one said a word.

The president looked directly into the camera. "I say to you now, my fellow Americans, your war with Aztlán is *our* war too."

The waitress sobbed, wiped her eyes with the hem of her apron.

"I say to Aztlán, both Belt and the Republic stand united," said the president. "Do not suppose for an instant that our religious differences will divide Muslims and Christians forever. We share a belief in one God, with a common line of saints and prophets. There's room in Paradise for all of us."

Rakkim wished he had postponed killing ibn-Azziz, just so the Black Robe could have lived long enough to hear the president say such a thing. Men had ended up on the Bridge of Skulls for lesser apostasies.

Two men walked in the front door of the diner, started to say something and were immediately silenced by the other patrons.

"As of today, the Republic will no longer send half the electric power generated by the Great Dam to Aztlán as tribute." The president gripped the podium as his hands started to shake. "As of today, the Republic is suspending all talks on relinquishing water rights to the Colorado River. What is ours will remain ours."

"What does that mean?" whispered Baby.

"It means war," Rakkim said, still watching the president.

General Kidd didn't move, stayed beside the president. Only someone who knew him as well as Rakkim did could have seen the tension in his face, the resignation. Kidd understood as well as Rakkim that Aztlán's air superiority almost guaranteed them victory. Amir, though . . . Amir seemed almost cheerful, the happy warrior. He leaned over and whispered in the president's ear . . . the president nodded.

"I call on President Raynaud to send an emissary to Seattle at the earliest opportunity," said the president, "so that we may map out a strategy for the future. Thank you . . . and may God bless us all."

The TV screen went gray for a moment, then cut to a Belt newsman looking stunned. He realized his camera was live, cleared his throat . . . and had nothing to say.

The diner echoed with conversation, people already arguing over what it meant, if the Republic could be trusted, and how long before the bombs started to fall.

Malcolm Crews appeared onscreen, standing on a street somewhere, the news kiosks behind him already replaying President Brandt's speech. A female reporter held up a microphone, and Crews said something about a time to heal old wounds, and prepare to fight the new enemy. "Like the man there said," Crews said, voice rising, "we Christians don't sing the same hymns as the Muslims, but at least we both pray to one God, not some unholy cafeteria of pagan deities like the Mexicans. That's got to count for something."

Rakkim stared at the TV, aware of Crews but still seeing Amir whispering in the president's ear. Still seeing the president respond to what he had been told without even thinking. *I don't know who the Old One's inside man is,* Jenkins had said, almost his dying words as the gulls circled the Bridge of Skulls. *I don't know who he is . . . all ibn-Azziz said was he had the ear of the president.* Amir had done the same thing at the presidential inauguration a year ago, embracing Brandt, then said something in the smaller man's ear that pleased him.

"What is it?" said Baby.

Could Amir really be working for the Old One? Hard to imagine . . . *the ear of the president* . . . a common phrase.

Meant nothing . . . but there had been something in their body language on the podium just now, some unseemly deference on Brandt's part. A small thing, but Rakkim had survived on the basis of noticing things others didn't: a glance, an intonation, the slight tightening of the jaw before a smile.

"What's wrong?" said Baby.

No . . . it couldn't be Amir. The Old One was attuned to every weakness, every human flaw—given his charm and powers of persuasion, he might have convinced even Amir to follow him, but General Kidd despised the Old One, recognized him for what he was. Amir might betray his country, but he would never betray his father. Never.

"Nothing," said Rakkim.

"You never tell me *anything*," said Baby.

CHAPTER 44

Hector Morales, Aztlán secretary of state, burst into the presidential suite as soon as the electronic locks disengaged. "El Presidente," he huffed, having raced down the corridor from his own office in the executive tower. "Have you seen . . . ?" His voice trailed off as he saw the row of televisions all tuned to President Brandt's speech.

"How kind of you to join me, Hector." Presidente Argusto sat with his chair tilted back, riding boots up on the desk, puffing away on a long Cuban cigar.

"E-Excellency," sputtered Morales, "I had no idea that Brandt—"

"Of course you didn't." Argusto released a perfect smoke ring into the air. "That would require some competency on your part, which we both know is alien to your nature."

Morales watched the smoke ring float toward him. "This . . . speech of Brandt's is totally out of character, Excellency. It makes no sense."

"It makes *perfect* sense, Hector. I just never credited Brandt with either the insight or the cojones to act upon it." Argusto puffed happily away on his cigar. "It is, of course, too late for such dramatic action on the part of the *yanquis* to succeed, but still . . ." A pillow of gray ash from the cigar tumbled onto the white carpet. "One must admire the courage."

"Excellency, I have already placed a call to my counterpart in the Republic."

"You do that, Hector." Argusto beamed. "Talk, talk, talk until you and your fellow diplomats are hoarse. Meanwhile I have already put our air units on high alert." The cigar jutted up from the side of his mouth. "*Discreetly*, of course."

Morales felt his legs quiver. "Are we going to war, Excellency?"

"It will not be much of a war, Hector, but there will be blood enough to satisfy the gods . . . for a time, at least." Argusto swung his legs around, put them on the windowsill, stared out at the great pyramid of the sun that dominated the skyline of Tenochtitlán. "I had thought to devour *el norte* in tiny bites, but Brandt has given me all the excuse I need. We shall take back the land stolen by the *yanquis* in one great gulp."

"The combined armies of the Republic and the Belt . . ." Morales moistened his lips, which had become quite dry. "Excellency, they are a formidable enemy."

"Airpower, Hector." Argusto waved his hand in dismissal, still staring at the great pyramid. "We shall sweep their armies away like dust beneath our feet."

"Did you know this was coming?" said Spider after the president had finished his speech.

Sarah shook her head.

"This was what you wanted, though, right?" said Leo. "Reunification."

Sarah watched the TV reporters interview people on the street. "That's what I wanted."

"Then why aren't you happy?" said Leo.

Sarah didn't answer. The three of them sat on the flat roof of Spider's house, cooling off in the night air. Gray clouds drifted over the city. From the backyard she could hear Michael playing with two of Spider's younger children, their voices high and giddy.

"*Sarah?*" said Leo.

"I don't know," said Sarah.

"I feel the same uneasiness," said Spider, pulling a blanket over his knees. "Aligning ourselves with the Belt against Aztlán is a huge gamble, particularly now, and President Brandt has never impressed me as being courageous."

"So maybe he rose to the occasion," said Leo. "People *do* that, you know. Even the ones everybody thinks are scaredy-cats, sometimes they surprise you."

"It's not about you, Leo," soothed Spider. "It's about the president and the reasons behind a very aberrant decision."

Sarah walked over to the edge of the roof, looked over the parapet. While Spider and Leo continued to talk, she watched Michael play hide-and-seek with the other kids in the big backyard. They were older than he was but he was better at the game. He found a quiet spot, peeking out from under an overturned wading pool. A creepy place to hide, damp and dark, probably home to spiders and other bugs, but he didn't seem to mind. Jonah, who was "It," wandered the yard and either spotted the other kids hiding, or waited until they gave themselves away by giggling. Michael stayed quiet in the darkness under the wading pool, stayed quiet and unmoving even when Jonah stood just inches away, stayed there until Jonah finally gave up.

"It's nice to see you smiling," said Spider. "It's been a while."

"I know," said Sarah.

Leo's pale skin was blotchy. "So . . . do you think Aztlán's going to declare war on us?"

"We may not get a formal declaration," said Sarah, serious again. "It may just happen."

"Perhaps Brandt's declaration of support for the Belt, presenting a unified front, will give Aztlán pause," said Spider. "It might at least buy time."

"Did you see General Kidd?" said Sarah. "He looked even grimmer than usual. At least compared to Amir."

"Young warriors are always eager for battle." Spider wrapped the blanket tighter around himself. "Old warriors know better."

"Do you want to go in?" Sarah asked him.

"I prefer it out here," said Spider. "I like hearing the children."

"Rakkim's got the cross," Leo said abruptly. "That's got to help."

"Are you getting religion, Leo?" Sarah teased.

"Whatever works, that's my philosophy," said Leo. "I don't care if it's magic beans or a prayer cloth dipped in the Jordan River."

"The cross *will* help," said Spider. "When Rakkim gets back he can turn it over to the president. Then Brandt can present it to the Belt president in a formal ceremony. Prove to the people of the Belt that Brandt's statement wasn't just words."

"The cross will do more than affirm Brandt's good intentions," said Sarah. "You have no idea the symbolic power it has for Christians."

Spider shrugged.

"I haven't heard anything from Rakkim in days," said Leo. "Has he contacted you?"

Sarah shook her head.

"Are you worried?" asked Leo.

Sarah went back to the parapet, looked down on the kids playing. "Always."

"You should learn to *relax*, Ibrahim," said the Old One. "Enjoy life."

"I am busy insuring my salvation." Ibrahim edged closer to his father as the crowd surged outside the Mighty Neptune Hotel and Casino, thousands of people pressed up against the railing surrounding the expanse of blue water. "Can we not *leave* this place?"

"Las Vegas is the happiest place on earth, that's what everyone says." Like many in the crowd the Old One carried a plastic trident and wore a seashell crown on his head. "Aren't you happy?"

"We've been here a week and I've hated every minute of it," said Ibrahim.

"I like this city and its endless enthusiasm. It makes me feel . . . it makes me feel young again. Hopeful. Have *fun*, Ibrahim. Life is short."

The crowd roared as Moby Dick surfaced from the center of

the lake, the white whale spouting water two hundred feet into the air, a rainbow mist in the twilight. Japanese-made, of course. They made the best creatures.

The Old One cheered along with the crowd, waved his trident overhead. "Smile, my son, what you see before you is the handiwork of Allah."

"*Father.*"

The Old One swept the trident across the water. "Over thirty billion gallons of freshwater. The largest man-made lake in the world, right here in the middle of the desert. Drained an aquifer to fill it and keep it filled, but did that stop the builders? No, it did not. They simply found another aquifer and piped it in. Where does such ambition and expertise come from other than Allah?"

Moby Dick rushed toward them, dove, its tail fluke kicking up a vast wave that broke over the crowd, drenching them.

The crowd howled with delight, none of them louder than the Old One, his clothes soaked, water dripping off his nose and ears.

Ibrahim looked miserable, his shirt soggy.

"I should have left you back in Miami," said the Old One.

"Doubtless you would have had a better time with the whore," muttered Ibrahim.

"Don't speak that way of your sister."

"My *half* sister," said Ibrahim.

"Baby is blood of my blood, as are you."

"Father—"

The Old One hooted as the *Pequod*, a full-sized, three-masted sailing ship, emerged from the casino and out onto the lake, sails catching the wind. Captain Ahab strode the deck with his peg leg, commanding the sailors while a tattooed man with a harpoon took a position near the bow. A tourist beside them hoisted a small boy onto his shoulders so he could see better, the boy wearing a pirate hat and waving a plastic scimitar.

"Avast, matey!" the Old One shouted at the child, shaking his trident.

The boy stared at him, then turned back to the *Pequod.*

"I hope you know what you're doing with Brandt," said Ibrahim. "His speech today—"

"Brandt's irrelevant. He could barely stand up without Amir beside him."

"Amir is irrelevant without General Kidd," said Ibrahim.

The Old One glanced at his son, then turned away, peering at the surface of the water, trying to determine exactly where the whale would resurface. As often as he had seen the show he could never be sure. The whale's central processor used random selection to heighten the excitement. Leo could probably work out the math to predict its exact appearance, but . . . He jabbed a finger at the lake. "Thar she blows!"

Moby Dick shot straight up not too far from the spot he had indicated, twisting in the air before landing in the water with a huge splash. The wave raced across the lake, sent the *Pequod* bobbing, Captain Ahab fighting to retain his balance.

The crowd whistled and applauded as the whale headed for the ship.

"I fear that you underestimate Aztlán, Father," whispered Ibrahim, water still dripping from his beard. "Their air force rolled back the Central American military in less than a week, and two days of aerial bombardment was enough to convince Venezuela to cede Aztlán their offshore oil wells."

Moby Dick picked up speed, the enormous sperm whale rushing through the water. On the *Pequod,* the tattooed sailor reared back with his harpoon.

"Study your history," said the Old One, watching the great white whale charge the sailing ship. "In 1967, the Israelis destroyed the entire Egyptian air force in one single afternoon. The whole war was lost while the Egyptian commanders sipped tea."

The tattooed sailor launched his harpoon deep into the white whale, but Moby Dick barely slowed, crashing into the *Pequod* midship, rending the wood planking. The crowd fell silent as the ship split in half, started to sink, the child beside them clutching his father's hair while Moby Dick slowly circled.

The Old One looked at Ibrahim. "So tell me, boy . . . do you think we are any less capable of smiting our enemies than *Jews*?"

"I . . . I just feared we were taking an unnecessary risk, that's all," said Ibrahim hurriedly.

"I'm leaving for Seattle tonight to ensure the takeover proceeds smoothly in the weeks ahead." The Old One scanned the crowd. "I want you to go back to Miami."

"Father, *please—*"

"Seattle is rainy, my son," said the Old One. "You might catch your death of cold there. I would never forgive myself."

CHAPTER 45

"How can you drive in this slop?" said Baby as the rain beat against the windshield, the wipers barely able to keep up. "It's raining cats, dogs and every other animal on the ark."

Rakkim leaned forward, blinking in the glare from the oncoming headlights.

Baby gnawed a pork rib thick with meat, takeout from a barbecue joint about ten miles back. "Might as well look for a motel. Even if we made it to the airport tonight, no way they're going to have flights leaving for Miami in this mess."

"You're probably right."

"Baby's probably right? That's a first." Seat tilted back, Baby propped her long legs on the dash. She tugged at her short shorts, the inside of her tanned thighs glowing in the red light from the instrument panel. "I must be getting to you, Rikki."

Rakkim glanced at her, then back at the road.

"You can admit it." Baby scraped her front teeth along the curve of the rib, peeling off meat. She had a tiny smear of barbecue sauce above her lip. "I won't tell anyone."

Rakkim smiled.

"I saw that," said Baby. "I got you now."

Rakkim reached over, snatched the last chunk of cornbread from the basket in her lap. She went to slap his hand, but he was too quick.

Thunder crashed in the distance, lightning zigzagging across the night. The rain came down even harder now—a red neon sign flashing *Kim's Cabin* shimmered through the downpour as though it were underwater. Like one of the inundated restaurants in New Orleans that Moseby had talked about, sea urchins pincushioning the stools and counters, moray eels curled up in the open cash registers. Rakkim was sorry he never had a chance to dive in the sunken city. Moseby promised to take him some-day, promised to show him the spots—shopping mall grottos alive with iridescent fish, and coral reefs festooned along miles of parked cars. Beautiful, terrible things, Moseby had said. Never going to happen now. Another thing Rakkim was sorry for.

"I wish we had been able to get Moseby to a real hospital," said Baby. "I wish he was here with us now."

"I . . . I was just thinking about him too."

"Really?" Baby shook her head, choked up. "I didn't know him like you did . . . but the man . . . he made an impression."

Rakkim watched the wipers slap back and forth, the rain coming down so hard he could see the fat droplets falling through the high beams. "Moseby told me this story once . . . about when he was first courting his wife. It was love at first sight, for him anyway. Annabelle was more practical."

"Women have to be." Baby's tongue snaked out, licked the barbecue sauce from above her lip. "We give in to foolishness, the consequences are much worse than for a man."

Rakkim cracked his window, just enough to let the cool, moist air in. "Moseby was a shadow warrior . . . sent to check out reports of the Belt manufacturing biotoxins in the delta." He shook his head. "He found out within two weeks it was a phar-maceutical plant. Most dangerous items coming out of it were these aphrodisiac pills made from stingray cartilage—Chinese men swore by them." He could barely see the road. "Moseby said they worked too." He drifted off, listening to the rain, steering by instinct more than anything else.

Baby put her hand on the back of his neck. "I like hearing how folks fell in love."

Rakkim felt the heat of her touch as the wipers kept their steady stroke back and forth. "Moseby was supposed to be invis-ible, the kind of person you notice only after they're gone . . . but after he saw Annabelle he started showing up where she was . . . always being in the right place at the right time. One thing led to another. Moseby had a good cover job, salvage diver, and he was patient, never pushy, had that deep voice . . . drove women crazy . . . but Annabelle, she was tough, and her father was even tougher." Far ahead of them, taillights blinked in the rain. "Moseby made her a deal. Told her to hide one of her earrings in her house. Hide it *anyplace* she wanted, and he'd find it within one hour. If he couldn't do it, he'd leave and never come back, but if he found it . . . she'd marry him."

"Just *one* hour?" said Baby.

"Took him ten minutes." Rakkim looked at her. "Annabelle cheated. Her eyes led him right to the earring. He knew she would if she really wanted to marry him."

"I *like* that story," said Baby. Thunder clapped closer, seemed to be right inside the car, the air sizzling, and Baby cried out, clung to him.

Rakkim put his blinker on, turned off into the Castaways Motel parking lot, barreled through a huge puddle, water shooting out both sides of the car.

"Leo!"

Leo jumped, tripping over his own feet. "You *scared* me."

"Pardon me, it's just that I've been hoping to run into you," said the Old One.

"Well . . . this must be your lucky day," said Leo, his face still red. The after-work crowd in the Zone broke around them, security blimps ringing the sky over Seattle. Leo was edging toward Wally's Game Emporium. "Harry Voigt, right? Harry Voigt Investments. Geneva, Shanghai, Nairobi."

"Very good, Leo. Not that I'm at all surprised at your memory." The Old One listened to the music pounding from the Kit Kat Klub, felt it through his shoes. It had been too long since he had been in the capital. He might keep it the capital of the reunited nation when the time came. From the palace he planned on building, he would look out at the snow-covered mountains . . .

"How did that encryption problem work out for you?" said Leo.

"Everyone was quite impressed with your solution," said the Old One. "Overwhelmed, actually. I wish you could have been there."

Leo blushed.

"I really hope you'll consider coming to work for me," said the Old One. "I like to think that one of the secrets of my success is my ability to recognize and nurture talent, the best and the brightest. I can guarantee you, Leo, that you will never feel unappreciated were you to work with me. Note, I didn't say work *for* me. I see us as equals, collaborators, as it were. We're adults, aren't we, you and I?"

Leo's face shone like the full moon. "I guess . . . yeah."

"Of course we are, and that's the beauty of our friendship: I respect you. You don't mind if I consider you my friend, do you? I hope I'm not being presumptuous."

"No . . . no, it's nice. Most people . . . I get on most people's nerves."

"Nonsense." The Old One clapped Leo on the back. "I've heard Hop Singh's has the best noodles in the Zone. Let's get dinner and discuss adequate compensation for your service." The Old One hooked his arm in Leo's, the two of them strolling down the crowded sidewalk. "I'm sure your father is generous, but a man who wants to be married needs his own money."

"That . . . that's true." Leo sniffed. "So did you actually try out my solution on your encryption yet?"

"Not yet," said the Old One as the crowd parted before them, "but any day now."

Rakkim lay in the bathtub, bubbles up to his chin, listening to the thunder. The light in the small, blue tile bathroom was dim, the water warm, and he half closed his eyes, giving in to the fatigue in his body. Been days since he had slept . . . He heard the door between his and Baby's adjoining rooms open, started to get up, then sank back under the bubbles, recognizing her footsteps. "Did you get lost?"

Baby stood in the door to the bathroom wearing a long-sleeved shirt, white lace panties peeking out from between the shirttails. Her hair was still damp from her shower. "I was just checking on you."

"I'm alive and well. No danger of drowning."

Baby walked over, sat on the side of the tub, trailed a hand in the water. "Nice to meet a man who enjoys a bubble bath. Shows confidence."

"Why don't you wait for me in the other room?"

The rain beat down on the roof of the motel room, thunder echoing. "You modest, Rikki?"

"That's right."

"You shouldn't be. Not with me." She scooped bubbles out of the tub, made herself a mustache, drew one on him too, and he let her. "I've seen you naked before, remember? I bathed you when you were in the field hospital."

Rakkim blushed. "I was unconscious then. I'm wide awake now."

"Why should that make a difference?" Baby lowered her eyes. She looked too young to have stopped Gravenholtz from beating him to death, too shy to have defied the Old One. "You . . . you have a really nice body, Rikki. I liked looking at you while you slept . . . liked taking care of you."

"Baby . . . you should go back to your room."

Baby shook her head. "I don't like my room."

"We'll switch then. You can have this—"

"That's not it." Baby played in the bubbles, her hand hovering just above him. She was looking into his eyes and he felt himself sinking into the depths of hers. "I . . . I don't like being alone."

Rakkim tried not to look at her but he couldn't tear himself away. He felt himself stiffen, grateful for the bubbles hiding his arousal.

"Please, Rikki?"

"I'm not very good company."

"No, you don't understand," said Baby. "Thunderstorms *scare* me. Have since I was a kid." Thunder rattled the windows and she flinched.

Rakkim put his hand on her shoulder, soapsuds on his knuckles. "Let me get dressed and we'll watch TV."

"My mama had a boyfriend when I was seven or eight, a real mean son of a bitch. He used to tease me. . . ." Baby wrapped her arms around herself, trembling. "He said . . . he said God liked to strike pretty little girls with lightning bolts, liked to burn them to a crisp to teach them a lesson for their nastiness." She rested her head on the cool side of the tub, her hand drifting through the water. "I know it's not true, but I still . . . I still can't abide thunderstorms."

"Go back to your room and I'll join you as soon as I get out of here," said Rakkim. "I'll stay with you until you fall asleep."

"Promise?"

"Promise."

Baby handed him a bath towel, discreetly turned her back on him until he stood up and stepped out of the tub.

Lightning crashed closer, almost in the room with them, and Baby screamed, clutched at him, nails digging into him. The towel was somewhere . . . on the floor, as she pressed herself against him, whimpering into his chest.

"It's okay," said Rakkim, holding her close as the rain pounded on the roof. "I'm right here."

Baby kissed him, tentatively at first, then eagerly, and he kissed her back. Baby tore off her shirt, buttons popping, rolling across the tile, kicked off her panties, as naked as he was now, her hands on him, her lips on him . . .

Rakkim pulled away, shaking his head. "This . . ." He couldn't catch his breath. "This is a mistake."

Thunder shook the windows again and Baby didn't flinch this time. She barely reacted, her eyes on him, one arm hooked around the small of his back.

"Sorry . . . I'm sorry." Rakkim disengaged himself. Grabbed the towel off the floor. "We can't do this."

"Speak for yourself," said Baby.

Rakkim walked into the room, and Baby followed him. He pulled on his pants.

Baby lay on the bed, nude, watching him. "You don't know what you want, do you?"

"It was my fault," said Rakkim. "I shouldn't have kissed you back."

"But you *did*." Baby stroked her belly. "Doesn't that tell you something?"

"It tells me I'm human."

"Oh, you're a lot more than that, Rikki." Baby patted the bed. "Come on over and talk to me. I promise not to bite." She held out her hand. "Come on. We can still talk, can't we?"

Rakkim sat on the edge of the bed. Her damp hair curled around her long nipples. She caught him looking and laughed. He smiled too. "Maybe we should get back in the car. It's safer."

"I'm tired of safe and sane," said Baby. "Tell me you don't want to make love with me."

"If I did it would be a lie," said Rakkim.

"So . . ." Baby ran a fingernail down his bare back. "What's the problem then?"

"I told you. I'm married."

"So am I . . . technically."

"Why don't you go get dressed and we'll get back on the road?" said Rakkim. "It's late, and what with the storm, maybe the traffic will have thinned out."

Baby pulled a pillow under her head, stayed where she was. "Either Aztlán stopped jamming our communications, or the Belt found some way to override their signal, because I got through to Miami loud and clear before I came in here. There's been a change of plans."

"What's going on?"

"You still want me to go back to my room?"

"No more games," said Rakkim.

"Fine." Baby glared at him. "Lester's not going to Miami with the cross. He's on his way to Seattle . . . to join the Old One. So that's where we should be headed."

"What's the Old One doing in Seattle?" said Rakkim. "If war comes with Aztlán, that's the last place he should want to be. Miami is *neutral*. Why would he leave?"

"Makes no sense, but Daddy's no fool," said Baby. "So if he's there, he must have important business."

"*Daddy?*"

"Shoot, I call all older men daddy." Baby scratched her ankle.

"I never heard you use it like that before."

"I called the Colonel daddy. You're not careful, I'll call *you* daddy too."

"You didn't say it the same way to the Colonel," Rakkim said quietly. "Different inflection."

"You're making a big deal out of nothing, silly."

"I once made a big deal when a man said *dinner* instead of *supper*," said Rakkim, "because it told me he wasn't from where he said he was. That nothing saved my life."

Baby stretched out a leg, wiggled her toes. "You keep this up, I'm going to be afraid to say anything to you."

"Daddy? It's a strange thing to call the Old One, that's all," Rakkim said, cool and calm inside as a mountain lake. "I met him once, and he had all these young men surrounding him, but no women. Yet, you stayed with him in Miami for a year. That's strange too."

"You think too much, Rikki."

Rakkim shook his head. "No . . . that's not my problem."

"Quit *looking* at me like that." Baby pulled the sheet around herself.

"It's just . . . *Daddy*, the *way* you said it . . . with that certain tone, that very distinctive inflection," said Rakkim. "When his sons spoke to him, it was *Father*, very respectful, very formal . . . but *Daddy*? That's as intimate as it comes. That's the kind of thing a daughter—"

Baby blinked back tears. "You're ruining everything, Rikki."

"What am I ruining, Baby?"

"We could have been happy, you and me," said Baby.

"No . . . I don't think so."

"Something's not right with Daddy, just like you thought, and Ibrahim doesn't have the balls to hold it all together."

Rakkim slipped off the bed, started putting on the rest of his clothes.

"Don't do this, Rikki." Baby got out of bed, trembling, put her hands on him. "I took care of you. I could have left you, could have taken the cross, but I didn't. I *stayed*."

Rakkim nodded.

"Doesn't that mean anything?"

"Yeah," said Rakkim, "but I'm still not sure what."

"Daddy's right about most things, but I didn't need him to tell me you were something special. So am I, Rikki, I'm special too." Baby put her arms around his neck. "Between the two of us . . . there's nothing we couldn't do."

Rakkim slowly untangled himself from her. Stepped into his boots.

"Don't do this," said Baby. "*Please?* You're making a big mistake."

Rakkim stepped outside into the rain, closed the motel room door behind him. He could hear her crying inside. In a night of surprises, it was the most surprising thing of all.

CHAPTER 46

"You're one busy lady these days," said Anthony Colarusso, taking a lick off the remains of a triple-decker ice cream cone. "Can't turn on the TV without seeing you being interviewed by somebody."

"The president's doing a brave thing by supporting the Belt," said Sarah, sitting beside him on the park bench. "I wanted to do everything I could to help him."

It was ostensibly business as usual in Seattle, but there was an air of hurried uncertainty in the city, everyone waiting for hostilities to break out. People talked too loudly, bought things they didn't need, and argued over the smallest things. Everyone watched the sky, waiting for the air raid warnings to sound.

"Marie thinks you're also promoting your own agenda, putting yourself out there like that," said Colarusso. "I told her our Sarah would never try to influence events like that."

"Smart lady you're married to, Anthony."

"Yeah, sometimes makes me wonder why she settled for me, but then, being Catholic, it wasn't like she had a lot of better options."

"That'll be changing too," said Sarah. "If the alliance holds against Aztlán, there won't be any more room for such bigotry."

"Yeah, well, you believe what you want to. I live in the real world." Colarusso looked up at all the newly added security blimps ringing the city. "I sent Marie and the girls off to stay with Marie's sister in Wenatchee until things work themselves out. Nothing there worth bombing except apple trees. Every year her sister sends us that Aplets and Cotlets candy for Christmas. Supposed to be a healthy treat, but it sticks to my molars." He sucked at a tooth. "You and Michael are welcome to join them."

"I'm needed here."

"Me, I'm needed too. I get tempted sometimes to let people take care of themselves." Colarusso belched. "Last time I was here, I was with Rikki. You hear from him?"

"A few garbled messages. He and Moseby evidently found what they were looking for."

"*Really?*" Colarusso fished out his Saint Christopher medal, kissed it. "What I wouldn't give to see that. *Touch* it. You got no idea what that would mean to me."

"Yes, I do." Sarah fingered the crucifix around her own neck. "My mother was Catholic."

"Of course. I knew that." Ice cream dripped off the cone and onto Colarusso's hand. "Every time I think about what Rikki is bringing back . . . I can't hardly think straight."

"That's the idea." Sarah saw his expression, touched his arm. "I didn't mean it that way. I just meant that religious icons operate outside of rational thought."

"No offense taken," said Colarusso. "I've seen what rational thought leads to. Dumbest people I ever met were intellectuals. Present company excepted, of course."

"Of course."

"That one interview you did with what's his name . . . Robert Legault?" Colarusso watched her. "He seemed sweet on you, but maybe that's just me. Never met a cop who didn't have a dirty mind."

"It's just TV," said Sarah.

Legault had initiated the media campaign that had put Sarah on TV almost constantly ever since the president's speech three days ago. Legault's productions were flawless, dramatically lit, giving her a gravitas far beyond her years. He said she was the perfect advocate for reunion—smart, well-spoken, the beautiful niece of Redbeard, the head of State Security who had kept the Republic safe from terrorists during its early days. In her own right, Sarah was a free-thinking Muslim, advisor to the former president, and a historian able to put Brandt's initiative into context. Vietnam had once been divided, so had Korea, Germany, South Africa, greater Russia. All of them had reunited and grown stronger because of it.

For good or ill, the president's speech had altered the geopolitical landscape. The armed forces had been put on high alert, all leaves canceled, but with the trade embargo between the Republic and the Belt lifted, the stock markets of both nations were up over 15 percent. The president had called Sarah twice, thanking her for her support and suggesting that she share the stage with him at a national town-hall meeting next week.

Getty, a friend and high-level government official in Atlanta, had contacted her, told her that the Belt president was hunkered down in the bomb shelter under his mansion and refusing to make decisions. Getty and other senior staffers had formed a war cabinet led by the Colonel to deal with the impending hostilities. *It's a roller coaster livin' in excitin' times, isn't it?* he had told her. *I haven't had so much fun since Truman Capote weekend the year I graduated Duke.*

A young couple approached, moderates, the woman short and rounded in a shimmering yellow chador, pregnant, the man tall and serious in a gray suit with a REUNION! button on his lapel.

"It *is* you," said the young man.

"I told him but he didn't believe me," said the young woman. "We're so proud of you."

Sarah pressed her fingertips together in a blessing. "We have some tough times ahead."

"We'll get through them," the young man said eagerly.

"My grandpa told us stories about when we were one country," said the young woman. "Was it really that wonderful?"

"No," Sarah and Colarusso said at the same time.

"They were trying to make it better, though," said Sarah. "Maybe soon we'll get another chance."

The young woman touched her belly. "I'm sure of it."

They watched as the couple left, the young woman turning

once to wave at them. Fourth time Sarah and Colarusso had been interrupted by well-wishers since they sat down.

"*Look* at this," said Colarusso, ice cream dripping onto his suit. He tossed the soggy cone into a trash can, licked his fingers. "My own fault for getting a triple. They price things so the third scoop costs hardly anything, but you got to eat so fast you get a brain freeze." He wiped his hand on his pants, sat down. Took a slow look around. "Well, here's something you might not know—police and State Security busted up five planned terrorist attacks in the last forty-eight hours. Black Robes."

"I'm sure ibn-Azziz isn't pleased with the president kissing up to the Belt."

"That's what I wanted to ask you about," said Colarusso. "We can't connect ibn-Azziz to the planned attacks. Seems to be the work of individual imams acting on their own. State Security intercepted a confidential fatwa from New Fallujah ordering no Muslim to interfere in any way with the president's overture to the Belt."

"Probably disinformation. Ibn-Azziz must have *wanted* it to be intercepted."

"Maybe." Colarusso shrugged. "Whatever the fatwa's intention, it seems to be working. Things are quiet at the mosques. In fact, captain at State Security told me it was ibn-Azziz's people who tipped them off to the planned attacks. How fucking crazy is that?"

"It's a *hudna*," said Sarah. "That's what ibn-Azziz assumes the president is *really* up to with the Belt. That's why he doesn't want to interfere."

"A what?"

"*Hudna*. It's an Arabic word that means calm . . . or a peace treaty. A *temporary* cessation of hostilities, not because the war is over, but so Muslims can regroup or redirect their strength. To ibn-Azziz, our immediate enemy is Aztlán, but our long-term enemy remains the Belt."

"So we're pals until we defeat Aztlán, and then we turn on the Belt?"

"I don't know anybody who expects us to defeat Aztlán, but together we might persuade them to rein in their territorial ambitions."

"You think that's what the president is doing?"

"I don't know."

"*Hudna.*" Colarusso shook his head. "Where I grew up we called that a stab in the back."

"It's considered a morally acceptable Muslim battle tactic," said Sarah. "At least when used against infidels."

"I'll never understand you people."

"Yes, your people are ever so superior, Anthony. Like that lovely Borgia family that just moved in down the block. The sister, Lucrezia, brought by the most marvelous-looking raspberry tart cake yesterday, you'll have to try it."

The two-seat helicopter caught the sunset as it angled across Perdue Airbase outside of Atlanta, skimmed over the trees and set down gently not far from a small private jet idling nearby. "Go!" shouted the military pilot.

Rakkim darted out of the chopper, keeping low as he ran.

"In!" barked the military aide in the gray uniform, a machine gun slung over his shoulder. He half lifted, half threw Rakkim into the open hatch of the jet, then jumped in after him, secured the door. The jet was already taxiing down the runway before Rakkim got seated.

Rakkim's belt snaked across his lap as the jet took off at a steep angle, pressing him back into his seat, the noise so high his ears hurt. The jet penetrated the reddish-orange cloud cover, still climbing, still accelerating, tiny pretzel-wheel snacks rolling down the aisle.

Rakkim had gotten lucky after he left Baby at the motel. The storm had kept most traffic off the road and he made good time.

It took a dozen phone calls but he finally got through to the Colonel, who had sent a helicopter for him.

"Pilgrim!" said Malcolm Crews, grabbing Rakkim by the shoulder, so tall he had to incline his head to avoid bumping the ceiling of the plane. "Glad you could make it. I was starting to fret." He beckoned. "Come on back and sit with me in the luxury suite."

Rakkim followed him to the back of the plane, past an inner door guarded by a couple of young soldiers reading the Bible. "Where's the Colonel?"

"Sit down," said Crews, indicating a sofa that filled the small suite. "Get you a drink?"

"Just water. I was supposed to meet the Colonel."

"Water for our guest, bourbon and a splash for me, James," Crews said to the aide that had lifted Rakkim into the jet. "The Colonel's in Texas, which is where I'm heading. He said you wanted to get to Seattle. I can't help you with that, but I can drop you off in Las Vegas. The Belt's still sealed off from the Republic, but you can hop a flight home from there."

"Good enough."

The aide brought their drinks and left them alone.

Rakkim hefted the cut crystal glassware, turned it so it sparkled. "You've moved up in the world, Malcolm."

"I've been washed in the blood of the Lamb." Crews peered at him. "You look tired."

"A little."

Crews took a long swallow of bourbon. "The Colonel's disappointed you're not going to spend more time with us, help us out with this war about to start."

"I appreciate the lift. You get me to Vegas, I'll find my way home."

"Of course." Crews sprawled on the sofa, legs crossed. The Man in White, they called him, but lately Rakkim had heard him called another name: "our new Lincoln." It seemed ridiculous the first few times he heard it, but seeing him like this, close up, long arms and legs, that bony horse face and thatch of black hair . . . well, there *was* a physical resemblance. Crews bobbed his head as though reading Rakkim's thoughts. "Never know what life has in store for us, do we? A year ago you and I were at each other's throats . . . now here we are, couple of civilized men enjoying a drink at ten thousand feet."

The jet bumped along on turbulence, ice cubes tinkling in their glasses.

"How's the mobilization going?" said Rakkim. "The Colonel have some plan to deal with Aztlán's air superiority?"

"I'm no military man," said Crews, "but the Colonel thinks it's best to disperse the men across the whole front, then wait for the inevitable air assault and then counterattack in small, hit-and-run raids. Strike fast and retreat, wear them down. Whether or not it works . . ." He shrugged, took a fat, hand-rolled joint out of his jacket pocket, fired it up.

"I thought you were clean as a newborn lamb or something," said Rakkim.

"You have to learn to forgive people their trespasses, pilgrim." Crews puffed away on the joint. "Colonel got a call about an hour after you reached him." He exhaled a plume of smoke. "Baby. She didn't have nice things to say about you."

"Oh, darn."

"The Colonel called me right after talking with her—might have placed some stock in the things she had to say . . . and pilgrim, *really*, you should be ashamed of yourself, she is a married woman."

"Nothing happened."

"*That's* too bad. A waste of quality pussy." Crews stretched out his legs, eyes shiny, enjoying himself. "Don't worry, I set the Colonel straight. Told him Baby was working for the Old One."

"How did you know that?"

Crews offered the joint, and Rakkim declined. "I know because the two of them showed up at my place in the country a few months ago, them and Lester. Let me tell you, that redheaded bastard is everything they say about him and more. Went through my boys like shit through a goose."

"What did the Old One want?"

"Always in a hurry." Crews shook his head. "It was the Old One and Baby that helped me become the man I am today. *They* were the ones wanted me to talk up the Colonel in my sermons, keep the waters boiling." He took another hit off the joint. "Crazy world, ain't it. Most preachers say the nature of God is unknowable, but I'm certain of one thing at least." He leaned toward Rakkim. "God Almighty has a sense of humor."

"Yeah, and unfortunately for us, it's mostly slapstick and irony."

Crews laughed and so did Rakkim.

"I missed you, pilgrim," said Crews. "Most folks are safe as milk, but you got an edge to you."

"You going to ask me to the prom, Malcolm?"

"See, that's just what I'm talking about."

"Why did the Old One want you to support the Colonel?" said Rakkim.

"Best way to cause trouble, I suppose," said Crews. "Baby said they were bringing hard times and fever dreams to the world." Smoke trickled from his nostrils. "They said me standing by the Colonel, riling up the rest of the country, would bring the hard times on faster."

"Sounds like she had *your* number."

"I suspect she's got all our numbers," said Crews. "I'll admit, I was always a great believer in burning down the village to save the village, whether it needed saving or not." He took a last pull on the joint, tossed it in his mouth.

"So why are you telling me about the Old One and Baby? Why tell the Colonel?"

"It's a funny thing. . . ." Crews smoothed his pearly white jacket. "Baby was the one who told me to dress like this . . . that whole Man in White thing, said it would make folks think I was part of the anointed . . . but it had the same effect on me.

I started thinking maybe I wasn't the evil fuck I always thought I was." He clutched Rakkim's sleeve. "It's not so bad being one of the good guys, is it? Long as we can still have fun." He pulled Rakkim closer. "The Old One was right about me . . . he saw straight to my dark heart. I *am* always listening for the trumpet blast announcing Armageddon, but shit and shinola, pilgrim, as long as we're having us a war, I might as well be on the side of the angels."

The sunset poured in the window, their faces like burnished bronze.

Rakkim turned toward the window, felt the warmth on his face. The Old One favored anything that destabilized the established order, and if it didn't happen naturally, he was happy to help, whether it was nuking D.C. or poisoning the Moscow water supply. Stirring up a war between the Belt and Aztlán was just the sort of thing he would do . . . but there had to be more. Brandt's speech supporting the Belt . . . did that help or hurt the Old One's plan? He looked at Crews. "The Colonel have any idea when Aztlán's going to launch their attack?"

"He's surprised they haven't *already* attacked." Crews leaned closer. "I hear you went into D.C. looking for something. You find it?"

"Found it and lost it," said Rakkim.

"Isn't that always the way. Did Baby take it?"

"No. Gravenholtz did."

Crews folded his hands across his flat belly. "I'd let it go then if I were you."

"You're not me," said Rakkim.

"Send him in," said the Old One.

Gravenholtz was ushered into the Old One's holo-suite in the New Mandarin Hotel, the most modern and luxurious hotel in Seattle. He looked around, whistled, the suite an exact replica of the Doge's palazzo in Venice.

The Old One gestured and his servants left them alone.

"Good to see you, Lester. I trust you had a pleasant flight. It took some doing."

"Yeah . . . thanks." Gravenholtz looked up at the ceiling three stories above him. "I could get used to this." He grinned his yellowed teeth at the Old One. "Except for all the statues of naked men. I don't go that route."

"What's wrong with your voice? I can hardly understand you."

Gravenholtz's eyes blazed. "My *tongue*," he said slowly. "Rakkim . . . cut . . . my tongue." He pulled out a crusty handkerchief, spit blood into it.

The Old One beckoned him closer. Held out his hand.

Gravenholtz pulled a small wooden case out of his jacket. "I'm making up a list of the things I want," he said carefully, trying not to slur his words. "It's one fucking long list too." He gave the box to the Old One. "You want my advice, I'd take Baby to the woodshed if I was you." He spit again into the handkerchief.

"I'm sure you would." The Old One didn't open the box. "You may leave me, Lester."

"That's it?" Gravenholtz walked out, grumbling.

The Old One climbed the thirteen steps leading to the ornate gold throne and seated himself. A perfect simulation, but nothing like the reality cube, part of the hotel wing that he had reserved, a cube three hundred feet in every direction with a gigantic pool at the center. A virtual beach. The cube alone cost $500,000 a night and worth every penny. The ultimate in Chinese technology, one of only five in the world. Anytime, anywhere at his fingertips. No special suit required, no implants, the cube instantaneously responded to the brain waves of the primary guest, but was experienced by everyone within the cube. The Old One had spent last night alone at an oasis in the desert land of his birth, where he had gone as a child with his fathers and brothers, all of them swimming in the warm water at the center of the retreat. Last night he had again felt the windblown sand against his face, felt every grain, and heard the date palms rustling as he floated on his back, the stars burning overhead—stars so sharp and clear in the night sky it was as though he were watching from Paradise itself. Such a long, long time to get from there . . . to here.

He hefted the box, so light it could have been a dream. Opened it at last . . . and took out the small piece of wood festooned with tiny white flowers, let it rest in the palm of his hand. He sighed as a warmth flowed through him like electricity. He noted the numerous striations in the ancient wood, the delicacy of the white flowers. His senses were more acute. His vision clearer. His sense of taste and smell heightened. He felt the knots in his body smooth out, the tightness in his chest leaving him. Most important of all, he felt the fear dissipate, the fear he had never acknowledged in these last few months, not once. For the first time since Massakar had told him he was dying, the Old One was certain of his destiny. He knew who he was.

CHAPTER 47

Presidente Argusto stood in his command center watching his air armada leave to destroy the combined armies of *el norte*, and wished he were in the lead bomber group. He stood with his hands behind his back, hair black as Monterrey crude. The war board was a mass of blinking red lights, wave after wave of red lights moving slowly toward the border. Nine hundred and fifty-seven red lights, nine hundred and fifty-seven combat airplanes, long-range and short-range bombers, fighters and electronic-jamming jets, each one linked to the command-and-control system buried deep in the heart of the Cerro San Rafael Mountains in Coahuila.

It had taken three years to dig the base out in secrecy—a futile hunt for silver, the locals thought—while the world assumed the base was being built under the foothills outside Tenochtitlán. A typically cautious move on the part of Argusto, who believed that great risks could be undertaken only after great preparation. He had mortgaged his nation's economy to pay for the air armada and the command center that ordered them into battle—money well spent. With that air armada he had wrested the Panama Canal away and the rich oil fields of the Isthmus. Soon he would replant the Aztlán flag on the lands of the north, lands that had once belonged to the Mexicans.

The lights on the war board blinked steadily, a soothing consistency as his planes raced across the dry landscape of Arizona, New Mexico, California, Texas, more squadrons taking off across the Gulf, wave after wave of titanium warbirds on their way toward targets in the Belt—power plants and population centers, military bases and manufacturing plants—bringing pain and destruction to *el norte*. A lesson about to be taught, a hard lesson that would not soon be forgotten.

Argusto rocked gently on his high heels, surrounded by technicians and generals, utterly alone with his dreams and ambitions.

Situated on an outcropping of red sandstone in the Sonora Desert, the Old One's small technical team picked up the first wave of Aztlán's armada moments after takeoff. Dietrich and his band of programmers immediately beamed Leo's encryption-busting equation into the onboard computer of one of the lead planes.

A simple operation. The proper vector, the proper sequence, a momentarily open door . . . and it was done, the results irrevocable. The team could disappear, be taken out by a cluster bomb, or be chopped to pieces by angry villagers wielding hoes . . . it didn't matter. Dietrich looked directly into the rising sun, tears running down his face from the harsh glare. In thirty-seven minutes, *inshallah*, the world would change.

Emilio Guzman watched the *Queen Mary* explode as he banked over Long Beach harbor, the tourist attraction splitting in half before slowly sinking into the filthy water. He would have liked to compose a rhyme to salute his first strike, but his mind was whirling, fear nosing around the edges of his consciousness.

All the years spent pretending to be a loyal subject of Aztlán, the tests passed, the clearances breached. Paradise better be everything it was cracked up to be. He smiled as Rosario, the squadron leader, directed them to take out the offshore oil rigs, Guzman following the command instantly, his afterburners briefly kicking in. A beautiful plane. A beautiful day, the sky the same deep blue as the Pacific, a perfect circle, no up, no down.

He had broken network security twenty-nine minutes ago, at precisely 6:58 A.M., right after takeoff, closed it up three seconds later. Just as the Old One had ordered. A brief enough interval that the command center monitoring the armada would consider it a simple electromagnetic glitch. Short enough to be undetected, long enough for the Old One's code-breaking program to be inserted into his onboard computer. A Trojan horse instantly sent to the command center in the constant back-and-forth between them. The program was already doing its mischief, transferring command to the Old One. In eight more minutes, command authority would shift abruptly from Argusto to the Old One. He only wished he could be there to see El Presidente's face.

Guzman hadn't asked what the Old One would do once he had control of the armada. He didn't need to. He was only grateful that the Old One had waited until Aztlán had drawn first blood, so that Guzman had gotten to utilize his hard-won skills. Doubtless the Old One had his reasons for waiting . . . to give time for the whole armada to be in the air, or to inflame *el norte*. It didn't matter. Only this moment mattered.

Eight minutes. He sped over the waves toward the offshore oil rigs, wondering as he often did what Paradise would be like.

Amir ushered President Brandt into the emergency elevator of the palace as the air-raid warnings sounded, a metallic bleating that could wake the dead. He gripped the president's shoulder, practically had to hold the coward up. In his ear he could hear his father coolly giving orders to the Fedayeen ringing the capital, then switching over to coordinate the defense of the other major cities. The doors closed and the floor seemed to fall away with the speed of their descent.

"Amir, has the president been secured?" said General Kidd.

"Almost, Father."

"Do your duty, my son."

"Always, Father." Amir broke the com-link as they descended farther underground.

The president clutched at Amir. "You said we would be safe."

Amir watched the levels whirl past on the digital readout.

"You assured me that Aztlán's planes would never reach us," said the president, voice cracking. "You . . . you *gave* me your word."

The elevator stopped with a slight bump. The doors hissed open.

Amir stepped out first into the bunker. "Everything's under control, Mr. President."

Sarah held Michael's hand as they filed down to the basement with Spider and his family, feet scuffing on the wooden steps. "It's going to be okay," she said.

Michael looked up at her, kept walking.

She should have taken Colarusso up on his offer and sent Michael to stay in Wenatchee with Marie and the girls. She had told herself that the war might be avoided, some last-minute diplomatic agreement, a postponement of hostilities. But it was her own selfishness that kept him here, her not wanting to be separated from her son.

Michael squeezed her hand. "Don't worry, Mom."

"Isn't it lovely?" The Old One stood in the rooftop garden of the New Mandarin Hotel, the café empty, chairs overturned in the patrons' haste to seek shelter. The streets below should have been packed with the morning rush, but instead they were deserted, the few cars abandoned. The security blimps ringed the central core of the city, gleaming in the sun. Out in the sound he could see ferryboats chugging full-speed to port. "We have the whole city to ourselves."

"Big fucking deal," said Gravenholtz. The view would have been better if Karla Jean was beside him, which was stupid—the woman *had* tried to kill him—but, he couldn't help himself. She had held out his last best chance for another life, but that chance was gone now, another lie, another betrayal. A hard rain was coming, a rain of blood loud enough perhaps to drown out the memory of her.

"It *is* lovely, Daddy." Baby gripped the Old One's arm. "I feel like you just gave me a present wrapped with a big red bow."

"It's not really for you, darling," said the Old One.

"I . . . I know that, Daddy. . . . I was just saying—"

"Lester has more cause to bask in my favor," said the Old One, still watching the ferries racing toward shelter. "He brought me the relic."

"I would have brought you the piece of the cross if *he* hadn't stolen it," said Baby, hanging on to him. "I would have brought you Rikki too."

The Old One didn't look at her. "Yes, but you *didn't*."

Rakkim was about to board the plane to Seattle when the reader board at Las Vegas International Airport flashed ALL FLIGHTS CANCELED—due to a just-declared state of war between Aztlán and the North American Alliance.

The waiting line dissolved into a grumbling mass heading for the airport's bars and restaurants, but Rakkim didn't move, staring at the TVs, which had just started showing footage of a burning city.

Argusto bathed in the pulsing red lights of his air armada as they moved inexorably across the map. Los Angeles . . . its oil depots burning, black smoke blotting out the sun. Houston's antiaircraft defenses down, its financial district collapsed. The downtown core of Baton Rouge . . . gone. Each of them damaged, but not destroyed. Argusto's planes targeted critical installations that would do maximum military and psychological damage, but leave the essential infrastructure unharmed. He would need the bridges, dams and reservoirs once the Republic and the Belt surrendered.

He turned, hearing rapid footsteps.

General Sanchez, the computer scientist in charge of the command center, hurried over, a thin, gawky man with wireless spectacles and foul breath. "El Magnifico . . ." he panted, his hands clenching and unclenching.

"What is it?"

"There's a slight . . . anomaly with the system." Sanchez swallowed. "You should call back the armada."

Argusto stared at "General Chicken Neck," as his bodyguards referred to the man. "Don't be ridiculous. What sort of anomaly?"

"I'm—I'm not sure." Sanchez cracked his knuckles. "There seems to be . . . a breach of some kind. I can't tell if it's a systems error or an outside attack on the command center itself."

"Do we have control over my birds?"

"Yes . . . for the time being. But I'm concerned—"

"Go away and take care of the anomaly." Argusto turned back to the war screen. The third and fourth waves were approaching Dallas and Sacramento, Nashville and Atlanta, while the first two waves stayed over their initial targets, awaiting further orders. The final fifth and sixth waves had just taken off for Seattle and Portland and New Detroit, Richmond and Louisville.

"The anomaly is spreading exponentially, Excellency," stumbled Sanchez, tugging at his thin mustache. "That . . . that's what I'm most concerned with. Unless we recall the armada immediately—"

"Are you still here?" said Argusto, still watching the war screen.

Group leader Jaime Rosario felt his light attack bomber shudder as he fought in vain to override the computer. Upside down, he felt himself pressed back against the seat as the plane accelerated directly toward the earth. All manual controls were dead. Through the canopy he could see the city burning, palm trees ablaze. Los Angeles, City of Angels . . . fiery angels today. He could hear the voices of the rest of his squadron on the comlink as they struggled to regain control, men he had known for years, all of them working with a grim professionalism, their superb training evident in the calm determination with which they continued their efforts. Even Guzman, the new man, who regaled them with obscene limericks at breakfast. One by one their voices abruptly stopped, usually in the middle of a curse or a prayer. Guzman came on the link, the last voice now: "There once was a man from Veracruz—" A crackle, then silence. Rosario thought of cool water as the burning streets below rushed toward him.

"*Do* something!" Argusto shouted at Sanchez, voice echoing in the command center.

Sanchez threw up his hands. Dozens of technicians tapped away at their consoles behind him, trying to regain control. "It is too late, Excellency."

Argusto could see lights winking out all across the war board, dozens of red lights going dark as the planes crashed all across the map. He grabbed Sanchez and shook him. "Restore control dominance to the pilots then! You can do *that*, can't you?"

Sanchez shook his head. "I've tried. The system will not allow—"

"The *system!*" Argusto pushed him away, Sanchez tumbling to the floor. "I control Aztlán, not some system."

"Excellency . . ." Sanchez adjusted his glasses as he got slowly to his feet. "I must report . . . that is no longer the case."

Lights continued winking out across the board, dozens, hundreds, the pride of Aztlán splattered across the landscape of *el norte*.

Argusto heard mutterings from the officers, heard fear in their voices—not fear of him, which he was used to, but fear of the people, fear of the army and navy, which had been starved of money and manpower to feed the needs of the air force. An air force that until now had never known defeat. Argusto drew himself to attention, chest thrust forward, one hand on his sword, as the last of the lights blinked out.

CHAPTER 48

"A three-day war," said Robert Legault, wearing a natty sports coat for the midmorning TV audience. "So tell me, Sarah, speaking as a historian, and a member of the president's inner circle, has there *ever* been a victory so sudden, so complete, so . . . *transformational*, as our victory over Aztlán?"

Sarah didn't snicker at "the president's inner circle" hyperbole. She had learned that much since Legault had spotlighted her in his news reports, her and Amir, "the new fresh faces of the Republic." It was necessary. She had no regrets.

"Sarah? *Is* our victory unique?"

Sarah thought of Thermopylae, Saratoga, Gettysburg, the outflanking of the Maginot Line in World War II and the encirclement of Baghdad in Gulf War II, but that wasn't the answer Legault wanted, and it wasn't the answer she wanted to give either. "No, Robert, the last seventy-two hours have been quite unique. In a three-day period, a unit of Fedayeen computer wizards destroyed the Aztlán air armada, and the combined ground forces of the Belt and Republic collapsed the Aztlán army. I think it's safe to say that God has smiled on both our nations."

"*Inshallah*, ladies and gentlemen, there you have it," Legault smiled into the camera, "the nation's premier historian has spoken." The camera lights blinked red and he turned to her. "Wonderful as usual, Sarah."

"I think I'm done for the day, Robert. I don't remember the last time I slept."

"I don't think anyone in the city has slept since the victory," said Legault, looking buoyant as ever. "Even the fundamentalists are dancing in the streets . . . although I wouldn't call that dancing." He patted her hand. "You *are* going to the embassy party tonight?"

"I had forgotten."

"You have to go, Sarah. I'm doing a live shot outside, and interviewing everyone. You don't want to lose your momentum with the public."

Sarah would rather be home with Rakkim and Michael, but Rakkim was still stranded in Las Vegas, unable to get a flight out. Maybe tomorrow, he had said. "I'll be there."

"That's the spirit," said Legault. "For God and country, eh?"

We must talk. Late-night prayers. Tonight. Abu Michael. Rakkim wiped out the message to General Kidd. He still didn't trust the Fedayeen com system and he had business to take care of tonight anyway. If that didn't work out, no reason to stand Kidd up. Instead Rakkim recorded a longer message outlining his concerns about Amir, and affirming his own respect and love for the general. Set it to be transmitted tomorrow at 9 A.M. Then he recorded another one for Sarah and another for Michael. Said his good-byes. A Fedayeen tradition before every mission, in expectation of death.

Rakkim walked out of the Blue Moon Club, the sidewalks of the Zone drifting with confetti and streamers from the three-day victory party. He had arrived in Seattle last night, decided to sleep in his old room at the Blue Moon instead of going home. He didn't want to see Sarah yet. When he did, he knew he'd have to tell her the truth about what had happened between him and Baby, how close he had come . . . no, he couldn't allow himself to be distracted. Not now. If he survived the next twenty-four hours, there would be time enough for the truth.

Two men sitting on the curb eyed him as he passed, bleary-eyed moderns, their fine clothes filthy.

Mardi, his former partner at the club, had contacts at all the luxury hotels—the Old One could easily blend into a city like

Seattle, but a man like Gravenholtz stood out no matter where he was. The redhead had been spotted at the New Mandarin, the finest, most modern hotel in Seattle. The Old One would have to be there too. With the piece of the cross that Moseby had died for.

Tonight Rakkim was going to pay them a visit.

General Kidd bent over, rested his palms on his knees, out of breath, his gasps echoing across the training arena.

Amir saluted him with his knife, high black cheekbones gleaming, his tunic spattered with blood. "Well done, Father."

General Kidd nodded, straightened up, feeling the blood ooze from more than a dozen light slashes along his arms and legs. "I . . . I shall comfort myself . . . with the knowledge that humiliation . . . humiliation is good for the soul."

In truth their combat practice had been more evenly matched than Kidd let on. Amir was quicker, more agile, but he was reckless in his attacks, leaving himself vulnerable. Amir had delivered three times as many cuts, but Kidd protected his vitals better, his own blade penetrating Amir's defenses to inflict two potentially killing wounds.

Amir wiped blood from the cut along his femoral artery, flung it onto the sand of the arena. Another inch deeper, he would have bled out in seconds. "I know, I know."

"I didn't say anything."

"You didn't have to," said Amir.

"You rely on your speed too much," said Kidd, as he always did. "A young man's vanity. An old man learns to absorb pain and wait for an opportunity."

"I'll remember," said Amir.

Kidd nodded.

"I always say that, don't I?"

Kidd nodded again.

The arena was attached to the family compound, a spartan

sixty-by-eighty-foot structure of mud-colored brick, the floor a treacherous expanse of sand and boulders designed to trip the unwary or the inattentive. Cool and quiet, it smelled of sandalwood and dry earth, the lighting controlled by panels in the roof. Kidd and his sons fought in everything from noon glare to pitch darkness. Often the women and younger children were allowed to watch, but today it was just the two of them.

Amir wiped his shaved head and checked his wounds, avoiding Kidd's gaze. His expression remained focused, his movements smooth, but Kidd knew him too well. Under that grim calm, Amir was uneasy.

They hadn't trained together in months—their busy schedules and obligations provided an easy explanation, but in truth, the growing tension between them had made the intimacies of training awkward. Today, when Amir had requested a session, Kidd had eagerly agreed, hoping to reestablish their bond, or at the least forget their differences. He had missed their time in the arena as much as his son. They were never so close as when they fought, knives flicking out, attack and retreat, twisting this way and then another, their breath the only sound in the stillness. Afterward they would sit side by side, basking in their own heat . . . content.

Amir offered cool water and Kidd drank, passed the bottle back. He sprawled on a bench, kneading the kink at the back of his neck, the result of a sudden maneuver to avoid a carotid slash. Amir paced, restless, toying with his knife. He turned his face up to the sun coming through the skylights and stayed there, immobile now, his muscles almost sculptural, his lips oddly delicate . . . with a different father he might have been an artist.

Looking at his son, Kidd had to fight not to show his pleasure. The boy had developed into a true warrior—resolute, daring and devout. A little temperamental, too easily misled by his passions, but he got that from his mother. Launching the technical team that had cracked the Aztlán code, funding it without

Kidd's knowledge, had been a breach of discipline, but Allah had smiled on the boy's boldness and brought victory to them all. Given time . . . given time Amir might develop the caution and calculation required in such perilous times. Perhaps someday he would become the leader the Fedayeen needed.

Amir saw Kidd watching him and bowed.

Kidd inclined his head. Sooner or later, he would have to relinquish command of the Fedayeen. Rakkim had resisted Kidd's offer to name him as his successor . . . and Rakkim had been right that passing over Amir would have profound consequences. The problem was that Rakkim was ready *now* to assume command, but Amir was not. Were something to happen to Kidd . . . He looked around the arena, took in the long rows of empty bleachers, remembering happier times.

He had started training Amir in this very place when he was three years old, a chubby little boy with big feet and quick hands, but he had showed promise early, defeating his older brothers, insisting on using edged weapons years before any of them, and with the scars to match his ambition. Amir was over six foot four now, handsome and graceful as a cat. A few more years . . . if Kidd could hang on for a few more years, perhaps Amir would be ready and he would not have to prevail upon Rakkim to do his duty.

Amir stared back at him.

"What's wrong?" said Kidd.

"I . . . have done things, Father."

"All is forgiven," said Kidd. "As I told you, I would never have attempted cracking the Aztlán command code. You took the risk, you deserve—"

"It wasn't my idea," said Amir.

"Whose idea was it?" Kidd said quietly.

"The Mahdi," said Amir. "It . . . it was the Mahdi's idea, and all glory to him and to God for it. It was necessary to hide his role in our triumph. Soon it will not be."

Kidd saw Amir's lips move . . . he knew what he was saying,

but he couldn't hear the words—there was a roaring in his ears so loud that all sound was canceled out.

Amir seemed in pain. "Father . . . I beg you . . ."

Kidd finally realized what the sound was. It was his heart pounding, thrashing around in his chest as though trying to break free.

"Father, let me take you to the Mahdi. I know . . . I know when you get to meet him that you will recognize that he is truly the one we have been waiting for."

"He's here?" said Kidd. "He's in the city?"

"He's come to claim that which Allah has promised."

Kidd laughed.

"Please, Father, you must . . . you must declare your allegiance to the Mahdi."

"Or what, my son?"

Amir locked eyes with him.

"Or *what*?" said Kidd.

"Or step aside, Father, relinquish command and let me do my duty." Amir didn't blink, seemed to grow even taller. "With the backing of the Fedayeen the Mahdi will be able to assume power, directing President Brandt until the time is ripe to reveal himself." His dark eyes bulged slightly. "The kaffirs in the Belt will learn soon enough the price for reconciliation. Convert or die."

"Why?"

"Why what, Father?"

"Why would this Mahdi of yours need the support of the Fedayeen if he has Allah on his side?" said Kidd.

Amir started to speak, went silent.

"Ask yourself that, Amir. *Think*, boy."

Amir lifted his jaw. "Too late for such word games."

"Your Mahdi is a perversion of Islam," said Kidd. "He's the lord of *lies*, not the lord of the earth. I've rejected that fraud's entreaties for twenty years—"

"Enough, Father." Amir slowly shook his head. "*Enough*."

Kidd felt a weariness descend over him, the leaden weight of shame . . . and worse. He saw Amir again as a small boy, covered in the dust of the arena, refusing to submit against an older brother twice his size, fighting on until he was knocked senseless and carried to bed. Too late for that now.

"You can still go back to the motherland, Father," pleaded Amir. "I won't let anyone raise a hand against you. Take your wives and your glory, and bask in the sun."

"You've dishonored yourself," said Kidd. "I'm placing you under arrest."

Amir went into a fighting crouch, knife held close to his body.

"Amir . . . don't do this."

Amir eased toward him, not making a sound on the hard-packed sand.

Kidd barely avoided Amir's sudden attack, dodged and twisted away. Amir kept coming. Kidd's own movements were feints, not meant to draw blood as much to keep Amir off balance. Their bare feet kicked up sand as they circled each other, knives flashing in the sun, back and forth. Amir jerked forward, leaped aside at the last moment and opened a long cut in Kidd's side. Kidd didn't make a sound. Another round of attack and counterattack, both of them breathing hard now. Amir cut him twice more, a third time, shallow wounds but painful. Kidd's own actions remained purely defensive.

"You can still stop," said Kidd. "It's not too late."

"Is there time to be forgiven, Father?" snarled Amir. His blade snaked out, drew blood. "Still time to receive your blessing?" Another strike. Another. Fresh blood trickled down Kidd's body, soaked his tunic. Amir's eyes glistened with tears. "Is there time for that? Or have you already given your blessing to Rakkim?"

Kidd danced out of reach, taking advantage of the shifting topography of the arena floor.

"He's back, Father, did you know that? We're all here now . . . you and I, Rakkim, the Mahdi." Amir circled, darted in, his shoulders loose and relaxed, a hunting posture that Kidd had taught him.

Kidd still hadn't launched an attack, hadn't touched him with his blade.

Amir moved fast, so fast, shifting his feet to come in from the side . . . there was an instant he left himself open, but Kidd couldn't bring himself to strike, and took yet another cut across his chest as he retreated across the arena. He pretended to limp slightly, favoring his right leg.

Amir's face dripped with sweat, droplets shimmering on his eyebrows like pearls. A beautiful boy . . . the most beautiful of all his many sons, so serious, always so serious, always in a hurry, as though worried that everything he had been given, everything he had achieved, would be snatched away from him at any moment.

Just under the main skylight, Kidd backed into a shallow depression, his right leg seeming to give way, and Amir moved in with a high thrust, knife hand arcing down from above his head. It was what Kidd had hoped for, the attack leaving him open for a brief moment, but Amir was too fast . . . His blade should have struck Kidd at the juncture of shoulder and neck, an instantaneous killing blow, but at the last instant Amir hesitated and Kidd drove his knife between his son's ribs and into his heart.

Amir gasped. That was all. Just a single, surprised gasp, his eyes wide.

Kidd lowered him to the sand, his hand still clutching the knife, warm blood running across his fingers. He knelt beside him, feeling Amir's heartbeat through the hilt . . . fading . . . fading.

"F-Father?"

Kidd caressed his face.

"I . . . I couldn't . . ."

"I should . . ." Tears ran down Kidd's cheeks, splashed onto Amir's lips. "I should have known."

Amir sighed, his eyes drifting shut.

General Kidd sang softly as his son died in his arms, offering Amir his blessing, calling him by his childhood nickname as he rocked him back and forth. A cloud slid across the sun, throwing the arena in shadow as Kidd begged Allah's mercy for a boy who had been led off the path to Paradise, a noble warrior betrayed by a false prophet.

CHAPTER 49

The balding French ambassador brushed her hand with his dry lips. "Congratulations to your marvelous country, Madame Sarah. You have rid the world of a dangerous threat, and inspired free people everywhere."

"Give the credit to our brave armed forces and President Brandt," said Sarah.

The French ambassador winked at her. "With all due respect, your President Brandt would never have challenged Aztlán without the counsel of someone wiser and more experienced in matters of state." He winked at her again and she wondered if he had a tic. "You have spoken and written on such matters for years. The diplomatic community is quite aware of who deserves the credit." He clicked his heels together, bowed, then turned to Colarusso. "Charmed to meet you, Monsieur Detective."

"Back at you," said Colarusso, gulping his champagne. He waited until the ambassador had left. "Your ass must be getting sore from being kissed all night."

"Thank you for your concern, Anthony. You should have considered a career in the diplomatic corps."

"I'll talk it over with Marie. Never too late, and the food's a hell of a lot better than at a police potluck." Colarusso handed his empty glass to a passing waiter, grabbed another one off the tray. "You heard anything from Rikki?"

"He's on his way back, that's all I know."

Sarah looked around the packed ballroom of the Brazilian embassy, decorated tonight like the Amazonian rain forest, wild orchids blooming in the lush green canopy overhead, enormous butterflies fluttering above the tropical flowers, and caged parrots squawking from the dwarf banyan trees. Colarusso had spent the first hour there wandering around with his head tilted back saying, *What the fuck?* She knew just how he felt. The two of them glided across the room, Colarusso in a rented tuxedo a little small on him, Sarah in a sea-foam green silk ball gown that rustled faintly with every step, the tiny seed pearls across the bodice gleaming softly in the light.

The international elite were here—billionaires and ambassadors, kings and queens, presidents and pashas, everyone eager to congratulate the victorious regime on vanquishing the evil empire. The very same empire that they had courted and cajoled for the last ten years. Everyone loved a winner, and the French ambassador wasn't the first one to compliment Sarah as being the hidden architect of the rapprochement with the Belt and the defeat of Aztlán. Legault had been relentless in promoting her contributions on television news specials, and it hadn't hurt that President Brandt had been incapacitated for the last two days with the flu, leading to all sorts of ugly jokes and rumors.

"He'll be fine," said Colarusso.

"I beg your pardon?"

"Rikki." Colarusso jerked as an iridescent blue hummingbird zipped past him. "He'll turn up, don't worry."

"I'm not worried," said Sarah, not caring that they both knew it was a lie. She looked around. "I'm surprised Amir isn't here."

"Something's going on with the Fedayeen high command," said Colarusso. "I'm hearing rumblings, but nothing clear." He hitched up his trousers. "You mind if I find some more of those prawns? Fucking things are the size of Shamu."

"Go ahead, Anthony."

"You'll be okay, won't you? They got more security here—"

"I'll be fine." Sarah kissed him on the cheek. "Go on."

She waited until he wandered off, then made her way through the crowd, forced to stop several times to be praised shamelessly, before stepping out onto one of the balconies off the ballroom. It was cooler and quieter out here, room to breathe.

Alone now, all she could think about was Rakkim. Her

longing for him was always there, just under the surface, kept at bay by her relentless schedule, the constant spinning of different possibilities. Busy making history and no way to know how her efforts would work out until it was too late, whether she had created a heaven or a horror show.

She waved away a waiter who approached with food and drink. She had lost five pounds since Rakkim had been gone, too nervous to eat, barely sleeping. There was a reason her uncle Redbeard had never married, all his attention taken up with matters of state security. *I'm married to the future*, he had told her once when she asked him why he didn't have at least one wife. She hadn't understood then, but she did now.

Legault approached, leading a young woman by the hand. Probably a budding newsanchor, or producer, or spokesmodel. She was beautiful, of course, moved like she was stalking something, lean and tan and healthy in a pale pink dress, her honey blond hair to her shoulders. The woman every man wanted and every woman hated. Particularly a married woman. Sarah smiled at her.

"Sarah, I have someone here who's dying to meet you," said Legault. "Sarah Epps, I'd like to present—"

"Pleasure to make your acquaintance, Sarah," drawled Baby, slipping her hand into Sarah's and giving it a gentle squeeze. "My name's Baby."

"Baby?" Sarah stared at her. "Are you . . . are you the Colonel's wife?"

"Don't look so surprised, sweetie, Christian wives get to travel and—"

"Don't call me sweetie."

"Oh my, Rikki said you were touchy, but you're really kind of a bitch."

"Sarah, I . . . I had no idea," stammered Legault. "Baby said—"

"Shoo now, Robert," said Baby. "Sarah and I got some girl talking to do."

"It's all right, Robert," said Sarah, "I can handle this." She looked past Baby, saw the Old One walk into the ballroom with the Russian ambassador. He had changed his appearance since the last time they met, what . . . five or six years ago, but it was definitely him.

Baby followed her gaze. "You don't miss nothing, do you? Just like Rikki." She waved to the Old One. "Hi, Daddy!"

In spite of the distance and the sound level in the ballroom, the Old One paused in his conversation with the ambassador, looked around until he spotted Baby, and waved back.

Baby turned back to Sarah. She still didn't know what Rikki saw in her. She was pretty enough, but she had lines around her eyes and you could see the veins along the backs of her hands. Daddy said Sarah and Rikki had a kid. Case closed. She could see Sarah checking her out too, but Baby didn't mind. Eat your heart out, lady.

"*Daddy?*" said Sarah. "Is that a pet name?"

"Don't be mean now," said Baby. "He's my father."

"My sympathies."

Baby had to hand it to her, she didn't let things throw her. Just processed the new information and moved forward like a shark.

"Is the Colonel here?" asked Sarah.

"Not that I know of," Baby said airily. "I think he's busy driving the Mexicans back across the Rio Grande."

A parrot cawed in the ballroom, the sound echoing. "You must be very proud of your husband."

"Well, tell you the truth, I'm more proud of yours." Baby saw Sarah's mouth tighten. "Golly, that just slipped out."

"Golly gee," said Sarah.

Baby brushed past her, stood at the railing of the balcony, letting the cool breeze tickle her skin. Headlights and spotlights all across the city, horns blaring, songs echoing through the streets, just one big party. Quite a change from three days ago, when everybody hunkered down waiting for the bombs to drop. Judging from Sarah's surprise when she saw Baby, the little woman didn't know anything. Rakkim was still probably trying to get home—if he had made it out of the Belt he'd be here now. Ignorance is fertile ground, that's what Daddy said, and Baby wasn't about to let the opportunity pass.

"I talked to Rikki a couple hours ago," said Baby, still looking out over the city. "I told him I might be running into you."

Sarah moved beside her, but didn't take the bait.

A waiter stepped onto the balcony. Sarah shook her head, but Baby beckoned him over, took a couple of champagne glasses from the tray. She handed one to Sarah.

"That's a real pretty dress you got," said Baby. "Flatters you."

"What do you and the Old One want?"

"You know Daddy, same as ever, he wants it all, every last bit of it," said Baby. "Me, I'm still trying to decide."

Sarah watched the bubbles rise in her champagne glass.

"Robert says you got the whole country in the palm of your hand," said Baby. "Politicians falling all over themselves to—"

"Whatever you're here for, you and your father, it's not going to happen," said Sarah. "The Old One's going to have to find another ugly little dream."

"I'll be sure and tell him, thank you kindly." Baby sipped her champagne, felt it fizz gently down her throat. "I wonder, though . . . you being so busy with interviews and politics, doesn't really leave much time for you and Rikki, does it? A man like Rikki, he won't stand for playing second fiddle to a wife's ego."

"Rikki told me all about you when he came home last year," said Sarah. "I'd repeat what he said, but I'd have to wash my mouth out."

"Here I was hoping we could be friends," said Baby.

"I *know*," said Sarah, pushing out her lower lip. "I'm disappointed too. I was looking forward to inviting you to my next slumber party."

"Daddy used to think you were really something." Baby

slowly shook her head. "I'm going to have to tell him he was misinformed." She sipped her champagne. "Gosh, I almost forgot. Don't be counting on that piece of the cross. Rikki gave it to me. Kind of a . . . pillow present after our first night." Fireworks exploded across the city.

"You and your father must be scared of me for you to go through this," said Sarah. "Or is lying as natural to you as breathing?"

"Sweetie, a woman who doesn't know how to lie is never going to keep a man." Baby peered at her. "Maybe *that's* your problem."

Sarah laughed. "I'd love to stand out here and listen to your quaint cornpone expressions, but I've got more interesting things to do."

"Rikki's penis surprised me no end."

Sarah stopped, turned back to Baby.

"I thought for sure he was going to be circumcised," Baby said, running her finger lightly around the rim of her glass, the hum rising and falling. "I heard all Muslim men are circumcised, but there was Rikki with this cute little sleeve on Mr. Johnson." She dipped her finger in the champagne, sucked it. "I asked him and he said he was born Catholic. Only became Muslim when he moved in with you and Redbeard." She batted her lashes, watched the flush rise up Sarah's neck. "Is *that* interesting enough for you?"

"I don't believe you."

Baby knew better. "Rikki's got a real nasty streak in bed. I like that in a man."

Sarah tossed champagne into Baby's face.

Baby's eyes burned as Sarah walked back into the ballroom.

"*Anthony*," said Sarah, greeting a big, sloppy guy with tough eyes, and a gigantic king-crab leg in each hand. "I could use some good company."

CHAPTER 50

"You're leaving the party early," Rakkim said softly, so close behind them he didn't need to raise his voice.

Sarah jerked.

Colarusso already had his gun out before he saw Rakkim
standing in the shadows "*Jeez*, Rikki, you almost gave me a coro-
nary."

Rakkim would have answered but Sarah threw herself into
his arms, kissing him like he was a drowning man. She pulled
back for an instant, looked like she was about to slap him, then
kissed him again, hanging on, and Rakkim clung to her, inhaled
her, folded himself into her heat and wished they didn't have to
speak.

They stood beside Colarusso's car just down from the Brazilian embassy, the police badge embossed into the bulletproof
windshield guaranteeing the best parking spot. A light rain had
started falling, the street mirrored with oily rainbows. Traffic
cops and security guards hunkered down in their windbreakers,
sipping coffee from cardboard cups. Music from the embassy
filtered through the drizzle.

"Good to see you, Rikki," said Colarusso, ignoring the
weather, rain spattering his stained topcoat. "You lovebirds going
to need a ride?"

"I'm not staying," said Rakkim, feeling Sarah tighten her grip
on him. "Just wanted to talk to Sarah for a few minutes. You can
take her home."

"Sure." Colarusso leaned against his car. He pulled a napkin
full of tiger prawns out of his coat pocket and started munching
away.

"Where are you going?" said Sarah, rain dripping down her face. "You should come home."

"I have to take care of some business first," said Rakkim, leading her deeper into the shadows.

"Can't this business wait?" said Sarah.

Rakkim shook his head. "I just wanted to see you first."

"Don't say it like that," said Sarah, her lower lip quivering. "You know I hate melodrama."

"I saw you with Baby."

"She's beautiful." Sarah watched him.

"Did she tell you that we had slept together?"

Sarah started to speak. Stopped herself.

"We didn't."

"I . . . I knew that."

"We *didn't*, Sarah." Rakkim gently wiped the rain from her cheeks. "I was close to making a mistake . . . closer than I ever want to get again, but I thought of you."

Sarah kissed him, her lips cool with rain but fiery underneath. "I knew . . . I knew she was lying . . . I knew you wouldn't . . ." She swayed against him. "I missed you, Rikki."

"Aren't you going to ask me if I have the piece of the cross?"

Sarah pulled back slightly.

"That's why you sent me into D.C.," said Rakkim. "That's what Moseby died for."

"What's wrong?" said Sarah.

Rakkim watched her standing in the rain, concerned, dark hair plastered around her face, and he could still see her as a little girl that first day Redbeard brought him home. She had been so happy to see him—a playmate, a friend, an ally—but even at six years old, she already knew how to hide her feelings, greeting him formally, welcoming him to her home. Redbeard had trained her well, even better than Rakkim . . . or perhaps Sarah just took to the training more than he had. "When were you planning on telling me?"

"Tell you what?"

"The truth."

Sarah hesitated only an instant, which was something. She knew how to lie, but she also knew when to cut her losses and tell the truth. "When I thought the time was right."

"What time is it now?"

"How did you find out?" said Sarah.

"I just kept putting the pieces together—I'm good at that. I remember when you first showed me the footage from D.C. and the zombie ripped his suit. He looked into the camera and said he was sorry, and I remember thinking, who is he apologizing to? His wife, that's what I figured. Then I met her and she told me what a tough guy he was, never shed a tear. She had such wonderful things to say about you, how you had paid for their kids' operations, and arranged for their schooling in Canada. You did all that *before* Eldon found the cross. It didn't make sense . . . until I realized you weren't paying him for finding the cross, you were paying him for *planting* the cross. Eldon was apologizing to you, Sarah, apologizing to you for ruining the big onscreen moment."

"If . . . Eldon hadn't torn his suit I wouldn't have needed you and Moseby to retrieve it," Sarah whispered, raindrops gleaming on her eyelashes. "I never intended to bring you into this."

"But you *did*. I'm just glad Moseby didn't realize he was dying for a fake."

"The cross . . . the cross is a symbol, Rikki, an emotional construct, a national lifeline," said Sarah, "and a symbol can't *be* a fake."

"What happens when the Belt finds out?"

"They're not going to find out."

"That piece of wood is going to be analyzed and reanalyzed."

"Let them." Sarah took his hand. "Spider's taken care of everything."

"Spider was in on this?"

Sarah nodded. "He wanted me to tell you the truth . . . if that matters."

"What about Leo?"

"No . . . just Spider." Sarah shivered, her evening clothes soggy around her. "It's going to work, Rikki. The president is going to hand it over to the Belt leaders and they're going to take it and put it on public display and be *grateful* to us for finding it and returning it to them. Miracles and visions will be attributed to it. Children will be healed. We all want to believe, Rikki. The Belt needs reunion just as much as we do, and no one's going to look too closely at the things that hold us together."

"We'll be held together with a lie."

"Here's a dirty little secret that most historians don't talk about." Sarah clutched his hand to her chest and he could feel her heart pounding. "Most wars start with a lie, good wars, bad wars, they start with a lie, and the peace that comes afterwards, those promises of forgiveness and cooperation and fair play for all . . . those are lies too, lies wrapped in hope. So if it took a lie to bring us together, I'll take it, and hope for the best."

Rakkim stared at her, saw the strength and certainty in her eyes. This was as close to an apology as he was going to get. He kissed her, his lips barely touching hers, kissed the rain from her eyes. "I love you."

"Rikki, don't be . . . *Rikki?*" called Sarah, but he was already gone.

CHAPTER 51

Rakkim was leaning against the railing overlooking Niagara Falls when he heard them come in. Just after 2 A.M. A virtual beach, they called it. He also liked Point Break, East of Oahu and Lake Como, all previously selected by the Old One and accessible, but you really couldn't beat Niagara Falls for sheer power. A place for honeymooners, that's what they called it. Danger and power and beauty. Prelude to a marriage.

He had been there for over an hour, waiting, enjoying the feel of the cool mist against his skin, and thinking about Sarah. When he confronted her outside the embassy, he hadn't even been sure that the cross was fake. Had half expected her to deny it, and would have been happy to accept her answer. *People want to believe, Rikki* . . . She was right, as usual. Instead, she had told him the truth. A small blessing with a sharp edge. He watched the three of them enter the cube, the mist floating around them.

"It *is* him," said Gravenholtz.

"Don't act so surprised, Lester, it reveals your ignorance." The Old One strolled into the cube, dapper in a lightweight dark blue suit that followed his every movement. "I expected you yesterday, or the day before, Rikki."

"I got delayed in Las Vegas," said Rakkim.

"Well, you're here, that's all that matters," said the Old One.

"Yeah, he's here," said Gravenholtz. "Light the candles on my birthday cake."

Rakkim watched them through the haze, the waterfall crashing behind him. Seeing Gravenholtz made him miss his blade even more. The New Mandarin was the only hotel in the Republic fitted with the latest Swiss security filters, able to detect even a Fedayeen DNA knife. No knives, no guns, no explosives . . . the system screened for eighty-seven poisons and biotoxins too. One big happy family at the New Mandarin.

The Old One looked around, the breeze from the falls stirring his fine gray hair. "A good choice, but have you tried . . ." He fingered the remote, the falls flickering for an instant, revealing the actual enormous swimming pool at the center of the cube, before popping to a clear lake surrounded by black volcanic rock, stars everywhere, the night air instantly colder.

"Where are we?" said Rakkim.

The Old One kicked off his shoes, rolled his pant cuffs up and waded out into the water. "Lake Neruda, in the Andes. Elevation so high and the soil so acidic that there's almost no life in it . . . hence its spectacular clarity."

"Fuck the travelogue," said Gravenholtz. "Is he on board or not? Because if he's not, I want to take him out."

The Old One looked at Rakkim, rolled his eyes.

Rakkim laughed.

"Are you going to let me in on the joke?" Baby stood in the doorway in a low-cut party gown. Rakkim hadn't expected to see her. "Don't worry, Rikki, I don't hold a grudge."

Rakkim ignored her, turned to the Old One. "You have the piece of the cross?"

The Old One patted his chest. "Right next to my heart." He splashed Rakkim. "Come on in, the water's fine."

Rakkim took off his boots, splashed out beside the Old One, the water numbing his feet, the gravel shifting slightly under his bare feet. He looked back at Gravenholtz glaring at him from the shore, his features brutal in the moonlight, and Rakkim couldn't tell if he was in a swimming pool in Seattle or in a lake on the other side of the world.

"Why don't you go out there and keep them company, Lester?" said Baby.

"No thanks," said Gravenholtz.

"Realistic, isn't it?" The Old One went under, came up spitting a fountain into the air. Tiny insects buzzed around them, their wings silky in the sunlight. A dragonfly landed on the Old One's outstretched hand, drying its wings before flying away. "Three-hundred-and-sixty-degree technology, every sense taken into account."

They were in bright sunshine now, the water warmer, the beach composed of smooth, flat rocks instead of gravel. Wooden cabanas and snack stands loomed behind Gravenholtz and Baby, men and women in bikinis waiting in line for cold drinks, the signs in French. "This is Cannes, on the Riviera of my youth. It doesn't exist anymore . . . except here." He sniffed. "You can actually smell the salt air and crisped potatoes."

"*Ask* him," said Gravenholtz.

"Lester, honey," drawled Baby, "shut the hell up and let Daddy handle things."

Gravenholtz kicked at the rocks, sent a couple of them scudding into the water.

Rakkim watched the ripples approach, *felt* them.

"I'm afraid Lester has a point," said the Old One, wading farther out, the water at his knees. "I asked you once before to honor me with your allegiance. You declined then, but I was hoping you might have changed your mind."

Rakkim watched the vendor walking down the strand selling ice cream bars to the sunbathers from a tiny icebox, an African immigrant . . . his features reminded Rakkim of Moseby, and for an instant he wondered if the Old One had programmed the holo display for maximum upset. He waded out to where the Old One stood.

"Leo is such an interesting young man," said the Old One. "He looks at the universe like a child presented with a new toy he can't wait to unwrap."

"You've spoken with him?"

"Don't be scared, Rakkim."

"I'm not scared."

"I think if I treat Leo right . . . treat him with care, I think he's going to be incredibly useful," said the Old One.

"You're not going to get the chance," said Rakkim.

"Don't threaten me, Rakkim—it demeans you." The Old One dragged a hand in the water, let it trickle through his fingers. "I could have had you killed on many occasions. You and your family. Didn't you ever wonder why I kept you safe?"

"I had all these questions when I came here," said Rakkim. "I was going to ask if Amir had signed up for your two-bit caliphate, and how the war with Aztlán fit in with your long-range plans. I really wanted to know what the puzzle was supposed to look like." He reached into the water, picked up a large rock, threw it at Gravenholtz, who tried to duck . . . the rock shimmered as it went right through him and clattered onto the beach. "Now . . . now I don't care," said Rakkim, unnerved by how real the rock had felt in his hand. "Answers would be nice, but I didn't come here for answers. I came here to kill you and Gravenholtz. That's good enough for me."

The virtual beach flickered, the scene at Cannes winking out, and Rakkim glimpsed again the Olympic-size swimming pool. Then he and the Old One were on a fine, white sand beach at dawn, the air already humid. Rakkim could see Sugarloaf Mountain and massive high-rises dotting the hills behind them. Rio.

"Why don't you wait a while to kill us? It's such a lovely morning." The Old One took off his suit jacket, tossed it onto the sand. He spread his arms, eyes half closed, his diaphanous white shirt flapping in the warm breeze off the Atlantic. "Relax, Rikki, enjoy the moment."

"Wheeeeeeee." Baby raced past them and high-stepped into the surf, completely naked, her white ass flashing in the sun as she dove in.

Rakkim looked back, saw her clothes strewn on the beach. Gravenholtz sat on the sand, knees clasped, glaring at him.

The Old One sat in a canvas lounge chair as Baby frolicked in the waves. "She's amazing . . . and even more beautiful than her mother." He drew on a sketchpad with a fountain pen—the breeze whipped his shirt, exposing the piece of the cross hanging around his neck on a silver chain, most of the tiny white flowers gone now. "Baby is part of the offer, Rikki," he said, not taking his eyes off her as the pen flew over the pad. "You can marry her with my blessing."

Rakkim watched Baby backstroking farther out. "What does she have to say about that?"

The Old One wiggled his toes in the sand. "It was her idea."

"Lester!" called Baby. "Come on in!"

"I *told* you, I don't want to," said Gravenholtz.

Rakkim felt the wind in his face.

"When I was a student at Oxford, I listened to professors argue whether it was a confluence of events or great men who changed the course of history," said the Old One, sketching away. "Whether Rome was brought down by overextension of the empire or the murder of Julius Caesar, whether it was slash-and-burn agriculture that collapsed the Mayan civilization or the inability of a single warrior-king to unite the cities. The sophistry of scholars." He glanced over at Rakkim. "The *secret* is to create the conditions for change, a process that sometimes takes decades, and then use certain men as pivot points, a fulcrum to move history." He went back to his drawing. "That's you, Rakkim. That's why you're here."

"Was Malcolm Crews one of your pivot points?" said Rakkim. "Because if he was, you're going to have to sit in the sad chair. Turns out Crews likes being the good guy."

"Well, I rather doubt that will last," said the Old One, "but no matter, Pastor Crews has served his primary function." His dark features were intense in the morning light, his mouth a thin slash. "Crews is a secondary player. Not easily replaced, but certainly replaceable. There's a country singer in Tupelo, Mississippi, drawing large crowds. Pretty girl, skin like cashew butter, sings gospel songs so sweetly you'd think she believed it." He watched Baby diving into the water. "Everyone's replaceable, Rikki. So what *do* you want?"

"You look tired," said Rakkim. "Vulnerable, somehow."

"Nonsense," said the Old One.

"No, it looks good on you," said Rakkim. "Nobody lives forever, do they? I bet when you lie down at night you can hear the clock ticking. Tickety-tock, tickety-tock."

The Old One's pen scratched away at the paper.

"It must hurt," says Rakkim. "All those years, all that effort, and what do you have to show for it? Just money and a line of corpses stretching on forever. If Allah chose you as the Mahdi he must be rather disappointed, don't you think?"

"Allah doesn't make mistakes," said the Old One.

"Exactly," said Rakkim.

Gravenholtz stayed on the sand, glaring at them.

Baby splashed into the shallows, waxed and smooth as a pink doll, a speargun in one hand, a large fish wriggling on the barbed tip. She tossed the gun up onto the beach as a fresh wave broke over her, white water foaming around her thighs.

Rakkim watched the fish flopping on the sand, its gills opening and closing.

Baby stayed at the waterline, squeezed out her hair—water ran down her breasts, collected in a sparkling arc at the bottom of her belly button . . . the promise of the dawn.

Rakkim turned to the Old One, who was as transfixed by her as he was. "Sending Baby and Mr. Ugly for the cross . . . you thinking of converting?"

The Old One showed the drawing to Rakkim. It was Baby, of course. Baby naked in the waves, precisely rendered. Baby, slim and sensuous, her expression playful, knowing just what she was doing. "A man picks up many skills over the years. . . ."

"I wouldn't blame you for going Christian," said Rakkim. "Sure seems like Allah's fed up with you. Ibn-Azziz? Dead. Malcolm Crews? Born again. All you have left is the man with the ear of the president. Maybe that's Amir and maybe it isn't, but I'm talking with General Kidd tomorrow."

The Old One tore off the sheet of paper. "Amir's dead." He released the drawing to the wind, Baby's image rolling down the beach.

Gravenholtz started after it, stopped himself.

"How?" Rakkim's voice broke. "How did he die?"

"He tried to murder Kidd and the general killed him." The Old One shrugged. "I'm not surprised. Kidd is forceful, and Amir . . . well, it's always difficult for a son to take his father's life. Doubts creep in and slow the hand, divert the intention. Kidd evidently had no qualms killing his son."

"You don't know Kidd."

"No, I don't—not like you do, Rikki. The general has great affection for you, which is understandable. I feel the very same way about you, and with the traumatic events of today, I suspect the general is ready to relinquish control to you very soon now. So he can grieve, of course, perhaps make a pilgrimage home to that desolate stretch of dirt on the horn of Africa."

"I see. You thought you had it covered both ways," said Rakkim. "No matter who won, Amir or Kidd, your man would be in place."

"*Are* you my man, Rakkim?" The Old One stood up, tossed the sketchbook onto the chair. "The world is a big place, too big for even me to rule by myself. Time to decide whose side you're on."

Rakkim's index finger inadvertently twitched, a well-honed killing reflex.

The Old One noticed. "Do you miss your knife?"

"I don't need a blade," said Rakkim.

"Don't be like that, Rikki," said Baby, walking toward them, water glistening along the curves of her body. "Daddy's right. I see things in you . . . things you could become. You and me . . . there's no limit to us."

Gravenholtz rushed to Baby, wrapped a heavy white towel around her. "This ain't right," he said to the Old One, his face flushed. "You're treating him like the fucking prodigal son. *I'm* the one who brought you the cross."

"Well, Rakkim?" said the Old One.

Rakkim backhanded the Old One, sent him sprawling.

Gravenholtz smiled. A warthog smile, tufts of red hair sprouting from his skull.

"Lester Gravenholtz, you settle down right now," said Baby, helping the Old One up. "Rikki, why don't you go in the water and cool off."

Gravenholtz closed in on Rakkim.

Rakkim backed toward the water, saw Gravenholtz slow. "Come on, Lester, what are you waiting for?"

Gravenholtz charged.

Rakkim dodged, drove the bottom of his foot against the side of Gravenholtz's knee. Any other man would have been lying in agony on the sand, crippled by the blow. Gravenholtz limped slightly, his smile still in place.

They went back and forth on the beach. Rakkim was faster, much faster, but his kicks and punches barely affected Gravenholtz, who kept trying to narrow the arena. Twice Gravenholtz almost grasped him, his nails gouging Rakkim's arms. Rakkim landed a solid strike to Gravenholtz's face, snapped his head back. It should have killed him. Gravenholtz spit blood on the sand and kept advancing, circling . . . except whenever Rakkim backed into the water. Then Gravenholtz waited for Rakkim to come out. Rakkim glanced over at Baby.

"It's not too late to change your mind, Rakkim," said the Old One.

"The *fuck* it isn't," said Gravenholtz, blood leaking from his nose.

Rakkim sidled into the water.

Gravenholtz hesitated, came after him.

Rakkim backed farther out, waves lapping against his back.

Gravenholtz stayed put. "I'll make it quick. Just like I did for your buddy."

Rakkim stepped back. The water was chest-high now. "You scared of a little water?" He whipped his hand across the waves, sprayed Gravenholtz's face. As the redhead rubbed his eyes, Rakkim dove, grabbed both of Gravenholtz's ankles, jerked him under, Rakkim on the bottom now, and pulled the both of them into deeper water.

Gravenholtz bent his body, trying to get free, trying to reach him, but Rakkim just kept walking backward along the bottom, still hanging on to Gravenholtz's ankles. Rakkim had once held his breath for nine minutes.

Rakkim tried to keep him under but Gravenholtz was paddling hard with his hands, stirring up silt, the two of them rising slowly. Rakkim let go of Gravenholtz's ankles, clawed his way up the man's bulky body, fighting for every inch, trying to hold him down. Face-to-face now, Gravenholtz snarling, bubbles pouring from his mouth . . . Rakkim drove his fingers deep into the redhead's eyes, deeper, scooping through the warm jelly as Gravenholtz bellowed, trying to escape; deeper, Rakkim pushing his way right into the sinus cavity, opening him wide. Water poured directly into Gravenholtz's throat now, unstoppable, flooded into his lungs as he struggled, the water pink with blood.

The last of Gravenholtz's air dribbled out his nostrils. Weakened now, blinded, a sac of skin filling rapidly with water, he still managed to flail around, found Rakkim and wrapped his arms around him.

The two of them tumbled underwater, yellow viscous fluid from Gravenholtz's ruined eyes trailing behind them as they sank toward the bottom. Gravenholtz clung to Rakkim in a cruel embrace, their faces inches apart, slowly crushing him. Rakkim tightened his chest, but felt his ribs cracking, giving way. Lightheaded, Rakkim watched a school of tiny orange fish zigzag around them, curious, nibbling at the bubbles of blood that floated past. A fish scooted in, nibbled at Gravenholtz's cavernous eye sockets.

Rakkim slammed the knuckle of his thumb again and again into Gravenholtz's temple, a killing strike that didn't kill him, but scared the fish away . . . and Rakkim would have laughed, but it hurt too much, and his vision was narrowing . . . narrowing . . . Terrible to die looking into Gravenholtz's face.

Then . . . then Gravenholtz released him, the redhead's arms drifting free, riding the watery currents. Rakkim coughed, a smoke ring of blood . . . but he didn't smoke. He feebly kicked toward the surface.

Rakkim broke through the waves, gasping, made his way to shore, crawled up onto the sand, exhausted. Breathing hurt, but not breathing hurt even more. He lay back in the morning light. Going to be . . . a great day in Rio.

Baby bent over him, kissed him. She had her party dress back on. Too bad. Rakkim rolled over, got onto his hands and knees. Baby helped him up.

"You . . . you knew he . . ." Rakkim coughed up pink water. "You knew he was too heavy to swim."

"I saw him about piss himself in a glass-bottom boat this one time," said Baby.

"Move away from him, Baby," said the Old One, pointing the fountain pen at Rakkim.

"You . . . you going to draw my picture?" Rakkim bent over again, coughing.

"That's not necessary, Daddy," said Baby.

"Move away from him *now*," said the Old One.

Baby moved away.

"Very impressive, Rakkim," said the Old One. "Killing Lester with your bare hands . . . that's quite a feat."

"Save the applause until . . . after I . . . kill you," said Rakkim.

"Your friend Jenkins told ibn-Azziz this ridiculous story about you killing Darwin," said the Old One. "Doing it by *yourself*. I didn't believe it, of course, but seeing what you just did . . . well, it makes me wonder."

"Jenkins . . . would have said anything to buy a little . . . little more time," said Rakkim.

"Did you do it, Rikki?" said the Old One. "Did you kill Darwin?"

"Come closer, I'll whisper in your ear," said Rakkim.

The Old One smiled. "I'm going to miss you, Rakkim."

"Daddy, *no!*"

The Old One aimed the fountain pen. "I offered you the world and you turned it down." Thin white strings streamed out of the pen. "Remember that as you die."

Rakkim tried to push aside the white strings but they were *so* sticky, wrapping around him, squeezing him even tighter than Gravenholtz. He felt his ribs splintering . . . tried to scream but there was no breath left in him.

The Old One kept spraying those silky white strings . . . until the moment that his chest exploded. He staggered . . . gingerly touched the sharp tines of the titanium spear protruding from his breastbone. Looked behind him.

Baby rested the speargun against her shoulder. "I asked you *nice*, Daddy."

CHAPTER 52

The world stopped. The Old One could see Rakkim staring up at him, the white polymer strings encasing him, and Rakkim's face was frozen in surprise, a single drop of water dripping off his earlobe, hanging suspended in space.

The surf froze, the waves immobile, about to crash on the virtual beach. The world as a snapshot. No such thing as snapshots anymore, they were as much an illusion as this stretch of sand, but the Old One remembered snapshots, photographs taken by tourists and lovers on holiday, snapshots taken with cheap cameras. Lovers would wait days to see what shining instants had been immortalized, precious moments to be tucked away in memory albums. *Here we are at Cannes, darling, here we are at Miami, at Honolulu, at Bali, at Sydney, at Capetown. Here we are, here we are, here we are.* The photographs were no more permanent than the newlyweds, yellowing and cracking over time, eventually fading to dust . . . like the lovers themselves.

The Old One bent over Rakkim, but he didn't react, just kept staring past him, and the Old One turned to see what had captured this new assassin's attention . . . and saw *himself*, arms flung to the sides, eyes wide, saw himself with the tip of a spear bursting through his chest in a spray of blood, each individual droplet shimmering like a ruby in the sunlight.

He moved closer, standing an inch from his own face, but got no reaction . . . this other self, this impaled self as immobile as the world. Behind him he could see Baby holding a speargun, her hair caught by the breeze, another frozen moment. She looked out of breath. No . . . not out of breath, exhilarated. Pleased. Proud.

The Old One walked toward her, moving quickly, his

footsteps not even stirring the sand. He smacked her across the face, wanting to slap the joy out of her, but his hand . . . his hand passed through her as though she were just another illusion on the beach. He looked at his fingers, flexed them.

He looked closer at her, examined the speargun. It was one of the guns they had used yesterday when they went diving off the old airliner that had crashed into the bay. Baby's idea, the expedition booked through the hotel. The dive had been interesting, the submerged fuselage crusted with barnacles, sea anemones waving in the current, fish darting through the broken windows. The dive captain had been smitten with her, of course, eager to show her everything, and she had come back to the boat with a salmon wriggling on her spear. He wondered if she knew yesterday that she was going to use the speargun today, wondered if today had been an accident or an impulse.

No, no, of course it had not been an impulse. What was he *thinking*? This was no time to go soft-headed, no time . . . no time at all. It had taken foresight and planning to smuggle the speargun past hotel security. The dive captain had probably helped her do it, not even knowing what he was doing, accepting whatever explanation she gave him.

The Old One looked into Baby's eyes but he couldn't see his reflection, no matter how he twisted and turned.

He walked back to his other self, his doomed self. Put a finger on one of the droplets of blood bursting from his chest. His finger went right through it. He moved closer, looked into his own eyes. He couldn't see himself either, but he could see pain in the other's eyes. And surprise. The surprise was worse than the pain. The Old One couldn't afford to be surprised. Not like this. It showed a lack of awareness. A man could get hurt that way, and though the Old One was chosen by Allah, he was still a man. He would have to be more careful in the future. This was a lesson. He would not make this same mistake again. Yes, never again.

The sun . . . the sun seemed dimmer. Twilight at the beach, not at all what he expected. Have to . . . have to lodge a complaint with the management. He strolled along the tideline in the growing darkness, comforted by the feel of the sand on his feet and the warmth of the water. He wished he could see Gravenholtz bobbing along the bottom but the light . . . was almost gone. Maybe tomorrow. He wanted to see Gravenholtz's expression in death. *That* would be a look of surprise, and unlike the Old One, Gravenholtz would not get the opportunity to learn from his mistake.

Rakkim had killed Gravenholtz with his bare hands. Amazing. Too bad the boy had let his ego carry him away. Refusing the Old One's offer of a place at the table? Absurd. A fatal lack of imagination. Might even . . . might . . . even be characterized as blasphemy.

The Old One couldn't see a thing now, but he kept walking through the shallows. Must keep walking. Walk until the sun came up if he had to. He hated the dark. Always had. No one knew. Another of his secrets. The water was colder. Something else he hated. In utter darkness, he turned toward the beach, but the water got deeper, past his knees now, and when he turned in the opposite direction it got deeper still . . . and colder . . . much colder. Shivering, he kept on trying to find his way back, but it was so dark, and no matter what he did . . .

The Old One toppled onto the sand in front of Rakkim.

The beach at Rio blinked out, replaced by an enormous pool. Float a sailboat in that thing. Crystal-clear water. He could see Gravenholtz's body on the bottom, arms waving. No sand. No waves. No sunshine, just indirect lighting. Not that it mattered. Rakkim's eyes fluttered.

"Just a minute," said Baby.

Rakkim saw her bend down and pull the spear through the Old One's chest. Then she hurried over and used the sharp edge of the spear to cut away the strings from around him. He closed his eyes.

"Don't go to sleep," said Baby.

"Okay."

"I *mean* it."

"I thought . . . the speargun was fake."

"If it was fake, I couldn't have killed Daddy, now could I?" Baby helped him sit up. "The *fish* was fake, but I kept the speargun just in case."

"In case . . . in case of *what*?"

"In case I needed it, silly." Baby patted his cheek. "You notice how whenever Daddy talked about dividing up the world, and pivot points, it was always *you* he was talking about and not me? When you get right down to it, Daddy just didn't respect women."

Rakkim breathed shallowly, breathed as if he were sucking air through a straw.

"So . . . what do you want to do now?" said Baby.

"Like to . . . keep . . . breathing."

"I mean later. *Us*."

Rakkim shook his head. "No such thing as us."

"Your loss." Baby must have had something in her eye.

"Are you . . . are you really afraid of thunderstorms?"

"Terrified." Baby wiped her eyes. "Damn you, Rikki, don't you make me miss you, or I'll kill you, I *swear* I will."

"I believe you."

"You better."

"I want . . . the piece of the cross," said Rakkim.

"Do you now?" Baby walked over to her father and nudged him onto his back. The piece of wood was suspended on a thin silver chain around his neck, tiny white flowers spattered with blood. "Didn't do Daddy much good, but if you want it, I'm going to have to get a kiss in exchange." She leaned over him, gently kissed him, her tongue tickling him, warm and sweet. She slowly broke the kiss. "That wasn't so bad, was it?"

"Compared . . . compared to what?"

"You really don't know what's good for you, Rakkim Epps." Baby walked to the edge of the pool and washed the blood off her hands. "You can stay here if you want, but me, I'm going back to Miami. Don't worry about me taking over the world or anything, that was Daddy's dream." She tossed her hair and it was as if somebody had thrown a handful of dirty gold into the air. "I got better things to do."

Rakkim watched her leave. His mouth tasted rusty. He stood up, dizzy, listened to the waves lapping against the sides of the pool, stirred up by the filtration system. Gravenholtz bobbed along the bottom, facedown, flotsam on the tide.

He looks better like that, said Darwin. *Most folks do, but him more than most.*

Rakkim saw Darwin standing beside him, the assassin almost transparent.

You could at least act surprised, Rikki.

"I don't have the energy. You could have helped me before. I almost got killed."

I don't have the energy either. Besides, you had the girl to help you with the Old One . . . and Gravenholtz, you didn't need me to take care of him either. Surprised me too. Dug right into the sticky stuff, didn't you? Couldn't have done it better myself. You didn't even need a blade to kill him—the best ones don't. Guys like us, we don't need anything.

"What . . . what are you doing here?"

I just stopped in to say good-bye.

"Where . . . where are you going?"

Anyplace but here, Rikki. I'm done with it.

"I thought you didn't like being dead."

You get used to it. Darwin looked down at the Old One. *You would have had fun working for him . . . and then there's the daughter . . . that would have been doubly sweet. I would have jumped at the chance if I were you.*

"No thanks."

Darwin's lips moved but no sounds came out.

"What?"

I said . . . Darwin's face thinned out, only his eyes remaining sharp as ice. *Only thing I miss about life is the killing. I was good at it. Good as God. Better maybe.*

"Me . . . I'm tired of killing."

Darwin said something.

"I can't hear you."

Darwin faded, fell apart like smoke, and Rakkim was alone.

EPILOGUE

Three Months Later

"I'm *dizzy*," said Sarah as Rakkim swung her round and round to the music from the wedding reception, wild music, Belt music, all bass and thump, the sound bouncing off the surrounding mountains. "Give me . . . just a minute."

Rakkim put her down, her pale blue bridesmaid's gown swirling around her. They held hands on the hillside, watching the reception below.

"Leo's quite a dancer," said Sarah, still out of breath.

"I thought he was having a seizure," said Rakkim.

The head of Abraham Lincoln hovered over them, a massive outcropping of granite more than sixty feet high, the sixteenth president stern and stoic as teams of workmen put the finishing touches on him.

Anthony Colarusso trudged up the path to join them. "Me . . . I'm just a big, dumb cop, and I don't know anything about art or sculpture, but . . ." He nodded at the monument where an engineering crew rooted around in Lincoln's nostrils with pulsating laser drills. ". . . but that just looks *painful* to me." He touched his own nose. Winced.

"You look a little drunk, Anthony," said Rakkim.

Colarusso grinned. "Couple of fellas in the Belt ambassador's entourage had some bourbon they wanted to share and I didn't want to hurt their feelings."

"Good for you," said Rakkim. "Wouldn't want you to cause a diplomatic incident."

Colarusso belched into his fist. "Heaven forbid."

Leo and Leanne had gotten married in the Black Hills of

South Dakota, right under the ongoing restoration of Mount Rushmore. The Black Robes had dynamited the original monument forty years earlier, saying human representation was blasphemous, but the Black Robes' opinions no longer counted for much. Lincoln was almost finished. Washington was still a work in progress. The other two faces were being left in their damaged condition until a bilateral committee determined who belonged up there with his head in the clouds. President Kingsley was the clear choice for the Republic. The Belt wanted either the Colonel or Elvis. Mount Rushmore was government property, off-limits to the public, but after it was learned that he was the one who cracked the Aztlán command code, Leo could get almost anything he wanted.

"Nice wedding we got going here," said Colarusso. "Good food, good weather. Marie's been introducing our girls to everyone in pants. Spider even gave the bride a spin around the floor before he had to stop and rest."

"He's happy," said Sarah.

"Probably more relieved than anything," said Colarusso. "Leo may be some kind of genius, but let's be honest, the boy needs a keeper. Wish the Colonel could have come. I'd like to meet him."

"The Colonel's got his hands full running the Belt," said Rakkim.

Sarah brushed cake crumbs off Colarusso's jacket.

Colarusso flushed. "You two coming back down?"

Sarah glanced at Rakkim, then back at Colarusso. "Not now."

"I know that look. Don't you go outraging public decency, Sarah." Colarusso scratched at a smear of cake icing on his necktie. "Something about a wedding that puts females in a lather. If I could bottle it, I'd never have to work again."

"Maybe you better stay here and protect my virtue, Anthony," said Rakkim.

"Too late for that, troop." Colarusso sucked dried icing off his fingernail. "*Long* past it." He started back down the path as a new song started up.

"What kind of music is that they're playing?" said Rakkim.

"Prewar classics," said Sarah. "Motor-Town they called it . . . no, Motown, that's it."

Rakkim rubbed the nape of her neck, felt her yield to his touch. Her dark hair was piled high—he preferred it down, but he liked being able to see her long slender neck. He brushed his lips across the sensitive spot under her ear, and she half closed her eyes.

"Maybe . . . maybe when things settle down we could have another baby," she said.

"If we wait for things to settle down we'll *never* have another one," said Rakkim.

Sarah kissed him, a brief kiss but there were promises behind it.

Michael ran up the path, making race-car sounds as he ran right past them at full speed, shirttails flying.

"Ibrahim bin-Salah was found dead at a hotel in Nueva Florida yesterday," said Sarah, as Michael continued up the trail, kicking up pebbles. "Evidently your little friend in Miami has finalized her hold on the Old One's financial empire."

"My little *friend*?"

Sarah laughed. "You were friends, weren't you?"

"The Belt makes people do crazy things," said Rakkim, "but I wasn't *that* crazy."

"Well, it's a good thing you turned her down in that motel, Rikki." Sarah took his hand. "If I hadn't killed you, eventually she would have."

Rakkim watched the party below; saw Colarusso bellowing along to the music while his wife tried to quiet him. Nobody else seemed to mind. "You were right about the cross," he said quietly. "That chunk of wood did everything you hoped for."

"Yes, it did. When President Brandt turned it over to the Colonel and the head of the Baptist Synod . . . that's when I knew it was just a matter of time until reunification."

"Highest TV ratings in history."

"By far." Sarah squeezed his hand. "Both in the Belt and the Republic. The line to view it at that church in Atlanta has never been less than a mile long."

"Congratulations."

Sarah pointed at the monument. "The workmen up there, they come home at the end of the day filthy, covered in dust and dirt and rock fragments, hands scarred from laser slag, but the tourists observing the result someday will see only the strong, comforting faces of great men. Studying history is for tourists—polite, tidy people with clean desks and clean consciences. *Making* history is for people willing to get their hands dirty, to make mistakes and lie when necessary, so that someday historians can sit quietly at their desks and act shocked."

"You don't have to convince me." Rakkim put his arms around her.

"What's strange, though," said Sarah, resting her head on his shoulders, slow dancing, "what's really strange are the flowers blooming on the cross. I don't know *how* that happened and neither does Spider. The wood . . . it looks different too."

"You think it's *real?*"

"I don't know what's real anymore, and I don't care." Sarah looked up at him. "I just know we needed a symbol and you brought one out of a dead city, you and Moseby, and that's miracle enough for anyone."

The workmen scurried over the presidential heads, moved across the rock on a lattice of thin steel cables as they etched in Lincoln's beard. Behind them, the sky was a rich, deep blue—the face of God, empty and infinite.

"Have you changed your mind about General Kidd's offer?" asked Sarah.

"I don't want to be head of the Fedayeen."

"General Kidd's heart is broken over Amir . . . and it's a profound honor." Sarah broke their embrace. "Like being offered the presidency."

"I don't want to be president either. Why don't *you* be president, Sarah?"

"Not yet," said Sarah.

"How nice you're willing to wait."

"What *do* you want to do, Rikki?"

"I'm waiting for God to give me a clue." He smiled. "It's a good thing I'm patient."

The two of them watched the cloudless sky framing the stone faces, holding hands. A more perfect union, that's what Sarah said Lincoln was after—well, maybe this time they'd do a better job of it. If anyone could make it happen, it was Sarah. He could hear Michael hollering as he approached, his voice echoing off the mountains.

"He needs a brother or sister," said Sarah.

"I'm willing to do my part."

"How noble of you." Sarah stroked the inside of his arm. "I still can't get used to you not wearing your knife. It's been a part of you for so long."

"An old friend told me something the last time I saw him. He wasn't right about anything else, but he was right about this. . . ." Rakkim drew her to him, held her so tightly it was as if the same blood rushed through the both of them. "I don't need a blade anymore."

ACKNOWLEDGMENTS

It's been over six years since I started the Assassin Trilogy and I had no idea where it was going to take me. I feel like I've been gone a long time and I'm not the person I was when I started . . . thank God.

Many people are owed my thanks, and here's a few of them.

Thanks to my family for putting up with my moodiness and distraction during this time, for covering for me when I forgot the names of people I've known for years, and reminding me by their every action why it's good to be home.

Thanks to my agent, Mary Evans, for her insight and determination.

Thanks to my editor, Colin Harrison, for his talent and ability to see to the heart of what I was trying to accomplish. He made the trilogy better and I am grateful.

Thanks to my publisher, Susan Moldow, for her creativity and unwavering support for a difficult project. When writers get together, we mostly talk about how clueless publishers are. Susan left me with nothing to say.

My research led me to the work of many fine writers and thinkers. The five I feel most indebted to are Samuel P. Huntington, Bernard Lewis, Robert D. Kaplan, Mark Steyn and the columnist for *Asia Times* who writes under the name Spengler. I would also like to thank Hugh Hewitt, law professor and broadcast journalist, whose nationally syndicated radio show both informed me and exposed the Assassin Trilogy to a broader audience.

Thanks to my readers who, by buying the books, have allowed me to finish the trilogy. And put a new roof on my house. A special thanks to the many readers who have written me—your encouragement meant a great deal. I didn't even mind when you asked me to write faster.

Finally, I would like to thank my characters, Rakkim and Sarah, Anthony Colarusso, Spider and Leo, the Colonel and John Moseby and General Kidd. Thanks to the Old One too, and Baby, of course, and preacherman Malcolm Crews, Satan's own holy roller. Lester Gravenholtz, you sick, redheaded warthog, you belong dead. But you're not, of course, not you, not any of them, least of all you, Darwin. I created every one of you, but you outgrew me and I can't follow. The best dialogue you wrote yourselves, whispered it in my ear as I typed. You cracked me up, scared me, made me cry at the Tigards' farmhouse and again at Graceland. I had the best seat in the house because of you, and I couldn't wait to get to the keyboard in the morning. Thanks for the ride.